BEFORE WE GROW OLD

CLARE SWATMAN

Boldwood

First published in Great Britain in 2022 by Boldwood Books Ltd.

Copyright © Clare Swatman, 2022

Cover Design by Leah Jacobs-Gordon

Cover Photography: Shutterstock

Every effort has been made to obtain the necessary permissions with reference to copyright material, both illustrative and quoted. We apologise for any omissions in this respect and will be pleased to make the appropriate acknowledgements in any future edition.

A CIP catalogue record for this book is available from the British Library.

Paperback ISBN 978-1-80280-654-0

Large Print ISBN 978-1-80280-650-2

Hardback ISBN 978-1-80280-649-6

Ebook ISBN 978-1-80280-647-2

Kindle ISBN 978-1-80280-648-9

Audio CD ISBN 978-1-80280-655-7

MP3 CD ISBN 978-1-80280-652-6

Digital audio download ISBN 978-1-80280-646-5

Boldwood Books Ltd
23 Bowerdean Street
London SW6 3TN
www.boldwoodbooks.com

For Mum and Dad. Thanks for everything

Dear William,

I can't believe you're gone. I can't believe I'll never get to hold you again, to feel the softness and warmth of your skin against mine, to press my lips into your hair. To watch you become the amazing man I know you'll one day be. To be a part of your life, the way we'd always imagined.

My arms will feel empty forever.

I have no more words. I'm sorry.

I'm broken.

I hope you'll have a happier life than I can give you.

I love you. Always.

Fran

1

August 1982

Mum reached up and pressed the doorbell firmly, an apple crumble balanced precariously in her left hand. I stood to her right, slightly behind her, and studied the scratched red paint on the door.

When it swung open I peered up to see a lady standing in the doorway, blonde hair piled up on her head, pink lipsticked mouth stretched into a smile. She looked as pretty as my favourite Sindy doll and I smiled back shyly.

'Hello, I'm Stephanie Gordon, and this is my daughter, Francesca,' Mum said, slightly too loudly. 'We've just moved next door so I wanted to come and say hello. Oh, and I've made you this.' She held the crumble up and the lady looked at it for a moment before reaching out and taking it.

'Thank you! How very kind. And how lovely to meet you, Stephanie – and Francesca, was it?' She bent down and peered at me behind my mother's waist.

I nodded.

'Wonderful. I'm Kathy. Kathy Poulton.' She stepped back. 'Oh, how rude of me, would you like to come in? I've just put the kettle on.'

'Thank you, that would be lovely.' Mum's voice sounded different, a bit like the queen when she does her speeches.

We stepped into the house that was the mirror image of ours, all the doors and rooms on the wrong side of the hallway, and followed Mrs Poulton into the kitchen. I stared at the wooden cupboards and cream worktops, which were much nicer than the ones we had in our new house. Mrs Poulton put the crumble on the side and opened the back door.

'William, James, can you come here a moment please?'

Seconds later two boys, one about seven, the same as me, and one much younger, both with blonde curls and scuffed knees, appeared at the door.

'Is it snack time?'

'Not yet. I want you to meet Mrs Gordon and Francesca. They've just moved in next door.'

Both faces turned to me. ''Lo,' the smallest boy said. 'I'm Jim.'

'James,' Mrs Poulton corrected.

'Jim,' he repeated, giving a wave and running back into the garden.

'William, aren't you going to say hello?'

'Hello. Want to come and play?'

My face burned with embarrassment. I'd never been friends with a boy before and I looked down at my shiny black shoes. But there was something about the piercing blue eyes and impish smile of this boy that made me want to say yes more than anything else in the world. I glanced up at Mum. 'Can I?'

'Go on, off you go,' she said, almost pushing me towards the back door.

I walked shyly across the kitchen and followed William outside and into the garden, leaving Mum and Mrs Poulton to drink tea and pretend not to eat biscuits.

'I'm Will, by the way, not William. Mum hates us shortening our names but we ignore her.'

I nodded.

'Did you say your name was Francesca?'

I nodded again. 'Yes, but everyone calls me Fran. Apart from my mum.'

We grinned at the shared secret and headed to the end of the garden.

'We're playing football, winner stays on,' Will said. 'Want to go in goal?'

I agreed even though I'd never played football before.

And that was that. That was the day I met William Poulton. That was the day I met my best friend.

And for the next eleven years, we'd hardly be separated.

2

NOW

October 2018

The café was packed and the steam that blurred the windows so thick that it was impossible to make out anything in the street outside. It looked as though we were floating in the clouds, and if I could make it so that was the case, I definitely would. It would certainly be infinitely more interesting than what was going on with my life right now. It was all just so *meh*. A job as a legal secretary I neither loved nor hated, but which I knew inside-out and that paid the bills; a thirteen-year-old son I adored but who seemed to have forgotten I existed most of the time; a best friend I rarely had time to see, and – well, that was it. That was the sum total of my life. I knew I should have been grateful for what I had, but the truth was I felt as though, without me even noticing, my life had closed in so tightly around me that it had become this tiny, narrow strip of existence from which I had no means of escape. My wings were well and truly clipped.

I let out a long sigh, my cheeks puffing out with the effort, and checked the clock above the counter. Twenty minutes until I needed to be back in the office. Would anyone even notice whether or not I went back? What would happen if I just stayed here, in this café, and never returned? Nothing, I suspected. Nothing at all. The lawyers would just keep on lawyering, and they'd find someone else to do all their admin for them without even batting an eyelid. It wasn't a great feeling to know you were so dispensable.

I closed my eyes, trying to block out the sounds around me: the braying tones of the yoga ladies-who-lunched at the table next to me; the whines of a small child desperate to climb out of its highchair; the low murmurs of the pensioners two tables across playing a card game; the indignant tones of a young woman whose boyfriend had cheated on her but she didn't know what to do about it. *Dump him*, I thought, but then flicked my eyes open in a panic. Had I said that out loud? I seemed to talk to myself a lot these days, probably because I spent most of my time on my own. But I was safe this time. No one had noticed a thing.

Sighing heavily again, I picked up my mug of hot chocolate and lifted it to my lips – then without warning there was a searing pain down my arm and hot chocolate was dripping from the table into my lap. I leaped up with a yelp, smacked my thigh on the table and knocked even more scorching liquid across the tabletop as I did so. For a moment I just stood there, watching the drip, drip, drip of the milky brown liquid as it flowed across the table and poured onto the floor.

'Oh God, I am *so* sorry,' said a deep voice. A hand briefly touched my elbow and I flinched, turning to see where the voice was coming from. 'I tripped, on that.' The man pointed vaguely towards a bag that was poking out from underneath the table next to me.

In one swift movement he grabbed a wodge of napkins from the counter and started patting them across my clothes, over my sleeves and down across my hand, which was pink from the heat of the drink.

I snatched the napkins from him and pushed his hands away. 'It's fine, I'll do it,' I said, trying to keep the annoyance out of my voice. After all, it wasn't his fault that other people couldn't keep their belongings under the table and he clearly felt bad about it. But then again, he wasn't the one who now had to go back into the office covered in hot chocolate, either...

The next few seconds were a scramble of wiping the table and floor, and apologising and stammering. Which is why it took me so long to actually look at the man who'd accidentally bumped into me in this busy café. I noticed his mop of expensively cut blonde hair first, peppered with streaks of grey and tousled into subtle spikes. Then I noticed his smile: the friendly mouth and glistening white teeth, followed by his sparkling blue eyes, which lit up as he looked at me.

'Oh...' I stammered, and almost fell into my seat, my mouth open like a goldfish.

'Fran?'

'Will.' I stared at him for a moment too long. 'I – do you want to sit down? I think it's dry now.' I looked at him again and indicated the seat opposite me as my stomach rolled over. 'If you have time, of course.'

'Let me get you another drink and get myself a coffee and I'll be right there. Don't go anywhere.'

I nodded mutely.

He joined the end of the queue and I took the opportunity to study this man: a man I hadn't clapped eyes on for twenty-five years.

Good grief, William Poulton. I never in a million years imagined I'd see him again.

When he disappeared from my life, it had been so unexpected, so sudden, I'd been shattered into a million pieces. It had taken me a long, long time to put myself back together again, piece by piece – to become whole again.

We'd been love's young dream. Best friends from the age of seven when my family had moved next door to his; our mothers always joked we'd get married one day. For years we couldn't imagine anything worse. We were best friends, and best friends didn't get married. Instead we frustrated them all by continuing to hang out together almost every day, without giving them even a sniff of romance. When Will brought his first girlfriend home at the age of fifteen – Katy, I think she was called – I'd thought his mum was going to cry. She invited me for dinner that night too, and I watched her eyes as they flitted from me to Will, to Katy and back again like she was watching a tennis match, the frown in her forehead deepening every time Katy moved anywhere near Will. So when Will and I did finally become a couple a year later, our mothers were both equal parts relieved, and equal parts smug about having been right all along.

Will had been my world. And for those eighteen months that we'd been together, we'd believed our love could never end. Even the prospect of university looming couldn't destroy our dream. We were going to be together forever, come what may. We were invincible, Will and I.

Then everything went spectacularly wrong when his mum died, and his dad decided to up and leave, taking Will and his brother Jim with him across the other side of the world, and leaving me heartbroken.

And now here he was, twenty-five years later, standing in front of me, holding a steaming mug of hot chocolate and giving me that smile that was so familiar it made my heart flip-flop.

I took the drink from him with shaking hands and we both sat down. I stared at the tabletop for a moment, trying to compose myself. What did I say to him after all these years, after everything?

When I finally raised my eyes to look at him, I saw he was watching me, waiting.

'I can't believe it's you.' My voice was almost a whisper.

'Me neither. But it definitely is.' He took a sip from his coffee and winced. 'Shit, that's hot.' He smiled and I smiled back.

I cleared my throat. 'So. You're not in Australia.'

He shook his head. 'No. I was, but – well, I came back.'

'How long ago?'

Will searched my eyes as though wondering whether I really wanted to hear the truth. 'I've been back about ten years.'

My stomach lurched. 'In London?'

He nodded. 'For most of it, yeah.'

'Oh.' I didn't know what to say. As an eighteen-year-old, Australia might as well have been another planet. The distance had felt insurmountable, and so I'd worked hard to put Will out of my mind, to accept that I'd never see him again, and to mend my shattered heart. And yet how would I have felt if I'd have known he'd come back? Would I have tried to find him?

I shook the thought from my mind.

'So.'

'So,' Will repeated. He leaned forward and rested his chin on his hands. 'What have you been up to over the last twenty-five years?'

I smiled weakly. That was a loaded question. The truth was I was a very different person to the one I'd been the last time Will and I had seen each other. But in front of this man I knew so well, it also felt as though nothing had changed at all.

I took a deep breath. 'Not much.' I picked up a packet of sugar from the bowl in front of me and tapped it on the table. 'I left university, got a job, had a baby...' His face drained of colour and I stopped, realising what I'd said. 'It's not... I didn't mean...'

He shook his head, then held his palms together, pressing his fingers to his lips.

'And is it... is he... or she...' His words trailed off and I saved him by shaking my head vigorously.

'He's thirteen.' I looked up from the table to meet his eyes. 'He's called Kieran.'

He nodded slowly and blew out through pursed lips. 'Wow.'

'Yeah.'

A silence hung between us for a few moments, the weight of the past making the air heavy and difficult to breathe. The hiss of the coffee machines and the tinkle of the bell above the door seemed louder than usual. I wondered whether he might say anything more. But then he straightened up and ran his hand through his hair.

'Well, Francesca Gordon. Of all the cafés in all the world you had to come into this one.'

'Nice line.'

'Thank you.'

I blew across the top of my hot chocolate, watching as the cool air skimmed across the foamy surface. Okay, so he'd decided not to talk about the past. That was fine with me. More than fine, in fact. That was good. It was too early to be raking over old ground. Besides, what would be the point?

And yet my hands still gripped my mug so tightly that my knuckles turned white, as the words I wanted to ask him hung in the air between us, unsaid.

'What about you?' I blurted.

'Me? Oh, not much. I work in a bank. I know, I know, it's a bit different to being a professional footballer but, well... it didn't happen, in the end. When we moved away...' He stopped, met my eye, and carried on. 'When I got to Australia, I went off the rails a bit and didn't bother joining another team. English football wasn't a big thing over there. A shame but I doubt I'd have made it anyway.' He shrugged. 'And yeah, banking is a long way from being the job of my dreams but it does pay well at least.'

I felt a pang of sadness as I remembered how much Will had loved his football. He'd been picked for all the school teams, played for the town by the time he was fifteen; there had even been mutterings of him playing for the big local team youth side. I'd spent hours watching him training, shivering in my parka, my hands turning numb as he raced around under the floodlights – waiting for him, my breath cold in the winter darkness, as he stripped out of his muddy kit, washed the sweat from his skin, then came and hugged me as his teammates teased him. He never cared, though. 'They're just jealous,' he whispered into my ear as he snuggled into me, and I swelled with pride as my body pressed against him for warmth. We'd all thought he was destined for great things. He *had* been destined for great things. And then life had got in the way.

'And do you—' I cleared my throat. 'Do you have kids?'

He gave a nod and his eyes lit up.

'Yes. A little girl. Elodie. She's six and a real sweetheart.' He picked up his phone from where he'd dropped it on the table and held it up to me. 'This is her.'

The little girl on the screen was pretty with masses of blonde curls, just like Will's had been as a young child. 'She looks like you.'

He peered at the picture. 'Do you think so?'

'Yes. It's the eyes. And the hair.'

'Ah, yes, the bane of my life.' He smiled and ruffled his now-tamed hair affectionately.

'And her mum?'

He hesitated a split second and I wondered whether I'd put my foot in it.

'We're not together any more,' he said carefully.

'I see.'

'We're still friends, though. We look after Elodie together.'

'That's good.'

'Yeah. Yeah, it is.' He looked for a moment as though he wanted to say something else, but then stopped.

He pocketed his phone and took a sip of his coffee. 'So, tell me about him.'

'Who?'

'Your son. Kieran, was it?'

I paused. I didn't know what to tell him. Since Kieran was only a few months old it had been just me and him. I'd always been protective of him, but now he was a teenager I felt even more so, and was reluctant to talk about him to people who didn't know him.

'Yes, Kieran, that's right. Well, he's lovely. He's a teenager so he's – well, you know. Things can be difficult between us sometimes but he's everything to me.'

'And his father?'

'Sean. We're not together. Haven't been for years. It's just me and Kieran and we live in a little flat in Crouch End, which I bought twenty-odd years ago before the prices went completely crazy, and we love it. But I have to work four days a week to make sure I can provide for him.' I looked down at my hands and noticed I'd been picking the skin round my thumb and it was bleeding. I stuck my hands under my thighs. 'I always assumed that as kids got older things got easier because they needed you less. It's not true, though. When they're thirteen and hormonal and tired, they always want you there and make you feel guilty that they have to let themselves in after school and wait until six o'clock for you to be home.' I looked up at him. 'It's never easy, is it?'

'No. No it isn't.'

I picked my mug up with both hands. The chocolate had gone tepid now and I took a big gulp. Opposite me, Will grinned.

'What?'

'You've got a foam moustache.' He reached his finger out across the table and wiped it across my top lip. 'See?'

But I couldn't answer. To my shock – and, I have to admit, embarrassment – the touch of Will's finger on my skin had sent a jolt through me. I could try and convince myself it was just the fact someone had touched my lip, but I knew it was more than that. It was Will's touch.

I felt blood rush to my face and I dipped my head down to cover my cheeks. Too late, though, it seemed.

'Are you okay? You look a bit flushed.'

'Me? Yes, I'm fine, just...' I looked round frantically. 'It's a bit hot in here.'

'Yeah, it is a bit steamy.' He tipped his head back and drained the dregs of his coffee. 'Listen, I'm so sorry, Fran, I really have to get back to work now. But are you free later? I'd love to catch up properly.' He stopped, his eyes flicking down to the table. 'If you fancy it, of course.'

I glanced at my watch. I was late back for work. 'I'd love to.' I stood and shrugged my coat on. 'Sorry, I've got to dash too but text me and we'll sort it out later.' I scribbled my number on a clean napkin and shoved it across the table at him. 'See you later?'

'Definitely.' He picked up the napkin, glanced at the number then placed it carefully into his suit pocket. Then I grabbed my bag and ran out of the door, the cool air outside slapping me in the face. I had no idea whether I'd ever see William Poulton again, but I hoped so.

3

NOW

October 2018

'Will?' Mags didn't even try to keep the disdain out of her voice when I rang her from outside the office.

'Uh huh.'

'As in the Will who moved halfway across the world and left you heartbroken, not to mention—'

'Yes,' I said, cutting her off before she could reach the end of her sentence. 'Yes, that Will.' I cleared my throat. 'But hear me out before you say any more.'

Mags had known me for a long time, which meant she was one of the only people in the world who could say it like it is and get away with it.

I could hear her sigh of exasperation down the phone but she didn't speak. I knew what Mags was going to say anyway: that the fact I needed to defend myself was proof enough that I was making a mistake; that he'd hurt me once, why did I think he wouldn't hurt me again. But this time I didn't want to hear her sensible advice.

'He's just like I remember him, Mags. He looks the same, except his hair is better, and he's not wearing a football shirt any more.' I smiled at the memory of Will's obsession with Arsenal, one that he clashed with my Chelsea-loving dad about on more than one occasion over the years. I listened to Mags's breathing down the phone and carried on. 'He hasn't changed. He's still the Will I always knew. I just…' I paused, unsure what I wanted to say. 'Something about him seemed – I don't know. A bit sad.'

'We're all sad, Franny. It comes with getting older. It's just the weight of the past lying heavy on us.'

I rolled my eyes. Mags was the happiest person I knew. She rarely thought badly of anyone, and always tried to see the bright side of things. If she didn't like someone, you knew you were in trouble.

'I knew you'd say that. But you know what I mean.'

I heard Mags breathe out. 'You're going to see him again, aren't you?'

'I have to, Mags. I can't stop thinking about him.'

'But you hardly know him.'

'Mags, it's Will. I know him better than I know myself.'

'You used to, you mean.' She sniffed. 'The truth is you haven't seen this man for twenty-five years, and you don't know him from Adam these days. Anything could have happened in that time.'

'I'm fairly certain he hasn't become a serial killer.'

'Well, that's a start.' I heard the smile in her voice. 'Listen, Franny. I just want you to promise me you'll be careful. Don't go rushing into anything.'

'I won't, I—'

'I remember how you were, you know. After everything.'

Her words stopped me in my tracks. 'I know.'

'And I don't want to see you in that state again. You were broken, Franny, and I don't think you'll survive being that broken again.'

'I know.' My voice felt shaky, like a glass balanced precariously on the edge of a table, about to fall. 'But I'm older now. Wiser, I hope. I'm not going to throw myself at him like some lovestruck teenager. But I have to see him again. I have to. You understand, don't you?'

A hesitation, and then: 'Yes. I do. But promise me one thing.'

'What?'

'Be careful. And don't let him hurt you again.'

'That's two things.'

'I'm serious, Fran.'

'Sorry. I promise, Mags. I won't let him hurt me.'

'Good.' She hesitated. 'And have you told him about—'

'No. Not yet.'

Her silence said it all. I heard her swallow, then she said, 'Make sure you ring me and tell me all about it tomorrow.'

I smiled. 'I will.'

But as I ended the call and headed back to the office, I couldn't stop Mags's words from repeating themselves on a loop in my head: *You won't survive being that broken again.*

She was right. But he wasn't the only one who'd broken me.

* * *

Sometimes, when you're waiting for something, it feels as though time has stood still. As though the clocks have stopped and you're the only one who has noticed. That's how the afternoon felt for me. I filed cases and spoke to clients and made endless tea, yet all the time I wasn't really there. Instead I was back in the past, thinking about the boy who had disappeared from my life so many years ago, and about how I'd never truly believed I'd see him again. How for a long time I'd hoped I would, hoped with everything I had that he would turn up in my life again. But slowly, that desperate need began to subside like a spring tide, until it felt as though he were nothing more than a wisp of memory, waves lapping gently on a shore, and I didn't need him any more.

And yet now, *bam*! Here he was again, bringing back so many memories, some welcome, some I'd rather had stayed where they were, buried deep.

I kept expecting to wake up.

Finally the clock ticked over to four o'clock. At the same time my phone beeped. I glanced at the message, and the breath left my body.

Fancy dinner? We could meet in town? 7pm? Will x

I felt as though my insides had coiled tightly. Would the relative ease with which we'd chatted earlier be shattered when we met up again? Would I say something I shouldn't, reveal something I didn't mean to?

And then, of course, there was Kieran. In the earlier excitement of feeling like a teenager all over again, I'd forgotten I couldn't just spirit myself away for the evening. I needed to be home for him, ideally before it got too late. I tapped out a reply to Will, hoping he wouldn't think I was being too forward.

I'm really sorry, I forgot I have to get home for Kieran. I don't suppose you fancy coming to mine, do you? I promise not to poison you. F x

I composed the message quickly and sent it before I even had time to think about the ramifications of inviting a man I hardly knew to my house. Sure, I'd known Will as a teenager, but Mags was right, twenty-five years was a long time. I shook the thought from my mind. This was Will, for goodness' sake.

That didn't stop me from spending the next twenty minutes surreptitiously googling his name, though. I'd resisted it, for all these years, determined not to think about him, or to try and find out anything about him, in case it was something I really didn't want to know. Or in case I was tempted to try and contact him again. I'd often wondered whether things might have been different if we'd had Facebook, or Skype or mobile phones back then. Perhaps Australia wouldn't have seemed so far away. And yet now here I was like some sort of manic stalker, combing through every piece of information I could find.

There was surprisingly little, in fact. It appeared he didn't use Twitter or Instagram, and, like me, his Facebook page was sparse. I scrolled through the photos it allowed me to view. There were one or two of him with his younger brother, Jim, and I smiled seeing his familiar face, and there was one of Will on a yacht somewhere wearing shorts and no top. I tried not to stare too much but couldn't help noticing he still had a footballer's physique. Oh God, what was I doing? I shut the picture quickly and scrolled through the remaining few bits I could find about him. There were reports from financial papers about his past successes and promotions, and a photo of him with his local South London football team winning a cup final and holding a trophy aloft several years ago, but other than that it appeared Will Poulton was a man of mystery. Unusual these days, when most people splattered their comings and goings all over social media. I wondered if there was a sinister reason behind it, then shook the thought away. After all, I didn't use social media much either, and that didn't mean I had anything to hide. I also wondered whether Will was googling me too.

It took almost half an hour for Will's reply to come, by which time I'd convinced myself he'd changed his mind.

I'd love to. Send me your address and I'll be there. 7ish ok?

My heart in my throat, I typed a reply. Will was coming to my house. I tried to remember whether I'd left the place tidy this morning before chastising myself. Why did it matter? He wasn't coming round to admire my furnishings or assess my housekeeping skills. He was coming to see me.

Good grief.

At bang on five o'clock, I left the office and raced for the bus, a knot of tension deep in my belly. The stars were clearly aligned because the bus was waiting for me, and as I climbed on board it set off almost immediately. Thirty minutes later I was in Crouch End and I ducked into the Co-op to grab something for dinner, slinging aubergines, sweet potatoes, a jar of curry paste and a bottle of Sauvignon Blanc into my basket.

As the door to my flat swung open a few minutes later, the sounds of a computer game drifted down the hallway from the living room.

'Hey, Keeks, good day?' I said, popping my head round the door. The room was in darkness, the blinds pulled tight against the darkening evening, a small puddle of light from the TV screen surrounding Kieran's outstretched frame. It hit me again, as it did most days, how grown-up he looked. It seemed only five minutes since I was sitting on that sofa with him nestled into my chest, sucking greedily from a bottle of milk. Now here he was, nearly a man, and my heart clenched with the undeniable knowledge that I was slowly losing him.

He grunted at me, barely turning his head from the screen where computer-generated players were kicking a football round a pitch.

'Can you pause that a minute, love?'

Nothing.

'Kieran.'

A huge sigh, then the action on the TV halted and he turned to look at me, his face stern. 'What?'

'Lovely to see you too, darling. Yes, thank you, my day was great, how about yours?'

I didn't miss the eye roll, but to his credit a hint of a smile did flit across his face. 'Hi, Mum, how was your day?'

'Surprising, thanks for asking.' I didn't tell him any more details and I was confident he wouldn't ask. Instead I held up the carrier bag in my hand. 'I'm making curry for dinner, want some?'

'Ugh, no thanks. Can I have a pizza?'

'For a change? I suppose so. Have you done your homework?'

'I'll do it in a minute. I'll just finish this game.'

I sighed. He knew the rules were homework first, Xbox second, and once again the realisation that there was nothing I could do about it while I wasn't actually in the house hit me. I felt like I was letting everyone down these days.

Leaving him to it, I went into the kitchen. I'd recently spent a bit of money modernising the kitchen and it was my favourite room in the flat. It was only small but I'd managed to squeeze in an island and two stools, which meant that Kieran could sit and chat to me while he ate his breakfast in the morning, giving us time to properly catch up. At least, that was the theory, although it only worked when he was out of bed in time for breakfast.

I heaved the bag onto the worktop and emptied everything out, then I flicked on the radio and started to chop vegetables, trying not to think about the night ahead. I still had to break the news to Kieran that I had a friend coming round. I suspected he'd react by locking himself in his bedroom with his headphones on rather than attempting to make conversation, but at least it made life easier if he wasn't sitting at the end of the table grunting or, worse, talking about his latest *Fortnite* battle.

As I fried the onions, my mind drifted back to one of the last times I'd seen Will, before things had gone so wrong between us. I hadn't thought about those days for a very long time, finding it easier as the years had passed to block them from my memory rather than go over them again and again, torturing myself with what ifs. It had been one of our last happy times, just before I left home to go to university in Portsmouth. Will had deferred his place at university after his mum had been diagnosed with cancer a few months before, wanting to be there to look after her during her final few months, and it truly felt as though life would never be the same again. If only I'd known then how much it was about to change.

We'd lain on Will's single bed, face to face, our noses almost touching. The cool wall was pressed against my back and from the corner of my eye I could make out the gold blur of Will's football trophies lined up along the shelf above his desk. The room was stiflingly warm, and I felt hot as Will's hand rested lightly on my hip.

'I'm going to miss you,' I sighed.

'I'll miss you too. It won't be the same around here without you.' His breath warmed my face as he spoke.

I longed to tell him about the ache in my heart, about the terror I felt that he'd forget about me the moment I left. I wanted to tell him that I'd never think about another man, that if I could, I'd stay, and be with him instead. But I knew he'd tell me to go, that he had to look after his mum anyway, that we'd be together soon enough. He'd tried to reassure me endlessly all summer, and I didn't want to upset him any more. He had enough on his mind.

'You'll write to me, won't you?'

'Course I will.'

'Every day?'

He pulled back slightly so I could focus on his face. The face that was almost more familiar to me than my own, the face that I'd loved for eleven years. 'I don't think I'll have enough to say every day. My life's not *that* interesting.'

I smiled sadly. 'Every other day, then.'

His lips pulled into a smile and he moved his hand up to my cheek. 'I'll write and tell you everything I've been up to. Not that it will be very exciting compared to your new life.' He stopped and a frown flitted across his face.

'What's wrong?'

He shrugged. 'I just don't want you to forget about me when you meet all your new friends.'

My heart surged with love. 'William. How could I ever forget about you? It would be like trying to forget I had a right arm.'

He pressed his lips against mine and they felt so familiar, so warm. How could I leave this man, even for a second, let alone the next six weeks before I could come home to visit?

If only I'd known then what was to come. Maybe I'd have stayed after all.

Now, I tipped some tomatoes into the pan and kept stirring

mechanically, my mind years away, lost in the past. I swallowed down a
sob. It was as though seeing Will had unlocked a box full of painful
memories, which were being released one by one to entangle themselves in my mind.

I added some spices to the curry, gave it a stir, and turned the heat
down. The kitchen smelled delicious, the aroma filling the air. I
checked the clock above the cooker. Six thirty. I had half an hour.

A quick shower and change of clothes and I was ready. My stomach
was in knots as I applied a slick of mascara, and it wasn't until I went
back downstairs to check on the curry that I realised I'd forgotten to
tell Kieran about Will coming round.

He was still playing his game when I pushed open the living-room
door.

'I'm nearly done,' he said, and I rolled my eyes. Did he really think I
didn't know he'd played at least two games since he last promised to
turn it off? I let it go this time. I'd learned to pick my battles.

'Fine. Can you just pause it a sec?'

I waited while he stopped the game and turned to face me.

'I've got a friend coming round in a few minutes. Do you want to eat
with us?'

'Who is it?'

'Just someone I used to know at school. He's an old friend.'

I tried to make it sound casual, but the truth was I rarely went out
on dates, and the few times I had started seeing someone more seri-
ously over the years, I'd been reticent about bringing them home. I
didn't want to introduce Kieran to a string of men I had no intention of
seeing more than a handful of times. So for him, this was a big deal.

I watched his face as my words sank in and for a split second he
looked as though he was about to say something else. But then his face
changed again and he said, 'Can I just eat in my room, then?'

I hated him eating anywhere other than at the table, but tonight I
desperately wanted him to co-operate.

'All right, just this once. But please be polite and at least come and
say hello, won't you?'

'I'm always polite.' He grinned at me and batted his eyelashes.

'Sure you are.'

'I'll turn this off now. I need to go and get my maths done for tomorrow.'

'Good boy. I'll give you a shout when your pizza's ready.'

The room plunged into darkness as the TV went black, and he uncurled himself from the beanbag. As he stretched to his full height I was struck by how extraordinarily tall he was becoming and, sadly, how like his useless father he was beginning to look. I glanced up at him as he passed and reached up to ruffle his hair.

'Get off!' he said, ducking away from me like he used to when he was little.

I waited until I heard his door close, then I went through to the kitchen and filled a saucepan with water for the rice. I checked the wine was chilled and flicked through my playlists. What should you listen to when someone you used to love but hadn't seen for years was coming round?

Finally I settled on Amy Winehouse, and as the first notes of the familiar song filled the room I poured myself a glass of wine. Why was I so nervous? I was a grown woman, for goodness' sake. I'd been through childbirth, heartbreak, illness – all sorts since I'd last laid eyes on William Poulton. Surely I could cope with a night in his company?

If only it didn't feel as though there was so much at stake.

I took a gulp of wine and wiped my lips then almost jumped off my stool when the doorbell went. I tugged at my top, smoothed my hair down and walked to the front door. As I pulled it open I held my breath, not sure what I was going to say.

'You made it!'

'I did!' The light from the security lamp behind him threw his features into shadow, and as he stepped forward into the flat and handed me a bunch of beautiful white roses I could see a smile on his lips. I stood back to let him pass and as he did he pressed his hand against my upper arm and leaned in to plant a gentle kiss on my cheek.

I closed the door behind him, keen to turn away and hide the glow from my face.

'Right, follow me,' I said, marching down the hall. God, what was wrong with me? I was behaving like a schoolmarm. I needed to relax, remember it was Will. No one special. Just Will.

It wasn't working. There was no 'just' about it.

'This is lovely,' Will said, glancing round as we entered the kitchen.

'Thanks. I've just had it redone.' I placed the flowers in the sink for the time being then pulled the wine from the fridge. 'Please, sit down.'

He pulled himself onto one of the stools and finally I stopped and looked at him again. It hit me how strange it was that this man was so familiar to me: the contours of his cheekbones, softened with age yet still relatively sharp and sculpted; the bow of his lips, the glow of his eyes. His face was more lined, of course, and his hairline wasn't quite as full as it once was, but I knew this man standing in front of me like I knew myself. I'd loved him, once.

I shook the thought away and screwed the top off the bottle of wine.

'White okay? I wasn't sure what you drank. I assumed it wouldn't be cider and black these days.'

He grinned at me and nodded. 'I don't know, maybe we should have a couple of bottles of Mad Dog for old times' sake?'

'Ugh, don't. I can't even think about that stuff any more, not since that party.'

'The one where you vomited so much it seeped through your bag and into your shoes?'

'That'll be it. Enough to put anyone off for life.' This was good. Nice, safe, affectionate teasing. This was a good start.

I poured Will a large glass and topped my own up. 'Cheers. To old times.'

'To us, and this morning's fortuitous meeting,' Will said, and we chinked glasses. I tried not to think about an 'us'.

We sipped our wine in silence for a moment and I hardly dared look at him. Suddenly Will spoke again.

'Is Kieran in?'

'Yes, he's upstairs. I've got to take him his pizza up in a bit.' It felt like a good sign that he'd remembered Kieran's name.

'Oh. I hope that's not on my account?'

'No, don't worry. He's a thirteen-year-old boy; I can't imagine there's anything more lame than having to spend time with your mother and an old friend. He's more than happy stuffing himself with pizza in his room and WhatsApping his mates, believe me. Although I have warned him he'd better come and at least say hello.'

Will waved his hand in front of his face. 'Not for my benefit. It might be a long time since I was a thirteen-year-old boy but I can still remember what it was like, and I totally get it, don't worry.'

'Thanks, Will.'

I shoved Kieran's pizza in the oven and set the timer for ten minutes, trying not to think about Will at thirteen.

'So, tell me about him. What's Kieran like? Is he anything like you?'

I shrugged. 'In some ways. He's stubborn.'

I looked up to see Will grinning.

'What?'

'Nothing,' he said, putting on a mock-serious face.

'Are you saying I'm stubborn?'

'Well...' Will's face broke into a grin again, unable to hold it back any more and I tried not to notice how his eyes lit up when he smiled. 'I mean, I can remember a couple of instances when your stubbornness came out, yes.'

'Go on.'

Will held out his hands and counted onto his fingers. 'Firstly, that time when you accused me of kissing Leanne Stacey at that party and when we both told you it had never happened and that it had been an entirely different boy she'd been snogging, you refused to apologise even when it was clear you were wrong.' He paused, as if to think. 'Then there was that time you refused to come with me to the fireworks because your mum wouldn't let you wear your cool new pixie boots and was trying to make you wear your wellies.'

'I was nine!'

'Be that as it may, it doesn't change the fact that's who you are and who you have always been.' He paused, suddenly more serious. 'Of course I have no idea what you're like now, and I wouldn't presume to guess. I mean, life changes us all, and I reckon I'd be doing you a disservice if I assumed you were anything like the Franny I used to know and love. Especially after...' He trailed off.

I nodded briskly, keen to steer the subject away from where I sensed it was going. 'I suppose the stubborn thing is a fair accusation.' The words came out quickly. 'Not much has changed there. Sometimes when I'm shouting at Kieran for exactly that, I feel as though I'm just arguing pointlessly with myself. But you're right. So much has happened since I was eighteen that I probably wouldn't even recognise myself if I met me then.'

Will's shoulders hunched and he rubbed his hand over his face. 'No, I don't suppose I would either.'

A beat passed and I caught Will's eye and looked away quickly. If only he knew the half of it.

I lifted the lid off the curry pot and let the steam blur my vision for a moment.

'Anyway,' I said. 'You were asking about Kieran. The truth is yes, he's stubborn, and yes he can drive me mad sometimes, but he's a teenager and that's what they're meant to do. And although life got a little bit tougher when he was born and my ex buggered off and left us as he "didn't want the responsibility"' – I made the quote marks in the air with my fingers – 'Kieran is a loving, kind, funny, caring boy under-neath and I wouldn't be without him for the world.'

I looked up to see Will watching me, a strange, unreadable expres-sion on his face. I held my breath, wondering what he was going to say next. Then the look cleared and he gave a small nod and a smile, and relief flooded through me.

'The curry smells amazing,' he said, leaning over the pot.

'Thank you. It's nothing special.'

'Remember that time you tried to cook for me, before?'

'Oh God...' I shook my head, my face flaming at the memory. 'Did you have to remind me?' When we'd first gone from being friends to being girlfriend and boyfriend we'd only been sixteen, but I'd wanted to prove to him how grown-up I was by cooking for him for our first official 'date'. Mum and Dad had gone out for the night and we had the house to ourselves. I'd picked a recipe I'd seen on a Delia Smith cooking programme and followed it, so I thought, to the letter. Except the soufflé didn't rise, the lasagne burned to a crisp and set the smoke alarm off in the middle of our candlelit starter, and the dog pooed in the kitchen because I forgot to let him out into the garden.

Will nodded, his eyes full of mirth. 'It sounded so romantic on paper. I'll never forget having to waft the smell of burning food and dog poo out of the window with napkins while the smoke alarm almost deafened us and the dog went mad.' He was laughing so much he could hardly get the words out and I couldn't help myself, and started giggling too. It had all been so ridiculous, and I hadn't thought about it for years. I'd been mortified at the time, of course, and had made him promise not to tell anyone, and as far as I knew he'd kept his promise.

'Hopefully tonight will be a bit more successful than that,' I said, wiping the tears from my eyes.

'Well I don't know, it turned out all right in the end, I reckon.' He reached for my hands and I remembered how we'd shared our first kiss that night, and how I'd felt as though I was going to explode with happiness. 'Maybe tonight will be a repeat of that after all.'

I looked at him for a moment, unsure whether he was joking. There was no tell-tale lopsided grin, and his face looked deadly serious.

But before I could answer the mood was broken by a loud, insistent beeping and I jumped.

'Oh, the pizza!' I said, whisking my hands away from his and opening the oven door, steam billowing round my face. At the same time the kitchen door opened and Kieran walked in.

'Is that mine?'

'Yes, just a sec.' I plonked the hot pizza on the counter and found a plate. 'Sorry, Kieran, this is my friend Will. We went to school together. Will, this is my son, Kieran.'

Will stood and held his hand out to Kieran, who, to his credit, only hesitated a split second before reaching out and shaking it. 'Lovely to meet you, Kieran. Your mum told me lots about you.'

Kieran just nodded.

He looked relieved when I handed him his plate. 'Go on, you can take it upstairs if you like.' And before I could even get to the end of the sentence he was gone.

'Sorry, he's not big on small talk,' I said, turning to Will.

'Don't apologise for him. It's fine. He's thirteen. Who wants to spend time with a couple of old gits like us when you can be chatting to your mates?' He paused. 'Anyway, who knows, there might be plenty of time for me to get to know him better.'

I didn't answer. How could I? I'd been on my own for so long now, and me and Kieran had our routine, our way of doing things, and there didn't appear to be any space for anyone else. Not to mention that fact that, until this morning I hadn't seen this man for twenty-five years, and we still hadn't talked about the most important thing that had happened to us both back then.

Instead of replying, I lifted the lid from the rice. 'I think it's almost ready.'

'Well then, what can I do?' Will jumped up. I handed him cutlery and plates.

'You can put these on the table.'

I was glad of the few seconds to compose myself as he turned his back and laid the forks and spoons carefully down on the small wooden table. I took a deep breath in and let it out with a slow puff of air.

'Right, let's eat.' I placed the curry and rice on the table in bowls and we sat down opposite one another across the table where Kieran and I had spent so many hours chatting over dinner, making a mess with paints and crafts, or arguing over homework. It felt strange to have someone else here.

'Well, this turned out better than before,' Will said, grinning.

'Just a bit. And I haven't got a dog so you don't need to worry there.'

I lifted a forkful of curry to my mouth and watched him for a moment. He was still so handsome, and I could see the old Will under the years of change. I wondered what my mum would say if she could see us now. She always loved Will but never understood the intensity of my feelings for him. She only had her and Dad's marriage to go on, I suppose and, while they loved each other, it was a comfortable kind of love, a love of cosy slippers and matching waterproofs and bracing walks holding hands in the countryside. I could never have imagined theirs being a passionate affair, not even at the beginning, although I suppose it might have been once. I wondered whether Mum would understand how conflicted my emotions were right now, given what had happened all those years ago, or whether she'd just tell me to steer well clear.

'I am sorry, you know,' Will said, looking up to meet my gaze.

I didn't reply, the curry suddenly a dry lump in my throat. I didn't want to talk about the past, to make it all real again. It had taken me a long time to get over it.

'Don't.' My voice cracked. Will put his fork down and reached his hand across the table towards mine. I moved it away, without even realising I was going to do it. He left his there, next to my plate, and I stared at his hands, his long fingers and bitten nails. Finally, I lifted my gaze to meet his.

'Why can't we talk about it, Franny?' he said, using the name only he and Mags ever called me.

I could feel tears sting my eyes and I blinked several times. 'I...' I stopped. 'I don't know. I just can't.'

'Well, can you at least let me explain?'

I shook my head, tears falling down my face now, splashing into the rice. Images flashed into my mind like bolts of lightning: Will's angry face as I walked away from him for what neither of us could have known was the last time; the letter he wrote to tell me he was moving to Australia with his dad and brother; the tears that had smudged the writing across the page from the endless re-reading long after he'd gone.

Will waited, the curry cooling between us. Then he said, 'I was wrong, leaving you like I did. I mean, writing you a letter. I should have come to see you, explained it better. I should have done more. You didn't deserve it.'

'It doesn't matter now, Will. It was a long time ago.'

'Of course it matters. I was such a coward.' He took a sip of wine. 'I wanted to ring you. I wanted to come and see you, tell you the news in person. No, scratch that. I never actually wanted to leave. But I...' He stopped. 'I was just so messed up, with Mum dying and Dad moving us away like that. I couldn't think straight. And then I was ashamed.'

'Ashamed?'

'Of how I'd behaved. Of everything.' He shook his head. 'I was so angry, Fran.'

'At me?'

He shook his head vigorously. 'God, no. Not at you. Never at you. At my mum for dying. At my father.' He stopped again and I waited for him to gather his thoughts.

'After Mum died, Dad fell apart. Looking back I think he must have had a nervous breakdown. But at the time all me and Jim saw was an angry father we resented, who we blamed for everything. I understand now that he needed to get away – he missed Mum as much as we did, and needed a fresh start. But at the time I was furious at him for ruining my life. I just couldn't bring myself to explain it all to you. Especially given...' His breath hitched.

'Will, it's fine. Really it is. We would never have stayed together. We were too young. We needed to get out there and see the world, to live a bit, to make mistakes.' I smiled. 'God knows I made plenty of them. But we're here now, and maybe this is when we were supposed to meet. Maybe this is our time instead?'

My heart hammered so hard I was amazed he couldn't hear it. I couldn't quite believe I'd just said that. I hadn't known I was going to say it, hadn't thought about it at all. But now the words were out there I knew it was what I wanted to say. I knew that, even though I had Kieran to consider now, I meant every word.

Will was here, I was here; maybe this was our time, and what was in the past could stay there.

Suddenly a loud screeching sound ripped through the air and I leaped up, my hands shaking.

'The smoke alarm!' I yelled, grabbing a tea towel from the worktop and wafting it wildly above my head. The room filled with smoke and I looked round to find Will pushing the oven door shut quickly.

'I think you might have forgotten the naan breads,' he said, his mouth stretched into a huge grin. He reached up and switched the oven off just as the kitchen door burst open.

'Mum, what's going on?' Kieran said, his hands clamped against his ears.

'Nothing, love, I've just burned something,' I said, wafting madly while Will opened the window. Kieran slunk back upstairs, shaking his head.

Finally the alarm stopped and the silence was so sudden it made us both jump. Exhausted, I slumped down onto the nearest stool and put my head in my hands.

'I know we've been talking about the last meal you cooked for me, but I hadn't expected you to try and recreate it in quite so much detail,' Will said, his voice full of mirth. I looked up at him, and when I saw his face I burst out laughing. For a few moments neither of us could breathe as tears streamed down our faces. My cheeks ached and my belly hurt, but eventually I started to calm down, and as we both managed to pull ourselves together, the smoke cleared and the air turned chilly from the cold October air pouring through the open window. Will stood and closed it then sat back down opposite me and rested his elbows on the table. He held his hands out, palms up. 'So what happens now?'

'With what?'

'With us, Fran.' A frown creased his forehead and lines fanned out from the edges of his eyes. I wished I could stare into those deep blue eyes and discover his story, find out what had happened to my Will over the years since we'd been so close. The good things and the bad, the loves and laughs and heartache he'd suffered. But even though I didn't know any of these things, not yet, it still felt as though I knew this man almost as well as I knew myself. And I knew right then that I wanted, more than anything else, to see whether, this time, we could go somewhere. Together.

4

February 1989

'Mum reckons we'll get married one day.'

'What?' I looked up from the book I was trying to read and stared at Will.

He shrugged. 'I know. Gross, right? But I heard her talking to your mum yesterday and that's what they said.' He grimaced as another thought occurred to him.

'What? What else did they say?'

His face flushed bright red and he feigned sticking his fingers down his throat. 'They were talking about what our baby would look like, if we had one.'

'Eeewww!' I threw the book down on the carpet in disgust and leaned forward to rest my elbows on my knees. 'Why would they even say that?'

'I think they'd had a couple of sherries.' He grinned and I grinned back. Our mothers were as thick as thieves, and we knew they snuck sherry into their mugs when they were pretending to drink coffee because they got all silly and giggly.

'Oh God, I feel sick.'

'Me too.'

We both went quiet for a while. I didn't know what Will was thinking about, but I was thinking about what it might be like to lean over and kiss him, right now. He might have thought it was gross that our mums had talked about us getting married and having a baby one day, and until recently I would have shrieked in horror along with him. But I was thirteen now. Will and I had been best friends for six and a half years, and I was starting to look at him in an entirely different light.

It didn't help that my best girl friends, Mandy and Jane, were besotted with him.

'How can you not fancy him?' they said as we watched the boys play football, Will running rings around everyone. 'He's lush.'

'He's practically my brother, that would just be weird,' I told them.

And I'd meant it. At first. But the more time that passed, the more I started to see what they saw. Will *was* lush.

I picked my book up and feigned reading it again, but my mind wasn't on it at all. Instead, I surreptitiously peered at Will over the top of my book every now and then, and let myself fantasise. I might not be ready to think about getting married just yet, but there was no harm in thinking about kissing him, was there?

It was just as well he couldn't read minds.

5

October 2018

Later in the evening as we sat on the sofa together, close but not quite touching, Will took a sip of his wine and turned to me.

'Do you ever wonder what they might have been like?'

I felt my breath leave me and my body froze.

I knew exactly what he was talking about, but I couldn't have this conversation. Not now. Not ever. It was the one I'd been avoiding all night.

And yet here it was, unavoidable.

I couldn't speak. Every time I tried, the words got stuck in my windpipe and I swallowed them back down, frantic.

I was aware of Will watching me, waiting.

'Fran?'

I sucked in air and felt breath rush into my lungs, and my heart pound against my ribcage. It was taking me everything I had not to stand up and run away from the room, and the fact that there was nowhere else for me to go was the only thing stopping me.

'Fran, are you okay? You've gone really pale.'

I shook my head. 'I'm fine.'

'I'm sorry, I didn't mean to take you by surprise like that. But it had to come up at some point, didn't it?'

No. Why did it have to? Why couldn't we just keep it in the past, where it had been buried for the last twenty-five years? Why did we have to talk about something neither of us could ever change?

But I didn't say any of that. Instead I shrugged like a belligerent teenager and waited for him to say something else. Beside me, I felt Will shuffle round to face me, his leg touching my thigh. I felt its warmth seep into my skin.

'I think about our child all the time,' he said. There it was. Our child. The thing I'd never wanted to talk about again. 'Don't you?'

'No.'

'No?'

'I try not to.'

I heard Will suck in his breath, saw his hands clench. 'Well, I do.' He looked down at his hands. 'I – don't blame you, for not wanting to keep it. You were right, in the end. But I've often wondered what they might have been like, our son or daughter. Whether they'd have looked like you, or me, whether they'd have been sporty or academic, funny or serious, blonde or dark...' He trailed off. 'I look at Elodie sometimes and I can't help wondering...'

'It was the right thing to do, Will.' My voice was sharp.

'I know, Fran. But it doesn't stop me thinking about it. I just mean... I suppose I sometimes wonder what our lives would have been like if things had been different. If we'd have stayed together, and kept the baby.'

'I would have been a single mum and would have had to leave university, that's what. Because you didn't stay, Will. You left, and you never came back.' The suppressed anger wasn't as well buried as I'd hoped; I could feel it bubbling to the surface, as fresh as the day I'd discovered I'd been abandoned.

We'd been abandoned. Me and our baby.

The memory came back now, the pain as acute as the day it happened. I'd come home from university to see Will but his mum had taken a turn for the worse and he'd rung and told me she didn't have long left. I'd felt bereft and couldn't begin to imagine how Will must have been feeling, but I'd had another reason for coming home too: I'd had something I needed to tell him.

And so, when we'd got home, I dragged him up to his room and we sat side by side on the bed, facing the wall. 'I'm pregnant.' I didn't look at him as I said it.

The words had hovered in the air between us for a few seconds and I felt dizzy as I wondered what he was going to say. I'd already decided there was no way I could keep this baby and I'd assumed he'd feel the same.

'That's amazing,' he whispered eventually.

'What?' I felt my pulse thump in my temple.

He turned to face me and he held out his hands, palms up. 'Isn't it?'

'No, Will. It's not amazing. It's a total disaster.'

'But – but I thought you were telling me because you wanted...' He trailed off.

I reached out for his hands and held them in mine. 'I can't keep this baby. We can't have a baby now.'

'Why not?'

'Are you really asking me that?'

He nodded.

'Will, we're eighteen. I'm at university, neither of us have jobs, your mum's dying...' I counted the reasons off on my fingers one by one.

'Okay!' He snatched his hands away and tucked them in the pockets of his jeans. 'You've made your point.'

'I just...' I stopped. 'I can't believe you think this is a good thing.'

He shrugged. 'I just thought... it would be nice.'

I shook my head. 'No. It's totally wrong. One day, it would be amazing. But not now.'

'So what? You're just going to have an abortion?'

I flinched at the word, at the anger in his voice. This wasn't going how I'd imagined this conversation would go.

'I think I have to.'

He stood up suddenly, the whole bed moving. 'I can't deal with this right now. My mum's in the next room dying, and you come and tell me this.' He shook his head.

'I didn't plan the timing.'

'I know but I can't do this now, Fran.' Then he walked away, out of the room, leaving me to go and see his mum with my head whirling.

Things hadn't improved for the rest of that weekend, and by the time I left to go back to university two days later we'd resolved nothing, and Will was barely speaking to me. As I climbed into Dad's car to go to the coach station, I saw Will watching me from his bedroom window, his face unreadable from that distance. He hadn't come to say goodbye, and that told me everything I needed to know. He wasn't with me on this. I was on my own.

Over the years that followed I wished I'd taken some more notice of him that night. I wished I'd taken in the curl of his hair in the light from the lamp post, that I'd noticed what he was wearing – was it a football shirt as usual, or a crumpled T-shirt? Was he smiling or sad? Did he love me, or not?

Because that was the last time I saw him. Shortly after that his mum had passed away, and his dad had decided to move the family as far away as they could possibly get. Will had told me by letter and by the time I next came home, he was gone.

Now, beside me, Will nodded and my hands shook.

'I'm sorry, Fran. For all of it. For the letter, for not talking to you about it. For not supporting you. I should have been there for you, when you...' He trailed off.

'When I got rid of our baby?' My words were sharp, like daggers.

He nodded, his eyes cast down.

'Yes, you should have been there for me. For us. But I had Mags. I was fine, in the end.'

He didn't speak for a moment. Then he said, 'I wrote to you, you know, after we left.'

I nodded. 'I know.'

'Did you read the letters?'

'No. I made Mags burn them before I could open them.'

He nodded sadly. 'I tried to come and see you once too, before you – before you had the abortion, just after you left.'

'Did you?'

He nodded. 'But I chickened out.' He caught my eye. 'Would it have made any difference, if I had have come?'

Would it? The truth was I had no idea now. But maybe it would have been enough to have saved us. To have stopped all of this. 'I don't know. It was a long time ago.'

'I can't believe it all went so wrong.'

Silence fell again. Will's hand reached out to mine and I let him take it, entwining my fingers with his.

'Let's not talk about it any more. It's done. It's in the past.' I turned to him. 'Let's just concentrate on us now.'

He looked at me for a moment, sadly, then smiled.

'Can there be an "us", then?'

'I don't know. Maybe.' Something occurred to me then. 'There isn't any reason why we can't try, is there?'

'What? No, of course not. What do you mean?'

'It's just that you changed the subject quite quickly when you mentioned Elodie's mum earlier, so I wondered…'

'Oh I see! I haven't lied about that, I promise. I just – well, there is something I should probably tell you.'

'What?'

Will rubbed his hand across his face. 'Me and my ex Amy, well, we're…' He stopped, took a deep breath. 'We still live together.'

I stared at him stonily. 'Right.'

'We are separated. That bit's true. We're trying to get divorced. But we just – I haven't moved out yet.'

'Oh.'

'I know it sounds weird but it's a big old house and the mortgage is enormous and I couldn't really afford to pay rent as well, so we agreed I should stay there, for now. It makes things easier with Elodie as well. It's just – well, it was fine. Neither of us had met anyone else. Until now.'

I nodded, unsure what to say. 'Does she know you're here tonight?'

Will frowned. 'No. Why would she?'

'I don't know. It just feels...' I stopped. How *did* it feel? We weren't cheating on anyone; Will had just told me he and Amy weren't together any more. So why was I feeling so guilty?

'It's fine,' Will reassured me.

'I guess.'

'I'd like to see you again. If you'll have me?' Will said.

There was so much we had left unsaid, and I knew seeing Will again would be difficult. I didn't know if it was a complication I needed in my life right now. But on the other hand, every fibre in my being wanted to see him again. I might have thought I'd got over Will more than twenty years before, but it turned out the feelings had been there all along.

'I'll think about it,' I said.

November 2018

'Don't you think it's a bit odd that he just happened to be in the same café as you, at the same time, on the same day?' Mags said, taking a sip of her mint tea.

'I can't believe you of all people are saying this to me. Don't you believe in fate?'

'I do. But sometimes coincidences are a bit too big.' She took another sip and gulped loudly. 'Think about it. London's a big place – there's what? Eight million people living here? And he doesn't live or work anywhere near where you were. Don't you think that's a bit odd?'

'I do now you've said it!'

'Sorry. I'm just looking out for you.'

'I know.' The truth was, it felt as though that's all Mags ever did – look out for me. She'd been my best friend since we met during the first week of university and I'd passed her a note saying 'yawn' in the middle of a lecture. She'd been there through everything since, including what had happened with Will. She may never have actually met him but she'd always understood my love for him. She'd also seen how heartbroken I'd been when he'd left so I understood why she was a little wary now.

'Have you asked him?'

'Asked him what?'

'Whether he bumped into you accidentally-on-purpose?'

I watched the steam rise from my own tea and shook my head. 'Course not. We had too much else to talk about.'

Mags nodded. 'And did you talk about – you know. Everything that happened?'

I shook my head. 'No. We talked about some of it but I didn't tell him all of it.'

'So as far as he's aware, you were pregnant, you were getting rid of it, and then he never saw you again?'

I nodded.

'Wow.'

'It sounds pretty bad when you put it like that.'

'It was bad, Fran. Do you really not remember? Because I do.'

'Of course I do. But it was such a long time ago. A lot's happened since then.'

'I suppose so. I just want you to be careful, Franny. I know I keep saying this but you don't know him any more. He could be anyone. He could have his own secrets. In fact, I'd be surprised if he didn't.'

I shivered. I didn't want to think about secrets. There'd been enough of those to last me a lifetime.

'I know. I'll be careful, I promise.'

'So you are going to see him again, then?'

I'd thought about nothing else since the night Will had come round. I had my doubts; I was cautious about introducing just anyone into Kieran's life, not to mention the fact that it was all so much for me to take on too. But on the other hand, it felt like fate, as though somehow Will and I were meant to be together. And although I still wasn't convinced I was making the right decision, I *had* decided.

'Yes. Next week. It's just dinner.'

Mags studied me for a second. 'That's good. At least that will give you a chance to get to know him a bit better – to get to know the present-day Will, not the Will you knew as kids – before you throw yourself into anything.'

I'd always wished I had my head screwed on as much as Mags. When we first met I believed she could handle anything, but now I also knew her vulnerable side. I knew the things that niggled at her, that kept her awake at night – the thought of her kids being hurt, of her husband, Rob, leaving her, of her parents dying – and she knew I'd always be there for her if she needed me too. And while I knew she was right to be cautious about Will, I also knew I had to at least see him one more time.

'Thanks, Mags.'

'Don't be daft. Just remember – ring me if you need me, and don't stay if you're not happy. Deal?'

'Deal.'

* * *

'I've got something to confess.'

Will was sitting opposite me across a table in an Italian restaurant, his face pale. It was our first proper 'date'. I'd already been feeling nervous enough and now Will was making me feeling even worse as he twisted his hands in front of him.

'Go on.'

He looked down at his plate and then back up at me. His eyes were wide. 'I – I haven't been entirely honest with you.'

'Oh God,' I groaned, my heart lurching. Was I about to find out I'd made a terrible mistake, coming here? 'Is this about you and Amy? You're still married, aren't you?'

Will shook his head. 'No. Well, yes, we are still married, but you already knew that, but we're not together. It's not about that.'

'What is it, then, Will? Are you moving back to Australia? Are you in massive debt?' I felt the panic rise in my chest.

Will held his hands up. 'Hang on. Let me speak.'

'Sorry.'

He took a deep breath. 'It wasn't exactly a coincidence that we met.'

'What?'

'I mean, when we bumped into each other last week. It wasn't an accident.'

'You mean you stalked me?'

'Well, I wouldn't exactly call it that. But I did make sure we met again.' He grinned.

I twiddled my fork round on the tablecloth. 'Mags was right.'

'What?'

I looked up at him. 'My best friend, Mags. She said it couldn't have been a coincidence that we met the way we did, and she was right.'

'Right.' He glanced around as though looking for moral support. 'Are you cross?'

Was I? What difference did it make? In fact, wasn't it even better that he'd sought me out? Didn't it mean he actually wanted to find me, rather than being forced into it by chance?

I shrugged. 'I'm not sure why I should be. I suppose I should be flattered.'

He smiled. 'Good.'

Then something occurred to me.

'But why? What made you look for me after all this time? I mean, you said you've been back from Australia for ten years. Why haven't you tried to find me before?'

He didn't speak for a while. 'I – I don't know. I was scared, I suppose.'

'Scared of what?'

'That you wouldn't want to see me.'

'So what's changed? What made you think I'd want to now?'

'I don't know.' He looked at the candle on the table between us and I watched it reflected back in his eyes. 'But I'm glad I did.'

'So am I.' And I really was, I realised.

He breathed out a huge sigh and the candle flickered wildly. 'Thank goodness for that.'

'So how did you find me? I mean, I'm not really on social media and I know you're not—' I stopped, realising what I'd said as he glanced up, eyebrows raised.

'Oh?'

My face flamed. 'I mean. Well, I might have looked you up, after we met that day. I just – wanted to make sure you weren't an axe murderer or something.'

'And did you find anything?'

'Nope.'

'No. I hardly use social media either. I'm a bit of a dinosaur.'

'So how *did* you find me?' I was intrigued now.

'Old-fashioned detective work.' He glanced at me, a grin on his face. 'Oh, and Google. There aren't many Francesca Gordons around, it turns out, so it was pretty easy to find out where you worked. So one day I rang your office and asked to speak to you and pretended I was meant to be meeting you for lunch but had forgotten where. Your very helpful colleague told me you usually went to that café, so I hung around a few lunchtimes in the hope of finding you. And then, there you were.'

'Wow.'

'Yeah, it was pretty easy. You might want to ask your colleagues to be a little bit more discreet in future, although I'm glad they weren't this time.'

'Me too,' I said.

The spell was broken by the waiter. As we ordered our food and discussed wine, I tried not to think about what it meant that Will had waited so long to come and find me. Was Mags right? Was he hiding something else, or did he really just decide to go for it?

We ate our food and chatted. I filled Will in on my life, and told him about meeting Sean, and how he'd left when Kieran was just a few months old, deciding he didn't want to be a father after all. 'I always knew he was useless, but it took that to make me realise quite how useless he was,' I said.

'And does Kieran see his dad now?'

'Not much. Sean used to come and see him regularly, but when it started to fizzle out I did nothing to stop it, and in the end, he let him down one too many times and I told him to stay away.' I took a deep breath. 'I'm not proud of it but I needed to protect Kieran from being hurt.'

'And now?'

'Now I think I might have made a mistake. I mean, I adore Kieran but it's a shame for him not to have a father figure in his life.'

'It seems to me like you're doing a pretty good job by yourself.'

'Yeah, maybe.' I shrugged. 'It's just that sometimes I worry that his life – our lives – are so small.'

'What do you mean?'

'There's just nothing going on. I go to work, Kieran goes to school where he sees his mates, and then we're both at home, and on and on and repeat. We never go anywhere or do anything because I don't really have any spare cash, and I wish I could give him more, do more. I wish I could be more.'

'Oh, Fran. Has he ever said he feels he's missing out?'

'No. No, he's a good boy, and he never would even if he thought it. But that makes it worse somehow, as though I'm letting him down even more.' I stopped, worried I'd said too much. 'I'm very protective of him. I don't...' I coughed. 'I've never let a man into my life since Sean. I – I wouldn't want Kieran to be let down again.'

Will nodded. 'I understand.' He took a sip of his wine. 'I'm not asking you to let me intrude on your life, you know. I would never want to push you into anything. I just – I'd like to get to know you again, Fran. I feel like there could still be something there between us and I – I'd like to see if I'm right. But only if you want to.'

'I feel the same way too.'

'But?'

'What? There's no but.'

'It sounded as though there was going to be.'

I sighed. 'I guess I still don't really understand why you're here. Now, I mean, and not ten years ago, five years ago. I understand why we lost touch in the first place. It's not like we could email or text each other all those years ago. But now – I don't know. I just feel like there's something you're not telling me.'

Will was quiet for a minute, rubbing his hand across his head. He grimaced, then looked up.

'There's nothing. I promise. Okay?'

I nodded even though I wasn't convinced. 'Okay.'

The waiter arrived to take our plates away and handed us the dessert menus, and for a few moments we both buried our heads in them, gathering our thoughts.

'Do you still hate tiramisu?'

I peered over the menu at Will and saw him grinning at me. 'Yes. Why?'

'I just wondered. I might order it so you can't steal any of it.'

'Oh that's romantic,' I said, laughing.

'There's nothing romantic about people stealing your pudding.'

I put the menu down. 'Do you remember that time your mum made some chocolate crunch cakes?'

Will creased his brow in thought for a moment, then broke into a grin. 'Yes! To take on a school trip, and they were inedible?'

'And we didn't dare tell her because she'd gone to all that effort, so we threw them out of the window of the school bus and you hit that duck?'

'That was you!'

'It was *not*!'

'It definitely was.' Will chuckled. 'God, they were bloody awful. Mum was normally great at making cakes.'

'My mum reckoned she'd forgotten to add any sugar, but whatever, they nearly broke my teeth.'

'Poor Mum.'

'Oh, I'm sorry, Will. You must still miss her.'

'Every day.'

'I think about her a lot too, you know. I loved your mum.'

'She loved you as well.'

It was true. Will's mum and my mum had been best friends, and my mum adored Will as much as his adored me. Our dads had got on too, but it was our mums who kept the two families so tightly bound together.

'Remember when you and your dad fell out and Mum let you come and stay for a few nights?' I said now, the memories tumbling out.

'God, yes. I'd forgotten about that.'

'What had your dad done?'

Will's face darkened. 'I've got no idea.' The mood had suddenly changed.

'Are you okay?'

'Yeah. I'm all right.'

'Have I said something wrong?'

'No. It's just – me and my dad don't speak any more.'

'Oh. Since when?'

Will cleared his throat and shuffled in his seat. 'I haven't seen him for twenty-four years.'

I froze. 'What? Since just after you left?'

He nodded.

'What happened?'

Will shook his head. 'I don't really talk about it. We just – we fell out. I was angry about leaving, and never wanted to go to Australia in the first place. But Dad had just lost Mum and so I went along with it for his sake even though...' He stopped. 'Even though there were so many reasons to stay.' He took a deep breath. 'Dad did and said some unforgivable things and in the end, I left.'

'Where did you go?'

'I stayed in Sydney. I didn't want to go too far away from Jim. He was still only fifteen and he needed me. I still saw him. I just never saw Dad. And I still don't.'

'Wow.' I couldn't even imagine what his dad must have said to hurt him so badly that they hadn't spoken for so long. But it was clear that now wasn't the time to ask.

'How is Jim? Is he still out there?'

'No. He came back to the UK before me. He and Dad came back together about twelve years ago. I came back because I missed my little brother so much. Plus there was nothing keeping me there in the end.'

I nodded, taking it all in. Will had done so much, been to so many places. My life felt even smaller in comparison. Would he still find me so interesting when he found out how little I'd actually done?

'Anyway, Jim's good. He lives in Cornwall with his wife, Karen, and their two girls, Soraya and Olivia. I think he missed the beach life so was never going to come back to town.'

'Do you see him much?'

'Not enough.'

We fell into silence for a few moments as we ordered dessert and drank our wine. I was enjoying getting to know Will again, but the more I found out about his life the more it hammered home just how much had happened in the years since we'd been together. The memories I had of him were of younger versions of ourselves – versions that were happy and full of hope and expectation. Now we were not only older, but we were weighed down by past relationships, pain and secrets. I wondered how we could get past that and move forward. Or whether we even could.

There was something else on my mind too, and as the evening came to an end, my stomach started to tie itself in knots. Will hadn't tried to kiss me yet, but I felt sure he would tonight. I wanted to kiss him too. So much so I couldn't think of anything else as we settled the bill and shrugged into our coats after our meal.

'I'll take you home,' he said as we shivered in the chilly air outside the restaurant looking for the orange glow of a free black cab.

'Don't be silly, you live at the opposite side of the city. I'll be fine, I'll just get a taxi.'

'Well, at least let me call you an Uber.' He pulled his phone out and pressed a few buttons before I could object. 'Right, done. It'll be five minutes.'

'Thanks, Will. Let me pay you for it.'

'Nope, it's done. No arguments.'

We stood for a moment, neither of us moving, and then Will stepped towards me and wrapped his arms around me, enveloping me in his coat. His body still felt slim, his arms firm, and I shivered. I pulled back and looked up at him, his face blurring in the lights from the restaurant. Behind us, someone whistled and shouted 'Get a room!' and we both laughed.

'Maybe we should?' Will said softly.

'Should what?'

'Get a room.'

I shook my head. 'Not yet.'

He ran his fingers across my cheek. 'You're right. But it's okay to kiss you, isn't it?'

I nodded almost imperceptibly and then Will's lips were on mine and they felt so soft and warm and he tasted of salt, red wine and a familiar taste I couldn't identify. I was suddenly sixteen again, and Will was kissing me for the first time in Mum and Dad's kitchen. My knees felt weak and my mind was filled with all the things I wanted to tell him and then – and then he pulled away and my lips were hit by the cold night air. I felt breathless with excitement and embarrassed too. I felt like a silly teenager again and I knew I was in trouble. I knew there was no going back, whatever happened, whatever reservations I might have had.

Will stepped away and turned to face the road. 'Your carriage is here, madame,' he said, gesturing to a sleek BMW that had just pulled up on the road beside us.

'Are you all right getting home?'

'I've got another cab coming, I'm fine,' he said, pressing his hand into my back and leading me to the back door of the taxi.

'Thanks for tonight,' I said, leaning into him.

'Thanks for forgiving me for stalking you.'

'You said you didn't stalk me.'

'You know what I mean.'

'Will I see you again soon?' I found myself holding my breath, praying he wouldn't say no.

'I'll ring you tomorrow,' he said, pressing his lips against my cheek as I sank into the car. The door was closed with a soft thunk and as the car pulled into the traffic I tipped my head against the back of the seat and watched the lights flash past through the rear-view window.

Will Poulton.

I'd met Will Poulton again. And he still made me feel the way he always had. I knew I was smiling and I closed my eyes and tried to conjure up his face in my mind, as it was then and as it was now, the two faces blurring in to each other, the past and the present inter-mingled.

My thoughts were interrupted by a buzzing from my bag. I dug my mobile out and squinted at the screen, my heart thumping in anticipation. Was it from Will already?

How did it go? Mx

It was Mags. I typed a quick reply.

Great. We kissed. Am seeing him again. You were right though. Our meeting wasn't an accident, he found me.

I knew it. Did he say why?

No. Just that he wondered how I was.

She didn't reply for a moment even though I knew she'd read it. Then a message pinged.

Just be careful and don't rush into anything. Promise me? x

I promise. Night night x

But despite my promise to her, I knew I wouldn't be taking things slowly. I'd be careful, if only for Kieran's sake, of course. But I was falling in love with Will all over again and I knew, just like a domino that's started a run, that there was nothing I could do to stop it.

24 December 2018

The lights twinkled on the tree, and the smell of mulled wine filled the room. I lay with my head back on the sofa, my eyelids heavy. If I could just have a quick snooze...

'Come on, lazy bones!' I woke suddenly, aware of someone tapping my ankle, and laughing at me. I sat up, disorientated, and tried to focus on the person standing in front of me.

'Will, what are you doing here already?'

'Sorry, I was a bit early and Kieran let me in. I hope you don't mind?'

'Course not. I just...' I stopped, and stared at him in horror. 'What the bloody hell is that?'

'What? It's my Christmas jumper.'

'You're not...' I paused, trying to stifle a giggle. 'You're not actually going to go out in public wearing that, are you?'

He glanced down at the reindeers dancing across his chest and shrugged. 'It looks as though I am.'

'Oh God...' I grinned and hauled myself off the sofa and pulled him towards me. Our noses were touching and I lifted my head to peck his lips lightly. 'I suppose I'll have to pretend not to know you, then, won't I?'

'How could you pretend not to know a gorgeous specimen like me?' Then he leaned in and kissed me deeply.

'Urrggghhhh!'

Kieran's disgusted voice broke the moment, and we leaped apart guiltily. 'Sorry, love,' I said, following Kieran into the kitchen, ruffling his hair as he tried to duck out of my way.

'You promised not to be gross,' he said, pulling a loaf of bread out of the bread bin.

'Sorry, Kieran, it was my fault,' Will said.

Kieran tutted and shoved two slices into the toaster.

'Wait, what are you doing? We're about to go out for dinner.'

Kieran shrugged. 'I'm starving. Just having a snack.'

I rolled my eyes. The appetites of a thirteen-year-old boy were a mystery to me. All I knew was that he seemed capable of eating three times as much as me and still staying as skinny as a rake.

'Well, hurry up, the table's booked for six. Gran and Gramps will be waiting.'

'Yeah, yeah. I'm totally ready.'

I glanced at his ripped jeans and Champion sweatshirt and decided not to say anything. There were battles to pick and this was not one of them.

Besides, I had enough to think about. My nerves were picking at the edges of my conscience, reminding me that this Christmas Eve meal was significant.

Will and I had seen each other a lot over the last couple of months, more than I'd intended. We'd been on a number of dates. He got on well with Kieran and, despite any reservations I might have had, I was happy. But today was going to be the first time Mum and Dad had seen Will since he'd walked out and left me heartbroken – not to mention eighteen and pregnant.

I'd finally plucked up the courage to ring them and tell them about Will two weeks before.

'You can't just not tell them. What are you going to do, hide from them for the rest of your life?' Mags had said, and I knew she was right. But knowing it and doing it were two entirely different things. Eventually I'd mustered up the courage, and my heart had thumped in my temples as I'd waited for them to react.

'I see,' Mum said, her voice tinny, distant. I'd asked her to put her phone on speakerphone so Dad could hear too so I didn't have to repeat the news, but she hadn't quite mastered the art of putting her mouth close to the speaker properly.

'You see good, or you see bad?' I cursed myself for the tremble in my voice. I felt as nervous as I had when I'd had to break the news to them that their teenage daughter was pregnant. I was forty-three years old, for goodness' sake.

'I think I need a little bit of time to digest the news, dear,' Mum had said. There was a wobble in her voice, then I'd heard a rustling sound and she'd said, clearly from some distance away, 'You talk to her for a minute, Pete.'

Then my father's voice, loud, in my ear. 'Your mother's gone to make herself a cup of something,' he said, and I could hear the smile in his voice. We both knew that meant she was pretending to make coffee, but that there would be something stronger in her cup to steady her nerves.

'So, what do you think?'

'I think it's great, love.'

'Do you really?' I hadn't expected that. My father had been furious when Will had left. He didn't say much, it wasn't my father's style, but the quiet fury was the sort that rarely burned out, just simmered gently until it was re-ignited. I'd felt sure my news would only stir his anger up again.

'I think it's great because I haven't heard you sounding this happy in a long time so he must be doing something right.'

'Aren't you angry?'

'Angry? No, too much time has passed for that.' He paused and I could hear the rattle of his breath in his chest. 'You're all right now, aren't you?'

'Yes. I am.' I cleared my throat, my voice scratchy, not wanting to make Dad feel awkward with a show of emotion. 'Do you – do you think Mum will be okay?'

'She'll come round, she always does. You know what she's like.'

I did. Lovely, kind and loyal, but sometimes that loyalty stood in the way of her seeing things from anyone else's perspective. It meant she could be blinkered, and hold grudges in a way I'd never known anyone to before.

'Anyhow, I wanted to ask you both something.'

'Go on.'

'Will and I want to have dinner with you at Christmas, and I – I need to know you're not going to say anything.' I didn't need to explain what I meant. Dad was silent for a moment.

'I won't say a word, love.'

'What about Mum?'

'I'll talk to her. She'll be fine.' I believed him. If anyone could talk my mother round, it was Dad.

'And you'll be nice to Will?'

'Of course we will; what do you take us for, Francesca?'

A silence fell for a moment, filled with all the things we could have said, but neither of us did. I knew my father would be remembering how broken I was when Will had left, how hard it had hit me, and worrying. But I loved him for not feeling the need to say that, and for supporting me instead.

Now, as we got ready to go and meet them, I felt completely unprepared, and worried Mum might say something she shouldn't, despite my preparations.

All I could do was pray it would go smoothly.

'Muuuum, are we going yet? I'm starving.' Kieran's voice interrupted us and I turned to see him waiting impatiently at the front door, slice of toast in hand.

'Come on, then, let's go.'

We stepped out into the chilly December air and, as we made our way to the bus stop, Will grabbed my hand. It felt cold in mine and I squeezed it and smiled at him.

'Okay?'

He nodded. 'Bit scared your dad might challenge me to a duel for breaking his daughter's heart, but other than that, fine.'

'I think you'll be fine. Hiring a hitman is more his style.'

He grinned.

We were the last to arrive at the restaurant and as we wound our way past the tables, ducking our heads to avoid the ridiculous amounts of decorations weighing the ceiling down, I saw the faces of all the people I loved watching our approach.

I knew my parents would be there already. They were never late for anything, thanks to my father's over-officious timekeeping. 'It's just manners, Francesca, nothing more,' he often said, in his soft Welsh accent. He hated tardiness. I must have driven him mad.

Now, Mum and Dad were sitting along one side of the table, Dad's thick grey hair swept off his face and held in place with the Brylcreem he'd always loved, and wearing his usual attire of jumper with a shirt and tie. Mum's hair was in the neat bob she'd worn for as long as I could remember, although grey now rather than the dark brown it had always been, and a dark green satin blouse. Mags, Rob and their girls were lined up along the other side and relief flooded through me; I'd begged Mags to come along to dilute the tension, and she'd readily agreed. Mags loved my parents, and they loved her. 'She's the best friend anyone could ever have,' my mum said, and sometimes I wondered whether she wished Mags was her daughter rather than me. Her presence today could only help.

I was also relieved to see that Rob had had the same idea as Will and was wearing an equally awful jumper with some sort of sparkly snowman on the front. Mags's face said it all.

As we approached the table, my heart hammered and it took everything I had not to turn around and run away from the restaurant, from my family, friends and everything this evening represented.

Surprisingly, it was Dad who broke the tension. As we reached the table, he stood, then leaned forward and hugged me awkwardly, slapping Kieran on the back. 'Hello, Kier,' he said warmly.

'All right, Gramps.'

Then he turned to Will and my heart leaped into my throat. A second ticked past, and then another... and then Dad held out his hand. 'Hello, young man,' he said, his voice formal. 'It's good to see you again.'

'You too, Mr Gordon,' Will said, shaking my father's hand.

'Call me Pete, please.'

Will nodded.

Next to me, Mum studied Will from beneath her fringe, her eyes searching his face. Then slowly she pushed herself up to standing. Will took a step towards her, his hand held out, and for a moment nothing happened. My stomach lurched. Was she going to make things difficult, despite her promises?

But then she stepped forward and cupped her hands round Will's cheeks. 'I'd have known that face anywhere. You've haven't changed a bit.' She smiled. 'It's good to see you again, William.'

'You too, Mrs Morgan.'

'Please, call me Stephanie.'

My heart thumped with relief as we took our seats. We'd done it. We'd got through the first obstacle. Now I just had to hope the rest of the meal would go as smoothly.

By the time our food arrived, I'd finally begun to relax.

'It's going all right,' Mags said quietly while Will was telling Mum and Dad about his daughter, Elodie.

'Don't speak too soon, I don't want to jinx anything.'

'Your Mum's behaving herself too. I never thought I'd see the day when she'd have a civil word to say to Will.'

'Me neither. I hope it lasts.'

'I think it will. She's softened in her old age, your mum. Besides, you know she always listens to me.'

I looked at her sharply. 'Did you say something to her?'

'I just told her how much this means to you, and that you were so happy she was being supportive.' She shrugged. 'That's all.'

I smiled. Mags knew as well as I did that my mum thought she was the best thing since sliced bread. No matter that Dad had already got her to agree not to say anything about the past – Mags asking her would have been the thing that sealed the deal.

I turned my attention back to the table where I could hear Mum's voice.

'So how's your father these days?'

'Mum!' I'd already told her that they didn't speak to each other, but she clearly couldn't help herself.

'It's all right, Fran,' Will said. He fell silent for a moment, and I watched his face as he struggled to work out what to say. 'He's fine, as far as I know,' he said, coughing into his fist. 'We haven't spoken for quite some time.'

'What, not at all?'

Will shook his head.

'Oh, is he still all the way over the other side of the world? That must be difficult for you.'

'No, he's back in England.'

'Oh. And you still don't see him?'

'No.' Will prodded a potato with his fork.

'Oh, what a shame. We might not see Fran as much as we'd like' – Dad threw me a look and rolled his eyes at Mum's obvious barb – 'but at least we speak to her whenever we want. We even get the odd text from Kieran sometimes, don't we, love?'

'Yes, Grandma.' Kieran looked down at his plate, awkward. Anger rose in me. I glanced at Dad, who shrugged helplessly.

'Mum, I don't think this is helping,' I said. 'I told you Will hasn't seen his dad for a long time, do you remember?'

I knew she did, but she looked shocked, her hand flying to her chest. 'Oh, I am sorry, you did mention it, but I completely forgot.' She placed her hand gently on Will's arm. 'Please forgive me for being so insensitive.'

'It's all right, Mrs Gordon. Stephanie.'

Mum was silent for a moment, clearly weighing up whether to ask what had happened, but when she saw the look on my father's face, she decided against it.

'How's your lovely little brother, James then?'

'Oh, Jim's the same as ever,' Will said, a smile spreading across his face. 'He's a teacher now, lives in Cornwall with his wife, Karen, and two girls, Soraya and Olivia.'

'How lovely. And do you see him often?' Mum said.

'Not as often as I'd like.'

'I know the feeling,' Mum said, spearing a sprout and popping it in her mouth.

We ate the rest of our meals in peace, the chatter of the other customers making the silence comfortable. I watched Mum across the table, wondering what was going through her mind. Despite her tricky questioning, I understood how she must be feeling. I knew if anyone hurt Kieran the way Will had hurt me, I'd want to tear them limb from limb. What must have made it worse was that Will was not only her best friend's child, but someone she'd always thought of as more of her son. I could hardly blame her for feeling angry.

As the waiter came to clear away the plates, I glanced across at Mum and found her watching me, the ghost of a smile playing on her lips.

'Okay?' I mouthed at her.

She nodded and I knew in that instant that everything was going to be all right. The past was firmly locked in the past and, if I had anything to do with it, that's where it was going to stay.

The meal finished, Dad raised his glass. 'A toast,' he said, and we all looked at him. He caught my eye and smiled. 'I'm not one for long speeches, as you know. But I just wanted to say thank you for a smashing day, and merry Christmas.'

'Merry Christmas!' everyone chorused at once.

As we left twenty minutes later, our bellies full, my heart swelled with happiness. I grabbed my coat and turned to Will, who looked pale, his face grey in the dim lights.

'Are you okay?' I said, slipping my arm into my sleeve.

He rubbed his hand over his face and grimaced.

'I think so. Just feel a bit dizzy and my head hurts.' He grinned. 'A bit too much wine, I think.'

'Me too. Let's get you home.'

I hooked my arm through his on one side and Kieran's on the other, who, to my surprise, didn't pull away. As we walked back down the street after saying our goodbyes, I smiled. I felt so lucky to have these two wonderful men in my life.

Life really was on the up.

* * *

I closed the front door behind us and collapsed onto the sofa.

'I don't know about you but I'm wiped out,' I said, pulling my boots off and flicking the TV on. 'Fancy watching a bit of crap Christmas telly?'

'I'm in,' Kieran said, flopping into the armchair and swinging his legs over the arm.

'Will?' I said, peering up at where he was still hovering in the doorway. His eyebrows were pulled in tight.

'I'm really sorry, but I think I'm going to have to go home after all.' He rubbed his head again. 'I just can't seem to shake this thing off.'

'Do you want some painkillers? I think I've got some in the bathroom?' I started to stand but he waved me away.

'No, it's fine. I'll just get going.' He swayed, holding himself up with the doorframe. 'I'll just have an early night and I'll feel better tomorrow.' He gave me an apologetic look. 'I'm sorry to spoil the night.'

'Don't be daft. Get yourself home and make sure you're feeling better for the morning,' I said.

'Will do,' he said, leaning down and pecking me on the cheek.

As he left, I turned to Kieran. 'It's just you and me then, son, the way it's always been,' I said, reaching over and squeezing his shoulder. 'Happy Christmas, darling.'

'Happy Christmas, you drunken fool,' he said, his smile softening his words.

* * *

Groaning, I rolled over and checked the clock. Seven o'clock. Ugh, still early.

I climbed out of bed and padded into the living room. I switched on the Christmas lights, made myself a cup of tea and sat and watched as it grew light outside the window, the sky turning from deep purple to pink, orange, yellow and, finally, a pale blue, like a light show just for me. I loved this time of day, when there was nobody around on the usually busy street – when there was a sense that you were the only person in the world, and you could watch as, one by one, in the flats and houses opposite, the world came to life again.

Of course, this morning there would likely be nobody out there, as everyone had either left London to visit families far away, or staying in the warmth of their homes to eat dinner and open their presents. I took a sip of my tea and let the steam curl round my face, warming me.

'You're up early.'

I turned to find Kieran in the doorway, clutching the stocking I still insisted on putting together for him every year even though he'd stopped believing in Father Christmas several years ago.

'Hey, you,' I said, moving along the sofa to make room for him. He sat down and I felt the cushion tip so that I fell into him.

'Shall I wait for Will to get here before I open these?'

Will was spending the morning with Elodie and Amy before coming to us for the afternoon and evening. I'd cleared it with Kieran that it was all right for Will to spend the night for the first time too.

'It's up to you, darling. Why don't you open your stocking presents, just me and you, and then we can open the ones under the tree when Will gets here?'

His eyes lit up, still a child underneath the gruff teenage exterior, and I watched him as he happily unwrapped the small gifts. A book, a new onesie, a chocolate orange, some deliberately mismatching socks. When he got to the end and pulled out the traditional tangerine, he grinned. 'You know I'm only eating this so I can have chocolate next, don't you?' he said, peeling the skin off carefully.

'Course,' I said, leaning over and giving him a peck on the cheek. I watched his face as he chewed slowly, deep in thought.

'Penny for them.'

He looked up, startled. 'What?'

'You looked like you were thinking about something important.'

'Oh no. S'nothing.'

I watched him for a moment, his familiar face that had my eyes and his father's nose, his beautiful face that was changing too quickly from a boy to a man. He was slipping away from me day by day.

'If you could choose anything you wanted for Christmas, what would it be? If money was no object?'

Kieran shrugged. 'Dunno.'

'There must be something you want more than anything else in the world? A fancy holiday? A new Xbox?'

Kieran raised his eyes to the ceiling for a moment, thinking. Then he dropped them to look at the floor just by my feet.

'I guess there is one thing.'

'Go on.'

He shifted his gaze from the floor to the wall to the ceiling and back again and I began to wonder what on earth he was going to say.

'I'd like to see my dad.'

I felt as though the room had tipped away from me for a moment, and the walls were closing in. 'Oh... I...' I stopped, the words getting stuck in my throat.

Kieran continued to stare at the wall just above my left shoulder.

'I've just been thinking about him a bit recently. I'd quite like to see him.' He shrugged as though it was nothing important.

'I... I didn't know.' My voice came out as a whisper and I cleared my throat. 'Since when, Keeks?'

He looked at me now, and shrugged again. 'A while.'

'Why didn't you tell me?'

He stared at his toes. 'I knew you'd be upset.'

My heart clenched. My own son wanted to see his father and was too scared to tell me? What sort of mother was I?

Kieran continued. 'I know he's not that bothered about me, but it would be nice to know him better.' He rubbed his eye nervously. 'I mean, he's out there, and he's part of me. It seems weird not to know him.'

'Oh, love.' I stood and walked the few steps across the living room to the chair and crouched down next to him and rubbed my hands across his forearm. 'I'm so sorry. I never meant to keep him away. He just – we...' I stopped, unwilling to tell him that, actually, his dad just wasn't that interested in seeing him. 'He's just quite a difficult man. But maybe in the new year we can see if we can get in touch with him, try and meet up.'

Kieran stared at the TV, but nodded. 'Thanks, Mum.'

I stood and planted a kiss on the top of his head.

'Let's get some breakfast, shall we?'

'Yeah, okay.'

I walked into the kitchen and made some more tea. As I poured the milk, I thought about what Kieran had said. Even though it wasn't my fault Sean had left, guilt still overwhelmed me. I hadn't exactly stopped Kieran seeing his dad, but I definitely hadn't encouraged it either. When Sean had left I'd been angry and hurt, and seeing him every now and then on the odd visit, seeing him getting on with his life without us, made my anger levels soar. I didn't make it easy for him, I knew that. But I just couldn't bring myself to. He'd hurt me so much, I needed to make him hurt too. It had never occurred to me that Kieran was that bothered. He'd never really mentioned him.

But I realised now how naïve I'd been. Of course he missed his dad. Of course he wanted to see him.

What boy wouldn't?

* * *

Will stretched his legs out in front of him and sighed. 'God, that was delicious,' he said, rubbing his belly. 'I'm not sure there's any room in there for my lungs to breathe, though.'

'You're such a lightweight,' Kieran said, reaching over and shoving the last roast potato into his mouth. His cheeks bulged as he chewed.

'It's all right for you, you're still growing. If I keep eating like this I'm only going to grow outwards.'

I grinned. Will was still so lean, his footballer's fitness never having left him, and the thought of him getting fat was slightly absurd. But I knew what he meant. I was so full I wasn't sure whether I'd be able to move from the sofa for the rest of the day.

'I'm glad your headache cleared,' I said, stretching out beside him.

'Me too.'

'What do you think caused it?'

'What? Oh, nothing, it was just one of those things, I think.'

'Maybe it's the stress of meeting me and my family again.' I grinned.

'That'd be enough to make anyone ill,' Kieran said, and I threw a selection box at him, hitting him squarely on the head.

Some quiz show on TV soon caught Kieran's attention and I turned to Will.

'I'm so glad we got to spend today with you,' I said.

'Me too. Thanks for making me dinner.'

'No problem.'

I leaned my head back and closed my eyes, memories of Christmases past floating into my mind – some more welcome than others. I pushed away the memory of the Christmas Will had left and instead thought back to the Christmas before that, when we were in love and thought we had the rest of our lives together. We'd spent the day at our house, our families having started taking it in turns to host Christmas dinner several years before, and had been desperate to get away and spend some time alone, just me and him.

'Where are you two lovebirds going?' his mum had asked as we'd stood and pulled our coats on. We'd glanced at each other, sheepish.

'We're just going for a walk.'

'Well, don't be long, I'm making sandwiches soon.'

'But we've only just had lunch.'

'That was hours ago.'

'Okay, okay, we'll be back in half an hour.'

'Good. Wrap up warm.'

We'd rolled our eyes as the front door shut behind us, exasperated at the way our parents still treated us like children even though we were seventeen.

I closed Will's hand in mine, feeling the coolness of his skin even through my woolly gloves. 'So where are we going, then?'

'I dunno, anywhere.'

We walked along the dark street, empty apart from a cat slinking across the road and the occasional shout from an open kitchen window. Suddenly Will had pulled me up a dark alleyway and into the woods behind our houses.

'What are you doing? We can't go in here in the dark.'

'Why not? Are you scared?'

'Yes, a bit.'

We walked deeper into the woods and Will stopped. An owl hooted somewhere above our heads, and something rustled in the undergrowth, but other than that it was completely silent. Will pulled me to him and I felt the thump of his heart through his padded jacket, slow and steady. I breathed deeply. This was where I wanted to be. Suddenly the woods didn't feel so scary any more.

'I love you, you know, Fran.' His words were muffled, his mouth pressed against my hair. I lifted my face to look at him, our lips almost touching.

'I love you too, Will.'

'You'll never leave me, will you?'

I pulled away slightly. 'Why would you say that?'

'I don't know. I just see you sometimes, with other boys, and I see them looking at you and I wonder...' He stopped. 'I wonder what it will be like when we both go away to university next year.'

'Will Poulton, I'm not interested in anyone else. You must know that, right?'

'Most of the time.'

'All of the time. You're the only person I'll ever love.'

'Do you promise?'

'Of course I do. And anyway, it might be you that leaves me.'

'Never. Nothing could ever make me leave you, Franny.'

I stood on my tiptoes and kissed him gently on the lips.

'Good. Now come on, let's walk, it's freezing in here and I want to get back and see how many After Eights I can stuff down my throat before your dad spots them.'

'Bet I can eat more than you.'

'You're on.'

That had been the last Christmas Day we'd spent together, and the best I'd ever had.

Until now. I opened my eyes and looked at Will, then at Kieran, and a feeling of contentment washed over me. What had I done to deserve this?

* * *

Later, when Kieran was in bed, Will looked thoughtful.

'What's up?' I said, leaning over for another slice of cheese that I definitely didn't need.

'Oh nothing. Just...' He stopped. 'It makes you think, doesn't it? Christmas time, I mean.'

'About what?'

He shrugged. 'Families and things. You know.'

I thought back to Kieran asking to see his dad. 'Yeah, I guess it does. Kieran asked to see his dad the other day.'

'Did he? And will you let him?'

'I promised I'd sort it out, yes.'

Will sighed. 'I don't blame him. I can't stop thinking about my father either, it must be catching.' His fingers drummed on his thigh. 'I mean, I'm lucky at the moment, being able to see Elodie all the time. But I can't stay there forever, living under the same roof as Amy. And when I move out, what's going to happen then? How often will I still see her? How can I live with not seeing my little girl every day? It's not right. And I know it's different when your kids are older, if they've chosen not to see you rather than being kept away against their will, but...' He sighed again. 'I don't know. I just wonder how my father must feel sometimes. About everything that's happened.'

I placed my hands on his. 'What did he do, Will? Your dad? What did he do that was so terrible you can't forgive him?'

He waited a beat. 'He...' Will picked at a loose fingernail. 'When Mum died we were all heartbroken, me, Dad and Jim. I was only eighteen but Jim was only fourteen, for God's sake. We needed Dad, both of us. We needed time to grieve, to talk about Mum, to remember her. But instead of letting us do that, Dad shut down. He wouldn't talk about her and he wouldn't let us talk about her either. It was as though a brick wall had gone up in his mind. Jim and I were both furious when we moved away. Dad claimed it was because we needed a fresh start, because the memories of Mum in that house were too hard for him. For *him*. But he never once considered what was right for us. I needed those memories, to be able to walk into a room and remember a time when I'd been there with Mum, when she'd been in my room and read me a bedtime story, when she'd brought dinner to the table and when she'd played games with me at the dining table. Every single piece of furniture, every single room, held a part of Mum, for us. And Jim and I both needed that. But instead Dad decided we had to go halfway round the bloody world before we had even really had a chance to let it sink in. We'd gone. Just like that.'

I held his gaze, searched his eyes. All I could see there was hurt.

'In the end, though, I think we would both have forgiven him. But he started drinking. And with the drink he became aggressive. He'd always been volatile – we often heard him and Mum shouting at each other – but as far as I knew he was never physical. But the booze changed him. He became bitter, and nasty. He neglected us. I was old enough to look after myself but Jim – he was still only young, vulnerable. I ended up looking after him as best I could but in the end I...' He stopped. 'He said some terrible things. Made some accusations that I could never ever forgive him for. If he could think that of me, then he didn't know me at all, and I didn't want to be part of his life. And so I left, and the day I walked out I vowed I'd never speak to Dad again. And I never have.'

'What things did he say, Will?' What could he possibly have said that was bad enough to cut him off for twenty-five years?

But Will just shook his head. 'It doesn't matter.'

It was clear he didn't want me to push him any more.

'So where is he now?' I asked instead.

'Now? I honestly don't know. I know he's in the UK because he came back with Jim. But I made Jim promise not to talk about him. It was easier that way.'

'So, what's changed?'

He shrugged. 'I don't know. Me and Amy falling apart. Spending Christmas with you and Kieran and him wanting to see his dad. Realising that, actually, maybe I do care about my father, underneath it all. Or at least, maybe I should.'

Will let out a long breath, and his body sagged, as though exhausted.

'Wow.' I was shocked. Will's dad had always seemed so lovely. So kind, and welcoming. I remember the day he told me I was like the daughter he'd never had and I was so chuffed to feel like a real part of the family. He worked hard, but it always felt that when he was there he was really there, teaching us to play cricket, building a treehouse in their garden, taking us to the zoo. In my mind he was funny and silly and did everything he could for his family. But maybe there had been a darker side to him after all. Maybe Will's mum dying was just a trigger for it all to get out of hand.

But I knew I couldn't tell Will what he should do. All I could do was be there for him, and listen.

'If you decide to see him, I'll support you,' I said now.

He squeezed my hand. 'Thank you, Fran.'

I hoped he'd make the right choice.

* * *

Later, as we made our way to bed, the nerves began to kick in. Although we'd been seeing each other for a couple of months, we'd both wanted to wait a while before sleeping together. Now, I wondered whether tonight might be the right time. We certainly felt closer than ever before.

We stood either side of the bed, facing each other.

'Well,' I said.

'Well indeed.' A smile played on Will's lips.

'What's so funny?'

'Oh, nothing. I just – I never in a million years thought I'd be spending another night with you. Twenty-five years.'

'Don't.' I glanced down at my belly, swollen with Christmas food. Maybe today wasn't the ideal time to be doing this after all. What would it be like to be intimate with this man who I'd last touched when I was a teenager? Would expectations be too high? Would he still find me attractive or would my looser skin, my less-taut belly, my wider thighs, put him off? I looked up and studied Will's face. I could still see the handsome boy I'd fallen in love with all those years ago in the long lashes, in the curl of his hair and the arch of his eyebrow. Something in my belly fluttered.

I thought of the first time we'd shared a bed, as innocent eight-year-olds excited to be having a sleepover with our best friend. Back then we'd found it funny to press our cold feet against each other's warm skin to make the other one scream, and we'd covered the sheets in crisp crumbs as we munched our way through a midnight feast we were convinced our parents knew nothing about. We slept at each other's houses often, back then, and our parents never gave it a single thought. But then one day it began to feel awkward, as though we were doing something wrong. We were probably about fourteen, and it had never occurred to us that sleeping in the same bed might be strange until a school friend pointed it out. From then on, we didn't share a bed but blew up an air bed whenever we stayed over, one person shivering on a tiny mattress on the floor, just so nobody thought we were up to anything untoward.

I thought of the first time we'd shared a bed as girlfriend and boyfriend. We'd been seventeen, and home on study leave. Will's parents had gone away for the weekend, trusting us to look after Jim while they were gone. But unbeknown to me, Will had arranged for Jim to stay with a friend so that we could spend the night together in his bed. And even though it wasn't our first time, and even though I knew his body almost as well as I knew my own by then after the times we'd spent getting to know each other in his parents' car, in the woods, in any place we could find to be together, there was something special, forbidden, about staying in his bed together.

Our parents found out, of course. But rather than getting angry, as we'd expected, they'd instead sat us down to talk about the new 'arrangement', as they'd called it. Which basically meant that they'd let us stay together sometimes as long as we promised to be careful. We were mortified, but pleased. But nothing had ever compared to that first, illicit night together, when I'd felt the warmth of Will's skin against mine, and we'd spent the night curled up, as one.

Would it be the same now?

Will sat on the bed and gestured for me to do the same. He reached out and snaked his arms around my waist and pulled me to him. His forearm rested lightly on my stomach, his chin scratching my neck. The fabric of his T-shirt and my vest top felt like a barrier between us and I pressed myself to him.

'You okay?' His voice was scratchy, his throat sounding dry.

I half-turned my head towards him. 'Yeah,' I whispered.

He pulled me closer and pressed his lips against my neck and I sighed. I turned round to face him and he opened his eyes.

'You look like a Cyclops this close up,' he said.

He pressed his lips against my nose and traced a line of kisses along my jawline and down my neck. I shivered at his touch. It had been so long since we'd been this close, but he still felt so familiar. His body still fit against mine perfectly. His lips carried on their path, down across my collarbones, across my breast, his lips brushing them gently through my T-shirt.

'I think this should come off,' he whispered, and I pulled it over my head and unclipped my bra.

I thought I'd feel exposed, self-conscious, being naked in front of him after all this time. We still had ghost memories of the old us, but would we both like what we saw, all these years later? Will's body still had the muscle tone from his footballing days and looked as lean and strong as ever, if a bit fuller, softer. I hadn't done any exercise for years, and after twenty-five years and a baby, I worried he might not like the middle-aged woman I'd become, the soft rolls of skin where there'd once been none, the breasts that were hopelessly struggling to defy gravity where once they'd been pert.

But as we kissed and fell into a rhythm that felt as sexy as it did familiar, I barely even gave it a thought.

And as we lay together afterwards, staring up at the ceiling, my heart pounding, I remembered what had happened on one of the last times we'd slept together. We'd made a baby.

I wondered whether Will was thinking about it too.

8

Late January 2019

I've never been one for New Year's resolutions. I mean, did people ever stick to them anyway? What was the point in choosing January to try and change everything you disliked about yourself? Surely you were destined to fail.

This year felt different, though. This year felt special. And although I didn't exactly make a New Year's resolution, I did make a vow to myself. This year, I would let myself be happy.

But then Will had some news.

He'd been acting strangely for a few days, avoiding eye contact, going quiet on me, making excuses not to come round. I was beginning to worry he'd changed his mind, that actually this was all too much for him, too soon, so I'd decided to sit down and talk to him about it. Which was where we were now – sitting in a bar, glass of wine in hand, me ready to have it out with him.

'Whatever it is, Will, it can't be that bad. If you want us to slow down, take things a bit easier, I'd rather know. Please tell me.'

He continued to stare at his hands, which were clenched in his lap, condensation dripping down the side of his pint glass as it warmed in the thick air of the pub. My throat tightened as I watched him. Surely nothing he could say was going to be as bad as the things I was imagining?

But then he raised his gaze to meet mine, and I knew I was right to be worried. I'd never seen him look so scared, so haunted.

'Will, what is it? Please tell me.' I reached forward for his hands but he pulled them away, almost flinching from my grasp. 'You're scaring me.'

'It's...' He stopped, swallowed, and started again. 'There's something I need to tell you. I – I haven't exactly been honest with you.'

I felt faint, as though I might fall off my chair, and I gripped the edges with my fingers and waited for him to explain. I tried to stop myself imagining his next words.

'Fran, there's no easy way to tell you this. I...' He stopped again, looked down and then back up. 'I'm dying.'

I gripped the chair tighter as the whole room closed in around me. The walls bulged, pressing down on me; the chatter around us faded to nothing. It was just me and Will, and his words, like shards of glass to my heart.

I swallowed. 'What do you mean?'

'I have cancer. A brain tumour. They can't operate.'

I stared at him for a moment, my eyes boring into his head as though it would show me where his tumour was. I couldn't speak; my throat closed up, my words snatched away.

'Aren't you going to say anything?'

I grabbed my wine glass and took a huge gulp, the liquid burning the back of my throat. I slammed it back down with shaking hands, a few drops splashing over the edge and landing on the table.

'What do you want me to say?'

'I don't know. Anything.'

I breathed in deeply through my nose and out again, trying to contain the panic I could feel rising in me. *This* was why I never got close to anyone. Because they always let you down. I should have known this would happen. It's not as though Mags didn't warn me he must be hiding something. It's not as though he'd never let me down before.

'How long have you known?'

Will watched me carefully as he told me. If he was worried about my reaction, he was right to be.

'Since last summer.'

Rage built in me now, burning like a fire in my belly, working its way up through my throat to my mouth, my tongue, my lips.

'How fucking *dare* you,' I said, the words hissing through my teeth as I struggled not to cause a scene. My body began to shake, and I tried to swallow down deep breaths to stem the fury.

'I'm so sorry, Fran. I never meant for things to get so far, I...' He stopped.

'You're sorry? *You're* sorry?' I gripped my glass so tightly by the stem it was a wonder it didn't shatter. 'Do you know what I'm sorry about, Will?'

He shook his head.

'I'm sorry that I ever let you come anywhere near me again.' I took a deep breath through my nose. 'I mean, it's not as though you haven't got form, is it?'

He reached out to me and I snatched my hands away, not caring how much I hurt him. A part of me was aware that I needed to find some sympathy, to comfort him. The man I loved was dying and soon, that fact would hit me. But that part was buried for now beneath so much fury, anger and betrayal that it couldn't find its way out.

'I'm sorry, Fran. For not telling you before.'

It was the deceit that got me. The fact that he'd told me there was no reason for seeking me out, that he'd made it seem as though he'd just felt like looking for me.

'What were you trying to do, by finding me again? Were you

looking for some sort of redemption before you go off to see your maker?' I knew I was being cruel, my words like bullets, but I couldn't help myself.

'No. It wasn't like that.' Will paused, thinking. 'I always felt so guilty about what I did to you. Leaving with my dad, and not even coming to tell you in person. Writing you a letter like a massive coward, not being there with you when you had the abortion, I... I always wondered how you were. I'd thought about trying to find you several times since coming back to England but I just couldn't do it. I suppose I didn't want to ruin your life again.'

'So why have you now?'

'Even when I married Amy, I always wondered whether I should come and find you first, just to make sure I was doing the right thing. But I didn't and then too much time passed. But then this summer... this summer I got this news and – well... it felt like the right time. I only planned to make amends, and see that you were happy. Make sure you had the life you always deserved. I didn't plan to fall in love again.'

A tear slid down his face and he brushed it away. Every part of me wanted to reach over and hug him, to tell him I loved him too, but I held back. I still felt betrayed and angry, and I needed time to process his news.

'How long have you got?'

Will looked at me, his eyes shining. 'The doctors aren't sure. They've said the tumour's growing slowly at the moment. It could be months, but more likely a few years.'

'Months?'

'Yes. But I think it will be longer. I'm feeling good at the moment, better than I have for a long time. I get the odd headache but apart from that I feel normal. Healthy.'

I closed my eyes and took a deep breath. I couldn't deal with this. I needed to get out of there. I stood, the stool scraping harshly across the tiled floor. My legs felt wobbly. 'I need to go.'

'Fran.' Will stood too. 'Please don't leave like this.'

'I have to, Will. I can't do this.'

'But I love you. I—'

'No. Stop. You have no right to do this. You can't let me fall in love with you all over again and then tell me you're dying and expect me to think that's okay. You can't do that. I can't do it.'

I picked my bag off the floor and walked away, my legs shaking, my head spinning. I didn't look back once, and as I marched back towards the house where Mags was looking after Kieran, I let the tears fall freely down my face.

* * *

Hours later, as I lay curled on the sofa, my head tucked into Mags's lap, I felt exhausted, wiped out. I could feel Mags's fingers gently caressing my hair, the gentle hum of canned laughter from the TV, turned down low in the background. I felt the buzz of her mobile, and her lap shook slightly as she picked up her phone and tapped a few buttons. I opened one eye and squinted at the clock above the TV. It was 1 a.m.

I pushed myself up to sitting and turned to look at my best friend, who was watching me, concern etched on her face.

'Hello, sleepyhead,' she said, smiling.

'It's so late. Why are you still here?'

'I couldn't leave you in that state.' She pushed my hair back where it had stuck to my cheek. 'You feeling any better?'

I shrugged. Was I? I'd got home and told Mags what Will had said, and then I'd cried for what felt like hours. My eyes were puffy and sore and my chest felt heavy. But the anger had subsided now, leaving in its place a numbness.

'A bit, I think.'

'Good.'

'You should go home now.'

'I will in a bit.' She picked up her phone. 'Let me just reply to Rob.'

I waited while she let her husband know that everything was okay.

'So, want to talk about it?'

'Haven't I bored you enough?'

'I mean properly talk about it. You've only told me what he said.'

'It's late.'

'I know. But this is important, Fran. Anyway, I haven't got work until late tomorrow so don't worry about that.' She rubbed her eyes. 'Do you want to know what I think about it, now I've had time to absorb Will's news?'

I always wanted to know Mags's take on something. She was almost always right, and even when she wasn't she helped me work out my own feelings. She was my voice of reason, and the person I trusted more than anyone else in the world. I nodded. 'Yes please.'

'Okay. So you feel angry and betrayed. Of course you do. But maybe this is a good thing.'

'How can it be good? The man I love is dying and tricked me into falling for him again. I can't see anything good about that.'

Mags held her hand up. 'Hear me out.'

I waited for her to carry on.

'Think about it. You know I've never been Will's biggest fan – I mean, all I ever knew about him was that he left you, and broke your heart. I was there, remember, picking up the pieces with you? But I really don't think he's done this on purpose. I don't believe he set out to hurt you, or trick you.'

'Aren't you going to say "I told you so"? I mean, you did say he must have something to hide.'

Mags shot me a look. 'When do I ever say "I told you so"?'

I shook my head. 'Sorry. You don't. Go on.'

Mags took my hand and held it in her lap. Her touch felt soft, comforting, familiar.

'I think you need to give him a chance to explain, Fran. The man's dying. Maybe he just wanted to see you. Maybe he just didn't want to get to the end of his life with any regrets. And what he did to you is likely to be right up there in his list of those.'

'I suppose so.'

'He probably didn't expect to fall in love with you. I know what you had as teenagers was intense, but people change. But then – well, it happened.'

'But he should have told me earlier.'

'When would have been a good time? The first day you met? "Oh, hi, I haven't seen you for twenty-five years, and guess what, I'm dying?" Or what about after your first kiss, or Christmas Day or...' She stopped. 'You know what I'm saying.'

I did. She was right. Now my anger had subsided I could see how this might have happened, but it didn't mean I was ready to forgive him yet.

'I can't see him any more. I just can't. I can't let myself go through it all again. I need to protect myself, and Kieran.'

'Fair enough. But maybe, when you're ready, you could give him a chance to explain himself. Imagine how awful you'd feel if he died before you'd seen him again.'

My heart clenched at the thought of it. A few months ago I'd thought I was fine. I had no one apart from Kieran to worry about, and no one to break my heart. Everything was safe. But then I'd opened myself up to Will, let myself get involved, fallen in love. I'd even got Kieran involved. And now this.

I didn't think I was strong enough to go through it all again.

'I'll think about it.'

'Good.' She pushed herself up to standing. 'Listen, darling, do you mind if I call a taxi?'

'No, course. You have to get some sleep.'

After Mags had left, I lay down on the sofa and stared at the ceiling, my thoughts still racing. I thought about Will, and how he'd made me feel when I saw him again, about the look on his face when we'd kissed. I thought about the tumour growing in his head and how scared he must have felt when he was told about it, how worried he must have been about telling me. I thought about the headaches he'd been having, the terror he must have felt, and then I remembered how I'd felt when he wrote and told me he was moving halfway across the world, leaving me to deal with my pregnancy all alone. I picked up a pillow and screamed into it, letting out the anger, the tension, the pain and the confusion, until my throat hurt and I felt spent. I didn't know what I was going to do yet. I still felt too raw, and too angry at him for keeping this from me to even think about it. But I knew I'd have to face Will sooner or later.

9

THEN

September 1993

All teenagers think that nobody could possibly have ever loved as much as they love their first love, and as I sat with my head on Will's shoulder and tears dripped into my lap on the night before I left for university, that's exactly how I felt. I loved him so much my heart felt full, swollen.

All the memories of the things we'd done together over the last eleven years swirled around my mind. The camp we'd set up in the garden aged nine that we'd abandoned by ten o'clock because we'd terrified each other so much with stories of axe murderers; the first time I'd been so drunk I'd thrown up and Will had held my hair off my face as I vomited in a hedge; the race to A&E after I'd eaten an oyster, which, it turned out, I was allergic to; the trip to London where we'd been frogmarched out of Covent Garden after Will had tried to put the street performer off his act one too many times; the fancy dress party where me and Will had turned up as Scooby Doo and Shaggy only to discover the party theme wasn't cartoon characters but movie stars. All of it was coming to a close now, and it felt like the end of the world. The end of my world.

'I'll still be here when you get home,' Will said, stroking my hair. My chest hitched with another sob. 'Nothing has to change.'

'I know. I just – I'll miss you so much.'

'I'll miss you too. But it's only six weeks till you're home again.'

I lifted my head and looked into his eyes. 'Will you be okay here without me? Do you want me to stay?'

'Don't be silly, you're leaving tomorrow. Anyway, I'm going to be looking after Mum most of the time. You need to go and do your course, have fun. I'll still be here when you get back.'

'But what if you're not? What if you don't want me any more?'

He lifted my chin with his fingertips. 'Why wouldn't I?'

I shrugged. 'You might meet someone else.'

'Yeah, all these wild nights out I'm going to have while I'm looking after my dying mother will be the perfect opportunity for romance.' His voice sounded sharp.

'Oh, Will, I'm sorry, you're going through all this and I'm being pathetic.' I sat up, straightened my shirt. 'We'll be fine, course we will.' I looked round his room, the room that had barely changed since I'd first come into it as a shy seven-year-old and we'd built a Lego castle and Will had got cross because I'd made it red instead of blue, and I breathed in deeply.

The truth was I couldn't imagine a life without Will in it. He was part of me, in the same way that Mum and Dad were part of me.

I knew we'd be all right, no matter what. Because nothing could come between us.

Nothing.

10

February 2019

When your world is small like mine – work, Kieran, Mags, repeat – it feels safe. There's very little that can go wrong, apart from an occasional mistake at work or the odd niggle from your teenager, and as a result, there's very little that can hurt you. My life was simple, uncomplicated, and I'd spent many years making sure it stayed exactly that way. But as soon as I'd unwittingly opened a door to the past, it had completely blown things apart.

Over the next few days I tried to close the doors again, to batten them tightly against pain, heartache and disaster. But somehow, the ghosts of the past kept battling to keep them open, to force me to confront the very things I'd tried so hard to ignore.

I lay in bed, staring at the ceiling, the curtains drawn tightly against the brightness of the day. It was Saturday lunchtime. Kieran was at football training and was going into town with his friends afterwards, which gave me some time to wallow in the misery I'd been trying to hide from him.

Bloody Will bloody Poulton.

All those years I'd spent trying to forget him, and then I'd just let him waltz back into my life and hurt me all over again.

'You can't tar all men with the same brush,' Mags had told me many times over the years. 'Not all men are going to hurt you.'

'I never thought Will would, though,' I'd replied. Will had been everything to me. My best friend, my childhood, part of my family, and yet he'd still gone, just like that, knowing I was scared and pregnant with his baby.

I rolled over and pulled my knees up to my chest. I closed my eyes and tried to blank out how Will had made me feel when we'd been together over the last few months. Was it really only ten days since I last saw him? It already felt like another lifetime. This was doing me no good. I had a couple of hours to wallow, then I'd need to pull myself back together and be a mum.

The duvet was pulled up so tightly over my head that it took me a few minutes to realise that the faint banging sound I could hear was coming from my own front door. A delivery driver? They could leave whatever parcel they had on the doorstep, but the knocking didn't stop, and when I realised it was becoming more insistent, I lifted the duvet from my head and tried to tune in. A banging: rhythmic, then stop. And again, a heavy hammering, followed by an insistent ringing on the doorbell.

I wasn't expecting anyone. I could just ignore it. I pulled the duvet back over my head, but now I'd tuned into the sound I couldn't block it out. Whoever it was didn't sound like they were giving up. Sighing heavily, I threw the duvet off me and swung my legs out of bed and walked quickly to the front door, ready to give them short shrift.

I reached the door and yanked it open but when I saw who it was, I gave a shout of surprise, making us both jump.

Will, standing in front of me on my doorstep, held his hands up in front of him in mock surrender.

'Don't shut the door, please don't shut the door on me, Franny,' he said, peering round his hands.

I stood frozen to the spot, blocking his entrance. He stepped towards me and I flinched before backing away so he stopped.

'Franny. Can I come in?'

I shook my head.

He tipped his head to one side, a gesture so familiar it took my breath away. 'I need to talk to you. Please? Just for a few minutes.'

I stood my ground, determined not to give in. What good had it done me last time, letting this man back into my life?

'I can't.' My voice sounded rough, gravelly.

Will took a step towards me again and this time I didn't back away. He pressed his palm against my upper arm gently. 'Please, Franny? Just five minutes.'

I hesitated a moment longer and then, against my better judgement, I gave a curt nod and stepped back. He stepped inside and I led him into the kitchen.

'Sit.'

He sat obediently, like a dog, and I stood on the other side of the kitchen counter, my arms folded. I was suddenly painfully aware of my unwashed hair and ancient nightshirt.

'You've got five minutes.'

'Okay.' He rubbed his hand down his face and when he looked at me I saw the pain in his eyes. 'I'm so sorry, Franny. I never meant for this to happen.' He waved his arm around. 'Any of it.'

'What did you want, Will? I mean, you looked for me, you obviously wanted something from me.'

He nodded and looked down to where his toe was making circles on the tiled floor.

'I don't know. When I found out I was reaching the end of my life I realised I didn't want to die with regrets.'

'And I was a regret?'

'Hurting you was a regret. Not loving you. Never that.'

'And what, you wanted to make amends, set things right before you died, is that it?'

He shrugged. 'Sort of. But more than that. I wanted... I don't know.'

He shook his head. 'I wanted to see you. Call it selfish, but that's what it boiled down to. I felt – I felt I owed it to myself and to you to make sure everything had worked out okay for you, despite everything that happened.'

'And what would you have done if I hadn't been okay?'

He shrugged. 'I have no idea; I guess I didn't think that far ahead. But I didn't mean to hurt you again. I never meant to do that.'

My head swam so I placed my hands on the worktop to balance myself, and leaned forward.

'So what now?'

Will's face twitched as though he was about to speak, then he stopped. 'I guess that's up to you. I'm here if you want me.'

I let my thoughts bounce around for a few more seconds, then I made an attempt to keep them still for just a moment so I could think properly. On the one hand, all I wanted, all I'd ever wanted, if I was completely honest with myself, was to be with Will. So many times I'd imagined a future with him, seen us growing old together.

And yet...

On the other hand was everything else. The heartache and pain of our past. The decisions he'd left me to make alone. And the hurt he'd caused me again, the second time around.

But could I honestly say I didn't want to be with him too?

He looked around the kitchen and behind him, towards the door. 'Is Kieran here?'

'No. He'll be gone a while.'

Will nodded, then I watched, stock still, as he made his way towards me. My hands stayed where they were, against the cool wood of the worktop, and I held my breath as he walked behind me and wrapped his arms around my waist. My breath hitched as he buried his mouth into my neck and finally, I turned to face him, to press myself against his warm, firm body.

'I don't want to waste another second being without you,' he whispered, his breath hot against my ear.

'Me neither,' I said, lifting my face up to his and pressing my lips against his. They felt soft and warm, so familiar, and tasted of coffee and lemon.

He pressed me against the counter and kissed me more deeply. But before we went any further I needed to ask him something. It took all my willpower to press my hand against his chest and push him gently away.

'What's wrong?' he said, his brow furrowed.

'I need answers, first.'

He took a small step back. 'Okay. Come on.' He grabbed my hand and led me through to the living room where we sat next to each other on the sofa, not touching.

I took a deep breath. 'Tell me about your cancer.'

He let out a breath.

'Wow. Well, there's not much to tell.' He rubbed his eyes with his fists then looked up at me. 'I started having headaches about a year ago. About the same time as Amy and I were having problems. I didn't think much of it at first – I mean, I was working hard, at the office a lot. That was partly why Amy and I were arguing actually, and if I'm honest I was staying away more than I needed to just to avoid being at home. But anyway, that's a whole other story. In the end the headaches got so bad I went to see the doctor. He wasn't that worried at first, but said he'd send me for some tests just to rule some things out. So I had a scan and all sorts – only the tests didn't rule anything out. Instead, they ruled the worst possible outcome in.' He shook his head at the memory.

'So what happened? You said they told you they couldn't operate. Surely they can do something?'

He shook his head again. 'Unfortunately where the tumour is means it's too dangerous to try and remove it, so all they can do is give me treatment to prolong my life. But as the tumour is growing slowly and the doctors don't even know how long I've got, I don't see the point. The treatment will make me really ill, and I just don't want to spend my last few years or months or however long I've got left feeling awful.'

'But surely...' I trailed off as he held up his hand.

'Believe me, I've had this argument with almost everyone I know. For Amy it was the last straw; she thought I was being totally selfish not wanting to live longer to see Elodie grow up. And Jim – well, Jim was the way he always is. He was clearly upset but he didn't try and change my mind because he knew it wouldn't work. He knows how stubborn I am.'

'So that's it, then, you've given up?'

Will reached out for my hands and held them. 'It wasn't an easy decision to make. I mean, having chemo or whatever other treatment they could offer me, I know it could help shrink this thing for a while. But it will never disappear. There will always be something growing in my head that could kill me at any time and to be quite frank I don't fancy being weak and ill and have everyone feeling sorry for me for the rest of my life. I'd prefer to just enjoy the time I have left.'

I looked at our hands intertwined on the sofa between us and felt a pang – was it regret, pain, jealousy, or a mixture of all three? I could tell it was too late to try and convince Will that having treatment was the right thing to do, that it could save his life. Because, not only was it not true, but also I'd be saying it for entirely selfish reasons. Now he'd found me, I didn't want to lose him again, but I didn't know how to say that, so was relieved when Will spoke first.

'I understand if you want to call it a day now. It's not what I want but I'd totally understand.' He rubbed his thumb gently across the back of my hand and I shivered. 'The thing is, I honestly never meant for this to happen. You and me, I mean. I don't know what I was hoping for when I looked you up – forgiveness, maybe? The permission to forgive myself for the way I treated you? Who knows. But it was selfish. I know that now. Since I found you again I've regretted not telling you straight away but the longer I left it, the harder it got.'

For a moment Will's words settled round us, and neither of us spoke.

There was so much to think about. What if Will died soon? What if he didn't and I ended up caring for him? And what about Kieran? Did I really want to bring this into his life?

I knew the answer, though, deep down.

'I don't want this to end.' My voice broke on the last word and Will let go of my hand and pressed his palm against my face.

'Me neither.'

And for the first time since I'd become a mother – maybe even before that – I knew I had to make the choice that was right for me. Kieran would understand, I'd make sure he did. And perhaps it wasn't such a bad lesson to teach a teenage boy – that, sometimes, love is more important than anything.

* * *

Three cups of tea later and Kieran still wasn't home. Will and I had talked about everything – our lives, his cancer, Amy, his father, and I'd told him until I was blue in the face how worried I was about Kieran – until we had no more words left to say. My legs were tangled in his, my head tipped back on the sofa.

'I think I might write a bucket list,' Will said.

I snapped my head back up. 'What?'

'Why not? I've got no idea how long I've got left but there are so many things I want to do before I...' He stopped before saying what we were both thinking. 'Before I die.'

My head spun.

Suddenly Will sat up, disentangling his legs from mine and planting his feet on the floor. 'Do you remember that bucket list we wrote years ago?' he said.

'Of course.'

Will looked surprised. 'Do you? I didn't think you would.' He smiled. 'I wonder how many of the things we've actually done. I'm not sure I can even remember what we wrote on it.'

I pushed myself up to sitting, then stood. 'Wait there.'

I left Will looking confused and moments later returned with a tatty piece of paper in my hand. It had been folded and refolded so many times it was almost falling apart.

'What on earth is that?'

I thumped down next to him. 'Read it.'

He opened it up carefully and I watched as his face split into a grin.

'Oh my God, you kept it.'

'Yep.'

'I can't believe you kept this.'

My face flamed. 'I kept a few things, you know. Just memories I didn't want to throw away.'

He read the first line out loud, which was written in my scrappy handwriting.

'Twenty-Five Things To Do Before We're 40.' The '40' had been scribbled out and 'Old' was written in its place, in Will's writing.

His eyes scanned the page, and I leaned over to read with him. I could hear him breathing next to me as we read through the list we'd written when we were just eighteen years old.

'Go on, read it out loud,' Will said, nudging me in the leg.

I cleared my throat and took the scrap of paper back from him.

'Twenty-Five Things To Do Before We're Old, by Francesca Gordon and William Poulton.'

I glanced at him and smiled before continuing.

'Number one: run a marathon.' I looked at him, eyebrows raised. 'Done that yet?'

He shook his head. 'Nope. I've run a half marathon, more than once, does that count?'

'Maybe. Let's see how many others we've done first.'

'How about you?'

I shook my head. 'You know I hate running. I ran for the bus once; can I have that?'

'You'll be lucky. Come on, what's next?'

I glanced down at the paper and read out the rest of it without pausing: 'Number two: learn to ski. Three: go to New York. Four: go to a festival. Five: learn to cook. Six: go skydiving. Seven: get matching tattoos. Eight: take a hot-air balloon ride. Nine: do the longest zipline in the world. Ten: see the Northern Lights. Eleven: learn to surf.

Twelve: buy a Chanel bag. Thirteen: learn a circus skill. Fourteen: learn to do a backflip. Fifteen: have sex in a public place. Sixteen: build a sandcastle big enough to sit in. Seventeen: eat twelve doughnuts each in one go. Eighteen: finish a Rubik's cube. Nineteen: go skinny dipping. Twenty: see a shooting star. Twenty-one: get married. Twenty-two: order everything off the menu at a restaurant. Twenty-three: sleep outside. Twenty-four: save a life. Twenty-five: have a baby.'

I sat back, my mind whirring. I hadn't thought about this list for years, but suddenly an image of the day we completed it, lying in the sun in the park, my head resting on Will's belly, sprang into my mind. It was a couple of weeks before I'd been due to leave for university, and Will had already decided to defer his place to stay and look after his mum. We'd started writing it a few days before to take our minds off things.

'Mum's proof that life's too short not to have fun,' Will said. I felt his belly shift beneath my head and I shuffled to get comfortable.

'I wonder what she'd have on her bucket list,' I said. 'Whether there's anything she regrets not doing.'

Will didn't answer and I held the paper up between both hands, trying to stop it flapping in the summer breeze. This list had changed so much over the last few days but I reckoned we finally had it nailed.

'So is this our final one, then?' I said.

'Yeah, why not? There are loads of other things I want to do, but...' He shrugged. 'These are good for starters.'

'I wonder where we'll be in twenty-two years' time. Do you reckon we'll have kids?'

I felt his stomach muscles tighten as he sat up to peer at me.

'Do you?'

I looked at him and smiled shyly. 'I'd like to think so.'

He studied me for a moment before dropping his head back down to the grass. 'Me too.'

We'd been proud of that list, so sure we'd easily tick everything off. Now, Will looked at me, eyebrows raised.

'Well, we were ambitious, weren't we?'

I nodded. 'How many of these do you reckon we've actually done?'

'Have you got a pen? Let's go through it.'

I dug a pen from a pot on the windowsill and went through the points one by one.

'Okay, well we know one of them we've both definitely done.' Will gave a grin and I frowned, confused. I looked down to where his pen was tapping on the page. Have sex in a public place. My face flamed.

'Oh!'

He waggled his eyebrows like he was in a Carry On film.

'Stop it!' I said, looking around desperately for something to throw at him. I thought back to the day in question. *It had been amazing, and totally unexpected. We'd made love before, of course. Snatched afternoons after school at one of our houses, or whole luxurious evenings when my parents had gone out for dinner and we had the house to ourselves. But this time had been different. This time we'd been getting ready to say goodbye, trying not to think about what life would be like when we were hundreds of miles apart, after the following day. We walked through the woods behind our houses hand in hand, not speaking. I was trying to bottle up the memory of that moment: the squirrels scampering in the undergrowth, the feel of Will's warm hand pressed into mine, the familiarity of him there, solid, beside me, so I wouldn't forget it and it would last until I saw him again. Then suddenly he'd stopped and I'd stopped too, my arm tugging in its socket at the force. I'd looked behind me.*

'What's wrong?'

A grin had crept onto his face. 'Do you want to make some real memories?'

'What do you mean?'

'We could always...' He'd trailed off, and nodded towards a bush we always hid behind to kiss. But I still didn't get it.

'Always what?'

He sighed and rolled his eyes. 'Are you trying to make this difficult for me? We could – you know. Over there.'

'Oh. Right.' I'd felt myself flush. I mean, I could think of nothing I wanted

more than to feel Will's body on mine, right now. But here? In the woods right by our parents' houses where anyone might see us? Could we?

In the end, of course, we did, and it was everything I'd hoped it would be, including the brambles sticking in my bum and the terror of holding our breath as an old woman ambled past with her overweight terrier and praying she – or the dog – didn't spot us in the undergrowth.

'Well, we can tick that one off, anyway,' he said, drawing a huge red tick next to it. I hoped Kieran didn't find the list and think too much about his old mum having sex.

'Hmm,' I mumbled.

Will looked at me again. 'So, we've established that neither of us have run a full marathon, but I'm ticking it anyway. A half's good enough and I've done more than one.' He put another red tick on the page. 'How about skiing?'

I shook my head. 'No, I've never tried.'

'Me neither. New York?'

'Nope, never been, although I've always wanted to.'

'Me too.' He leaned forward and ran his finger down the list. 'I've been to a festival, one in Oz in 1995, just after...' He trailed off, unwilling to finish the sentence, even though we both knew when he was talking about. Just after he left. 'I've also learned to cook, got married, obviously and, er...' He ran his finger down to the end. 'I've saved a life.'

'Really? When?'

'A couple of years ago. A guy was drunk and falling all over the road and almost stumbled into the path of a speeding van but I pulled him out of the way just in time.' He flexed his muscles. 'Felt like a right hero. Shame he vomited all over my shoes and walked off shouting incoherently.' He looked at me. 'I've had a baby as well – well, not me but you know what I mean. So I've only done seven. That's pretty pathetic given I'm forty-three.'

'Hmmm.'

'So how about you? How many have you done?' He indicated the list.

I turned towards it and ran my finger down the piece of paper. 'Well, I've been to a festival too – Glastonbury 2004 and Reading 1996 – and learned a circus skill—'

'Have you? Which one?' His eyes were wide.

'It was a friend's hen do a few years ago. There was some sort of trapeze set up in the East End of London and we all had a go. It was bloody terrifying but pretty exhilarating.'

'Wow. Were you any good?'

'Absolutely useless, but it was great fun.'

'What else?'

I glanced back at the list. 'Hmm, even fewer than you. I've finished a Rubik's cube, I've had a baby.' I sat up. 'I think that's it. Four.' I sighed. 'God, nine between us. That's pretty tragic.'

Will nodded. 'It really is. I think our teenage selves would be ashamed of us, don't you?'

'They would. I mean, forty felt so old when we wrote this. How could we not have done all these things by now?'

Will paused a moment. 'You didn't say you'd been married.'

'That's because I haven't.'

'Oh, I assumed, when you mentioned your ex...' He trailed off.

'Nope. Me and Sean were together for seven years, but he never wanted to get married.' I shrugged. 'I wasn't too bothered so I never mentioned it. I assumed he loved me anyway. But then when I fell pregnant with Kieran he panicked and disappeared, leaving me alone to bring him up, and without anywhere to live. So it turns out I judged that one pretty badly.' I was aware my voice sounded angry, abrasive.

'Do you ever see him?'

I shook my head. 'He used to come round every couple of months or so when Kieran was little, hand over a wad of cash and then disappear again. Eventually even that tailed off. But...' I stopped. 'Now that

Kieran's asked to see him, I've been in touch with him again. I feel bad I've kept them apart for so long.'

'It doesn't sound like it was your fault.'

'No, not initially. But I never encouraged him to keep in touch. Maybe I should have done.'

'Well, you've done it now. I wouldn't beat yourself up about it.'

'No, maybe not. I've got to start letting him go eventually.'

I stared at the bucket list in front of us, the one we had written together all those years ago, so full of hope for the future. I tried to remember what I had imagined we'd be, back then, by the time we were in our forties. Did we picture having a huge house, glittering careers, fast cars, or that we'd hold grown-up dinner parties every weekend, go on exotic holidays and talk about politics and finances? What would we have made of the adults we'd actually become? I couldn't help thinking the teenage me would have been disappointed if I'd been able to see into my future...

* * *

The front door slammed and seconds later Kieran walked into the room, his tracksuit trousers smudged with mud, his football shirt creased and dirty. It always astounded me how he managed to make fairly expensive clothes look like they were being modelled by a vagrant.

'Hi, love,' I said, standing. 'Want a drink?'

'No, I'm good thanks.' He threw himself into his favourite armchair by the window and I grimaced as clouds of dust wafted from its worn covers. For the first time in years I was starting to see my flat through an outsider's eyes – the worn furniture that held so many stories, so many memories, that I'd never got round to replacing; the faded wall-paper in the hallway, slightly peeling at the edges where the damp from outside had seeped through the window above the door; the handle on the bathroom door that had been broken for years but I'd never bothered replacing because Kieran and I knew how it worked.

These things that I'd become blind to were making themselves known now that Will was spending so much time here, and I wondered what he made of it all.

I shook the thought away as I watched Kieran, who was scrolling through his phone, his legs dangling over the side of the chair. My heart surged with love.

'How was training, love?'

'Good.'

I nodded. 'Did you get something to eat in town?'

'Uh huh.'

He glanced up and his eyes landed on the table. He reached over and picked up the bucket list before I realised what he'd done.

'What's this?' His eyes scanned down the list Will and I had written when we were not much older than him.

'Oh, er, it's a bucket list. Mine and Will's.'

'A bucket list? Why, is he dying or something?'

My heart stood still. I'd wanted to tell Kieran ever since Will had broken the news to me more than a week ago, but hadn't been able to find the words, or the right time. Now, I leaned forward and rested my elbows on my knees. 'Actually, love, he is.'

Kieran didn't speak for a moment, but just looked at me with a puzzled look on his face.

'What do you mean?'

I took a deep breath and laid my hand on his thigh, his skin warm beneath the fabric of his trousers.

'Will told me something last week and I've been trying to work out how to tell you ever since.' I swallowed and met his gaze. 'You see the thing is, Will has a brain tumour.'

'Cancer?'

How did he know so much about life already? 'Yes, love. It's cancer.'

'But can't they do stuff? Cure it or whatever?'

I shook my head sadly. 'Not this one. It's there for good.'

Kieran said nothing for a few minutes. 'Has he just found out?'

'No. He's known for a while.'

'Oh right.' He blew air out through his mouth. 'Well, that sucks.'

I smiled despite myself. If only we could all see the world and accept everything in it as easily as a thirteen-year-old boy. Life would be so much easier to navigate.

'Yes, it really does.'

Kieran glanced down at the piece of paper in his hand. 'So this is why you've made this?'

'No, this is an old one. Me and Will wrote it when we were not much older than you.'

He studied it for a moment. 'And the ones you've ticked...?'

'They're the ones we've already done. Not many, eh?' I grinned as his face folded into a grimace.

He jabbed at the paper. 'Ew, this one... you've done this?'

I leaned forward and my face flushed as I noticed what he was pointing at.

'Yes, well, we were young once too, you know,' I said, leaning forward and reaching for the piece of paper.

He tugged it away and kept reading. 'Eat twelve doughnuts in one sitting... have you never done that?'

'Nope. I think that must have been Will's choice.'

'I'd totally do that.'

'Well, maybe you can do it with him, because he wants to get this list finished.'

Kieran nodded and handed the piece of paper back. 'Sounds cool.'

I grinned and read through the list again.

'What would you put on a list, if you were writing one?' I said.

Kieran raised his eyes to the ceiling for a moment, thinking. Then he looked at the floor just by my feet.

'I've pretty much got everything I want. I've got you, and now I've got Dad again too.'

My stomach tightened. After we'd talked about his father at Christmas, I'd kept my promise to Kieran to speak to Sean. It had taken me longer than it should have done – I hadn't spoken to Sean for years but I still kept tabs on him. I knew he was living in London, and working as a taxi driver, and so finally, I'd rung him a couple of weeks after Christmas.

'Fran,' he'd said, when he'd answered the phone, sounding surprised. 'Nice to hear from you.'

I bit back all the sarcastic replies I could have given, about how he could have called me, how he could have rung to see how Kieran was whenever he wanted, that it was his choice to abandon his son. But I was doing this for Kieran, and antagonising Sean wasn't going to help. I needed to do this right.

'Hello, Sean. How are you?'

'I'm all right, yeah. Good thanks. You?' I was glad to hear he sounded as nervous as I was.

'Good.' I took a deep breath. 'Listen, I'm ringing about Kieran.'

'Okay...'

'He'd like to see you. I know you haven't seen him for a while but – well, he misses you, Sean.'

I listened to the hum of the phone for a few seconds, the odd bang and shout in the background and I pictured Sean's face as he took in what I'd just said to him. I waited for him to say something.

'What's brought this on?'

'Nothing's brought it on. I think he just wants to see his dad.' I took a deep breath. 'He's thirteen now. He's at an age when he's questioning things. And one of those things seems to be why he never sees his father even though, as far as he's aware, his father is still alive.' I tried to keep my voice even and not let my anger slip between the cracks.

'Right.' I heard him suck in air and pictured him dragging on a cigarette, the tip burning too long and dropping down the front of his T-shirt. I'd always hated the habit but he'd never wanted to quit. I wondered whether he was ever going to reply.

'All right. When?'

I was so shocked I didn't know what to say at first. 'Oh, er...'

'Next week? I've got a couple of days off, was going to take off down the coast but, well, I could see the lad. Maybe take him with me?'

I realised as he spoke that part of me – a cruel part, obviously – had hoped Sean would just say no way and that would be that. I'd have Kieran to myself still and I'd never have to worry about him being away from me. But I knew that was completely unfair. This was what Kieran wanted, and it's what he should have in his life.

'Okay, I'll ask him.'

'Great. Actually, has he got a phone?'

'Of course. He's thirteen.'

Another sharp inhalation, then: 'I'll ring him myself, shall I? Sort it out?'

'Oh, yes. Okay then.' It was all going a lot better than I'd expected. Sean seemed almost happy to be seeing his son. I didn't know what had changed but I supposed I should be grateful I didn't have to battle with him. And Kieran would be made up.

'All right then. Let me have his number and I'll drop him a text.'

I recited Kieran's number and as I hung up a few moments later I realised that what I was feeling was jealous – that Kieran was going to be doing something that didn't involve me, that he might form a close bond with someone who wasn't me. I knew he went out with his friends to the local youth club from time to time, or spent the evening playing Xbox at his mates' houses, but he always came home to me; he still needed me. If he was with his dad, things could be, would be, different, and nothing to do with me.

But I also knew I needed to learn to let him go, especially given all the time I was now spending with Will.

And he had gone, and he'd had a lovely time. And now he was due to see him again, and was thrilled to have his dad back in his life. I was happy for Kieran, even though it was breaking my heart.

I placed my hand on Kieran's knee and he didn't push it away. 'I'm glad you're getting to know him, love. Just – be careful, all right? He's not the most reliable person in the world.'

'He's all right. I like him.' He looked at me earnestly. 'I think he actually likes spending time with me too.'

'Course he does. You're wonderful.' I leaned in and wrapped my arms around him, breathing in the smell of boy sweat, hair gel and Lynx body spray, the smell I loved more than any other in the world.

'Thanks, Mum.' He pulled away and turned his attention back to his phone, his own life, and I felt a pang for my little boy.

'You're sure you're okay about Will? About the cancer?' I said, worried it might be playing on his mind.

He glanced up, already lost to whatever virtual conversation he was having. 'Yes, Mum, totally. It's fine. Well, not fine, but – you know.' He shrugged and looked back down at his screen again.

I was so proud of how strong he was. I just hoped he realised how proud.

* * *

A few days later, Mags rang.

'How did Kieran get on with Sean this time?' she said.

'Oh, fine, I think.'

'You don't sound very happy about it.'

'God, I know. Am I a total cow? I just feel jealous that they're getting on so well.'

'Course you do, who wouldn't? But you also know full well that you're doing the right thing.'

'Yeah, I know, you're right.'

'I usually am.'

I grinned.

To look at her, Mags wasn't the most obvious choice of advisor. She wore her long hair in dreadlocks or plaits, and spent most of her time in tie-dyed T-shirts and dungarees. She still dressed like a 1990s teenager, the same way she'd always dressed, and I loved her for it. She just didn't care. She'd spent the last twenty-five years trying to get me to believe in all kinds of wacky alternative therapies – fads that had swung wildly from reiki to crystal healing, ear candling and flower therapies. She was never going to win me over, but that didn't stop her from trying.

'Are you going to offer me a positive-thinking elixir or something?' I said.

'Ha ha. No, actually, smart arse. I was going to ask whether you'd managed to sort any of your bucket list out yet?'

'What? No. Give us a chance!'

'That's exactly what I'm going to do.'

'What do you mean?'

'I might just be able to help you with one of them. One of my mum friends works at the indoor skydiving centre down the road and can get you three free goes, if you fancy it.'

'Oh, Mags, that would be amazing, thank you,' I said.

'I mean, it's not real outdoor skydiving, but I figured it was better than nothing.'

'No, it's perfect. Anyway, there's no way you'd get me jumping out of a plane.'

'That's what I thought.' I could hear her smile down the phone. She always teased me for not being brave. 'I also thought if I didn't help you get started you'd never bloody get on with it.'

'You're a star, thanks, Mags.'

So that was how one bright, cold February day, Will, Kieran and I found ourselves zipping into all-in-one bodysuits, helmets and plastic goggles, ready to tip our bodies into a tunnel of wind. Elodie was too young to join in but we'd promised to tell her all about it.

Will and Kieran were beside themselves with excitement, but I shook with terror as we waited on the benches watching the group before us have their turn.

'Oh God, I can't do this,' I mouthed to Will above the roar of the air rushing through the tunnel.

'Don't be silly, you'll be fine. You're totally safe, the instructor stays with you the whole time.'

I nodded numbly. At least this was preferable to actually throwing ourselves out of a plane at several thousand feet and tumbling uncontrollably to earth. I really didn't think I'd ever manage that. When did I become such a wuss? I inhaled deeply, trying to get a grip.

In the end, though, the experience was amazing and, as I floated around inside the vertical tunnel, the wind rushing across my body and buffeting it from side to side, lifting me up higher, higher, higher, and back down again, my spirits soared.

Afterwards, as we peeled off our suits and the adrenaline high began to subside, Will grinned. 'So, was it as bad as you thought it would be?'

I shook my head. 'No, it was brilliant.'

'See, Mum, I knew you'd love it,' Kieran said, a grin plastered across his face too.

'Yes, well, then you clearly know me better than I know myself.' I folded the suit up and placed it back on the rack. 'Anyway, I've got an idea.'

'Does it involve eating, because I'm starving?'

'Actually, love, it does. Follow me.'

Moments later we were in Wagamama, Kieran's favourite restaurant. 'Right, I think we should attempt to complete something else off the bucket list,' I said, placing my hands flat on the menu.

I waited a moment as the boys looked at each other, confused.

'I think we should order everything.'

Kieran fist-bumped the air. 'Yessss! This is the best day ever.'

Will raised his eyebrows. 'Here? Are you sure? I mean...' He pointed at the huge list of food.

'Listen, when we wrote this list this was one of your ideas. I know at the time you were more likely thinking of Pizza Hut but – well, we might as well do it here. Order one of everything and see how much we can put away. And let's be honest, we're much more likely to succeed if we have a thirteen-year-old human dustbin with us.'

Will shrugged, defeated. 'Okay then, you're the boss. I just hope you're hungry.'

'Starving,' Kieran said, rubbing his hands together.

A waiter appeared at our table. 'Have you decided?'

'Can we have one of everything from the menu please?'

He stared at me for a moment, unsure whether I was being serious. 'Really?'

I nodded. 'Yep. It's a challenge, don't worry, we haven't gone mad.'

'O – okay.' He shrugged. 'One of everything including the starters and side dishes?'

I glanced at Will, who shrugged. 'Don't ask me, this was your madcap idea.'

'Let's just stick with the main courses,' I said. 'Thank you.'

As the waiter left I pulled out a crumpled piece of paper from my bag and laid it on the table. Then I dug around and found a pen and put two huge ticks on the page. 'Two birds with one stone,' I said.

'You do know we're going to have loads of food left, don't you?' Will said.

'That's okay. Nowhere on our list does it say we have to finish everything from a menu. We just have to order it.'

'I'm going to give it a good go,' Kieran said.

'I'm sure you are, darling.'

It wasn't long before the food started to arrive, dish by dish, filling the table. As more and more came – plates of curry, steaming ramen, bowls of noodles – people started to glance our way, curious about why three people were ordering so much. I picked up my chopsticks and stuck them in the noodles and took my first bite. Across the table I watched as Kieran shovelled in mouthful after mouthful of rice and curry, and I felt a pang of nostalgia for the boy who had dreamed of this all those years ago. Will, just a few years older than Kieran was now, deciding that one of the things he most wanted to do before he got 'old' was to eat as much as he possibly could in one go. I doubted it was something he'd choose now, and I wondered what else he might change from the list if he could, now he knew he was dying.

I vowed to ask him.

11

March 2019

It was as though the cancer knew that something had changed, because it decided to take a tighter grip on Will almost immediately after he told me about it. So much so that, just three weeks after breaking the news to me, and before I'd had the chance to really let it sink in, Will's headaches started to get worse. Sometimes they lasted all day, just an underlying gripe that he couldn't seem to shake even with painkillers. Other times it was a searing pain that sent him to his bed for the rest of the day.

'I never take time off,' he groaned, when he'd crawled into my bed for the third time in as many weeks.

'You have to go and see your consultant about this,' I said.

'There's no point, they'll only try and make me start chemo again.'

'So you just say no. But you really have to go, even if they just give you something for the pain, to help you get back to work.'

'Maybe.'

I knew he was scared about what they might tell him – we both were.

And I knew he was thinking about his mum. His lovely, happy mum, who'd been the heart of their family, until she was diagnosed with cancer and it sapped her life away until she'd become a shell of her former self. Will hadn't spoken about it much since we'd got back together, but we'd talked about it constantly at the time. It had been one of the defining characteristics of our relationship back then – what made it even more intense, even more special, that he felt he could talk to me about his feelings, about how scared he was, watching his beloved mum fading away so quickly. Of course at that age you think you're invincible, and it never occurs to you that it might happen to you too.

But now here we were, middle-aged, kids of our own, and terrified that history was repeating itself.

'We'll be okay, Will,' I said, wrapping my arms around him. 'Whatever happens, whatever this bloody disease throws at us, we'll be okay.' I battled to keep my voice firm, to not let him see how petrified I was.

I watched as a tear slipped from the corner of his eye and trickled down his cheek. He swiped it away with his hand. 'I don't want you to have to go through all this.'

'I want to be there for you.' I held my hand against his, feeling the coolness of his skin against my warm hand.

'But it's my fault. I'm putting you through all this. I should have just stayed away.'

I thought about his words for a moment. What if he had stayed away and I'd never met him again? Would I have been happier than I was now, with the prospect of losing him again looming over us? Happier being just me and Kieran?

No, the truth was, as much as I adored Kieran, he had his own life to lead, and I'd been growing bored and lonely. I couldn't imagine carrying on like that forever. Whatever happened now, I was in it with Will for good. 'I want to be here, with you. I promise. I just...'

'Just what?' He pulled away and peered at me.

'I just wish you wouldn't dismiss the idea of having some treatment so easily.'

'I—' he started, but I held my hand up.

'No, I let you explain yourself last time; now you can listen to me. I know you're frightened and you don't want to spend the time you have left feeling terrible. I understand that, truly. But there are other people to think about too. People who care about you. Elodie for one.' I shrugged. 'Me and Kieran. I just – I don't understand why you won't at least speak to the doctors again, see if there's anything they can do to give you a little bit more time.' My voice trailed off as a sob clutched at my throat.

'You think I'm being selfish.' It was less a question than a statement.

'Yes, I do. Sorry. I just wish you'd at least think about it. For me. For us.'

Will studied me for a moment, and I wished I could read his thoughts. Was he furious with me, was he about to walk away in anger?

'All right,' he said.

'All right?'

'I'll think about it. I promise. Okay?'

'Okay. Thank you.' It was the best I could hope for. I just wanted as long as possible with him.

An idea struck me then. 'How are things with Amy?'

Will frowned, understandably confused by the sudden change in direction the conversation had taken. 'Er, all right. Why?'

'I...' I stopped, unsure how best to phrase it. Will had told me he was only living with Amy because he couldn't afford to move out. As far as I understood it, she'd agreed to let him stay because he was ill and she didn't want to make things any worse for him. But surely him staying there was unsustainable for the rest of his life – however long that was? I took a deep breath and tried to get out the words again.

'I wondered if you wanted to come here? To live?' My face felt warm as Will studied me. 'Oh no, you think it's a terrible idea. Forget it. It was just a thought, it's far too early, I...' I trailed off as a smile played at Will's lips. 'What's so funny?'

'You're funny,' he said softly.

'Thanks.'

He pulled himself up to sitting and took my hands. 'Do you mean it?'

'Well, yes.'

'Wow.' His lips split into a smile. 'I'd love to. But wait.'

'What?'

'Have you asked Kieran if it's all right with him?'

Kieran. I never did anything without making sure he was happy. How could I have made such a bold offer without even considering him? It showed how much Will's illness was already getting to me.

'No, but you're right, I'll ask him too – I'm sure he'll be happy about it, though.'

'Well, if he'll have me, then I'd love to come and live with you. Things with Amy are fine. She's a kind person and she'd never see me out on my ear. But it doesn't feel right to impose on her, especially now I spend so much time here. Me living here, with you, would be much nicer for all of us, I'm sure.'

'And what about Elodie?'

'We'll sort something out. Amy would never stop me spending time with her. She knows what it's like to have an absent father.'

'Well then, let me speak to Kieran. And if he says yes, let's do it.'

It was a huge step. We'd only been together – for the second time – for four months. But given our history and Will's diagnosis, there really didn't seem like any point waiting any longer.

Now all I had to do was hope that Kieran was happy.

* * *

Kieran wasn't sure to begin with.

'But you've only known him a few months.'

'Well, technically I've known him for many, many years,' I said, aware I didn't want to guilt-trip Kieran into agreeing to something he was unhappy about, but also desperate for Will to move in. 'But he needs me. He needs us.'

'But why can't he just live in his own house and stay here some-times like he's doing now?' He kicked a small yellow ball against the skirting board over and over as he spoke, bang, bang, bang.

'Please can you stop that!' The words came out sharper than I'd intended and he flicked a glance at me that told me now was not my moment to be negotiating with him. He stopped, and slumped onto his bed, stretching out like a lion sleeping in the sun. I watched as he lay staring up at the ceiling, processing my request. Of course he was anxious about it. Why wouldn't he be? For so many years it had been just me and him, and nobody else had come close to penetrating our tight little unit. And now here I was, throwing this huge responsibility onto him and expecting him to understand. I sat down next to him and stroked his hair back from his face. He didn't resist.

'I know it's hard to understand, Keeks. I know you haven't had much time to get to know Will but he means a lot to me. As you know, we were best friends when we were your age. He was like my brother.'

'Like Luca, you mean?' he said, referring to the boy he'd known since he started school at the age of three and who, despite their differ-ences, he'd stayed best friends with.

'Exactly like that. Except that when we got older Will became my boyfriend.'

'Ugh, don't.' He screwed his face up but then looked at me. 'So why didn't you see each other for so long?'

'Well...' I hesitated, unsure how to explain it to him in a way he'd understand. 'Will moved away suddenly. His mum died and his dad was so upset about it that he decided to move to Australia, and that was it. I didn't see him again until recently.'

'And he didn't even ring you, or text?'

I smiled. 'No, sadly, my little man, I'm such a dinosaur we didn't have mobile phones back then, and definitely not Skype or anything like that. The only way he could have contacted me was to write me a letter or ring me on my parents' phone as I was away at university. Besides, I think he was too embarrassed.'

'But why? It wasn't his fault his dad moved him away.'

'No, it wasn't. But there was – there were some things going on. I was very upset about him disappearing and then we just – we didn't see each other again. Until now. And now – well, now he's dying, and I just want to make sure whatever time he has left is good. That he's happy.'

Kieran stared at the ceiling a bit longer, his face unreadable. Then he turned his head to look at me.

'Do you love him, then?'

'I – um...' I trailed off, wondering how to answer him. Fortunately, I didn't need to.

'Ha, you do! You've gone bright red!' He grinned and pulled himself up to sitting and bent his knees, hugging them to his chest. 'So you're in love with him, and now he's ill and he wants to come and live here?'

'In a nutshell, yes,' I said. So much for not understanding relationships. Maybe I should give my boy more credit.

He nodded. 'Well, then I suppose it's okay. But...' He held his finger up between us. 'He's not allowed to ruin Film Fridays.'

I let out a laugh, relieved. Kieran and I loved our tradition of choosing a film every Friday evening and hunkering down to watch it under the cover of darkness, a bowl of sweet and salty popcorn between us. I held my hand out and Kieran shook it solemnly. 'Nothing will ruin Film Fridays, I swear,' I said.

He pulled his hand away and I immediately missed his touch. We rarely touched these days, and his once-prolific hugs were sporadic, at best.

'Then okay.'

'Thank you, Kieran.' I pressed my hand against his thigh. 'I love you.'

'I love you too, Mum.'

How I could ever have thought my life was empty, I have no idea. Right now I felt like the luckiest woman in the world.

* * *

The last of the bags were in, and finally, we sat down, exhausted.

'I thought you said you were only bringing a few things over,' I said, laughing.

'This is only a few things,' Will said.

I cast my eyes round the five or so bags and three boxes piled in my small living room, and rolled my eyes. 'I'd hate to see what you call a lot of crap.'

'I'll show you if you like?'

'No way. If you bring anything else over we won't be able to get in the flat ourselves.'

'Sorry, Fran. And thank you.'

'Please stop thanking me. Kieran and I are happy you're here.'

'Are you sure? Kieran really is okay with this?'

'He really is. He can be surprisingly mature sometimes.'

Will stood. 'Right, before I unpack, let me make myself useful and make a cuppa.'

'I'd prefer wine.'

Will checked his watch. 'Five thirty.' He shrugged. 'Why not?'

While I waited for Will to pour two glasses of wine, I sat and looked round my living room. It held so many memories, this room: of me with Kieran as a newborn, staring into the empty darkness during endless night feeds; of ripping open presents on Christmas mornings; of birthday parties. And of arguments, shouting, Sean leaving a note for me to find after he walked out when Kieran was only a few months old.

Now we were about to make a whole lot of new memories. It was the start of a new era. And despite everything, I couldn't wait.

'Here,' Will said, appearing at my side with a glass of white wine, condensation dripping down the side.

'Thanks.'

'What are you thinking about?'

'Oh, just us. And, you know. What the future's going to bring – however long it might be.'

'Lots of happiness, I hope. We've waited long enough.'

'I'll drink to that.' We chinked glasses and I sighed as the cold liquid slipped down my throat.

Neither of us brought up Will's illness. I didn't want to taint the happy atmosphere with worry.

Beside me, Will snored on and I propped myself up on my elbow to watch him as he slept. I could still hardly believe he was here, in my bed. Will, who had once been such a huge part of my life, and who had then occupied my thoughts for so many years. He was here. With me. For good.

I watched Will and traced the outline of his face with my eyes and wondered whether our child would have looked like him, but pushed the thought from my mind immediately. It had taken me a long time to stop thinking about what had happened but Will's return to my life had brought many of those memories back, and they weren't always welcome. For now, we had to think about the future. And tomorrow, we had a day out with Elodie planned.

'I've booked tickets to the zoo,' Will had said excitedly earlier that day. 'It's Elodie's favourite place.'

'Oh I love it too,' I'd said. I was nervous about meeting Elodie. She might only be six years old, but her approval was important to me. To us.

In the end, unable to sleep, I got up just as it was beginning to get light outside and made a cup of tea and watched the sun coming up behind the buildings opposite my flat. A new day, and one filled with hope and expectation.

'What are you doing up so early?' Will's voice behind me in the dim light of the kitchen made me jump.

'I couldn't sleep.'

He wrapped his arms around me and planted a kiss on my head. 'Me neither. I'm too excited.' He walked over to the kettle. 'Coffee?'

I'd already had two but something told me I was going to need all the energy I could get today. 'Please.'

The morning passed slowly, and I felt like a child waiting for Christmas to arrive. Will left early to pick Elodie up, and finally, the hands of the clocks ticked over to eleven o'clock.

'Shall we go, then?' Kieran appeared behind me and I squeezed his arm gently. He'd agreed to come along today, and I was more thrilled than I was letting on. I knew Will was too.

'Yes, love, let's go,' I said, pulling the front door open. The sun was out today, and despite there being little warmth in it, it made everything seem brighter, better. Half an hour later we were outside the zoo, twenty minutes too early to meet Elodie and Will. I clung to Kieran's arm tightly.

'Why are you so scared, Mum?'

'What makes you think I'm scared?'

'You're gripping my arm like a lifeboat.'

'Oh, sorry.' I loosened my fingers. 'I'm just a bit nervous about meeting Elodie.'

'She's only six!'

'I know. But what happens if she doesn't like me?'

Kieran pulled away and looked at me. 'Course she'll like you. You might be annoying sometimes but you're all right really.'

I grinned at the backhanded compliment. 'You're not too bad yourself.'

We didn't have time to worry any longer, though, because suddenly Will was walking towards us and beside him, reaching up to just above his waist, was Elodie, her blonde curls trying to escape from a bright red bobble hat, clutching her daddy's hand and smiling happily. She was looking up at him as if she was waiting for an answer to something.

'Hey, you guys,' he said. Then he crouched down beside his daughter. 'Elodie, this is Daddy's friend, Fran, and this is her son, Kieran. Fran, Kieran, this is Elodie.'

Elodie took a step back and hid behind her father's leg as he stood up again and I crouched down to her height and held out my hand. 'Hello, Elodie. It's really lovely to meet you. Daddy's told me all about you.'

She smiled shyly and stepped forward slightly and stuck her arm out straight in front of her. 'Hello.' She looked up at Kieran, who was standing awkwardly behind me, and smiled.

'Kieran, say hello to Elodie.'

''lo.' He held his hand up in a little wave and I realised he had no idea how to behave today either.

I stood up. 'Right, shall we go to the zoo, then?'

'Yes!' Elodie clapped her hands together and jumped up and down. 'I love the zoo!'

'Me too, Elodie. What's your favourite animal?'

And as we walked down the street towards the entrance, Elodie started to come out of herself, and regaled me with tales of all the animals she'd seen and all the ones she liked best.

I had a good feeling about today.

* * *

I've always loved London Zoo. There was something about the unexpected peace and tranquillity in this little oasis of calm, tightly wrapped inside its Victorian railings and buildings in the middle of one of the biggest, busiest cities in the world that really appealed to me. It was one of my happy places.

Today, though, despite the early-spring chill in the air, it was packed with clusters of tourists wielding oversized rucksacks and queues miles long outside every snack concession.

'I can't believe it's so busy,' I said, elbowing my way past a family of tourists blocking the entrance. 'It's freezing.'

'It's because the sun's out,' Will said, peering up at the pale sun that flickered dimly in the ice cream sky.

'Well, I wish they'd all bugger off home.' Crowds made me grumpy.

'Can we go and see the giraffes?' Elodie said, tugging on Will's sleeve.

'Yes, okay, sweetheart.'

'Can I go and see the bearded dragon too?' Kieran said.

'Course, love.' He'd begged me to let him have a lizard as a pet since he was seven years old and I'd always refused, unable to contemplate the idea of feeding it live insects. The least I could do was let him see one at the zoo.

'Shall we do that first?' I said, turning to Will. He looked pale and gaunt. 'Are you okay?'

He nodded. 'Yes, just feeling a bit dizzy.'

'Are you sure that's all it is?'

He nodded again, but then grimaced and rubbed his head. 'Sorry,' he said. He stood perfectly still as crowds of people pushed and bustled around us. 'My head's killing me too.'

'Come on,' I said, pulling his arm gently. 'Let's go and sit down for a bit; I'll find some painkillers.'

'No, it's fine. Elodie wants to see the giraffes.'

'We can go later, can't we, Elodie?'

'Yes, I don't mind, Daddy,' she said, following us as I steered Will towards a bench that had just been vacated by a family. Will thumped down on it. I sat beside him while Elodie stood behind us and Kieran hovered in front, awkwardly.

'Kieran, love, could you go and get Will a bottle of water, please?' I handed him a fiver and he trotted off, clearly relieved not to have to deal with whatever was going on here. Will leaned forward and pushed his head between his knees and took some deep breaths while I rubbed his back gently. After a few moments he slowly sat back up.

'Blimey, sorry about that, I don't know what happened.' He was still pale but his cheeks had regained a hint of colour and he didn't look as though he was about to pass out any more.

'I think we should go home.'

'But we've only just got here.'

'You're not well, Will.'

He shook his head. 'Absolutely no way. I promised Elodie a day out at the zoo, and that's exactly what we're going to have.' His voice was sharp and we both looked over to where Elodie was doing forward rolls in the small patch of damp grass behind us.

'But—'

'No.' He held up his hand. 'No arguments. I'm not letting this thing ruin anything else. I'll be fine.'

'Okay, well, let's at least rest for a few minutes,' I said, trying to spot Kieran among the crowds of people at the kiosk. The last thing I needed was for him to go missing now. Suddenly, there he was again, striding back towards us, two bottles of water and a packet of Doritos tucked under his arm.

'I'm guessing I'm not getting any change, then?' I said as he approached.

'What? Sorry, I didn't think you'd mind.'

I rolled my eyes and grinned as he opened the packet and dug his hand inside. I picked up one of the bottles of water, unscrewed it and handed it to Will. 'Here, drink this.'

'Yes, boss,' he said, but he didn't argue as he took some painkillers and tipped half the bottle down in one go.

Just then Elodie climbed up beside him and snuggled into his side. Will wrapped his arm round her shoulders and let her climb onto his lap. He looked happier than he had in ages.

'All right, sweetheart,' he said.

Her head nodded up and down, then she gazed up at him, eyes wide.

'I love you, Daddy,' she said.

'I love you too, Els.' He pressed his lips against the top of her head.

I tipped my head back and closed my eyes, letting the sun warm my face. A memory came to me then, unbidden, from our childhood, of me and Will, at another zoo, with Will's parents. We must have been only nine or ten and the details were hazy, but I could remember sitting on a bench just like this, the sun beating down on us as our skin slowly cooked in the heat of the summer, the factor four sun cream we'd slathered on doing nothing to protect our skin from burning to a crisp. We'd eaten our ham sandwiches, packed by Will's mum, and were crunching on packets of pickled onion Monster Munch, the sound filling my ears as I watched the lion dozing on the other side of the fence. I didn't dare take my eyes off him in case he got up and I missed it, although it didn't look likely.

'It says here that lions sleep up to twenty-two hours a day,' Will's dad said, leaning forward to read the sign next to the cage.

'I wish I could sleep that long and never have to go to school,' Will said.

'No you don't, love, what a waste of a life.' I glanced over at his mum as she said this, her face raised to the sun, her oversized straw hat tipped back on her head.

'I do.'

She shook her head. 'You'd regret it if you did. Imagine all those things you'd run out of time to do.' She shrugged. 'Life's short enough as it is.'

Back then, time had stretched before us like a road through a desert, nothing but endless days to fill, and we assumed it would be like that forever, the long summer days of boredom interspersed with trips to the beach, swimming in the river and listening to records in my room. But even then I thought I understood what she meant. That time would run out eventually, and if we slept through it all we'd never do anything or be anything to anyone.

I couldn't help thinking now of all the weeks and months and years Will and I had wasted already, not being together. At least now we had time to make up for it, however limited that time might be. Which was another reason I hoped he'd decide to reconsider chemotherapy, or whatever treatment would give us a chance of having more weeks, months, even years together.

'You okay?' I opened my eyes to find Will watching me with curiosity and I nodded and painted a smile on my lips.

'Yes, fine. Just thinking.'

'About what?'

I shook my head. 'Nothing really. Do you remember when we went to the zoo with your mum and dad when we were – what? Nine? Ten?'

Will frowned, trying to dredge up the memory. 'This zoo?'

'No, I don't think so. There were lions. And chimps. And we ate ice cream…' I trailed off, aware I wasn't helping his memory at all with my vague recollections.

'No, I don't remember. Why, what happened?'

'Nothing really, I was just thinking about it.'

'Do you think about it a lot? Our childhood?'

I nod. 'Yes, all the time. Do you?'

'More and more.' He turned to face me now, his expression serious. 'Do you know I always thought we'd get married?'

'Did you?'

He nodded. 'I just assumed that's how things happened. You married the person you liked most in the world, and you lived happily ever after. I never imagined, back then, that we wouldn't see each other again after the age of eighteen until…' His voice caught. 'Well, until now.'

Around us the crowds were beginning to thin as swarms headed for a show in the big tent. Beside me, Kieran was staring at a football game on his phone, and Elodie was back to doing forward rolls, her skirt flying over her head every time.

'I never knew.' My voice was a whisper.

'Well, it was on the list. But you weren't meant to know it was *me* I wanted you to marry,' he said, smiling. 'I wanted you to know it was there, though. The thought.'

'I'm glad.' And I was. I'd thought about it too, of course, just like any teenager in love. Only with Will it was different.

I leaned over and gave him a peck on the cheek and laid my head on his shoulder. 'Are you okay to carry on?'

'Yeah. It'll pass, and I can't let Elodie down. Let's stay a bit longer, and then maybe we'll head back and get hot chocolates on the way home.'

I nodded, but stayed there a few more minutes, breathing in the soft scent of Will mingled with the sharp tang of the icy London air. The hum of voices faded into the background, and through my half-closed eyes I watched people as they passed: a mum carrying endless bags in one hand, small children hanging off her like chimps; a couple strolling arm in arm, chatting; a small child running up to a cage of birds and poking his nose through the bars before being dragged away by his dad. Above us the sky stretched out, dotted with wispy clouds and the occasional bird, and an aeroplane trail streaked through the pale blue, the plane long gone, its passengers already well on their way to a week in the sun. Somewhere, the distant buzz of machinery crept over the boundary hedge, reminding us that we were still in the middle of a busy city, while my bottom felt cold and damp, the cool metal of the bench barely warmed in the early spring sunshine. I wondered whether the details of this memory would stick in my mind alongside the one from the zoo years ago. I hoped so. It would be like starting a photo album afresh.

'Right, let's go and see some animals,' I said, standing suddenly.

'Are we going to see the giraffes?' Elodie said, bouncing beside me, tugging on my hand.

'Giraffes first then bearded dragon?' I said, giving Kieran a glance.

'Sure.' He unfolded himself from the bench and I was struck again by how grown-up he seemed all of a sudden.

* * *

After paying visits to the promised animals, it was clear Will was feeling even worse. His face was ashen, and even though he thought I hadn't noticed, I'd seen him grimacing every time he made a sudden movement, rubbing the back of his head. But just as we were heading for the exit, Elodie stopped in her tracks.

'Can I go on those?' she said excitedly.

She pointed to some trampolines in the corner, lined up behind rectangular netting. Several children bounced up and down while a small queue snaked along the adjacent hedge.

'I think Daddy's tired,' I said.

'Pleeeease, Daddy? Just a quick go? I can show you my sit-down-stand-up move I learned at gymnastics.'

A frown flitted across Will's face as he considered it, then cleared. 'Okay, love. Just one go.'

We made our way over to the trampolines. 'Would you mind queuing with her while I go and sit down?' Will said as we approached. He looked ready to drop. I held my hand up to his cheek.

'Are you sure you don't just want to go home?'

'No, it's fine.'

I searched his eyes for a moment, knowing that he was putting on a brave front for Elodie's sake. 'Okay. Kieran, fancy it?'

'Yeah, okay then.'

I was surprised. I'd expected him to be too cool for the trampolines, but something about spending time with Elodie had made him stop worrying about that for the day. Not for the first time I was struck by how much he reminded me of Will at that age, all long limbs and hormones and worrying about girls. Except Will had had me as his best friend and hadn't needed anyone else, not for a while at least. I wondered how Kieran was coping with the minefield, and vowed to let him know he could talk to me whenever he wanted. For now, though, I was just grateful he could still sometimes just be my little boy behind the teenage façade.

'Come on then, you two, what are you waiting for,' I said, grinning as I raced away from them and left Will to find a space on a nearby bench. They easily caught up and we joined the back of the queue.

Ten minutes later we finally reached the front and I paid for the two of them.

'Can I come on with her?' I said.

'Yeah, just leave your shoes here.'

I slipped my boots off and followed Elodie and Kieran to the two spare trampolines at the end.

'Watch this!' Elodie said, bouncing up and down and falling onto her bottom gracelessly. She burst into fits of giggles. Beside her Kieran sprung so high I thought he might get his head caught in the overhanging branches, and I watched in amazement as he effortlessly tipped forward, flipped over and landed back on his feet.

'Where did you learn to do that?' Elodie said, her eyes wide with admiration.

'PE,' Kieran replied, flushing with pride.

'Can you teach me?'

He shrugged. 'It's easy.'

'It's not, I never managed it when I was a kid,' I said, laughing. 'I was the least athletic child in the world.'

'I bet you could do it now if you tried, Mum.'

'Nope. Definitely not.' Something occurred to me then. 'Although, do you think it would count as a backflip if I could manage it on a trampoline rather than from the ground?'

'Count? What do you mean?

'It's on the list,' I said, scrabbling around in my bag to find the tatty piece of paper with the bucket list on it. 'Look: learn to do a backflip. Now, I'm fairly sure it was one of Will's choices, but he said he's never done it, so do you think if I could do one now, on these trampolines, it would count?'

Kieran looked at me and back at the trampoline then, slowly, he nodded. 'Yeah, I reckon it would.'

'Well then, let's do it.' I put my bag down and stepped gingerly onto the stretchy canvas. It made me feel dizzy just standing on it as it bobbed gently up and down, and for a moment as I stood there swaying I wondered what on earth I was doing. I wasn't athletic, and I had no idea how I thought I'd ever be able to flip my whole body round on this thing. But I'd committed to it now, and I didn't like to give up.

'Right, so where do we start?'

'Well, first you need to get some height,' Kieran said, demonstrating for me on Elodie's trampoline.

I bounced gently and felt the material bow beneath me. Then I launched into the air and came immediately back down again, then up, and down, and higher and higher each time, my heart racing.

'Come on, Mum, your feet have hardly even left the trampoline,' Kieran said, laughing.

I stopped dead, my knees buckling beneath me. I was breathless. 'What? I was really high!'

Kieran shook his head. 'You need to be much higher than that before you can even think about flipping,' he said. 'Come on, try again.'

I started bouncing again, pushing myself up with my arms as I got higher, peering over the top of the netting and onto the heads of the people in the zoo each time I reached the summit, then falling back down into the soft landing, before reaching up to the sky once more. It was terrifying but exhilarating at the same time.

'What now?' I shouted, as Kieran and Elodie watched me, their heads bobbing up and down in time to my bounces.

'You need to lift your knees and tip them over your head and tuck your head in as you go over,' Kieran shouted. 'But stop first, let me show you.'

But I didn't want to stop now. I could feel myself getting higher and higher, and I knew if I stopped I'd lose my courage. And so I lifted my knees, then dropped them back down, then lifted them again into the next bounce, higher this time, trying to get the feeling of letting myself go. I was terrified, and had no idea how I was going to let myself just tip backwards and hope I landed back the right way round again. What if I landed on my head, and broke my neck, and was paralysed? What if I broke a bone, or fell through the springs, or badly injured myself some other way? I couldn't do this, I wasn't brave enough, I had to stop.

But then I noticed Will watching me, his eyes wide with astonishment, his head moving gently with my movement. His hands were clutched beneath his chin, and I knew he'd clocked what I was trying to do. I couldn't chicken out now.

I'd have to do it soon because I was struggling to breathe, my unfit lungs screaming for air as I bounced higher and higher. And so, without thinking about it too much, on the next bounce I lifted my knees, tucked them into my chest, stuck my head down and flung my arms up and threw myself backwards. There was a scream and a flap of arms and a bang, and a sharp pain in my wrist, and I fell onto the trampoline in a tangle of clothes, then bounced up again and fell back onto my bottom, more gently this time, and again, and again, until I finally came to a stop. My eyes were clamped shut and I could hear Kieran's voice above me.

'Mum, are you okay?' He sounded like he was trying not to laugh, and I opened my left eye and peered up at him. His face loomed into view and beside him, lower down, was Elodie, her little face scrunched up like a crisp packet. I turned my head and opened my other eye, squinting against the bright sunshine.

'Er, I think so?' It was a question more than anything. The wrist stuck below me was painful, but I was beginning to suspect it was my pride more than anything that was going to be hurt when I realised what had happened. I sat up and noticed everyone else had stopped bouncing and was watching me.

'Um, shall we go?' I scrambled to stand – tricky when you're on a trampoline and trying to hurry and your legs keep slipping from beneath you. My face burned and relief flooded through me as I felt Kieran grip me under the armpit and pull me gently to standing. I placed my feet on the solid ground between the trampolines.

'Did you hurt yourself?'

'My wrist hurts a bit.' I glanced around. Most people had given up watching now and were getting on with their day, but I couldn't stop thinking about how I must have looked: a middle-aged woman trying to flip over and landing unceremoniously on her face, her arse in the air. My face burned hotter with the shame.

'You stay with Elodie, let her finish, I'll see you in a minute,' I hissed, trying to regain some dignity as I wobbled off the trampoline, picked up my boots and hobbled over to where Will was still sitting.

Tears were rolling down his face and he'd turned bright red and for an awful minute I thought he felt so ill he was crying. And then I realised.

He was laughing at me. Properly, doubled over, killing himself laughing, so that he could hardly draw in enough breath. I stood and looked down at him, my arms crossed awkwardly in front of me as my handbag swung from my elbow. Slowly, he looked up, and wiped his face with the back of his hand.

'Oh God...' he stammered, more tears chasing down his face. 'I – I'm sorry.' Then he was off again, his face bright red, clutching his stomach.

I sat down next to him and crossed my legs, and waited for him to stop. When finally he did manage to get his mirth under control, I felt his hand on my forearm. I didn't snatch it away, but I didn't welcome it either.

'I'm sorry, Franny,' he said. 'Did – did you hurt yourself?'

I whipped my head round. 'Oh, now you care?'

'I did care! I do care! I just – I'm sorry, you just looked so funny and I wasn't expecting you to do that and...' He stopped again. 'What were you doing anyway?'

'I was trying to do a backflip. For you.' My voice was small.

'For me?'

I nodded. 'It was on the list and I thought – well, I thought I'd get another one ticked off, while I was there.'

His mouth was straight but his eyes were filled with laughter.

'I'm sorry. I didn't mean to laugh. It's just that...' He trailed off, his shoulders shaking. Despite myself, despite my shame, I found my mouth twitching upwards too.

'Do you think it counts?' My voice hitched as I stifled a laugh, not quite ready yet to let Will know I'd forgiven him. But he'd noticed, and he turned to me, grinning.

'Shall we just say it does, and never speak of it again?'

I couldn't help it any longer; the laughter exploded out of me and when I saw the relief on Will's face it made me laugh even more.

'Was it anywhere near there?' I stammered, shooting my words out through bursts of laughter.

'Almost. Halfway.'

I clutched my stomach and squeezed my sore cheeks and waited for the hysteria to subside.

'Anyway, it looks as though Elodie has mastered it.'

I looked up and squinted towards the trampolines and watched as, under Kieran's supervision, Elodie flipped herself forwards and landed on her feet again.

'Well, in fact, that's where you're wrong,' I said, grinning. 'You see she's performing a simple front flip, whereas what I was attempting to perform was a complicated backflip, just like it said on the list, and which is renowned for being much harder to carry off.'

Will nodded wisely. 'Oh of course, yes, I would never dare compare the two. I was merely pointing out that Elodie seems to be able to spin right over and land back on her feet again, neither of which things you managed.'

'Ha, I really didn't, did I?' I sighed, rubbed my face. 'I know it was a disaster, and I'm sorry. I should have just let you do it.'

'With this headache? No way.'

'Headache or no headache, you'd have still been far more successful than me.'

'Ah, but then it wouldn't have been nearly as entertaining.'

'True.'

'And anyway, I love you for trying.'

I slapped his thigh. 'Yes, well. Thanks.' I still hadn't quite shaken off the shame yet and I could feel the burn of my cheeks in the cold winter air.

'Oh, look at these two,' Will said, interrupting my thoughts. I glanced up to see Kieran and Elodie walking towards us. Elodie was clutching Kieran's hand and he didn't look too grumpy about it. My heart soared.

'Kieran taught me to flip over, did you see, Daddy?' Elodie said excitedly.

'Yes, darling, well done, you were brilliant,' he said letting go of me and pulling his daughter onto his lap. Kieran sat down next to me and I felt his warmth. 'Are you sure you're all right, Mum?' he said.

I nodded. 'Yes, I'm fine.' I shook my sore wrist, sure now it was nothing more than a bit of a bruise. 'Not much more than my pride damaged.' I grinned.

'You did look pretty funny. You just sort of landed in a massive heap.'

'But did I flip?'

He screwed his face up, thinking.

'Even a little bit?'

'Yeah, a bit.'

'So it counts?'

He nodded. 'It counts.'

And with a flourish I unfolded the list and ticked it off. One more down. Thirteen to go. There was no time to waste.

12

NOW

April 2019

When we were children, Will was always the one who came up with ideas for things to do. A day trip to the seaside, building a treehouse in the woods behind our houses, sneaking to a gig we'd been told we weren't allowed to go to. From the age of seven, I rarely had to think about how to fill my time: Will did it for me.

He hadn't changed, despite his illness, and now he had this mad notion of completing this bucket list in his head, he was determined to see it through to the end.

Given his unknown future, it felt churlish to argue with him.

Which was why Will was currently tapping away on his laptop as I watched a documentary about migrating birds with a beer bottle clutched in my hand and my feet tucked underneath Will's thighs.

'God, your feet are freezing,' he said, pulling away.

'Yup, that's why I want you to warm them up.' I grinned and took a swig of my beer.

'Right, booked,' Will said, pressing one final key with a flourish and sitting back with a satisfied smile.

'What's booked?'

He tapped the side of his nose. 'You'll see.'

'Oh come on, if you want me to do something you've got to at least tell me what it is.'

'Nope. You'll refuse if I tell you.'

'Oh God, that doesn't sound promising.'

He grinned and flipped the lid of his laptop shut. 'You'll be pleased once you've done it, though.'

As he walked out of the room I looked over at Kieran, who was scrolling through his phone playing some complicated-looking game. 'Any idea what he's up to?'

'Absolutely none.'

I soon found out when two days later I was standing at the bottom of a huge hill, feeling a little bit sick.

'There you go.' Will pointed through the glass and I tipped my head back… and back… and back. Finally, my line of vision reached the top of the slope of snow.

'Bloody hell, Will. No way. I can't do this.'

'Course you can. It'll be fine.' He squeezed my shoulders.

'But, but look at it. It's so… so… high. And steep. I'm going to break my neck. Or my legs. Or both.' I could feel my legs turn to jelly beneath me.

'You are not going to break your neck. I promise.' He grinned. 'Well, not on there anyway.'

'How do you know?'

He nodded to a tiny, much less steep slope behind a barrier. 'Because we're going over there.'

I punched his arm. 'You little shit!' He'd been winding me up all the way to the ski centre about how high the slopes were, and how much fun it was going to be whizzing down the snow at top speed. I'd felt increasingly terrified until, as we pulled into the car park, I'd almost chickened out. This was the final straw.

'Sorry,' he said, not looking sorry at all. He looked at me again. 'You didn't really think we'd be starting on there, did you?'

'Well, why not? I didn't know there was anywhere else!'

'Don't worry, we'll be on the beginners' slope. They won't put us on there for another few weeks.'

'Few weeks? I'm not coming more than once. That was the deal.'

'Come on, you might love it. It looks amazing.'

'I won't. It was your idea to add skiing to this list, not mine. I've never had an overwhelming urge to throw myself down a mountain out of control, funnily enough.'

'Oh, Fran, what's happened to you? You used to be so fearless.'

'Did I?' I was pretty sure that wasn't true. I felt as though I'd spent most of my life scared of almost everything.

But Will nodded. 'Don't you remember when we snuck into the school basement that time and got locked in?'

I smiled at the memory. The school was an old Victorian building and the basement was, as we well knew, strictly out of bounds for pupils. Rumours were that it was haunted by one of the orphans who used to live there, and Andrew Machin from our year swore he saw a little girl crying behind the doors once, although nobody really believed him. One lunchtime we'd dared each other to go down and find out what all the fuss was about. As we'd pushed the creaky old door open and crept down the dusty stairs, I'd felt my heart racing in my temples and held my breath. What was going to be in here? In the end, of course, it was a complete anticlimax: nothing more than a dusty store cupboard for old school play props and costumes and the odd ancient musical instrument. But there were no lights and the tiny windows had been painted over years ago, so when the heavy wooden door slammed shut behind us, we panicked. The handle seemed to have disappeared in the dark, and when we did eventually find it, the door wouldn't budge. We pushed and pushed, becoming increasingly frantic, worried we were going to be locked down there for days until someone found us, being slowly eaten by rats. Thankfully the care-taker had found us and as he opened the door and the light flooded in, we breathed a sigh of equal parts relief and terror about what our punishment would be. Of course he marched us straight to the head, who gave us two weeks of detention each. It was about as naughty as I ever got.

'I'm pretty sure that was your idea too,' I said to Will now.

He shrugged. 'Probably. But I remember you being more than happy to go along with it. And what about the time we graffitied the wall outside the Co-op?'

'Well then, I don't know about brave – an idiot, more like.'

Will leaned over and gave me a peck on the nose. 'Yeah, well, I liked it. So come on, find your inner idiot and stop being such a wuss, Francesca Gordon.'

'All right, bossy boots. Let's go.'

* * *

'Cheers.' Will held up his hot chocolate and chinked it on the edge of my cup.

'Cheers,' I said, a huge grin on my face.

'You don't have to look quite so pleased with yourself.'

'What?' I said innocently.

'Your face.' He blew on his hot chocolate and took a gulp, wincing as the hot liquid hit his lips.

'I don't know what you're talking about,' I said, watching the skiers whizz down the slopes through the window behind Will's head.

'Oh ha ha, smart arse. Just because you were better than me.'

'I don't know about that. I mean, it depends on your definition of better. If you were aiming for the most amount of time on your arse then you were definitely better than me.' I grinned as Will punched me in the arm. 'I'm sorry, Will, but this is the first time ever that I've been better at something than you. Well, something sporty, at least. You can't blame me for milking it.'

'No, true,' he conceded. 'But at least you don't like to go on about it too much.'

I grinned and drank my drink. 'Anyway, I thought you looked cute, sliding down the slope on your bottom.'

'You were too busy laughing to think about whether or not I looked cute.'

'Good point.'

'But it's something else to tick off our list. Well, sort of.'

'Why only sort of?'

'The list said "learn to ski" and I'm not entirely sure that what I managed out there qualifies as having learned to ski. More like learned to slide down a hill on my backside.'

'So are you saying you want to have some more lessons?'

'God, no. I'm going to be covered in bruises tomorrow; I'm not going through that again.' Will grinned and his whole face lit up. 'But I reckon you've learned, so we we'll tick it off anyway, shall we?'

'Definitely.' I stood. 'Right, we'd better go. We've got to be home before Kieran gets back.'

I sighed. Kieran had spent the day with his father and, while I was trying to be happy about all the time they were spending together, I couldn't dampen down the pang of jealousy I still felt whenever I thought about it. He was my boy, not Sean's. I'd brought him up, done all the hard work, all the sleepless nights, the worried doctor's trips, the middle-of-the-night dash to A&E when his temperature soared; I'd dried his tears when his best friend stopped speaking to him, cleaned his cuts when he fell and picked him up when he was down. I'd done all those things and more, every single day for the last thirteen years, and now Sean was waltzing in and trying to be a part of his life and I felt like the green-eyed monster. I knew it was wrong, and I knew it was good for Kieran, but that didn't make it any less difficult.

'He'll be fine, you know,' Will said now.

I nodded. 'I know. I just...' I stopped, not wanting to admit how hard I was finding it. After all, what kind of mother doesn't want their son to be happy?

But I couldn't hide anything from Will.

'I know how you're feeling, I do. But Kieran having a relationship with his dad won't take anything away from you and him. He loves you, Fran, and he always will.'

'I know. I feel horrible.'

'You're not horrible. You just love him. But you're doing the right thing.' He rubbed his head. 'I'd give anything to have a relationship with my dad still.'

I didn't reply. How could I? He'd made it clear how he felt about his father, and about talking about it. I just had to wait for him to be ready to open up to me.

'Anyway, where did they go today, Kieran and Sean?' Will said, changing the subject.

'I'm not sure. Sean mumbled something about taking him to the trampoline park, but Kieran's a bit old for that. See, he doesn't know him at all.'

Will hesitated a moment, then held his hand out.

'Well, let's get home before he does, and then we can find out, can't we?'

I took his hand gratefully, and followed him to the car.

* * *

Later that evening we sat in the living room, empty bowls of chilli discarded on the coffee table, the tick of a record spinning round on the turntable because none of us could be bothered to get up and take the needle off.

Beside me, Will sighed and I glanced over.

'You okay?'

'Yeah, just sleepy. And my head hurts a bit.'

I felt my stomach tighten as it always did when he had symptoms of his illness. 'Do you need anything?' I pulled myself up to sitting.

'No, I'm okay.' He rubbed his head and grimaced.

'Maybe you should go and speak to the doctor, see if there's something he can give you for the pain?' I didn't want to nag but I hated that he resisted going to the doctor all the time.

'Maybe.' He closed his eyes and tipped his head back, the pain clear on his face.

I turned to Kieran, who was laughing at something on his phone.

'Did you have a good time with your dad today, love?'

He looked up and nodded. 'Yeah.'

'Is that all I'm getting?'

'What? Sorry, Mum. Hang on, let me just finish this.' I rolled my eyes as his thumbs flew over the keys. Finally, he put his phone down and turned to face me. 'Sorry, what were you saying?'

'I was asking whether you had fun with your dad.'

'Yeah, it was good. We went trampolining.'

'Oh, did you?'

'Yeah.'

'You normally say it's too babyish.'

'Yeah well, I thought it was. But Dad seemed keen so I agreed, and it was fun, in the end. He came on with me. You should have seen him, showing off doing all these tricks. It was hilarious.'

I felt my heart clench at the affection in his voice. 'That's great, love. I'm glad you're getting on.'

'Yeah, we are. He's cool.'

I nodded, biting my tongue. *Not so cool when he buggered off and left us*, I wanted to say, but didn't. Kieran was happy and that was all that mattered. 'Well, good.'

Kieran's phone buzzed and I expected him to turn away and go back to chatting to his friends, but instead he turned to Will. 'You should try and make up with your dad, you know.'

Will's head snapped up so quickly I felt the sofa move, and he winced. 'What?'

'Your dad. I bet he'd want to see you, if you tried.'

'Kieran!'

'What?' He looked at me, bewildered.

'It's just…' I stopped, unsure what to say. Perhaps the unsubtle approach of a thirteen-year-old was just what Will needed to get him to stop hiding from whatever was bothering him.

Will opened and closed his mouth a couple of times like a goldfish, obviously considering what to say.

'I can't,' he said, in the end.

'But that's what I always used to think about my dad,' Kieran replied. 'That I couldn't see him, or didn't want to. And I thought I didn't care. But now I'm seeing him and I'm getting to know him and it's better than I thought it would be.'

Will gave a brief nod. 'That's great, Kieran. Really. But it's not right for me. It's an entirely different situation. My father had his chance, and he blew it. He had more than one chance, actually, and he blew them all. He doesn't deserve my forgiveness and he'll never get it. Not as long as I live.'

And with that Will pushed himself up to standing. He looked pale. 'I'm sorry, Kieran. I know you mean well. But it's not going to happen, okay?'

Kieran nodded, then looked down at his hands clutched in his lap. He looked sheepish. 'Sorry.'

'It's all right. Don't be sorry.' Will leaned over and ruffled his hair, then straightened. 'I'm going to bed. Night.'

And with that he left, closing the door firmly behind him.

* * *

It was Will's birthday, and I had a surprise for him, one I hoped would cheer him up. The trouble was, he was grumpy with me.

'What is it?' he said.

'Well, if I told you it wouldn't be a surprise, would it?'

'But I hate surprises.'

I rolled my eyes. 'You'll like this one. Now come on, follow me.'

I dragged him out of the house and towards the Tube station. All the way into town I refused to tell him where we were going, despite his constant nagging, until eventually, we arrived outside Brown's in Covent Garden.

'Is this the surprise?' Will said, looking up at the entrance as we approached.

'Part of it.' I watched him as we took our seats, voices buzzing around us. 'I wanted to do something nice for your birthday. It's the first one since we've been together again.'

'It'll probably be the last.'

'Don't say that.'

'But we both know it's true.'

I reached over and held his hands. 'We don't. No one has said that. You could still have years left. We don't know anything. So stop, just for today, okay?'

He dropped his head. 'Sorry.' He looked up again and I noticed how exhausted he appeared. The skin round his eyes was darker, and his cheeks were beginning to look sunken, rather than chiselled. My heart lurched. 'It's fine. But listen, let's try and make the most of it, okay? Try and enjoy ourselves.'

'Yes. We will.' He grabbed hold of the menu and scanned the wine list. 'Starting with a bottle of champagne. My treat.'

While we waited for our drinks to arrive, Will looked round at the groups of people huddled at tables – the families, the couples, the friends – and his eyes looked sad. My heart ached for him as I thought about everything he stood to lose.

Will looked back at me.

'So, what's the other part of the surprise, then? Are you ever going to tell me?'

I glanced over his shoulder and smiled. 'I don't need to. It's arrived.'

And before he could look round, a firm hand clamped Will's shoulder and an arm wrapped around his neck. Will jumped up instantly and returned the hug.

'Jim!'

'Will.' Jim pulled back, leaving his hands on his big brother's upper arms, and looked him up and down. 'You look knackered.'

'Wow, thanks, that's the kindest thing you've ever said to me.'

Jim grinned and turned to me. We hadn't seen each other since I was eighteen and he was just fourteen, but his face was still familiar, his angular features having settled into a handsome face with a strong jawline and lines round his eyes that crinkled when he smiled.

'Hello, Jim,' I said, holding my arms out.

Rather than pecking me on the cheek, he pressed his palms to my cheeks and planted a kiss on my forehead. 'It's so good to see you again, Fran. Thank you for looking after my big brother.' His eyes were filled with pain. His voice had a soft Australian lilt that Will didn't seem to have picked up.

'You're welcome. And it's good to see you too. You've changed a bit.'

He smiled. 'You haven't. Still the girl who's far too pretty for a big lummox like Will.'

Will punched him lightly on the arm as they sat.

Jim placed his rucksack under the table and clasped his hands underneath his chin. 'So, tell me the latest,' he said, watching his big brother's face carefully.

Will told Jim about us meeting, and moving in together, and how his headaches were getting worse. As they chatted I watched the pair of them together, and all I saw were the teenagers they'd been the last time I saw Jim: the slightly sad boy who'd lost his mum and was worried about losing his big brother too; Will, the funny little boy, lost beneath his grief, who always loved making people laugh, and who'd always meant the world to his little brother, despite the four-year age gap. They were like two peas in a pod.

Once they'd stopped talking, Jim turned to me.

'So tell me more about this bucket list Will's mentioned, then. I hear this is something you two came up with back in the day?'

I nodded, and explained what it was.

'We'd hardly done any of the things on it, so we've decided to try and get them all ticked off before I cark it,' Will said.

'Will, don't.'

'What? Not talking about it won't change anything,' he said, looking from me to Jim and back again.

'I know but...' I stopped, unsure what I wanted to say. What was the point of being coy? Will was going to die, there were no two ways about it, and whether it was in a few years or a few months, it was still going to be too soon. Avoiding the issue changed nothing.

'You're right. I'm sorry. I just find it hard to say.'

'Me too, Fran,' Jim said. 'I mean, how can this be fair? How can something like this snatch away the rest of your life without there being anything we can do about it? It's shit, that's what it is. Utterly shit.'

There was a beat of silence as the words settled around us, none of us disagreeing.

Then Jim turned to me. 'So, what's next on the list?'

I pulled the piece of paper from my handbag and handed it to Jim, who read through it, running his finger down the paper.

'Well, you're not doing too badly, but we need to get a bit of a shuffle on while you're still fit enough. What are you planning next?'

'I don't know.' Will shook his head. 'I can't believe it's taken my dying to get our arses in gear and actually do these things.'

Jim nodded, and I bit my lip.

Jim looked down the list again. 'What? No way!'

We both waited for him to elaborate. 'No way have you never learned to surf, Will!'

Will looked sheepish. 'I know.'

Jim shook his head. 'Wow. Fifteen years in Oz and you never learned to surf. I can't believe I've let that one slide.' He clapped his hands together. 'Well, that's sorted, then. You can come down and stay with us and we'll get loads of these ticked off.' He ran his finger down the list again. 'Surfing, tick... sandcastle, tick...' He stopped again. 'Skinny dipping?!'

'Ha ha, yes, I know. I'm not so sure I'm bothered about that one now, but there it is,' Will said, his face turning pink.

'Well, you can kill two birds with one stone and go naked surfing,' Jim said, grinning.

'Are you sure we can come and stay?' Will said. 'I mean, we'd love to – wouldn't we, Fran?'

I nodded. 'It would be amazing. If you have room.'

Jim and his wife Karen lived in a cottage at the top of some cliffs, right by a path that ran the length of the coastline so that people walked past their garden all day long. Will had shown me photos and the views looked amazing. I longed to see it for myself.

'We can squeeze you in. The girls can share and you can have one of their rooms. It'll be fine.'

'Well, then, thank you, Jim,' I said.

Jim looked back at the list again. 'Would you change anything on this list now, if you could?' he said. 'I mean, if you were writing it again, is there anything you'd want on there that you'd never have thought of before?'

Across the table, Will looked thoughtful, and I wondered what he was going to say. This list had grown to hold so much more significance now; it was an indication of what Will was capable of, a measurement of his eventual decline.

'I'm not sure,' Will said. He looked at me. 'What about you, Franny?'

I shook my head. 'Not off the top of my head.'

Jim was quiet for another moment, deep in thought. 'I'd like to add something,' he said, his voice almost a whisper so that we had to lean in to hear him properly above the buzz of voices. He looked at Will then, meeting his gaze directly.

'I'd want you to make amends with Dad.'

I saw Will's body stiffen and his expression close down. I watched him for a few seconds, wondering what he was going to do. Would he bolt, run away from the situation like he always did? Or would he get angry, refuse to talk about it? The seconds ticked by and none of us said a word. Then finally Will spoke.

'I can't.'

Jim slammed his fist on the table and the cutlery rattled. 'For God's sake, Will. I'm sorry, I know this is shitty, shitty situation, and I know you're ill, but why are you always so stubborn when it comes to Dad?'

Will pushed his chair back and threw his napkin on the table, but

Jim held his arm and pinned him in place. I watched in fascination at this scene playing out between the two brothers. From what Will had told me, Jim was careful never to mention their father around him. He'd learned his lesson years ago and so they skirted round the issue effectively.

But now things had changed, and Jim was clearly frustrated. I couldn't help agreeing with Jim, but I didn't dare speak.

'Don't, Will,' Jim said now. 'Don't just get up and storm off. I've spent years not talking about him around you, and I've accepted that you didn't want to hear what he was up to, but I can't just sit here and watch this happen.'

'Watch what happen? Nothing's changed. At least not with him. He's still the man he always was.'

'Everything's changed! Everything. You're dying, for God's sake, and nothing we say or do will change that. Don't you think Dad would want the chance to see you before you go? Don't you think he deserves the chance to say goodbye to his eldest son?'

'Deserves? He doesn't deserve anything after the way he behaved!'

Jim shook his head and took his hand away from Will's arm. Will didn't move.

'Listen, I've never understood why you're quite so angry with Dad, and I still don't. Especially now. I know he made mistakes. I know he was terrible to live with in those months after Mum died. But I don't think he did anything malicious. He was grieving too. We all were. I just think – now, given what's happened, given you won't be around for much longer, you should just think about seeing him. Even just once. To say goodbye.'

Will was looking down at the table, perfectly still. His face was a mask and his expression unreadable. Jim and I both waited, wondering what was going to happen next.

Eventually Will looked up at his brother. 'I'm not promising anything.'

It seemed to be enough, for now, and Jim gave a small nod and picked up the menu and handed it to Will, a conciliatory gesture. Will took it and studied the menu as though the words printed there were the most important words in the world.

The conversation was over. For now. But something told me that, once Will had had a chance to calm down and think it through, Jim might just have made a chink in the solid armour he'd spent so many years constructing around himself. I could only hope.

For the rest of the afternoon we put the conversation out of our minds and enjoyed our meal. We forgot about Will and Jim's father, we forgot about the cancer, we forgot about all the things that had gone under the bridge, and we just ate and laughed and drank like we were any normal group of people.

And, for that moment in time, we could pretend we were.

* * *

Later, back at home, I dug out spare sheets to make up the sofa bed for Jim while Will had a shower.

'Are you sure it's not easier if I just stay at a B&B?' he said, taking the pile of sheets and pillowcases from me.

'Course not, you're more than welcome here,' I said. 'As long as you don't mind a slightly lumpy sofa bed for a couple of nights?'

'I could sleep on a washing line.'

'I'm sure that can be arranged.'

Jim put the sheets down and stood facing me. He held out his hands and took mine in his and held them lightly. His face was serious.

'Thank you, Fran.'

'What for?'

'For looking after Will. I – I was so happy when he told me you two had met up again. He was so broken after we upped and left. I'd never seen him so vulnerable, and it took him a long time to get over it. I know it was wrong, leaving without telling you properly, but – well, you know… it was a long way, Australia, especially in those days. I think it was just easier to leave and never look back.'

'I know. We've talked about it a bit, since.'

He nodded. 'The thing is, this thing with Dad. I've struggled with it, I've got to be honest.' He let go of my hands and they dropped to my sides. 'I know how Will feels, but I still can't quite understand what Dad did to deserve the depth of his anger.' He looked up at me, his eyes pleading. 'Do you know what I'm saying?'

'I think so. He doesn't talk about it much, just that things were difficult after your mum died, and that your dad let you both down, that he said a few things to him, things Will can't forgive. I know Will felt guilty about leaving you.'

'I know he did. But he needn't have done. I was fine. Me and Dad rubbed along okay, in the end. But I still desperately want him to agree to see Dad.'

A thought occurred to me then. 'Does he know? About Will, I mean. Have you told him?'

'Who, Dad?'

I nodded.

'No. I haven't seen him for a while. He lives...' He stopped, clearly unsure whether he was going to put me in an awkward position with Will by revealing anything. 'He lives quite far away so I haven't seen him for a few months. And this is definitely something you want to tell someone to their face.' He stopped, shrugged. 'I'm sorry for upsetting Will earlier, though, bringing it up. I never normally do, but this feels too important now not to.'

'It's fine. I get it. Just – don't get your hopes up, eh? I know you think Will should see your dad, and part of me agrees. But I don't think pushing him to do something he doesn't want to do will help any of us. We just really want these last few months, however many we have left, to be special. To be happy.'

Jim nodded. 'I know. And I promise I won't do anything else to upset him. But if you do get a chance to mention it, you will, won't you?'

I nodded. 'I'll do what I can.'

'Thanks, Fran.' He picked up the sheets again. 'Now, where shall I put these?'

'Just leave them on the side there. I'll make your bed up later.'

He placed them carefully on the sideboard and sat down. 'Can I help you? With the bucket list?'

'Of course you can.'

'I mean I don't want to interfere with your plans, I'm sure you've got it all under control, but I'd love to help more, if I can.'

I sat down next to him. 'Jim, we'd love you to. You're Will's brother; why wouldn't we?'

'Should my ears be burning?' Will said as he came through the door and plonked himself down in the armchair.

'Course they should, we're always talking about you,' I said.

'I'm not that interesting.'

I watched Will as he flung his feet over the side of the chair, the same way Kieran sat in it. From a distance he could be the teenage Will I used to know. He could be the boy who'd chased me through the woods until I couldn't breathe because I stole a sweet from his bag, who'd made me laugh until I cried with his impression of Mr Simpson the English teacher who had a head shaped like a turnip and thought everything in every book ever written was a euphemism. As I watched him, my heart squeezed a little, because that teenage boy I'd known and loved for all those years was now here, a grown man still with so much life and energy to give, and yet... and yet his light was being extinguished, one day at a time, and I could hardly bear it. I still had so much I needed to tell him.

'Why are you both looking so serious?' Will said.

I glanced at Jim guiltily. 'Was I serious? Sorry.' I pulled my lips into a smile and bared my teeth.

'Very attractive,' Will said, laughing.

I stood, straightened my skirt out. 'Shall I make a cuppa?'

'Or shall we have something stronger?' Jim said, pulling a bottle of gin out of his bag and waving it in the air.

'Why not, you only live once,' Will said. And he knew more than anyone how true that was.

* * *

The almost-empty gin bottle sat on the table, a tell-tale sign that we'd all drunk too much.

'Ugh, I've got work tomorrow,' I said, as the street lights shining through the window blurred before my eyes.

'Yeah, sorry, I think we got a bit carried away,' Jim said, a gormless smile on his face as he lay flat out on the sofa bed next to me.

'I've got an idea,' Will said suddenly, jumping up and swaying a little. 'Oops.' Then he walked out of the room. I looked at Jim.

'Any idea what he's up to?'

'None at all.'

We didn't have to wait long to find out. A few minutes later Will came back into the room, a reluctant Kieran in tow.

'Me and Kieran are sleeping in the garden tonight,' Will said, his words a little slurry.

'What?'

'It's on the list, the bucket list,' Will said, waving his arms around wildly as though to indicate the list in my bag.

'Riiiiight.' I looked at Kieran, who shrugged helplessly. 'And are you up for this, Kieran?'

'I s'pose so. I mean, it will be fun, I guess.' He glanced out of the window. 'But is it warm enough?'

'It'll be fine,' Will said. 'Anyway, we can take loads of blankets outside.' He looked at me. 'You've got loads of blankets, haven't you?'

'I've got a few. And a couple of spare duvets. I don't think that's my main issue with this plan, though, Will.' I looked at Jim for support but he was just grinning madly.

'What's wrong with it? It's a great idea, get another one ticked off the list, and watch the stars with this dude.'

Kieran rolled his eyes, mortified at being called a dude.

'You're not expecting me to come out there as well, are you?'

'You can if you want. But we'll be all right just us two, won't we, Kieran?'

Kieran nodded.

'Fine. But make sure you get some sleep, you've got school tomorrow,' I said, standing and walking to the airing cupboard. 'Come and get some blankets and then I'll make you a flask of coffee to take out with you.' I glanced at Will. 'I think you need it.'

Will looked sheepish. 'What? I'm not that drunk.' He leaned in towards me and I could smell his warm smell, citrus mixed with a woody scent and the unmistakable waft of booze. 'I'll look after him, promise.'

'I know you will. And nothing much is going to happen in that tiny postage stamp of a garden anyway.'

'Thanks, Fran. It feels good, you know, getting things done. It feels like I'm achieving something. With you.' He planted a sloppy kiss on my forehead and grinned. 'Right, give me these, we're off outside.'

And with that he marched outside, spread the blankets across the small piece of lawn and lay down.

By the time Kieran got there with a flask of coffee and another one of hot chocolate, Will was snoring gently, his mouth open.

'Uh, does this mean I can go and sleep in my bed now?'

I looked at Kieran. 'Do you want to? I can stay out here if you like?'

'You two go to bed. I'll stay out here with my ridiculous brother.' Jim's voice came from behind us. I looked at Kieran and he gave a small nod.

'Thanks, Jim. I think we're both happy to get a good night's sleep. Are you sure you're okay out here? We could always wake Will and bring him indoors.'

'No, you go. Let him get his outdoor sleep ticked off. Keep the boy happy.'

And so Kieran and I went back inside and shut the door gently behind us, leaving the two brothers to sleep under the stars.

* * *

Two nights later, with Jim gone and Will and Kieran both in bed, I sat in the living room with a glass of wine and stared at my own ghostly reflection in the window. Everything was quiet outside and for the first time in a few weeks I had time to think. I wasn't sure I wanted to.

I thought about Will, and how much had happened since we'd met again. How much had happened since we'd last seen each other. And how I was going to cope with life going to back to how it had been once he was gone.

I took a sip of wine and watched as a plane crossed the sky above the roof of the flats opposite. My eyes followed the flickering lights of the stars, light years away, in other galaxies. It had always fascinated me, the thought that, whatever stars I could see, someone thousands of miles away could be looking at them at exactly the same time as me. All the hundreds of thousands, or even millions of people, staring at the same place, at the same time, all across the world.

A memory floated into my mind then of a time, many years before, lying on the flat roof of the garage between mine and Will's houses, watching the constellations and drinking warm cider. 'What's that one, then?' Will said, his words slurred, his arm waving wildly in the air.

'Dunno. Maybe it's that belt thing. You know, Orion's belt or whatever it's called.'

'Uh huh.'

We'd lain there for hours that night, the lumpy roof tiles digging into our backs, talking about our lives, our families, our future. We thought we knew everything life had to offer us.

Another memory flashed into my mind without warning, uninvited, unwelcome. Another night sky peeked through a curtainless window. A memory I'd always managed to suppress, to push away, with a little bit of effort, until it couldn't bother me any more. But not today. Today it was coming forcefully, and there was no stopping it.

I screwed my eyes shut and let it come to me in flashes, bracing myself.

Flash. Stars through a tiny window.

Flash. Bright lights, a hospital bed.

Flash. Screams. Mine.

Flash. A head full of blonde curls, a warm body, a tiny blanket.

Flash. My arms empty.

Flash. Curled up in bed, alone, broken... the stars through my skylight...

'No!'

The memories stopped, suddenly, and I opened my eyes, my heart pounding so hard I thought I might be sick. I leaned forward and tipped my head between my knees and took some deep breaths. Slowly, my pulse returned to normal, and I looked up and peered at my blurred reflection in the window again. I looked transparent, pale, a lost soul, barely real in a room full of ghostly furniture. If I reached out my hand, would I even be there?

It had been a long time since I'd allowed those memories to crowd into my mind like that but now they were back, and this time I didn't seem to be able to fight them off.

This time maybe it was time to face them head on.

The question was, how the hell was I going to tell Will the truth?

And when I did, would I lose him forever?

13

THEN

December 1993

Dear Franny,

I'm not really sure how to tell you this so I'm just going to come out with it. I'm moving to Australia. It's not my idea, it's Dad's but I can't leave him at the moment.

I'm not going to insult you by trying to come up with loads of excuses about why I'm not staying, or why I'm not coming to explain in person. I'm just not brave enough. If I see you I'll want to stay, and I can't. My dad needs me, and Jim needs me. I'm so desperately sorry.

I guess, given what a coward I am, you definitely made the right decision about the baby. You were right, we are too young and it would have ruined our lives. But I'll never forget what could have been.

I know Australia is a long way away but it's probably easier like this. I hope you'll write to me, though. I'll write to you anyway, whether you want me to or not.

I hope you'll be happy, Franny. I don't think I will be, without you. But you'll always be in my heart.

Be everything you can be, Franny. I'll always love you.
Your Will

I clutched the piece of paper in my fist, the crumples already etched deep from where I'd screwed it up then dug it out of the bin and flattened it out again.

My heart hurt.

I watched the dreary landscape of grey shop fronts and rundown terraces slip past the window of the bus and leaned my head against the glass.

I couldn't believe Will had gone.

Will had gone, and all he'd done was write me a letter.

Instinctively my hand moved to my almost-flat belly where our baby was growing inside me. Every day I imagined the tiny little being getting bigger and bigger, growing fingers and toes and eyes and a nose and lips.

How could Will leave us now?

We'd parted on bad terms. I'd gone home to see his mum a few days before she died, to say goodbye. The cancer had taken its final hold and I'd wanted to see her before it was too late.

But I'd also needed to tell Will about the baby.

I'd thought he'd be as horrified as me, and relieved when I told him I knew we couldn't keep it. But instead he'd been thrilled, and furious with me when I told him about the abortion. We'd argued about it all evening, going round and round in circles until there'd been nowhere else to go. I'd gone to see his mum, and then I'd left, with Will barely speaking to me. And that was the last time I'd seen him. As far as Will was concerned, I'd already had the abortion, and although he'd tried to ring me several times and I'd ignored his calls, he hadn't exactly tried hard to find me, to come along and support me.

I'd told myself it was fine, that we'd sort it out when I came home for Christmas, try and mend things then. Because there was something I wanted to tell him.

I'd changed my mind about the baby.

'Are you sure you're making the right decision?' Mags had asked.

'Not in the slightest,' I said. 'But I just don't think I can go through with an abortion either.'

'God. A baby. This is massive.'

'I know.'

The truth was I was fairly certain I was making a mistake, having this baby. I still believed it was the wrong time, that it would ruin the rest of our lives. But the more I'd thought about Will's excitement when I told him, as well as the reality of actually getting rid of a baby, I just knew I couldn't go through with it after all. I was still angry and upset with Will, but I'd felt sure we could sort it out, make a life for ourselves, the three of us. I knew he'd be thrilled, once I told him.

But now this letter had arrived and blown everything apart.

The bus pulled up at my stop and I got off. It was raining heavily now but I hardly noticed as I walked the five minutes to Mags's house.

'Come in, quick,' she said, bundling me in out of the rain. Her dreadlocks were piled on top of her head and her tie-dyed jumper had holes in the wrists where her thumbs poked through, and the familiar sight of her broke the dam of tears.

She pulled me into her bedroom and sat me on the bed where water dripped onto the dark brown carpet. She sat down heavily next to me and crossed her legs, elbows resting on her knees. 'Now tell me what on earth has happened.'

I shook my head and handed her the now soggy letter and waited while she read it.

'Fucking hell, Fran.' She looked up at me. 'This is utterly shit.'

'I know.' My voice was small, my throat tight.

Mags stood and paced up and down the tiny space of her bedroom, turning with a flourish when she reached each end, then taking the three steps back the other way. She waved the letter around in the air as she spoke.

'I cannot *believe* he's done this.' Turn. 'I mean, what a fucking coward.' Turn. 'Who ends a lifetime of friendship' – turn – 'let alone dumps his pregnant girlfriend' – turn – 'by fucking *letter*?' Turn, stop. I looked up at her, her anger clear on her face and if I hadn't been sure before, I knew without a shadow of a doubt now that Mags would be my best friend for life. I felt glad and proud to have someone so fierce, so loyal, on my side.

She sat down again and put her arm round my shoulder. 'This is a fucking outrage. I can't tell you how *livid* I am.'

'I think I've got the idea,' I said, smiling despite myself.

'Sorry. I just can't believe it.' She shook her head, a dreadlock slipping out of its tie and slapping her on the cheek. She pushed it away.

'So what are you going to do?'

I shrugged. 'I'll have to have the baby now, whatever. I mean, look at me. I'm almost five months gone.' I gestured to my belly where the slight swell was only obvious to someone who knew.

Mags nodded. 'You're right. But do you actually want to keep it?'

I snapped my head up. 'What?'

'Well, you know. I don't mean to be blunt, but what you said before still stands. This is a terrible time to be having a baby, but at least before you thought the baby's father would be around. He might say in this thing' – she indicated the letter – 'that he's going to write but what good is that? That's not being a father. You'll be doing this all alone.'

'But what if I tell him? He might come home...' I trailed off when I saw Mags's face.

'He's made his decision, Franny.' She pushed a strand of damp hair off my face. 'He's chosen his father and brother. I'm so sorry, but it doesn't sound like he's coming back.'

'Even if he knows? I mean, he still thinks I've – you know. Got rid of it.'

'No, darling. I don't think he will. He's in *Australia*, for God's sake. He's on the other side of the world now.'

She was right. Of course she was right. Although I knew Mum and Dad would do all they could, I also knew they were ashamed, and I didn't want to burden them with this. For all intents and purposes, I was on my own.

'I'll help you. Whatever you want to do, I'll help.'

I stared at the wall in front of me for a few minutes; Che Guevara stared back at me from the poster tacked to the wall. Could I do this, with Mags's help?

'What are the options?' I turned to face her. 'Tell me what I should do, Mags. I don't know what to do.' A sob escaped my throat.

Mags counted her on fingers. 'Option one, you have an abortion now. It's late, it's not ideal but it is an option.' I shook my head.

'I can't.'

'Well, then, you have two other options as far as I can see. You have the baby and become a single mum, and probably have to move back home. Although I can help you. Or you have the baby and you have him or her adopted.'

'Give it away?'

She nodded.

I looked down at my feet, stretched out in front of me in their scuffed Converse. I was still a kid, barely able to look after myself. How could I look after another human?

The truth was, I couldn't.

'If I decide to do that, will you help me?'

'Of course I will. I don't have the first clue how we'd go about it, but if it's what you decide you want to do, I'll help you all the way.'

'Thank you, Mags. I don't know what I'd do without you.'

And that was the truth. I really didn't.

I had a big decision to make.

14

May 2019

Some people – Mags included – believe in the power of positive thinking: if you think about what you want hard enough, somehow the universe will make it happen. I've never subscribed to it – and now I knew for certain that it wasn't true.

Because despite all my wishing that Will's tumour might slow down or even stop growing and give us much longer together than expected, doctors were telling us the exact opposite.

Will's tumour was growing quickly, and it was likely he didn't have long left.

After weeks of worsening headaches, Will had finally been convinced to go and see his consultant, who'd delivered the news in no uncertain terms. Not only was Will's tumour growing much more quickly now, but it was pressing on his brain, and the cancer had spread to his lymph nodes too. In fact the consultant had been surprised that Will's speech was still normal, and that he hadn't noticed any personality changes.

'So you haven't witnessed any violent or angry outbursts, or impatience at small things?' he'd said, directing the question at me.

'No,' I'd told him, shaking my head.

But as the days had passed since then, Will did seem to struggle to remember words from time to time, or, if he remembered them, he struggled to form them properly. He became angry and frustrated and I was scared this was the beginning of the end.

'I know you don't want treatment, but there is an experimental drug trial about to start, if you're interested,' the consultant had offered.

But after hearing about the possible side effects, Will had stuck to his guns.

'I don't want to spend my last few months feeling terrible,' he said. 'If I'm going to die anyway, I want to really live for as long as I can. You understand, don't you, Franny?'

'No, not really.' The lump in my throat made it difficult to get the words out. But I couldn't sugar-coat it. I couldn't understand why he wouldn't want to at least try and extend his life even a little. Just a few weeks would make all the difference as far as I was concerned.

He'd cupped my face in his hands. 'I love you and I want to be with you for as long as I can. But I don't want to spend whatever time we have left struggling, or being cared for by you. It's not how I want you to remember me – and it's certainly not how I want to spend the last few months of my life.'

I felt a tear slip down my cheek, but I nodded anyway. I did understand what he was saying. But it didn't stop me from wishing with all my heart that we could just squeeze out as much time as possible.

But the truth was, whichever way we looked at it, we were approaching the end of the road.

Will was dying.

'We're all dying,' he said, when I burst into tears over breakfast the next morning. 'I just have more of an idea of when the end is coming for me.' He tried to smile but his lips barely lifted and he gave up before he'd really got started. 'I'm sorry. I don't know why I always have to make a joke about everything.'

I shrugged. 'It's fine. I didn't mean to cry either.' Besides, humour was better than the alternative. I breathed in deeply through my nose and released the air slowly through my lips. I might have felt as though I'd been hollowed out, but it was my job to stay strong. Will needed me not to fall apart.

Will brought a croissant to his lips and took a huge bite, crumbs tumbling from his chin onto the plate.

'I've decided to stop working,' Will said through his mouthful.

'Since when?'

'Since yesterday. I've been thinking about it since we were at hospital and it's the right thing to do. I'm taking so much time off anyway, and I don't need as much money any more now the house is being sold. I just – I think it's time.'

I swallowed. It felt like yet another sign marking Will's inevitable decline and I didn't know what I could possibly say in response. Instead I took a deep breath.

'Have you told Jim that the cancer has spread?'

'Not yet.'

'You have to tell him. You can't wait until we go down and see him.'

'I know, and I will. I just – I needed some time. To process.' He waved his hand round his head in a whirring motion.

I thought about Jim all the way down in Cornwall, oblivious to what his big brother was going through, to how the end of his life had suddenly become a much closer, more threatening spectre, and I felt sick. This was going to break him.

'Do you want me to tell him?'

Will shook his head. 'No thanks. This is something I have to do on my own.'

'Okay.' I waited, unsure what to say next. Will stood up, crumbs dropping from his lap onto the kitchen floor. 'No time like the present, I suppose.'

'Good luck.' As he passed me I grabbed his hand and gave it a squeeze.

I sat for a moment, my mind whirring.

I couldn't imagine how Jim was going to take the news. He'd lost his mother young. Now he faced losing his big brother too.

If I thought this was awful for me, how much worse would it be for him? Not to mention Elodie. Breaking the news to Jim was one thing, but how could you explain it so a six-year-old could understand that she was about to lose her daddy? Kieran had been different. Although I'd been worried about telling him, concerned he'd feel as though he was being abandoned just as he'd accepted Will into his life, when I'd broken the news to him the day after we got back from the hospital, he'd been surprisingly mature. He'd leaned over and snuggled his head on my shoulder, something he hadn't done for a long time, somehow instinctively understanding that it was what we both needed. And as I'd breathed in the scent of Lynx body spray and an undertone of sweat, tears had filled my eyes. I loved him so much, but I couldn't help thinking it was lucky that Sean had come back into his life when he had. Maybe it would shield him from some of the heartache that was about to come our way.

* * *

Throughout all of this there hadn't been much time to think about anything else. But there was one thing that had been preying on my mind since Will had been told his time was running out, and I needed to address it, soon.

So the following evening, when Will was in bed and Kieran was out with his dad, I pulled a box from the back of the wardrobe that I hardly ever looked at. It was a metal box, locked, and I blew the thick layer of dust from the surface before I laid it down on my bed. I placed my hands on the top of it and felt the cool metal warm beneath my touch. The contents of this box contained information that could blow my life apart, and I wasn't sure whether I was ready to open it just yet.

But I had no choice.

Time was running out.

Taking a deep breath, I untaped the tiny key from the bottom of the box, stuck it into the lock and turned. I lifted the lid, slowly, and stared at the contents for a moment, wondering whether I had the courage to pull them out. It had been years since I'd looked at this, preferring to lock it all away both physically and metaphorically. That way, it was easier to pretend it had never happened and that it didn't matter.

But it did matter now. More than anything.

I lifted the small pile of papers from the box. There was a selection of folded letters, yellowed around the edges, cards, their corners bent and misshapen, and photographs, faded with time. As I placed the pile on the duvet, a photo slipped out and landed face up and I gasped. With a shaking hand I picked it up and studied it, running my index finger gently over it: across the blonde curls, long here, too long, flopped awkwardly over one eye. A pair of red dungarees, a white T-shirt, and a push-along bike, without pedals. My eyes followed the contours of the cheeks: round but not chubby, the baby fat already dropping away, the cheekbones taking on their edges. But it was the eyes that took my breath away. The dazzling blue eyes, with their gentle tilt at the corner, sparkling, full of mischief. Just like his father's.

Just like Will's.

This was our son. I'd called him William, knowing he'd probably have his name changed but always hoping he wouldn't, that he'd keep something of his father's whether he realised it or not.

Later, his new parents had called him Jacob, and they wrote to me faithfully a couple of times a year via the adoption agency, just as they'd promised, and sent me these photos. I'd almost wished they wouldn't, hardly able to bear the news of the son I'd given up, to see the photos of him growing up without me, a reminder of everything I'd lost. Yet I couldn't imagine not seeing them either, these images that I spent hour upon hour devouring, searching for all the similarities I could find, anything to link this young baby, then this boy, then this young man, to me. To Will. I wrote to him, just once, but never posted the letter. No words could express how empty I felt.

When Jacob turned sixteen, the letters stopped.

We feel it's time to let Jacob decide for himself whether to keep in touch, they wrote. *We're so sorry.*

And that was that. I never heard from them – or him – again.

But now, it was time.

I had to try find him, and tell him what had happened. Tell him that his father was dying. He had a right to know, and Will had a right to know about his son.

Even if it cost me everything.

I put the photo back in the pile and tore my eyes away from the rest of them. I picked up a soft piece of paper, folded several times and, even though I knew what it said, my heart thumped as I carefully opened it up. It was the letter I'd written to my baby, just after he was taken from me.

I can't believe you're gone. I can't believe I'll never get to hold you again, to feel the softness and warmth of your skin against mine, to press my lips into your hair. To watch you become the amazing man I know you'll one day be. To be a part of your life, the way we'd always imagined.

My arms will feel empty forever.

I have no more words. I'm sorry.

I'm broken.

I hope you'll have a happier life than I can give you.

And, remembering how wretched I'd felt as I'd written those words, tears dripped from my face and dampened the paper, spreading out slowly, dragging the ink with it. I bundled everything back into the box, unable to look at any of it for one more moment, and shoved the whole thing right to the back of the wardrobe. I knew what I had to do now. Go online to the Adoption Contact Register and see whether my son had put his name down – to see whether he'd ever wanted to find me. Because this was my only chance.

* * *

'This is ridiculous,' Will muttered as I rummaged through the holdall and checked it for the tenth time.

'I'm just making sure we've got everything,' I said, pulling out the contents one by one.

'I know but you've checked about a million times.'

I packed everything back inside the bag and sighed. 'I just want to make sure we don't forget anything. And you know, you need enough painkillers for the week, just in case.'

Will sighed. 'Whatever happened to the days of spontaneity, eh?'

'They went out of the window the minute I fell pregnant with Kieran.'

He smiled weakly. 'Yeah, I suppose so. It just feels as though everything is such a drama these days. Every trip out of the house has to be meticulously planned down to the last detail just in case it's too much for me, rather than just leaving and seeing where the day takes us.'

Irritation bubbled in my chest. I knew Will was feeling frustrated, and I understood why. In the last few days he'd quit his job, and agreed with Amy that when the house is sold she would buy something smaller, and I knew all these changes were hard for him. But I was doing my best to make life as happy as possible for him.

'It's not my fault,' I said now, my voice cracking.

Will looked up and hauled himself from the sofa and wrapped his slender arms around me. 'I know, my love, I'm sorry.' He nuzzled his face into my neck and I squirmed. 'I'm just so fed up with feeling so crap all the time, and knowing it's only going to get worse.'

My fingers found his face and stroked the stubble growing on his cheeks. 'I just wish...' I trailed off, not knowing which of the many things I wished I actually wanted to say out loud. I wished he wasn't dying? I wished we'd never split up? I wished we'd met again earlier? I wish, I wish, I wish. It made no difference.

We had decided to take the trip to Cornwall to see Jim as promised, in an attempt to take both our minds off everything, and try and have some fun with his family. We were also hoping to tick off a few more things from our bucket list, worried that Will might not have the

energy to complete the whole list if we didn't get on with it, even
though some of the things we'd chosen seemed silly and irrelevant
now. Why was learning to surf so important over reading more books,
or seeing more theatre, or spending more time with loved ones? Or
being reunited with your estranged father...?

There was one piece of good news, though. Elodie was coming to
Cornwall with us.

'It'll do her good to spend some time with her daddy,' Amy had
said.

So here we were, getting ready for the long drive down to Bude, and
waiting for Amy to drop Elodie off. Will's hands refused to stay still –
rubbing together, rubbing his face, picking at his nails. His nerves that
something would go wrong before we could even get on the road were
clear.

When the doorbell went he leaped up quicker than I'd seen him
move in days.

'Sit down, love,' I said, walking towards the front door. 'I'll get it.'

As I walked towards the front door, my heart hammered. This was
the first time I'd met Amy, and I didn't know how she'd react when she
saw me. I pulled the door open and there, in the blazing sunshine in
front of me, was a woman with her dark blonde hair scraped back into
a ponytail, dressed in pink gym gear. Beside her stood Elodie, clutching
her mummy's hand and staring up at me with big eyes and a huge grin
on her face. She was holding a small pink suitcase in the other hand.

'Hello, Amy, hello, Elodie,' I said, opening the door fully.

'You must be Fran,' Amy said, sticking her hand out. Trying not to
show my surprise, I took her hand and shook it.

'Lovely to meet you at last,' I said.

'You too.'

Amy crouched down and pushed Elodie's hair back from her face
and planted a gentle kiss on her nose. 'Now, be good for Daddy and
don't miss me too much,' she said.

'I'll be good, I promise,' Elodie said.

'Good girl. And make sure you ring me every day, okay?'

'Yes, Mummy. I'll do Skype, it will be like being in the same room.'

I smiled at the words Elodie was parroting that had obviously come from Amy.

Amy pulled Elodie into a hug and then released her and stood up.

'You'll look after her, won't you?' she said quietly.

'Of course we will.' I held my hand out to Elodie, who shyly let go of Amy's hand and took mine. She turned to her mum. 'Fran lets me have ice cream and go on the trampolines. We'll have fun.'

'Right, well. Let me know when you get there.'

I nodded, then Amy turned and jogged down the steps and into the street. She gave a little wave then we watched as she walked away, her shiny ponytail swinging behind her in the sunshine. I felt Elodie's hand squeeze mine tightly.

'Right, shall we go and find Daddy?'

'Yes!' she said, and followed me into the living room where Will was standing awkwardly. His face lit up when he saw Elodie and she ran into his arms.

'Daddy!'

'Hello, sweetheart,' he said into her hair. Tears shone in his eyes and I noticed how pale his skin looked next to Elodie's sun-tinted glow. He pulled away.

'Are you ready to go on an adventure?'

'Yes! And can we go on a trampoline again? That was funny.'

My face flushed at the memory. 'Yes, I'm sure we can.'

Will grinned as Elodie clapped her hands with excitement.

'Right, I'll pack everything in the car and then we can get going,' I said.

Will started to follow me. 'Where are you going?'

'To help you.'

'Absolutely not. You stay here with Elodie.' Will hated being treated like an invalid but there was no way he was strong enough to be lugging suitcases up and down the steps. And even if he did manage it, it would set him back for the rest of the day. He hesitated for a moment, caught between arguing and doing as he was told. In the end, he made his way back to the sofa and pulled Elodie onto his lap. As they started talking about all the things they were going to do on the beach, I went and knocked on Kieran's door. No answer. I poked my head round. Kieran was lying flat on the bed, headphones clamped to his ears, eyes tight shut. I tapped his foot and he jumped.

'Huh?' He yanked his headphones out of his ears. 'Are we leaving?'

'Can you come and give me a hand getting everything in the car please love?'

'Ohhh, do I have to?'

I crossed my arms across my chest. 'No, you don't have to. But otherwise I'll be doing it all myself.'

'Can't Will help?'

I raised my eyebrows and waited for him to think about it. He let out a sigh and swung his legs over the edge of the bed and slid his feet into his sliders. 'Okaaaaay.'

Fifteen minutes later the car was packed to the rafters with more than we could possibly need for a few days away in Cornwall, enough snacks to feed half the street (which Kieran would probably scoff his way through in the first couple of hours) and we were all climbing into the car.

'Everyone ready?' I said, slipping behind the wheel.

A mixture of delighted yells came my way and I pulled slowly out into the road. I couldn't wait to get away for a few days. I just hoped Will would be all right.

* * *

Seven and a half long hours later we were finally pulling into the driveway of Jim and Karen's house. Several stops and the inevitable heavy traffic had made it a longer journey than we'd expected, but at least we were here at last. Beside me Will was sound asleep, his lips slightly parted, his skin clammy. Kieran was listening to music and Elodie was watching *Frozen* for the third time on her iPad.

Before I'd even cut the engine, Jim, Karen and their girls were on the driveway to greet us. I opened my door and stood up, my limbs screaming as they straightened out after being cramped and folded in the car for hours on end.

'It's so wonderful to meet you at last,' Karen said, throwing her arms around me and hugging me as though we'd known each other our whole lives. She pulled back but kept her hands on my upper arms.

'I've heard so much about you,' she said. I took in this woman who had married lovely, caring Jim, and I could see instantly why he'd fallen in love with her. She radiated warmth, and the twinkle in her eye told me we were going to get on just fine. She turned to her daughters, one who stood shyly behind her waiting to be introduced, the other, older one jabbing at her phone and pretending not to be interested.

'This is Olivia...' The younger girl stepped forward and gave a small wave. 'And this is Soraya – who will definitely say hello if she can ever tear her eyes away from her screen.' Soraya looked up and gave a sheepish grin. 'Sorry. Hello.' She stepped forward and shook my hand, which was a surprise from a thirteen-year-old.

Behind me, Kieran opened his door and climbed out, unfolding his long limbs. 'Hi,' he said, when he noticed everyone looking at him.

'This is Kieran, my son,' I said, and everyone said hello. I watched him as he took in this group of people on the driveway in front of him, and when his gaze landed on Soraya, his face flushed. Ah, two hormonal thirteen-year-olds together for a few days in the same house. This could be interesting.

I went round to the other side of the car and let Elodie out, and she held my hand tightly as she was greeted by the family she'd barely had the opportunity to get to know because they lived so far away.

'Girls, why don't you take Elodie and Kieran inside and show them where they're sleeping,' Karen said, and we waited as the four of them trudged towards the house and disappeared inside.

Jim turned to me, his brow furrowed, and indicated the car with a small nod. 'How is he?' His voice was almost a whisper, as though he was worried Will might hear him through the closed doors.

I glanced inside. What should I say? Should I lie and tell them he was fine so they didn't treat him like an invalid? Or should I tell them the truth, that he had good days and bad days and on the bad days I was truly terrified that this might be the beginning of the end?

'He's – okay,' I said. 'Exhausted all the time, and in pain a lot, but he's determined to keep going and doing things. There was no way I was stopping him from coming down to see you, no matter what.'

Jim shook his head and rubbed his stubbled cheek. 'I can't believe it. My big brother.' His voice was filled with sadness.

'I know, darling,' Karen said, hooking her arm through his and resting her cheek on his shoulder. 'But we'll look after him.'

We all jumped as the car door opened and Will peered out, shielding his eyes from the sun that was slowly setting behind the house.

'Will!' Jim said, going over to take Will's hand as he started to climb out of the car. Will shook it off grumpily and I saw Jim flinch. 'I'm fine.'

Jim took a step back and waited as Will slowly levered himself up until he was standing upright on the driveway in front of us. 'See, we made it!'

Jim stepped forward again and wrapped his strong, tanned arms round his much frailer older brother and the contrast almost took my breath away. When you watch something happening every day, the changes are so small they're barely noticeable. But over many days, those small changes added up to make a much bigger difference, and although it had only been a month or so since Jim had last seen Will, a lot had changed in that time. I saw Jim draw in his breath as he held Will, his frame thin beneath Jim's arms.

'You look great,' Jim said, stepping back.

'For a cancer patient, sure,' Will said, and I flinched again as I saw the pain on Jim's face.

'Don't say that.'

'But it's true. I look good for a cancer patient, crap for anyone else. It's fine.'

Karen stepped forward and gave Will a squeeze. 'Come inside, you two, let's have a drink.' I was grateful to her for changing the subject, and followed the three of them into the house.

It was a stunning home. The living room opened up onto a huge open-plan kitchen, with windows that stretched the length of the house from one side to the other. But the view was what stole the show: a small rise of green, a patch of scrubby bushes, then a sudden drop of brown and grey and purple-streaked cliffs towards the sea, which sparkled and shone in the dazzling early evening sunlight.

'Wow, this is beautiful.' I stood and looked out of the window for a moment, drinking it in.

'It's fab, isn't it?' Karen said, coming to stand beside me. 'This was what sold the house to me. I grew up by the beach in Oz and I always wanted to live by the ocean when I moved to the UK. And look at it – who could fail to feel happy standing here and looking at that?'

I thought of the view from the window of my flat – a scrubby hedge and parked cars and the front windows and doors of the houses opposite, closed faces revealing nothing. Here the light felt different, the air brighter, and it made you believe you could achieve anything; it made you almost believe in miracles.

Behind me, Will lowered himself onto a dining chair. 'It's amazing, isn't it?'

'It really is.'

'Tea? Coffee? Wine?' Karen and Jim bustled around the kitchen pulling bowls from drawers and tipping family packets of crisps into them.

'Wine would be great,' Will said.

I paused. Will hadn't drunk alcohol for a couple of weeks because he said it made him feel sick. I hoped this was a good sign, rather than belligerence and being unwilling to let Jim see how ill he really was.

'Me too, please,' I said, standing. 'But first I'm going to get the bags in, before I get too comfortable.'

'I'll come and help you,' Jim said.

'Lovely, thank you.'

I knew Will was finding it hard to let us do things for him, but I was glad to see he didn't try and argue this time. Instead, Jim and I left them to it while we hauled the bags from the boot where Kieran and I had wedged them all in earlier.

'Blimey, you moving in?'

'Well, we thought we might if you don't mind,' I said, slamming the heaviest suitcase onto the gravel driveway. My skin was hot and I wiped my hand across my brow. Beside me, Jim was still. I turned to look at him quizzically.

'You could, you know. Move in, I mean.'

I didn't laugh, because I saw from the look on his face that he meant it.

'Thank you, Jim.'

'I'm serious, though. I mean, it's lovely here. You've seen it. And Will loves the sea, always has. And... and—' His voice broke and he sniffed loudly and cleared his throat. 'He doesn't have long left, does he?'

I felt tears prick my eyes again and I shook my head, directing my gaze just above Jim's knee so I didn't have to look at him. 'I don't think so, no.' I looked up now and shrugged, unsure what else I could say.

Jim gave a tight nod.

'What's really happening, Fran?' He coughed and clasped his hands together. 'I mean, do you really think there's no hope? That this thing can't be stopped?'

The desperation in his voice broke my heart, but how could I lie to him? I shook my head.

'I'm sorry, Jim, but it really can't. They're completely certain.' I took a deep, shuddering breath. 'The position of the tumour, and the way it's growing, means there's nothing they could do about it even if Will wanted treatment, and because it's growing quite fast it's hard to tell how quickly he'll go downhill. The only thing they can be certain of is that it will happen, and fairly soon.' I stopped. 'I mean, you can tell how much weaker he's got even since the last time you saw him.'

'Yeah. I...' He rubbed his hand across his face again, a gesture I'd noticed him do when he was trying to compose himself. 'What the fuck are we going to do without him, Fran?'

I shook my head. The words I wanted to say wouldn't come out; my mouth felt as if it was full of cotton wool. Jim dropped the bag he was holding and wrapped his arms around me and I cried onto his shoulder as he sobbed into my hair. It felt cathartic, somehow, to let it all out. Eventually, I stepped away and wiped my face with my sleeve.

'We just have to try and keep strong and give him the best time we can while he's still able to do things,' I said. 'He was desperate to come down and see you, so while we're here we're going to try and do all the things Will wants to do, whether we think he's up to them or not.' I shrugged. 'It'll make no difference, he'll be exhausted either way.'

Jim nodded. 'And what about your list? Have you given up on that?'

'The list? God, no. Will's more excited about ticking off some more from the list than anything else.' I grinned.

'Stubborn bugger. Determined to pretend he's fine just so he can get his own way.'

'You know Will.'

'I certainly do. So, what's on the list for this week?'

I pulled my phone from my pocket. I'd been concerned about the piece of paper getting even more damaged or going missing, and so I'd given in to modern technology and typed the list into the notes on my phone for ease. I clicked it open and scrolled past the completed ones.

'Right, here you go.' I squinted at the phone. 'This week he's hoping to learn to surf, go skinny dipping and build a sandcastle big enough to sit in.'

Jim shook his head. 'I still can't believe he's never learned to surf – all those sports he always loved.' He smiled. 'We'll get on it first thing tomorrow as long as the weather holds out.' He glanced upwards at the darkening sky. 'And even if it doesn't, we've got plenty of wetsuits; we won't shrink.'

I didn't tell him how worried I was about Will trying to surf. I was certain it was too much for him, but I also knew how determined he

was to give it a go and I couldn't ruin it for him. As for the other two –
well, they'd be simple in comparison.

'Anything else we can tick off while we're here?' Jim said, reading
through the list.

'Let's take it one step at a time,' I said, grinning. 'Anyway, we'd
better get these bags in before they think we've buggered off to the pub
for a drink.'

'That's not a bad idea,' Jim said, grinning back as he lifted the heaviest rucksack onto his shoulder, picked up the suitcase and headed into
the house.

* * *

The following morning I woke early. Unsure where I was for a
moment, I blinked as my eyes adjusted to the sun pouring through the
gaps in the blinds, creating stripes on the wooden floorboards.

I looked over at Will, who was still snoozing peacefully beside
me. He lay on his back, snoring gently, his left arm slung above
his head, the other one resting on top of the duvet. I watched as
his chest rose and fell beneath the covers. It was impossible to
imagine, in moments like this, that Will was losing his battle
with the illness that was eating him from the inside, that soon
enough, his heart would stop beating, and his chest would stop
rising and falling. How could this man, who was so full of love
and intelligence and hope and ambitions, be snuffed out so
easily?

I sat up, taking care not to wake him. Last night had been fun. Will
had been well rested after the long journey, which he'd slept most of
the way through, and had been on good form, laughing and joking
with Jim like they always used to as kids. It had been wonderful to see
him with some sparkle back again.

I knew Jim was going to be heartbroken when he lost his big
brother, and seeing them all together last night, it was clear that Karen
and the girls loved Will too, and would find it hard when he died. And

how would Elodie cope when her daddy disappeared from her life forever?

Every time I watched Will with his daughter, my mind kept wandering back to Jacob. It lay heavy on my mind, but I was anxious not to mention it to Will unless there was actually something concrete to tell him. I had no idea whether Jacob would ever get in touch even if he was on the Contact Register, and whether, even if by some miracle he did, Will would forgive me for keeping his existence a secret from him for so long. I didn't have a clue how I was ever going to tell him.

I climbed out of bed and went downstairs, leaving Will to sleep. He'd need as much rest as he could get if he wanted any chance of learning to surf.

The kitchen was empty when I got there, and I stood for a moment at the patio doors, watching the dip and lift of the surf, the white tips as they rolled toward the shore; I watched a seagull hover on the air above the water, then swoop low and fly off on some distant, unknown mission. I could hear the gentle roar of the sea as it reached the pebbles of the tiny beach directly below the house, and the louder rush as it slapped against the cliffs, gently today, with very little breeze. Not an ideal day for a skilled surfer, but perfect for us. I was relieved. It was almost as though the gods were smiling down on us.

I heard a noise behind me and turned to see Karen padding across the living room.

'Morning.'

'Oh, Fran, you made me jump,' she said, holding her hand to her chest. She walked towards me and stood next to me at the window. 'Just as gorgeous today, isn't it?'

I nodded. 'Beautiful.'

We stood in silence for a moment. Then Karen spoke. 'Jim told me what you told him last night. About Will's tumour.' I saw her turn her head towards me and felt her fingers reach for mine. 'I'm so sorry, Fran. For all of you. You, Will, Jim and Elodie. It's just...' She stopped, and looked back out of the window.

'I know. It's shitty.'

'It is.' She looked at me again and this time I turned to face her. 'You've known Will a long time.'

I nodded.

She paused, obviously battling with whether to say something... 'I just...' She stopped. 'I don't know whether I should even be saying this; Jim would kill me. But do you have any idea why Will won't speak to his father?'

I sighed. 'No, not really. He won't talk about it.'

She stood still, staring out at the view. 'Do you think there's any chance he'll ever agree to see him? Before he dies? Alan isn't too well himself and I know it would mean the world to him. It would mean the world to Jim, too.'

'I honestly don't know. A few months ago I'd have said absolutely not. But now – things have changed. I'd say go carefully, but that there might be a chance. A small one.' I shrugged. 'But who knows what goes on in someone else's mind. I can't imagine cutting someone out of my life like that forever, but who am I to judge?'

'True.' She took a step back towards the kitchen. 'Can I interest you in a coffee?'

'That would be brilliant, thank you.' I reluctantly turned away from what had already become one of my favourite views, and followed Karen into the kitchen.

'You sit there, let me make this, and then we'll think about some breakfast when the kids get up. Maybe some pancakes?'

'Sounds perfect,' I said, as I slipped onto the stool opposite the kitchen. 'Thank you.'

* * *

It was late by the time everyone was up, fed and showered, and as we stood on the driveway later that morning, the sun was already hot despite it only being May.

'Right, has everyone got wetsuits?' Jim said, bustling about in the shed, his voice muffled.

'I think so.'

Like everything when there's a big group of people, just getting to the beach felt like a major expedition.

I thought about what Will had said the day before, about nothing ever being spontaneous any more, and I got a pang for the days when we could just disappear off to the beach at the drop of a hat, whenever we liked. I remembered a day when we were about fifteen – a day just like today, the sun hot during the long summer holidays, when we'd still been just friends and nothing more. The knock on the door had come early, and I'd heard Mum moaning as she went to answer it. But then her tone had changed completely and I lay in bed listening to the rumble of voices, wondering who it was. I soon found out.

'Fran, Will's here!'

Part of me had wanted to roll over and pull the pillow over my head and go back to sleep, but the other part wondered what Will was so desperate to tell me at eight o'clock in the morning.

'Fran, hurry up,' he'd said, as I clomped down the stairs in my short pyjamas.

'What for?'

'Will says he wants to go to the beach, love,' Mum said, beaming beside the door.

I looked at Will, who I realised now was holding a rucksack on his back with a rolled-up towel sticking out of the side, a cap wedged onto his head.

'Fancy it?'

'Not really.'

'Oh come on, lazy bones.' He'd swung his arm up in the air. 'It's gorgeous and sunny and I'm so bored of sitting around doing chuff all every day. Come on.'

'But how will we get there?'

'There's a train – we go into London, round to Waterloo and then get the train down to Brighton. It doesn't take long.'

I'd thought about it and shrugged. Why not? I was getting pretty bored too.

'Give me ten minutes,' I'd said, and dived upstairs, throwing on shorts and a vest top and cleaning my teeth as I listened to Mum and Will chatting easily downstairs. When I got down to the kitchen I'd watched them for a minute, Mum telling Will off for some minor misdemeanour as though she was his own mum, and I smiled. She always said Will was like the son she'd never had.

'Ready!' I'd said, stepping into the kitchen. Mum handed me a Tupperware box full of sandwiches that she'd magicked from somewhere and I shoved them in my rucksack.

'Have you got any money, love?' Mum asked. I shook my head, and she rummaged around in her handbag and handed me a twenty-pound note.

'Now, you both be careful going into London on your own,' she said, giving us stern looks. We nodded obediently and I tried not to laugh as I saw Will looking at me from the corner of my eye. 'And be home by seven o'clock.'

'Okay, Mum.' I'd been thrilled. It gave us a whole day to spend at the beach, in the arcades, eating ice cream, and as we walked down to the station a few minutes later I felt filled with excitement for the long day that stretched in front of us. We'd had a blast, throwing a ball around on the pebble beach, whizzing round the rollercoaster at the end of the pier, and running away from the seagulls who tried to steal our chips.

Now, I felt a pang for the ease of the old us – the Will and Fran who could decide at the last minute to head to the beach, with nothing more to think about than whether we were going to spend our money on chips or waste it in the arcade. It felt like more than a lifetime ago. They felt like two entirely different people.

'Right, let's go, otherwise it'll be time to come home by the time we get there,' I said, clapping my hands and herding everyone into cars. The sun was already hot and the heat poured out of the car like liquid when we opened the doors. The steering wheel was too hot to touch and skin squeaked on leather as everyone climbed in. I glanced behind where Kieran was helping Elodie with her seatbelt.

'All right, sweetheart?' I said.

'Yes,' they replied in unison, and I smiled.

Beside me, Will was clipping his seatbelt in. He looked brighter today than he had in weeks and I wondered whether it was the sea air having such a positive effect on him. Whatever it was, I was thrilled, and looking forward to the day ahead.

By the time we got to the beach and found somewhere to park, it was packed, but we found a spot as close to the sea as we could, and spread towels and mats and deckchairs out across the soft sand.

'Here, you have this,' I said to Will, opening a deckchair for him and sticking it under one of the umbrellas we'd brought to shade us from the scorching sun.

'There's no time for sitting,' he said, flashing Elodie a cheeky smile. 'Is there, Els?'

'No, Daddy,' she said, picking up the bucket and spade we'd borrowed from Jim's girls and striding over to grab Will's hand. 'We're going to build a massive sandcastle.'

I glanced around. The place was so full there was barely a spare patch of sand to dig, let alone build a sandcastle big enough to sit in. I knew Will was desperate to get going with it, but I wasn't sure now was the right time or place.

'Are you sure you don't want to wait until the beach is a bit quieter?' I said.

'We're going down there,' Elodie said, pointing down towards the shore where the waves lapped gently against the sand.

'Are you coming to help?' Will said.

'Do you want me to?'

'I think we might need as much help as we can get, given Elodie's grand architectural plans,' Will said, grinning. 'Does anyone else want to come and help?'

'Me!' Olivia said.

'Kieran, love?' I said.

Kieran shrugged, and glanced quickly at Soraya, who was already stretched out on a towel in her swimming costume, sunbathing.

'You'll help, won't you, Soraya?' Karen said.

Soraya rolled her head to the side and shielded her eyes with her arm. 'I've just laid down.'

'That's okay, you've got all day for that. Come on, come and help your uncle Will make the best sandcastle in the world.'

Soraya reluctantly pulled herself upright, and Kieran stood too. 'Okay, I'll help as well,' he said.

I noticed that he barely looked at Soraya, and I suppressed a smile. I remembered those teenage days of feeling awkward and I wondered whether my boy had a bit of a crush.

Jim and I followed them all down to the shore while Karen stayed behind to guard the bags, until Will stopped and declared, 'This looks the perfect place!' I looked around. The little patch slightly to the left was quieter than the rest of the beach, the sand was firm and the tide was going out so the castle wouldn't be washed away before we'd had a chance to finish it.

'Right, what are we making? An actual castle?'

'I have a better idea.' Will stuck his spade in the sand and pulled it along, drawing a circle in the sand. 'We wanted something we could sit in, right?'

I nodded.

'Well, let's build a sand car!'

'But, Daddy, I wanted a princess castle!'

'Castles are lovely, but they're hard to sit in. How about we make a really cool car that a princess would drive, and we can all sit in it then. You can even pretend to drive it.'

Elodie's little face screwed up as she gave it some serious thought. Then she smiled and said, 'Okay then.'

I stood. 'Right, we have the royal seal of approval – car it is!'

'But a princess one!'

'Yes, Els, definitely a car for a princess,' Will said. 'Right, let's do this.'

For the next hour we all dug furiously under Will's direction, making piles of sand, patting it down, standing back to admire our work. For a long while it looked like just a few odd lumps here and there, but Will had a clear vision, and slowly it started to take shape. Will looked more full of life than he had in a long time.

An hour later, we stood back.

I heard a low whistle and realised it was coming from Kieran. 'That is cool,' he said.

He was right. The car we'd created *was* pretty damn cool. There were four seats, a steering wheel, and a windscreen with wipers etched into it, and it was sunk low into the ground.

'Daddy, can I get in?' Elodie said.

'I reckon we can all get in,' Will said.

'Er, I'm not sure it's big enough for everyone,' I said, laughing as Elodie and Olivia carefully stepped over the car door. Elodie sat proudly in the front seat, Olivia beside her.

'Getting in, love?' I said to Kieran.

'Nah, it's okay. I'll just take some photos.'

'All right, then, wait a minute.' I climbed in and Will followed, and we all posed as Kieran and Soraya snapped away.

And despite the achievement, and despite the look of happiness on Will's face at ticking another task off the list, I could only hope that we'd have time to tick off the rest before it was too late.

* * *

'Are we going surfing now?' Will said, as we re-joined the group.

'Why don't we have a rest and do it after lunch?'

'If you mean you think I need a rest, don't worry,' he said. 'I feel great today.' He stretched his arms out and yawned.

'I know you do, I just don't want you to overdo it.'

'I'm fine.'

'Well, I'm knackered after all that digging, so you'll have to give me a few minutes,' Jim said, and I shot him a grateful look. I understood why Will was being so stubborn – if he gave in to the tiredness, he'd be admitting how ill he really was. But I didn't want him to make himself feel worse just to prove a point.

'Okay, okay, if you're all going to gang up on me I suppose I have no choice,' he said, lowering himself down into his deckchair. Elodie settled herself beside Will's chair and began covering her legs with piles of sand so she looked like a mermaid. I sat down on the other side of him. Nobody spoke for a while, just letting the chatter of other families, the squawk of the seagulls above our heads and the gentle breeze wash over us. Elodie broke the silence.

'Daddy?'

'Hmmmm?' His cap was shielding his face from the sun and his voice was muffled. It sounded like he was dropping off to sleep already.

'Is that man over there a grandad?'

We both peered across the sand towards where Elodie was pointing.

'Who, love?' Will said.

'That man there, with the bald head. The one digging a hole.'

'Yes, I expect so. Why?'

Elodie looked down and watched her finger trail a circle round and round in the sand. Then she looked up, all wide-eyed innocence.

'Have I got a grandad?'

The silence that followed seemed to stretch for an eternity, and I wondered for a moment whether Will was going to answer, but then he sat up and pulled the cap off his face and leaned forward in his chair. He looked pale and I glanced at Jim, worried about what he was about to say. Jim gave me a look I couldn't read.

'Of course you've got a grandad. Grandad Fred.'

Elodie nodded. 'Yes, I know about him, silly. But that's Mummy's daddy. But everyone else has got two grandads – well, apart from Josie Williams, but that's because both of her grandads are dead and so's her dad, but we're not supposed to talk about it. But in my class the other day we were talking about family trees and loads of other people had two grandads and grandmas and I only had one of each. I know Grandma

died because Mummy told me, but she never told me about my grandad.'
She was looking at Will earnestly now, and my heart started hammering,
wondering how he was going to explain this to a six-year-old.

'Well, the thing is...' He stopped, looked down at the sand, cleared
his throat. 'The thing is, Els, you don't have a grandad. I don't have a
dad.'

Beside me I heard Jim give a sharp intake of breath and I didn't
dare look at him.

Elodie's forehead creased up. 'Why, did he die?'

Will didn't answer for a moment. 'I don't know, Els. I – my father
and I – your grandad – fell out a long, long time ago and we don't speak
any more and – well, that's it. I don't know where he is.'

'But...' Elodie looked at me as though I could explain things a bit
clearer. 'But, Daddy, how can you fall out with your own daddy? And
how don't you know where he is?'

Will looked as though he wanted nothing more than to just disappear so I thought it was time I came to his rescue.

'Sometimes, Elodie, people do fall out, even with the people they
love. It's not very nice but it happens, and sometimes people do things
to hurt you that you can't forgive. And that's what happened to Daddy
and his daddy.'

'Did your daddy hit you?' Elodie said, looking back at Will, her
voice scared now.

'No, people don't always have to hit people to hurt them,' Will said
at last. 'Sometimes they can say mean things that hurt people.'

Elodie thought about it for a minute. 'But what about "sticks and
stones may break my bones but words will never hurt me"? That's what
my teacher, Miss Dunhill, tells us all the time and she knows
everything.'

'I'm sure it's true most of the time, but thing is, sometimes, words
can hurt a lot. And sometimes, words that have been spoken can't be
taken back.'

She looked down at her legs and brushed the sand off them furiously. 'What did Grandad say to you that was mean, then?' she said, standing and letting the rest of the sand fall from her legs.

A heavy silence filled the air as we collectively held our breath.

Will took her hands and kissed them. 'I'll tell you one day when you're a bit older,' he said. 'But let's not worry about it now.' He pushed himself up with a struggle. 'Now, why don't we all go and get an ice cream?'

Elodie took a few seconds to decide whether she wanted to keep talking or whether she wanted an ice cream instead. And then she smiled.

'Okay, Daddy, but only if I can have a big cone with a chocolate flake in it too?'

'Course you can, darling,' Will said, scooping her up with relief and planting kisses all over her face, making her giggle.

'Too many kisses, Daddy!' she said, squirming until he put her back down again.

'Right, who wants one?' Will said. He was smiling but I could see the worry in his eyes.

'Me, and I'll come with you,' Jim said, jumping up.

My heart sank. I knew why Jim wanted to go with his brother, and it wasn't just to help him with the ice cream order. I could feel the fall-out coming and I was terrified it was going to ruin everything. But all I could do was sit and watch helplessly as the two brothers walked slowly up the beach, picking their way between towels and picnic hampers and small children, their feet sinking into the soft sand. They were deep in conversation, and I wished I could hear what was being said.

'What do you think they're talking about?' Karen said, glancing to make sure Elodie and Olivia were out of earshot. Kieran and Soraya had their earphones stuck in their ears so we didn't have to worry about them.

I shook my head. 'I wish I knew. I just hope they're not going to argue.'

Karen fell silent for a moment but I knew she was about to say something more. From what I'd seen in the less than twenty-four hours since we'd met, everything she said was considered.

'I think Jim's really angry.'

'About Will and his dad?'

'Yes.' She paused again. 'I don't think he even realises it. I see him when the subject of Will and their father comes up and his whole body tenses and his jaw kind of sets into a line. It's the only time I see him like that about anything.' She looked at me now. 'I think if he knew the truth, if he could understand what really happened between the two of them, then he could let it go a bit more.'

'I think Will just always wanted to protect him,' I said.

'I totally understand that. But Jim's a grown man now, and he just wants to know the truth.'

I picked up a handful of sand and watched as it ran through my fingers, slowly, slowly, speeding up towards the end until it became beach again, indistinguishable from the rest. 'I have a feeling Will's on the verge of something. I don't know whether he wants to see his father, but I do think he at least wants to know something about him, so he can make that decision. But I'm afraid if Jim pushes him now, he'll pull away again, and it—' My voice broke and I cleared my throat. 'And then it might be too late anyway.'

Karen nodded, and we both watched the two men we loved as they queued at the ice cream kiosk, still deep in conversation. They were too far away to make out facial expressions, but it was clear from Will's stance that he was defensive, angry. My heart ached as I watched them. They'd always been a similar build: tall and strong and athletic. If anything Will had been fitter than Jim as teenagers, and in the inter-vening years had kept up his fitness playing football. But looking at them now, side by side, the difference between them was stark. Jim was still tall and strong, and although he was carrying a bit more weight around the middle than he used to, his broad shoulders balanced it out. Beside him, Will looked shrunken, and older – as though, rather than the four years that separated them, there was a whole generation between them. Will's T-shirt was hanging off him like an old rag. His legs, always so strong and muscular, were thin, poking out of the bottom of his shorts like little sticks. My heart felt as though it might break in two.

My thoughts were interrupted by Elodie, who'd run back over to us and was tugging at my arm. 'Fran, Daddy's coming back, can I go and get my ice cream?'

'Yes, okay, but be careful of other people,' I said, glad of the distraction. I watched as Jim and Will approached, trying to work out from their faces whether they were still speaking to one another.

'I thought you'd gone to Italy to buy the ice cream,' Karen said, standing and taking a couple of cones from Jim and handing them to Olivia and Soraya.

'Yeah, I think half the population of Cornwall decided they wanted ice cream about five minutes before we did,' he said, handing another cone to Kieran. Ice cream dripped down his forearm where it had already begun to melt in the heat of the day.

Will flopped back onto the deckchair and I tried to catch his eye, but he kept his gaze locked determinedly on the cone in front of him as though his life depended on it.

'Are you up for trying a bit of surfing later?' I said quietly, moving closer so no one else could hear us.

He glanced at Jim and shrugged. 'Depends.'

'On what? Jim?'

He nodded and took another lick of his ice cream.

'Did you sort anything out?'

'Not really. He asked me what happened with Dad again, and I said I couldn't tell him. He got angry and said we'd talk about it again before I left. And that was that.'

'And will you?'

He glanced at me. 'Will I what?'

'Talk to him about it later?'

'No. Nothing's changed, Fran. I still don't want to tell Jim what Dad did, because there's no point.'

'Except you might turn Jim against you if you keep pushing him away about this.'

Will took a lick of his ice cream and angled his body slightly away from me, making it clear the conversation was over.

He might not want to talk about it right now but I wasn't about to give up. It might not be anything to do with me, but I loved Will and I didn't want to see him throw away the chance to make amends with his father before he died if it was what he really wanted, beneath all the fear and the hurt.

I just had to make Will see that.

* * *

It was early afternoon by the time we all pulled on our wetsuits and headed down towards the sea clutching a surfboard each. The wind had got up a bit, which Jim insisted meant the conditions were better, but which terrified me.

We'd all tried not to notice how skinny and pale Will looked as he pulled his wetsuit on, and how the rubber fabric hung off his body. Jim and Will had clearly decided to try and put their argument behind them for the afternoon too.

We reached the water's edge, and I watched as, what seemed like miles out, surfers stood effortlessly on their boards and caught the waves, riding on the crest all the way in to shore. They made it look so easy but I knew it wasn't going to be. I'd never even managed to successfully stand on a skateboard; I wasn't quite sure how I thought I was going to pull this off.

'Right, first things first,' Jim said, letting his board drop to the sand with a soft flump. Will and I did the same. 'First, I'm going to get you to stand up on the board when it's not moving.' He looked at me and to Will and back again. 'It's harder than it looks, getting up from lying down on a narrow piece of board, believe me.'

Will and I both lay flat on our bellies on our boards as the shallow water lapped around us. 'Right, copy me,' Jim yelled, lifting his chest up, then his left leg, his right leg and then coming up to stand. He made it look effortless. I tried lifting my chest and then trying to hook my left leg up towards my hand, as Jim had done, but it wouldn't get anywhere near. I kneeled on my right knee and hoiked it round that way, then stood, wobbling as the wind tried to tip me over.

'Not elegant, but you got there,' Jim said, grinning. 'Will, your turn.'

Will lifted his chest and hooked his left leg up with ease, before gently kneeling and standing. He looked pleased with himself as Jim gave him a clap, but I could see the effort on his face.

'Excellent. Right, let's go in the water now. But strap the board to your ankle first, like this.'

We did as we were told, attaching the boards to our ankles with Velcro straps, then waded after Jim into the shallows. We strode out, the waves trying to push us one way while we kept pushing the other, out towards the deeper water. I felt the cold water creep up past my knees, my thighs and over my belly and felt my heart rate pick up as we got deeper. Just as I thought we were going out of my depth, Jim stopped.

'Let's bodyboard back into shore first,' he said, and I sighed with relief. This sounded manageable. I watched as Jim jumped easily out of the water and slid his body onto his board. Beside me, Will did the same, the muscles of his arms straining as he pulled himself up. I jumped next, expecting my body to lift out of the water and land on the board just as easily. But instead the water pulled against me and dragged me straight back down again, leaving the board bobbing on the surface. I tried again, and the same thing happened.

'I can't get up!' I said, my face burning. This was the first step; how could it be so difficult? Jim paddled over and hopped off his board and placed his hands round my waist and lifted me as I jumped, and this time I landed inelegantly on the board, a tangle of arms and legs and shame.

'Don't worry, it gets easier,' Jim said. Beside me, Will grinned and I wanted to throw something at him.

The next hour was more fun than I'd expected as Jim explained how to catch a wave and ride with it into the shore. The gentle movement of the sea as we slid across the surface was soothing, and with my face down close to the water I felt safe. Every now and then I glanced over at Will to make sure he wasn't getting too tired. He was stubborn about admitting it at the best of times; Lord only knew how much he'd resist it with Jim, especially after their argument earlier. I knew he felt he had something to prove.

But he seemed fine. In fact, more than fine – he seemed to be revelling in his new-found skill.

'I can't believe I've never done this before,' he said, laughing as we all stood in the shallow water.

'Me neither,' Jim said. 'It's totally up your street.'

Will's face changed then.

'What's wrong?' I said.

'Nothing, I'm fine. I just – I can't believe I left it so late to discover how much I love this.' He looked round at the expanse of sea dotted with bodies, at the milky blue sky that arced above us, and wiped his face with his hand. It was hard to tell whether there were tears mingled with the salty water. 'Sorry, Fran. I just feel so fucking sad that everything's going to end so soon.'

I felt my breath catch in my chest and I gulped it down to smother the sob that threatened to escape. Will rarely talked about the approaching end of his life. I hadn't known whether that was because he wasn't scared or whether he was so scared he was blocking it out, but now it was clear. He was furious: at the world, the universe, at whatever this thing was that was eating him up from the inside. And I found at that moment that my fury matched his. How dare fate let us be apart for so long and then snatch him away from me again almost immediately?

I waded through the water towards Will, my surfboard dragging behind me and knocking into my shins, and flung my arms around him. I tried to imprint in my memory the feel of his body against mine, the sound of the waves slapping against us and the call of the seagulls above our heads, the feel of his arms around my body. I needed to guard this memory forever, wrapped up safe where I could call on it whenever I needed comforting. I knew it would fade in time, but I had to do my best to keep it alive. To keep Will alive.

I could feel Will's shoulder shake as he sobbed and I didn't dare look at his face. Instead I opened my arms up and gestured for Jim to join us. This was no time to be arguing.

None of us cared what we looked like as we stood in the shallow waters of the beach that day, kids splashing and laughing around us, three surfboards bobbing wildly round our shins, as we clung to each other as though we would never let go. Finally, though, Will released his hold and stepped back. He'd composed himself and dragged in a deep breath, flaring his nostrils as he let it back out again in a huge puff.

'Wow, that feels better.'

I still held his hand loosely in mine and I squeezed it now.

'I'm sorry, you two, I don't usually let it get to me. It's just – it's moments like this when it suddenly hits me.'

'Don't ever apologise, Will. You're being so strong.'

'Am I? I don't feel it. I feel like a coward, like I'm letting this thing beat me.'

'Don't be crazy,' Jim said. 'This isn't something you have any control over. This is something that's happened to you, and you know what? Most people would have given up, would have let the evil disease take over. But you're not. You're grasping the few months of life you have left, and you're wringing out every last inch of fun and love you possibly can. What on earth is cowardly about that?'

'He's right, you know,' I said, reaching up and pushing wet hair out of Will's eyes. When had his hair got so long, and why hadn't I noticed?

'I'm exhausted by it all, though,' he said, staring down at our entwined hands. 'The bucket list, and doing all these things with you, it's keeping me going. But I'm scared I won't be able to keep going long enough before the cancer takes over completely. I mean, look at me. I'm so much weaker now than I've ever been. How much time have I actually got left?'

'Oh, Will, don't worry about that. I'll help you do as much as we can, I promise, and Jim will too, won't you?' Jim nodded, the pain carved onto his face. 'But it doesn't matter. None of it matters. If we finish the bucket list then great. But if we don't, never mind. All that matters is that you're happy and you know you're loved.'

He nodded, then looked up. 'If I don't finish it, will you? The two of you? And Kieran?'

I paused for a moment, thinking about how hard it would be doing these things without Will by my side. But I knew how much it meant to him too.

'Of course I will. We all will. But let's not think about that now. Let's just pack in as much as we can while you're still able. Deal?'

He nodded, the determination back on his face again.

'Okay.' He looked at his brother. 'Are you going to teach me how to stand on this stupid thing, then?'

'Are you sure you're up to it?'

'Positive.' He looked at me, the cheeky grin back again. 'But I'm not so sure about Fran.'

'Oi!'

'Do you want to come back out with us, Fran?' Jim said.

The truth was, Will was right. There was no way I was going to be able to stand up and ride a wave by the end of the day. If ever. I shook my head. 'No, I don't want to hold you two back. I'll call it a day now – if you don't mind, Will?'

'I think it's for the best, darling, don't you?'

I stuck my tongue out and released my ankle from the Velcro strap. Then I waded back to shore, feeling relieved I didn't have to go through that any more, and relieved that Will had finally talked about how he was feeling.

I hoped it might mean he'd open up to Jim about everything else too.

* * *

Everything was packed and in the car. Wetsuits were peeled off and my sun-baked skin felt sticky with sea water and gritty with sand. My hair didn't bear thinking about. I was looking forward to a shower when we got back to Jim and Karen's.

Will, it appeared, had other ideas, though.

'You know what we haven't done yet, don't you?' he said, sidling up behind me and wrapping his hands round my waist. I could feel his breath on my ear.

'What?'

'Skinny dipping.'

I turned my head to look at him. His eyebrows were raised in a question.

'Now? Are you serious?'

His eyes glittered and his mouth tugged up into a grin. 'Why not? We're here, it's not too busy, it's the perfect opportunity.'

I looked round the beach. There were still several families dotted across the sand, some packing up, others still trying to catch the last rays of sun before it dipped below the horizon. I'd expected Will to be so wiped out he just wanted to go home and sleep. But he'd snoozed for an hour after his surf, and it had obviously regenerated him.

'I can't go now!' I hissed.

He turned me round to face him. 'Oh come on, Franny.' The name he always called me when he wanted me to do something. 'Why not? Are you scared?'

I was, truth be told, but I didn't know what of. I mean, what was the worst that could happen?

'Just me and you?'

He glanced back at Jim and Karen, who'd already climbed into their car. 'Yeah, I think so.' He walked across to the car and tapped on the window. Jim rolled it down.

'Would you be able to take Kieran and Elodie home as well?'

'It'll be a squeeze.'

'Go on, it's not far. There's just something that me and Fran need to do before we come home.'

Jim glanced at me as I smiled innocently, and he nodded. 'Come on then, climb in you two,' he said, and Kieran blushed furiously from his hairline to his toes as he squeezed in close to Soraya.

'Thanks, Jim, we won't be long.'

'Just don't do anything I wouldn't do,' Jim said, grinning as he drove slowly out of the emptying car park.

Will turned to me. 'Well, shall we?' He held his hand out and I took it and nodded.

'Let's do it.'

We walked hand in hand back down to the beach and onto the sand. The sea looked a long way off and I didn't know how close Will wanted to get before we stripped off. 'Let's go down by those rocks,' he said, pointing to the very edge of the beach where there was hardly anyone left.

'Getting shy all of a sudden, are you?' I said.

'Well, I don't want to flash my arse to the whole world. Nobody needs to see that.'

'I don't know, I think you've got a lovely bum.' I gave it a squeeze. He leaned over and planted a kiss on my lips and I felt myself melt into him, all the worry of the last few weeks disappearing for a few moments at the feel of his lips against mine. He tasted salty. He pulled away and gave my hand a tug.

'Come on, then.' Then he started walking briskly down the beach towards the rocks. I ran to keep up.

'Where's all this energy come from all of a sudden?' I said, jumping over stones and rocks.

'No idea, but I'm making the most of it,' he said. We reached the rocks, and stopped.

'Right, ready?'

I nodded. Why was I so nervous about this? I was being ridiculous. With a deep breath, I pulled my T-shirt over my head, unclipped my bikini top and pushed my shorts down, leaving them in a puddle on the damp sand. Will stood still, just watching me and I began to feel self-conscious standing there completely naked. I looked over my shoulder to see whether anyone had noticed. Nobody was looking our way. Yet.

'Your turn.' I nodded at him and watched as he peeled off his T-shirt, shorts and boxers. The first time we'd seen each other's bodies without clothes on when we were teenagers we'd been equal parts terrified and equal parts hysterical. We'd touched parts we'd never touched before in wonder, as though someone was going to stop us at any minute. This moment, right here on the beach, felt just the same, and I felt a surge of love and nostalgia that I thought might make my heart burst.

'I love you,' he said, reaching his hand out to touch my cheek. I shivered beneath his touch as he ran his hand slowly down my neck, to my chest and stopped on my left breast. Then he closed the gap between us and pressed his body against mine and I moaned.

'Let's go.' And as quickly as he'd closed the gap, he opened it again and raced off towards the water, sand flicking up behind his heels as I ran to catch up.

We didn't stop at the water's edge, both too keen to get into the water before anyone spotted us, and the cold took my breath away as it hit my thighs and stomach then chest. Finally, before it reached my neck, we stopped and Will turned to me and circled his arms around me. His skin felt warm against mine, the cold water enveloping us, trying to slip in between our bodies. A gentle breeze blew across the water, sending ripples around us, and I shivered.

'I'm so happy we're together,' Will said, kissing my nose, then my cheeks. His face was so close to mine I could make out his eyelashes, dark against his blue eyes, and the whiteness of his skin, almost translucent.

'Me too.' My voice was a whisper, whipped away on the wind.

'Promise me something, Franny?'

I nodded, rested my forehead against his.

'Promise me you won't grieve for too long?'

I shook my head. 'I can't promise that.'

'I know it will be hard, but I can't die knowing I'm leaving behind a trail of pain.' He paused. 'Do you ever wish we hadn't met again?'

I gasped and pulled away. 'No! Do you?'

He shook his head vehemently. 'Absolutely not. I'm happier than I've been for years. Since – well, since we were last together. I never thought I'd find this sort of happiness again and I feel so lucky.'

I put my hands against his cheeks and held him still. 'I'm happier than I've ever been too, despite what's happening. I could never regret being with you and having this time together. Never. I love you, William Poulton.'

'And I love you too.'

'Can I ask you something else, though?'

'Of course.'

'Can we get out now? I'm bloody freezing.'

And at that Will tipped his head back and let out a shout of laughter and pulled me with him towards the shore and back to the rocks where we shivered as we hurriedly pulled on our clothes over our damp skin.

Another one ticked off.

And another day closer to goodbye.

15

June 2019

Sometimes seconds, minutes, hours seem to move so slowly you can almost hear the tick, tick, tick of the clock. At other times, though, days slip away like water, until they become weeks and you've barely even had the time to notice.

After Cornwall, that's exactly what happened. It was as though time was speeding up like some cruel game to see if we had it in our power to rein it in, to slow it down.

Cornwall had been wonderful, but it had stirred up a lot of emotions too, and over the next few days I had an underlying ball of anxiety in the pit of my belly, as though I knew I was about to miss something but couldn't quite remember what it was. Will, however, was still refusing to give in, and was busily planning things to tick off his bucket list.

Which was why, one warm summer's day, Will, Kieran and I found ourselves waiting in a field to climb into the basket of a hot-air balloon.

'I can't believe how lucky we are with this weather,' Will said, tipping his face up towards the warm summer sun. His skin glowed, such a contrast to how wan and pale he'd looked recently.

'You've said that about twenty times this morning already,' I said, rolling my eyes.

He turned to face me, serious. 'I know, sorry. But I'm just so relieved. I mean, they fitted us in at the last minute as it is, so if the weather had been crap we'd have struggled to get it rebooked in time...' He trailed off. He didn't need to finish the sentence for me to know what he was about to say.

'Sorry, love, I'm only teasing.' I kissed his nose. 'You're right, we are lucky.' I glanced over to the huge balloon that was spread out, deflated, like a silk puddle across the grass. 'I've always wanted to do this.'

'Me too. I can't wait.'

'Mum, they're ready.' Kieran's voice interrupted us, and we made our way towards where he was standing by the instructors. I took hold of Kieran's hand and for once he didn't snatch it away.

'Excited?'

'Can't wait. Although I am bricking it a bit too.'

'There's nothing to be scared of. These things are really safe.' I said the words but actually I was pretty nervous too. I couldn't get Ian McEwan's novel *Enduring Love* out of my head, where the opening scene starts with someone plummeting to their death from a hot-air balloon, their body smashed to pieces by the impact.

While we listened to the safety instructions I could hear the roar of hot air behind us as the balloon was inflated. And then, finally, it was time to lift off.

We scrambled into the basket behind ten other people and made our way to the edge. There was a huge roar as the hot air was pumped into the silk and slowly, inch by inch, the red and orange fabric – and the basket we were standing in beneath it – started to lift off the ground: slowly at first, like an infirm old man, and then more and more as the air stretched the fabric and the balloon rippled above our heads like liquid. I gripped Kieran's hand tightly on one side, and Will's with the other and stood, feet planted firmly, as we lifted up into the air. The roar was so loud I would have had to shout to be heard, so instead I watched my two favourite people in the world, saw the delight on their faces as we climbed higher and higher towards the clouds. Once we levelled out the three of us inched forward and leaned carefully over the side. There below us, stretched out for miles, were fields and hedges and trees, getting smaller and smaller and, further in the distance, the high-rise buildings of London reaching up through the hazy sunlight. I gasped as we rose even higher, the view taking my breath away. We floated along with the breeze, the roar of the hot air and the wind blowing my hair and the feeling of Will and Kieran's palms in mine, and I felt a surge of happiness.

An hour later, as we slowly dipped back towards the field where we'd started, I felt adrenaline course through my body.

'That was amazing,' I said, tears filling my eyes.

'Mum, are you crying?'

I wiped my cheek with the back of my hand. 'Sorry, I just feel a bit emotional.' I grinned. 'Did you love it too?'

Kieran nodded. 'It was amazing.'

'Will?'

Will was staring up at the sky, watching the fluffy clouds slide along on the breeze. He looked back down and caught my eye. 'It was—' His voice broke and I realised he was feeling the same way as me. 'I just couldn't stop thinking about how I don't want to leave this behind,' he said quietly so Kieran couldn't hear.

'Oh, Will.' I didn't know what else to say. Nothing, no reassurance, no platitudes, would be enough. He *was* going to leave this behind, and soon – and in his wake he was going to leave a very big hole. I reached out and held him, my cheek pressed against his chest. I could feel the steady rhythm of his heart. And slowly, as we landed on the field with a bump, Will's body began to relax.

* * *

It had been years since anyone apart from my parents and Mags had remembered my birthday – at least without prompting. So when I found Will looking shady in the kitchen one morning a few days later, I wondered what he was up to.

'Has something happened?' I said, stepping towards him.

'Nope.' His eyes shone and he moved to block something on the worktop behind him.

'What's that? What have you got there?'

Will rolled his eyes. 'For God's sake, woman, stop being so nosy and just go and sit in the front room.'

Obediently, I walked to the living room and pushed open the door. And there, surrounded by dozens of helium balloons and hundreds of streamers, was Kieran. He grinned as I walked in.

'Happy birthday, Mum,' he said, stepping forward and kissing me on the cheek. I pulled him into a hug then released him.

'Did you do all of this?'

'I helped.' He shrugged. 'It was Will's idea.'

I turned at a noise behind me, and there was Will, a tray in his hands piled high with croissants, jam and a pot of tea. It shook as he placed it carefully down on the coffee table. 'Ta da!'

I felt tears prick my eyes and blinked them away. 'I can't believe you've done this for me,' I said. 'No one ever remembers my birthday.'

'I do,' Kieran said. I raised my eyebrows at him, the memory of last year's scribbled note with an IOU attached to it springing to mind. 'Well, sometimes.' He grinned sheepishly.

'Do you want to eat breakfast or open your presents first?' Will said, sitting tentatively on the sofa. He looked tired.

'Ooh, there are presents?' I looked round the room and spotted a pile of obviously hurriedly wrapped gifts in the corner that I hadn't seen before. 'I'll open these first,' I said.

For the next five minutes I happily tore paper from presents – some new books, my favourite Neil Young album on vinyl, a pair of pyjamas and a bottle of gin. And when I thought I'd finished, Will handed me another one, this time neatly wrapped and tied with ribbon. I looked at him in amazement and he smiled sheepishly. 'I didn't wrap it myself, obviously.'

'What is it?'

'Open it.'

I picked at the edge of the paper and tore a strip off, letting the pieces drop to the floor. Slowly, a black box was revealed, white writing along the top. *Chanel*. I looked up at Will.

'You didn't?'

'Just open it!'

I lifted the lid off and there, nestled in among black tissue paper, was the familiar black padding of a Chanel handbag, just like the one his mum had always used and that I'd always coveted. I ran my fingers along the edge.

'This must have cost a fortune!'

'It's the right one, isn't it?'

'Yes. But—'

'Then that's all that matters.'

I planted a kiss on his lips. 'Thank you, Will. It's amazing.'

'Well, there is an ulterior motive too.'

'What?'

'It means I get to tick something else off the bucket list.'

I smacked him gently on the arm. 'You and that bloody bucket list, you're going to drive me mad.'

'Can we eat now? I'm starving,' Kieran said.

'Of course! Thank you both so much for doing this. It's the best birthday I've ever had.'

'Even better than the one when you fell out of a tree and broke your arm and spent the day in A&E?'

I groaned. 'Definitely better than that.'

Kieran grabbed a croissant and stuffed half of it in his mouth. 'Happy birthday, Mum,' he said, his words muffled.

As I sat there with my two favourite people in the world, I felt like the luckiest person alive.

* * *

For all his mooching about and teenage grunting, sometimes Kieran surprised me. The next day he did just that when he walked through the door half-hidden behind a pile of white and green boxes.

He plonked them down on the kitchen counter and grinned.

'What's this?' I said, wiping my hands on a tea towel and peering through the cellophane covering on the top box.

'Thirty-six doughnuts,' he said.

'Er, what? Why?'

'Dur.' He poked his index finger at the boxes. 'It's on your list, remember? Eat twelve doughnuts in one go. I said I'd help, and this is me helping. Three of us, twelve doughnuts each. Thirty-six dough-nuts.' He held his hands out as if to demonstrate his point.

'Oh, good grief. At least I haven't cooked dinner yet.'

He looked at me like I'd gone mad. 'We're not having these instead of dinner – are we?'

'Well...' I shrugged. 'God only knows.'

'Shall I go and get Will, then? Where is he?'

'He's in bed. He was feeling a bit sick.'

'Oh.'

'Don't worry, love, I'll go and wake him up. You sort these out.' I started to walk out of the kitchen and then stopped suddenly. 'Keeks, where did you get the money to buy all of these? Krispy Kreme are not cheap.'

'I, er – I took the money from my money box.'

'But that's your savings!' I said.

Kieran shrugged. 'Yeah, I know. But this is important, and I didn't want to ask you.'

A pang of guilt twisted in my gut. We'd never been exactly poor, but money had always been tight, and Kieran had always known not to ask for anything expensive.

'I'll give you the money back, Kier,' I said.

'No, I don't want it. I want to pay for this.'

I looked at him for a second longer, then tapped my index finger against the end of his nose. 'To be discussed, mister,' I said, and left the room to find Will.

When we got back to the kitchen, Kieran had placed a box at each edge of the kitchen worktop, and a glass of water with each like some sort of televised eating challenge. He was waiting expectantly on a stool. I hadn't told Will what Kieran had planned, and when he saw the boxes his face lit up.

'Doughnuts!' he said, grinning. 'Did you do this, Kieran?'

Kieran nodded and looked at his feet. Will walked over to him and slapped his hand on his shoulder. 'Thank you.'

Kieran's face flushed bright red. 'S'okay.' He shrugged. 'I just wanted to help.'

'Well, you've made my day.'

Will sat on the stool nearest him, I took the other, and Kieran stood at the end of the counter next to the third box. Inside, the doughnuts glistened under the kitchen lights, spotlights reflected in the oozy pink and brown and white icing.

'Right, is there a time limit?

Kieran looked at Will, who shrugged. 'I'd say we need to get them eaten as quickly as possible, and we definitely can't take a massive break,' Will said. 'What do you think, Kieran?'

'Sounds about right.'

I gulped. How on earth would I eat twelve Krispy Kreme doughnuts in one go? But if it meant that much to Will, and to Kieran, I'd give it my best shot.

I picked up the first doughnut, a Nutella-glazed one, and took an enormous bite, crumbs dropping from my mouth as I chewed. 'Come on then, losers,' I said, the words muffled through my mouthful of food.

'Oh, that's attractive,' Will said, grinning, selecting a pink glazed doughnut and shoving a third of it into his mouth, while Kieran did the same with a sugared one. For a moment none of us could speak, rendered mute by mouths full of sickly dough. As I watched their faces chewing desperately, I wanted to cry and laugh at the same time.

* * *

As I lay in bed later that night, my mind whirred. The last couple of days had been wonderful, spending time with Will and Kieran, and we'd seen Elodie one afternoon too. Mags had popped round on my birthday and I'd even managed to get Mum and Dad on FaceTime, although I'd spent most of it talking to the inside of Mum's nose.

But making these new memories had also got me thinking about Jacob. It had been five weeks since I'd added my details to the Adoption Contact Register and, even though I knew it was still early days, every morning my stomach rolled with anticipation while I waited to see whether there would be an email, some sort of reply to let me know Jacob was interested in speaking to me; then every day would end with disappointment and a little bit more of me would give up, assuming that I'd lost my chance.

I knew I didn't deserve anything from him, but I'd always longed to let him know I loved him, that I'd never stopped thinking about him.

And now, of course, there was something even more important to tell him. His father was here, and he was dying.

All I could do was wait, and hope.

16

December 1993

The best thing about having a friend like Mags is that you know you're never going to be alone. Which was just as well once I'd made my decision about the baby.

'I can't tell anyone, though,' I told Mags.

'What, no one?'

I shook my head.

'What about your parents? Aren't you even going to tell them?'

'No. It's easier this way.'

Mags thought for a moment. 'I think you should.' Mags hadn't met my mum and dad yet but I'd told her all about them, so she of all people should have understood why I couldn't tell them about this baby.

'But they'll be so disappointed.'

'So what?'

'What do you mean, so what?'

· 'Most parents would be disappointed if their only daughter told them she was pregnant and that the father had disappeared and that she was having the baby but had decided to give it away.' She shrugged. 'I mean, it's not an ideal situation. But they deserve to know.'

I rubbed my belly. Mags was right. Of course she was. But the thought of saying the words out loud to Mum and Dad, of seeing the sadness, the disappointment, on their faces was almost too much to bear. How could I tell them – especially Mum – that the dream she'd always had of me and Will spending our lives together, of having a baby together, had gone so spectacularly wrong? And yet, how could I keep such a big secret from them?

'You're right.'

So I'd rung them that evening. To their credit they hadn't said much, although I could hear Mum's sniffles in the background once Dad came on the phone, and his voice had sounded tight, as if it was caught in his throat.

'I'm so sorry, Dad,' I said, my voice thick with tears.

I didn't go home that Christmas, and I made Mum and Dad promise not to come and see me, explaining that I'd go home once this was all over. I didn't want anyone else to know, and I didn't want to bring what my parents would consider to be shame on the family. Instead, I stayed in my student accommodation, and Mags stayed with me. We had Christmas dinner together, cooked on the temperamental stove in her student house, and clinked Appletiser-filled glasses together on New Year's Eve.

'I can't believe you're doing this for me,' I said. 'We've only known each other four months.'

'You're my best friend,' she said simply. 'Besides, it's not as though I have much to go home for.' Her parents were getting a divorce and it was less than amicable. She was glad to have somewhere else to be.

Over the next two months I carried on going to lectures, hiding my swollen belly beneath huge baggy jumpers. Finally, I was too enormous and too exhausted to carry on, and Mags went to speak to someone to arrange for me to have some time off. In fact, Mags helped me organise everything, including contacting the adoption agency to help me find a family for my baby.

'I'm not sure I can do this,' I sobbed, as we sat through meeting after meeting to talk about giving up my baby. I knew it was the right thing to do. I knew I couldn't give a baby any kind of a life right now. But the simple fact was, I didn't want to give it away. How could I? This baby was part of me now. How could I lose my baby as well as its father?

Will had written to me a few times, as promised, but I'd refused to read the letters and made Mags burn them before I changed my mind. And when it became clear I wasn't going to reply, the letters gradually fizzled out. There was only so many times he could tell me how sorry he was, I guess.

On 14 March 1994, with my belly as huge and round as a beach ball, my waters broke, two weeks before my due date. The sense of relief that it would all soon be over was tempered by the knowledge that, once this baby was delivered, it wouldn't belong to me any more. While it was still inside me, I could tell myself there was still time to change my mind. That I could run away from the hospital, and build a life for me and my baby away from everyone else.

Only I couldn't do that. For my baby's sake.

The labour was quick, but painful. There was screaming – mine – and gasping and panting and pain. But finally, my little boy came sliding into the world, and opened his lungs and filled the room with his cries. As I lay there being cleaned up, I watched as his tiny, pink body was wrapped in a blanket and handed to me.

'Here's your son,' the midwife said. 'Congratulations.'

Tears slid down my face as I buried my head in his blonde curls, and whispered my hello, and my goodbye. 'I'll love you forever, little man,' I said, and I thought the tears would never stop. 'Goodbye, William.'

After he was taken from me, I felt empty, as though the life inside of me had been drained away, leaving nothing but a bag of bones and organs. I didn't think I'd ever function again. What was the point?

Mags tried everything she could think of. I was back at Mum and Dad's by now but Mags was there every day, sitting with me, talking to me, making me eat. Plus there was the actual adoption to arrange. For now, William was with a foster family, waiting to find his forever home. I still had time to change my mind, if I wanted, and more than once I almost did. But deep down I knew I was doing the right thing, so I had to hold it together, spending hours going through adoption files, studying the faces of the couples who wanted to give my little boy the life he deserved. I could barely imagine it, and my heart ached as I pictured him leaving me forever.

But in the end I chose one. A lovely couple, Roy and Sandy Campbell, early forties, unable to have a baby of their own. I didn't know what it was that made me choose them, but perhaps it was to do with the longing in their eyes. Something told me they were kind, and that they'd love William the way he deserved to be loved. So even though I thought my heart might break, my little boy became their little boy just before he turned six months old. It was over.

It was Mags who made me get on with my life again.

'Come back to uni with me,' she said one day as I sat curled up in bed.

'I can't,' I sobbed.

She lifted my chin up to look at her. 'You can. You can do this, Fran. You're one of the strongest people I know.'

'I don't think so.'

'Course you are. Look at what you've just done. And you're still here.'

'I haven't smiled in months.'

'No, but you will soon, and then you will again, and again until you realise you really can smile at life again.' She smoothed my hair down and held her hand to my cheek. 'Come back with me.'

So finally, a few months after my baby was taken away, I went back to university. I couldn't go back to classes as I'd missed so much, but the university sent me the assignments I'd missed and I spent the next few months catching up, absorbed in my work. I was glad to have something to think about, but not to have to see too many people, to have to explain where I'd been. Mags was with me every day, getting me through bit by bit, putting me back together until, nine months after baby William was born, I felt as though I might be getting a bit of myself back again.

Then a letter had arrived, from William's adoptive parents via the adoption agency, and I was in danger of toppling all the way back to square one again. I'd said it was okay for them to contact me, but it was a shock all the same.

Dear Francesca, it said. *We hope you don't mind but we wanted to send you a photo of Jacob, as we have called him. This is him at his christening last week. He's growing so quickly. We hope this is appropriate. Thank you for everything you've done – you've made our lives complete. Yours, The Campbells.*

Not William any more. Jacob.

I dropped the letter on the floor as though it were burning my fingers. My hands shook, my whole body shook, and that's how Mags found me when she came round later that evening. She picked up the letter and the photo from the floor with her fingertips, as though it was something dirty, and placed it gently on the bed.

'Did you know they were going to send it?'

'I think—' My breath hitched. 'I think they asked if they could, yes. I just forgot, what with everything.'

She laid her hand on mine and squeezed it gently. 'You can ask them to stop, you know?'

I shook my head. 'No. No I need this.' I nodded with my whole body, convincing myself. 'Yes, I do. It will be good. To know, I mean. Know he's okay. He's happy.' My voice didn't sound like mine, but the more I said the words the more I knew I meant them. If I could have some connection to William – Jacob – then maybe it would make it easier.

And with every letter that arrived, I filed it away for when the future me needed to remember.

17

Early July 2019

The unopened email glowed like a beacon, and I felt my breath stick in my throat as I stared at it, frozen.

'Are you all right, love?' I slammed the laptop shut at Will's voice behind me, before my body jump-started back to life, the blood racing round my veins like a runaway train. I felt dizzy and clutched the edge of the table.

'I'm fine.'

Will looked at the closed laptop, at my shaking hands and at my face, which I had no doubt would be ashen, and frowned. If he was suspicious I was up to something he didn't say, but instead turned slowly away and sat across the other side of the room from me. I longed to sit down next to him, to open the laptop and read the email from the General Register Office together. But I couldn't, not yet. Instead I scooped up the laptop and scurried away down the hall to the toilet, where I locked the door behind me and collapsed onto the toilet seat, my heart hammering.

I waited for my hands to stop shaking, then I opened the laptop again and waited for the black screen to roar back to life. Half of me expected the whole thing to have disappeared, as if it had been nothing more than a figment of my imagination. It would have made life easier. But seconds later there it was again, the email that could change my life, whatever it said.

My hand hovered over the mousepad for a few seconds, while I conjured up the courage to click on it.

And then I did.

Dear Francesca,

Thank you for making contact with the Contact Register. I can confirm that Jacob Campbell is also registered and is happy to be put in touch with you…

The rest of the words slid off the screen as my mind processed what I'd just read. Jacob didn't hate me.

I might be about to meet my son.

* * *

While I waited to hear back about my first meeting with Jacob, life marched on. Will must have assumed it was worry about him that was making me quieter than usual, making me drift off in the middle of conversations, and he stopped asking me what was wrong. I felt terrible. I was consumed with anxiety about meeting Jacob, but it was too early to share anything with Will yet, for fear of disappointment.

Luckily Will was so happy and full of enthusiasm for the bucket list again, that I got swept along in it, which was why I found myself, just a few days later, unfolding myself from the front of Will's car after a long journey. Every limb ached and my neck was sore, and as I stretched my arms above my head I felt my spine click. I groaned.

'You sound like you're about a hundred,' Will said, climbing out of the passenger seat beside me.

'I feel it.'

The drive from London to North Wales had taken more than six hours with roadworks seemingly most of the way along the M40. I'd been unsure about taking such a long journey, but Will had been insistent.

'I'm ill, I'm not dead yet,' he said. 'Anyway, if you drive all I have to do is sit there and stare out of the window and change the music every now and then.'

'But why do we have to go so far? There are plenty of zipwires nearer London. Loads.'

'I know but it says here on our list "the longest zipwire in the world".' Not any old zipwire. The longest. And this is it!'

'But what happens if you fall ill while we're away? It's a bloody long way from home.'

'We'll cross that bridge if we come to it. But let's just assume I won't, shall we? Let's assume this stupid body will give me a little bit of respite.'

'Hmm.' I didn't say anything more, but the following day Will told me he'd booked it. 'And guess what? Jim's coming too, and Mags, Rob and the kids want to come as well. It's going to be epic!'

'Epic? Really?'

Will had shrugged. 'You know what I mean. Come on, Fran, it'll be amazing, you know it will.' He took my hands in both of his and gave me puppy-dog eyes.

'Fine. Let's do it.'

And now all eight of us were here after a long, tedious journey in convoy in two cars, ready to throw ourselves down the longest zipwire in world. What was I doing?

It was lunchtime, and as we ate in the café at the centre, Will was like a little kid, bouncing around with excitement. Watching him now, it was impossible to believe he was so ill – impossible to believe that, just a few days ago, he was so exhausted he slept most of the day. Cancer was such an unpredictable bastard.

Far too soon we were being driven to the top of the quarry in a huge jeep, bones jangling on the bumpy road. Harnesses hung loose, and helmets were balanced on heads ready for the descent. I tried not to think about why they might be needed, about plunging into the depths of the quarry below, bones snapping on rocks. I stared out of the open window at the scenery and tried to ignore my nerves and rubber-stamp this on my memory instead, ready to call on one day in the future when I felt lonely or sad. Because there was no denying it was stunning. The mountains of rocks rose steadily in front of us, the product of decades of work digging the slate from far beneath the earth. I tried to conjure up an image of how it must have looked all those years ago when it had been teeming with men, but now, dotted as it was with tourists and the odd mountain biker, it was almost impossible.

Beside me, Kieran looked excited, and I reached over and squeezed his hand.

'All right, love?'

'Uh huh.'

'Not scared?'

'No. Why, are you?' He looked at me, his eyes narrowed.

'Maybe. A bit.'

He studied me a moment longer. 'You wuss.'

A scream from above our heads silenced us and I peered into the cloudy grey sky to see four bodies flying past, whooping with delight. I swallowed nervously.

Finally, we reached the top and as we listened to the safety briefing I spotted Mags's kids, who seemed more subdued than Kieran, who was bouncing around in excitement beside me.

'Are they okay?' I whispered to Mags.

'Yeah, they're fine. They've been excited about this for days. I just think it's a bit daunting now they've seen it.'

They weren't wrong. I could hardly bring myself to look at the yawning chasm that stretched out in front of us just past the metal fence, which was the only thing stopping us from plummeting to earth. And while I knew all the safety measures were in place, and that, in fact, I'd be safer doing this than I would crossing the road in London, right now it didn't feel that way.

'I'm terrified,' I whispered, and Mags grinned and squeezed my hand. 'Be brave, little one. What's the worst that could happen?'

'Er, I could fall from the sky and my body could be smashed to smithereens on those bloody great rocks down there before being eaten by birds?'

'Well, apart from that. It'll be brilliant, you'll see. I bet you'll want to do it again.'

I wasn't so sure, but I swallowed down my fear and waited my turn. I felt like my body was a ball of anxiety – this immediate terror wasn't helping, but worry about Jacob and how I was going to tell Will about him was eating me up. I longed to tell Mags too. At least she already knew about his existence. But I couldn't tell her before Will; it wouldn't be fair.

I turned my attention back to today and watched as, one by one, people I loved threw themselves into oblivion. This was Will's day, so he went first. I watched with my heart in my throat as he stood on the metal platform, and inched his feet forward until his toes were teetering on the edge, dangling in the air. And then off he went! Soaring though the air, high, high above the rocks and the trees and the terrifying canyon, the roar of his voice fading as he disappeared into the distance.

I turned away. I wasn't sure I could watch Kieran leaping off the platform as well, and I refused to look again, listening to Mags's running commentary instead as she told me who was up next. Then it was my turn.

'Are you sure you don't want to go first?' I said, pleading with Mags. If she went first maybe I'd get away with not doing it after all. I could tell them I'd changed my mind and could just meet everyone else at the other end. But Mags could see right through me, and instead of agreeing, gave me a little shove closer to the edge.

I felt the instructor's hands on my shoulders, and I gripped so tightly on to the straps holding me into the harness that I could no longer feel my fingers. And then the instructor was counting backwards... three... two... one... and then I was off, falling into space,

swaying round wildly way above the treetops and the zigzagged path-
ways and the bright blue of the mountain lakes. As I released a puff of
air I realised I hadn't taken a breath since I'd leaped from the safety of
the platform, and the blood rushed to my head so I felt dizzy, but as I
settled, the wind rushing past my helmet, the cold air pushing my
cheeks back towards my ears so the skin flapped and wobbled in the
rush of wind, I let out a laugh. I felt my arms relax and the grip of my
fingers on the straps loosen and I looked around and took in the
breathtaking scenery around me. The tiny ant-like cars beetling far
below, the soaring blue sky and the greys and browns and purples of
the rocks, ragged and earthy beneath me.

Then, as suddenly as it had started, it all came to an end as the platform raced up to meet me. I stopped, and waited to be unbuckled from
the harness and I realised I had tears dried to my face and I grinned.
Placing my feet down carefully on the gravel surface, I stood for a
moment on jelly legs and looked at the others, who were watching me
and cheering. I'd done it! I'd actually done it. And far from dying up
there, I felt exhilarated.

'Can we do it again?' I said, running towards Will and wrapping my
arms around him.

'I told you it would be amazing, didn't I?' he said into the top of my
head. Then he pulled away and looked at me. 'Thank you for doing
this with me.' He looked at everyone else, standing watching us. As
Mags approached behind me, Will cleared his throat. 'Actually, I want
to thank you all for coming with me today. I know it's a bloody long
way from home, but it was something I really, really wanted to do
before...' He stopped. 'What I mean is, it means the world to me that
you all came with me. It's a memory I'll never forget.'

And I knew I wouldn't either.

* * *

The traffic was even worse on the way home the following morning,
and as Kieran and Jim dozed in the back of the car, Will and I took the

opportunity to talk. We'd stayed the night at a cheap B&B near the zipline centre, and had set off after breakfast – along with the rest of North Wales, by the looks of it.

'I can't believe how brilliant that was,' Will said for the hundredth time as we inched along behind a blue van that kept stopping and starting, its brake lights flashing like disco lights. I glanced over at him, the smile on his face seemingly permanent since he'd launched himself off the platform into the void. I wish I didn't have to think about the news I had to tell him.

'I'm glad you enjoyed it.'

He placed his hand on my knee and we drove in silence for a while. I assumed Will had fallen asleep, that the excitement of the last couple of days had taken it out of him, but then he spoke, his voice so soft I could barely hear him over the roar of the engine and the gentle chatter of the radio.

'What was that?' I said, and Will glanced over his shoulder at the sleeping figures in the back. They both snored softly on.

'I've been thinking about Dad.'

I nodded, unsure what to say. 'What about him, love?'

Will was silent for a moment and I didn't know whether he was trying to work out what to say or whether he'd decided he'd said enough already. But then his voice came again, just as soft as before so that I had to lean slightly towards him over the gearstick to hear properly.

'It was spending time with Elodie the other day that made me think about him,' he said. I counted the chevrons on the road in front of us as I waited for him to say more. 'I just – I know Dad's made some mistakes. No, more than that. He totally fucked up. But I can't help thinking about how I'd feel if I did something wrong and then I lost Elodie forever as a result.'

The road slipped by beneath us and I wondered whether now was the moment Will was finally going to tell me what had happened between him and his father.

'So... what does that mean?'

From the corner of my eye I saw Will's shoulders rise up and drop down. 'I don't know. Maybe nothing. But...' He stopped and sighed heavily. 'I don't know. I don't know if I can forgive him, but then again, I can't help thinking that I don't want to die and have any regrets.' He turned to face me again and I risked a quick glance away from the road. 'The question is, will I regret it more if I do see him or if I don't?'

I didn't know what to say but it was clear what both of us were thinking: time wasn't something Will had much of.

'Do you – do you think you might want to see him then?' I said instead.

Will shook his head. 'I don't know, Fran. I really don't. A huge part of me still doesn't want to. I mean, I've been fine without him in my life up till now. But there's another small, but growing, part of me that thinks it might be time. I don't want to be literally dying and then wish I'd done something different.' His voice trailed off and he looked behind him again to check on Jim and Kieran. Satisfied they were still asleep, he said, 'Don't say anything to Jim, will you? I don't want him to get his hopes up, in case I decide not to, and I don't want him to nag me about it either.'

'No, of course I won't. But can I say something now?'

Will looked at me. 'Sure.'

I kept my eyes fixed on the car in front of me, not wanting to catch Will's eye. 'Don't let stubbornness rule your head.'

'What do you mean?'

'I mean, just because you decided all those years ago not to have your father in your life, it doesn't mean you can't change your mind. You can, and if you decide it's for the best, you should.'

Will didn't reply, just stared determinedly at the road ahead without speaking.

That subject was closed for now.

Now I just had to work out how to bring up the subject that was consuming me. Time was running out.

18

Late July 2019

I'd never felt so terrified in my life as I did right now, seated on this cool plastic chair in a room that smelled of old coffee and rich tea biscuits. My leg jiggled beneath the table and Sarah, the woman next to me, smiled reassuringly.

'Nervous?'

'Petrified.'

'It'll be fine. Your son has asked to see you; that's more than lots of people get.'

I nodded and tried to steady my breathing. I'd been barely able to relax since I'd found out that Jacob wanted to meet me, and now here I was, waiting in an adoption centre somewhere just north of Brighton, which was where Jacob lived these days, waiting to meet my son. No wonder I was struggling to catch my breath.

Suddenly there was a light tap on the door and a tiny woman with red-framed glasses poked her head round it and smiled widely.

'Francesca,' she said, pushing the door wide open to allow the person behind to follow her. I watched, heart in my mouth, as the figure appeared, a silhouette at first, the glow from the window behind throwing him into shadow so that the only thing I could see was that he was tall, his shoulders broad.

And then there he was.

My William. Or Jacob as he was now. All my breath left my body as I stood, my legs feeling as weak as matchsticks beneath me, barely able to support my weight. But before I could move towards him, he was at the other side of the table, looking down at me.

'Hello, Francesca.' His voice was deep and rich.

'Hello, Jacob.'

A silence fell. I didn't know what to do now, how to behave as I took in the man standing in front of me. I didn't think my legs would take my weight as I drank him in. The blonde curls were gone, the short crop faded to a darker blonde. His skin was tanned and he wore a pale blue shirt, the top button undone, and a jacket with jeans. But I couldn't tear my gaze away from his eyes. A startling blue, they were almost more familiar to me than my own.

He was the image of his father.

'Lovely to meet you,' he said, thrusting out his hand. My bag was still clutched to my belly with both hands and I fumbled to release one of them to take his hand in mine. It was warm and soft and I felt a surge of emotion burn through me at his touch. It was the first time I had touched my son for more than twenty-five years.

He released his hand and we both sat down, awkwardly. Beside me, the social worker stood.

'I'll leave you to it for a bit,' she said, and then the two women left the room, closing the door behind them with a soft click. And then it was just me and Jacob.

I'd had so much I wanted to say to him, so much I'd imagined I'd want to say when I'd pictured this moment all those times over the years. But now it was happening I felt struck dumb, as though no words could force themselves out through my dried-up throat.

'I—'

'Thank you—' we both started at the same time and stopped, laughing awkwardly.

'Sorry, you go on,' he said, his fingers threaded together on his lap, thumbs brushing back and forth, back and forth against each other. I realised he was just as nervous as me. Of course he was. I cleared my throat.

'Thank you for agreeing to meet me. I didn't know whether you would.'

He nodded, looking straight at the table, and I wondered what he was thinking. Was he already regretting coming today? Was I a disappointment to him?

Then he turned his head towards me, those sparkling eyes, and smiled softly. 'Thank you for contacting me. I don't know what you want to tell me, but I'm glad to meet you after all this time.' He coughed into his fist. 'I didn't know whether I wanted to at first. But I made the right decision.'

'Thank you.' My words choked. 'I can't tell you how happy I am to see you.'

He smiled. 'I guess I look a little different to the last time you saw me?'

A mop of blonde hair, the warmth of a baby's skin.

'Yes, a little. But your parents sent me photos, over the years.'

'Yes. Yes, they told me. I'm glad they did.' He looked at me. 'I'm sorry I stopped, when I was sixteen.'

'It's fine. I mean, I understand.'

'I shouldn't have done. I was just – I don't know. A teenage boy, I suppose. And then it felt too late to start again.'

'It's fine, really. I know teenage boys, I've got one—' I stopped, aware of what I'd just said.

'Have you? How old?'

'He's thirteen. Kieran. He's – he's lovely.'

His hands stopped moving and he rubbed his face. 'Wow. I have a half-brother.'

I let the news settle for a while. 'Do you want to see a photo?'

'Can we... do you mind if we wait a while?'

'No, no, of course.' I needed to calm down, take things slower. I studied him for a moment, this man I'd spent my whole life trying to imagine. He was tall and slim, the same build as his father, with the same blonde hair. But there were flashes of me in there too: the lines each side of his mouth when he smiled, the tilt of his eyebrows and the shell-like curl of his ears. My heart ached to reach out and touch him, to hold him in my arms. But of course I couldn't. I didn't have the right.

He leaned forward then, and rested his elbows on the table. 'So, where do we start?'

I picked up my mug of coffee and took a sip. It was lukewarm now but I needed a moment to think. How could I start? There was too much to say, and the thought of giving any piece of information preference over another seemed overwhelming. I sighed and watched the froth on the top of my coffee float lazily in a circle.

'Well, I guess I've already told you about Kieran.' He nodded. 'I – he's a lovely boy. His father isn't around, so it's been just me and him for most of his life.'

'Being an only child isn't so bad.' He smiled kindly.

'No. I guess not. I was one too.'

He paused. 'I suppose I should really be asking you why you had me adopted. It's what I've always wondered. But now you're here, it doesn't seem to matter so much.'

'Let me tell you anyway, if you want.'

He studied me, his brow folding and unfolding just like Will's. 'Okay.'

'I was young. Really young.' I drummed my fingers on the tabletop. 'I was at university, and your father' – I stopped on that word, knowing what I still had to tell him – 'thought I'd had an abortion.' I flinched, and looked up at him. 'But I couldn't do it. And then your dad moved away, and I knew in my heart of hearts I wanted to have you, but I was eighteen, and I couldn't give you the life you deserved. And so I let you go, and I... I've regretted it every single day of my life since.' My words got lost in a sob. Opposite me, Jacob was watching me carefully. I knew my explanation wasn't enough but how could I possibly explain what had happened in just a few words?

'Where did he go?'

'Who?'

'My father.'

'He moved to Australia with his father and younger brother. His mum had just died, and they were all grieving, and his father moved them away and... well, I was too angry to write to him. He wrote to me but when I ignored him he gave up eventually. And that was that.' I looked at him. 'We'd been best friends since we were seven years old. I was heartbroken.'

A beat of silence, then: 'So, what was it you needed to tell me?'

I was thrown by his directness, but at least it made things easier. I breathed air in slowly though my nostrils and let it out again.

'Your dad – his name's William, the name I gave to you – he...' The story that had seemed so straightforward in my head was getting tangled on the way out. 'We met again... last year. We're together again and...' I stopped, and Jacob watched me, his eyes boring into me. 'He's dying.'

The word hung between us, hovering just above the Formica of the table between our coffee cups. The air felt thick, and I struggled to breathe it in. I laid my palms flat on the table and waited.

'Dying.' It was a statement more than a question so I didn't reply. He nodded slowly. 'What of?'

'He has a brain tumour. It's untreatable.'

'How long?'

'Not long. A few months, they think. I – I thought you should know.'

'Why?'

Why did I think he needed to know? Was it because I hoped for a happy reunion, a family reunited in grief? Or did I think he deserved to know, in case there was a chance it could be genetic – after all, Will's mum had died of cancer too, albeit a different type. The truth was, I didn't really know. It just felt like the right thing to do.

'It seemed important.'

He nodded. 'And does he want to meet me?'

'He – he doesn't know about you yet.'

Jacob sat stiffly opposite me. I didn't know what to do with this calm behaviour. Crying and shouting I could handle, I understood, but this calmness, this detachedness, I didn't understand at all. It made me want to babble to fill the silences, and I had to bite my tongue to stop spouting explanations and justifications at him. This was enough for him to take in, without that.

Suddenly, Jacob's hand was on mine, his fingers wrapped around my wrist. I looked up and was surprised to see tears on his face. Without thinking, I lifted my hand and wiped my fingers across his cheek.

'What happens now, then?' His words came out as a whisper.

I shrugged. 'I really don't know. I – I need to tell him about you, obviously, but I wanted to meet you first, to tell you.'

'Do you think he'll want to meet me?'

'Do you want to meet him?'

He paused, his face set. 'Probably.'

'Then I'm sure he will.' I didn't know this, of course. I had no idea how Will would react to this news. But I couldn't say anything else.

We sat in silence for a moment, the sounds of ordinary life outside these four walls feeling incongruous. How could everything else still be the same when everything inside this room had changed?

I didn't know what to say to this man sitting opposite me. This man who was in so many ways so familiar, yet in so many more a stranger. I knew nothing about him: whether he was married, had children, what his favourite film was, his favourite food, his funniest childhood memory. Was he good at sport like his father, or hopeless like me? Did he love music, theatre, books, or was his mind more practical? I knew I had to give it time but I wished I could instantly get to know him as well as I'd always longed to.

And what did he make of me? Had he thought about me, growing up? Had he ever wondered about me, hated me? It sounded as though his childhood had been everything I'd hoped it would be: safe, secure, happy, loving. I hoped this wouldn't hurt him too much.

A knock on the door broke into my thoughts.

'Sorry to interrupt, but time's nearly up.'

I glanced at the clock on the wall. Almost forty minutes had passed in a flash. I understood that they made these rules so that people had a chance to leave if they'd changed their minds, if the person they'd met wasn't all they'd hoped for. But it didn't stop me wishing we could stay here all day, just talking, and telling each other everything.

I looked at Jacob now, and he smiled.

'Would you...' I stopped, unsure how to ask him. 'Can we meet again? If you want to, of course...'

'I'd like that,' he said.

'Oh!' I didn't know what to say. 'Great. When?'

'When's good for you?'

Any time, I wanted to say. *Always, every day, tomorrow*. 'Next week? I feel there's so much more to talk about...'

'Me too. Next week would be perfect.' He reached into the pocket of his jeans. 'Here, let me give you my number.'

And just like that, my son was back in my life.

* * *

Five days later I was back in Brighton, waiting anxiously for Jacob to arrive. This time I was just as nervous, but I felt less scared. Because the worst bit was over with, and he didn't hate me, or resent me. I knew he must have lots of questions, but I was prepared for that. And I wanted to get to know him better too.

The last few days since we met had been so hard, keeping the secret from Will. I knew I had to tell him about Jacob soon, but I needed to be certain first. Lying to Will felt so wrong, and I knew he was suspicious when he saw me reading texts one evening.

'Found a new boyfriend to replace me?' he said, when my phone buzzed for the fourth or fifth time. It was Jacob, arranging where to meet.

'Yeah, a few.' I laughed. But he didn't seem convinced by my brush-off, and was quiet for the rest of the night.

I sat on my bench and watched as hundreds of pairs of feet passed my eyeline, walking, running, cycling along the promenade, the sea a sparkling blue in the background. It was a warm day and the sun burned the back of my neck, warmed my arms through the thin sleeves of my cardigan. Suddenly there was a shadow in front of me and I looked up to find Jacob standing there.

'You came!' I said, jumping up.

'Of course I came.' He touched my elbow lightly and leaned in to kiss my cheek. My skin jolted at his touch.

'Shall we sit here for a bit?' he said, indicating the bench. 'It's a nice day.'

'Why not.'

We sat down facing the sea, and the sun sparkled and bounced in my vision, but my mind was filled with nothing but the fact that my son was here, with me.

'I realised you're not what I expected,' he said, out of the blue.

'Oh? In what way?'

He shrugged. 'I don't know. I expected someone – older. Less kind-looking. I don't know, it sounds stupid saying it out loud. I expected not to like you. I'd always wondered what sort of person could give a child away but I suppose I'm beginning to understand that there are all sorts of reasons that I can't even imagine.'

This was one thing I'd quickly realised about Jacob. He wasn't one for small talk. I turned to face him.

'I never wanted to give you away, you know. It was just – I truly believed it was for the best. I was a very young, innocent eighteen-year-old. Barely able to look after myself, let alone a baby. And then Will – your dad – left and I was facing the prospect of bringing you up totally alone.' I stopped, the memories overwhelming me suddenly. 'When you were handed to me, after you were born, I imagined getting up and leaving the bed, and disappearing with you. Just you and me. I couldn't imagine letting go of you, and having you taken out of my arms and handed over to someone else to love. But I knew I had no choice if I wanted you to have the life you deserved. It broke my heart.'

'I had a good life, you know. Mum and Dad are the best. But do you know the one thing I always wished?'

I shook my head.

'That I had a brother or sister. It can sometimes be a lonely business being an only child, especially to older parents.'

'I know. I think that's why Will meant so much to me when we were young. We were like brother and sister. I mean, he had a younger brother, Jim, but for me our friendship was my world.' I stopped and risked reaching out to take his hands in mine. He didn't pull away. 'I'm sorry, you know. For everything.'

'I know. But you don't have to be.' He sighed heavily. 'It's just a lot to take in.'

I nodded. 'Shall we walk?'

'Yeah, let's.' He stood and picked up his jacket just as a gust of wind hit us.

I shivered and pulled my cardigan closer around me. 'Where to?'

He pointed towards the cliffs and I nodded, following him closely. As we headed up it got quieter, the crowds thinning, and the loudest sound that of the wind, which was getting stronger the higher we climbed. And as we walked, we talked. It was much easier, I found, when I couldn't study the expression on Jacob's face, or see his reactions, to just talk, and say the things we wanted to say, freely.

We talked about him: the fact that he'd just come out of a long-term relationship and was struggling to get over it; that he longed to have a family and settle down; that his parents were close but that they were old-fashioned. He told me about his job in IT, his love of old cars and football, just like his dad, and his penchant for terrible eighties music, and I told him about my job, about Kieran and Sean, and what it was like meeting Will again.

There was still something I needed to ask him. 'What do your mum and dad think about you meeting me?'

He hesitated. 'They're fine about it.'

'Really?' I didn't know whether I would be.

'Well, maybe not fine. But they understand. I think they always expected me to come and find you, so it's not a huge shock.' He glanced at me. 'Mum's struggling with it more than Dad, though. I suppose she worries you might try and replace her.'

'I'd never do that.'

'I know. And she knows it really. But – well. I understand how she feels.'

'Me too.'

A silence fell and I watched my feet stepping rhythmically, thinking about Roy and Sandy, and wondering what to say next.

'So how come didn't you get in touch before?' Jacob said suddenly. 'I mean, I understand why you have now, but why not before?'

'I just – I never thought I had anything to offer you. I mean, I'd given you away. What right did I have? I was a single mum, living in a small flat in London, doing a job I tolerated rather than loved. What could I offer, exactly?'

'You could offer you.'

I didn't know how to answer that. We'd reached the top of the cliff by then, the wind blowing our hair wildly round our faces, the sun sparkling off the waves, blinding us every now and then.

'So, tell me about my father's cancer. It's terminal, right?'

I nodded. 'Yes. I'm afraid it is. And the thing is, his mum died of cancer too. I just – I wanted you to know.'

He nodded. 'And what are you hoping? That we'll be reunited before he dies?'

That was what I'd wanted, and still did. But standing here right now, at the top of this cliff with my son, it felt like a ridiculous thing to admit. Was I being hopelessly romantic and naïve?

'If you'd like to be. But there's no pressure at all.'

'Okay.' He stood with his face tipped towards the sun, his hands clasped behind his back. It struck me that the coldness I'd detected from him earlier was something else entirely – it was his way of protecting himself against something that might hurt him. And I realised it was exactly what I did, too. How alike we were, in so many ways I still had to discover.

We spent the rest of the afternoon strolling back into Brighton, and then he walked me to the train station. As we said our goodbyes, he stood in front of me, his arms pinned to his sides.

'I'll be in touch, okay?'

I nodded.

'And you'll let me know what he says? William? My father?'

'Yes. Just give me a bit of time.'

He nodded. And then, unexpectedly, he stepped forward and wrapped his arms around me and I felt as though I might melt into the ground there and then. The feel of my boy's strong arms around me, his body pressed against mine... I breathed in his scent, so unfamiliar, a mix of soap, the sea and a lingering undertone of washing powder, and I tried to bank it in my memory, to call on when I needed comforting. I could have stood there, in the middle of the station concourse, and held him all day. But eventually he pulled away and as I stepped towards my platform and waved him goodbye my heart clenched with pain. A scream. A mop of blonde hair. A painful goodbye.

All I could do was hope that I'd see him again.

* * *

There was never going to be a good time to turn Will's life upside down. So much had happened to us both in the last few months: meeting again, Will's cancer. But this felt bigger than them all.

I had to just do it.

'Will, I need to talk to you.' I stood in the doorway of the living room, clutching a wodge of papers. Will was stretched out along the sofa, the early evening sun slanting through the blinds and creating stripes along his head and torso. His arm was slung across his face and he removed it now and lifted his head. He looked exhausted.

'This sounds serious. Should I be worried?'

I didn't answer, but came and stood by the sofa and waited for him to move his feet. He struggled to a sitting position and tucked his feet away so I could perch on the cushion next to him. 'What's the matter, Fran?'

I turned the words over in my mind once more, shuffling through them like a pack of cards, deciding which ones to deal out first. In the end, instead of speaking, I handed him an envelope from the pile of papers in my hands.

'What's this?' Will's face creased and a flash of memory came to me of Jacob pulling that exact same face as I told him about his father. My body trembled.

'Open it.'

I watched as Will lifted the flap of the envelope and pulled out some photos. The top one was the first photo I had of Jacob as a baby, and then the pictures I'd been sent every year. He stared at the top one, his face still creased, and then the next one, of Jacob on his first birthday. He looked up at me then, before looking at any more.

'What are these?'

'They're photos. Of—' The words choked in my throat and then came out as a whispered croak. 'Of our son.'

Will's face turned white and he looked down at the first photo again and then back at me. He didn't speak for a very long time and I began to wonder whether I ought to say something first, offer some sort of explanation.

'Is this...' He looked at me, his eyes hard. 'Is this some kind of sick joke?' He looked round the room, his eyes darting from one corner to the other. 'I mean, is this a trick of some sort? A test?'

'No, Will. It's not a joke. It's the truth.' I leaned over and pointed at the photos I'd studied so many times over the years that they were creased and dog-eared, the colours faded and insipid. 'This, here, is our son. His name was William but he's now called Jacob.'

I waited for the words to sink in. I didn't dare look at Will's face any more, instead staring at the pictures in his lap until he spoke again. Finally, realisation dawned.

'You had the baby.' It was a statement rather than a question and I raised my eyes to meet his and gave a nod.

'Yes.'

He looked back down at the photo and held it up, studying it, as I had so many times: the narrow nose and curled ears so like mine; the eyes, the blonde hair and the arch of the eyebrows so like his. He couldn't fail to see it, I was sure. He just needed time.

He looked at the next photo, and the next, and the one after that, and then all of them in turn until Jacob reached sixteen and they stopped. Then he placed them down in his lap and stared straight ahead.

'But you never told me.'

'No. I – I couldn't. I mean, you'd left. I'd planned to come home at Christmas and tell you I'd changed my mind, but you left and I – I didn't know what to do.'

'But why? Why did you change your mind?'

'I just – I couldn't go through with it. And then your mum, she—'

'My mum? What's my mum got to do with this?'

His words were angry.

'When I went to see her, just before she died. When I came home, and we argued about the baby, remember?'

'I remember.'

I paused. 'Well, she guessed I was pregnant. She just knew, Will, I don't know how, and I couldn't lie and she begged me not to get rid of it. To reconsider and...' I trailed off.

'But she never mentioned it to me. She wouldn't keep something like that from me.'

'I don't know why she didn't mention it. Maybe she thought you had enough on your mind; maybe she thought it was for me to decide. But her words stuck in my head and I realised I couldn't go through with it. And that actually, maybe we could bring up a baby together.

Maybe it was meant to be. But then your mum died, and then you left.'

The words had come out in such a rush it took a while for them to settle so I waited.

'So you had him anyway.'

'Yes. I had to. I – I just couldn't go through with it. But I decided – well, I decided it would be for the best if I had him adopted. I – I didn't want to, not really, but I knew I had nothing to offer him. And so it was all arranged.'

'And you never...' He stopped, cleared his throat, shook the words loose. 'You never thought to try and find me? To let me know? I don't know, maybe give me a chance to decide if I wanted to get involved?' His voice was getting louder and I flinched.

'You'd gone, Will, across the other side of the bloody world. I was heartbroken. And I was so young. You know that.'

He was sitting up properly now, his elbows on his knees, chin resting on steepled fingers. He stared into the empty fireplace, his expression dark. The minutes ticked by and I leaned back into the sofa and hugged my knees to my chest. There was no point in trying to justify what I'd done, not right now. Will needed time to make sense of it. So I waited, listening to the sounds of the outside world as it passed the flat: the swish of car tyres, footsteps, voices, laughter, music. There was no rush. Kieran was at his dad's and wouldn't be home for ages.

Finally, after what seemed like hours but must have been only minutes, Will spoke into the silent room.

'Why now?'

'Why now what?'

'Why have you told me now?'

'Why do you think?'

He twisted his body to face me and the look on his face frightened me. 'Because of the cancer, you mean?' He gave a bitter laugh.

'Yes, of course because of the cancer.'

'Ha.' He shook his head. 'And you thought that now, with everything else that's going on, now would be the perfect time to tell me I have a son I know nothing about and that I'll never get to meet?' He dropped his head between his knees and sighed. 'Really, Fran, what was the point?'

I had to tell him. 'I've met him.'

The words hovered between us and, slowly, Will turned his head to face me. 'You met him?'

'Yes.' I shuffled awkwardly, ran my hands through my hair.

'When?'

'A week ago. And yesterday.'

'A week? And you're only telling me now?'

'I've been trying to find the right time and—'

'The right time? Are you fucking kidding me? The right time would have been – oh, I don't know, twenty-five fucking years ago, Fran. That would have been the right time. Now, surely any time is the right time?'

I banged my hand against the arm of the sofa and made us both jump. 'For God's sake, Will, do you think this has been easy for me?'

'For you?' He uncurled his body and sat up straight now, facing me head on. 'No, Fran, I can't imagine it's been easy for you at all, keeping this secret from me for so many years. Not to mention all these months we've been together – nine months and you've never thought to mention it? It's only now that you see fit to tell me?'

'I couldn't! What would have been the point before? I didn't know whether he'd want to meet you, to meet us. God, Will, I didn't even know whether he was still alive.' I stopped, and stared at Will, watching his expression change from fury to confusion before softening to – what? Acceptance?

'You said you didn't know whether he wanted to meet me?'

I nodded.

'So what are you saying? You do know that now?'

I nodded again, suddenly mute. 'I...' I stopped. 'That's what I'm trying to tell you. I met him. And we talked, and I told him about you and he...he said he'd like to meet you. If you want to.'

Will's fury seemed to collapse like a deflated balloon, all strength leaving his body at once. He sank back into the sofa. I longed to reach out and comfort him, but I had no idea if he'd want that, so I stayed where I was.

'I...' he started, then stopped again, his eyes staring at a spot on the sofa between us. Then he raised his eyes and I saw the fear there. 'When?'

'Whenever you want. I just need to email him.'

He nodded. 'And he knows? About me?'

'Yes. I told him.'

He looked away and stared out of the window, through the blinds. Was he trying to imagine his son now?

'Okay. See what he says.' He turned his head to look at me and his eyes were heavy. 'I need to go to bed.' Then he stood and walked out of the room, leaving me with just my thoughts, racing round my mind.

But I'd done it. I'd told him.

And the world was still turning.

19

Early August 2019

This time, I didn't need to travel to Brighton, where Jacob lived. This time, he said he'd come to us. I couldn't imagine how the poor boy – man – must be feeling. Going from knowing neither parent to meeting both in the space of a few short weeks must be terrifying. But he wasn't the only one I was worried about. The truth was, I'd been worried sick about how Kieran was going to take the news. And so, a few days ago, I'd sat him down and told him all about his half-brother.

'What the hell?' were his first words.

'I'm sorry, love.'

He'd been silent for a few moments then, staring at the floor in front of him. 'But – where?'

'He lives in Brighton. He's twenty-five.'

I waited for the news to sink in. 'How come you've never told me about him before?'

I shook my head. 'I hadn't told anyone.'

'What, not even Grandma and Grandad?'

'Well, they knew. But we all agreed never to talk about him.'

'But why?'

'I was young, Keeks. I...' How could I explain it so a teenager could understand? 'Imagine if you had a baby now. Do you think you could look after it properly?'

Course not. But I'm only thirteen.'

'I know, love. But it's the same thing. It's how it was for me, then. I knew I couldn't give this baby the life it deserved, so I wanted someone else to.'

'But – but why the big secret?'

'It was easier I suppose. It hurt too much to talk about it.'

He nodded again and I wondered what was going through his mind. 'Does Will know?'

'Well, that's just it, love. I've just told him because – well, Jacob is Will's son too.'

'Oh.' He looked at his feet.

I explained everything to him then – how I'd met Jacob, and how he wanted to meet Will too. 'And then I hope you'll want to meet him too, Keeks. Do you think you will?'

He nodded. 'I guess so. I mean, he is my brother, right?'

'He is, love.' I blinked back the tears that threatened to overwhelm me and pulled my precious boy in for a hug. 'I'm so proud of you, darling,' I whispered, cherishing the few seconds I knew I'd get before he squirmed away from me.

And so now everyone who needed to know had been told, and Will was about to meet his son for the very first time.

'How do I look?' Will stood in front of me, nervously. He was wearing a short-sleeved shirt and jeans. Everything hung off him and it struck me again how diminished he looked; his cheeks were more sunken, and the lines round his eyes more pronounced. My heart broke for him: my Will, who'd always been so strong and capable. How must he be feeling about what the cancer was doing to his body?

I hoped he hadn't noticed just yet how much he'd changed.

'You look like a man who's just about to meet his son,' I said, smiling. 'You look great.'

He ran his hands up and down his upper arms and shivered despite the warmth of the day. 'I'm petrified, Fran.'

I stood and wrapped my arms around him. 'You'll be fine. He'll love you.' He felt so frail in my arms.

Since our meeting, Jacob and I had been in touch via email, arranging where to meet, and when. And although most of the emails had been practical, I did feel as though I was getting to know him a little, bit by bit. I was wary of pushing it and scaring him away, so I didn't ask too much. I had plenty of time to get to know him.

Unlike Will.

'Right, let's go,' I said, taking Will's hand. His felt damp in mine and I gave it a squeeze.

An hour later we were waiting in the place we'd arranged to meet Jacob: a nondescript café near South Kensington station.

'This reminds me of the day I met you – the second time,' I said as we sat down. We were early, Will determined to be there before Jacob arrived. He glanced round at the wooden tables and chairs, the counter filled with cakes and sandwiches, the imposing coffee machine that flashed and rumbled behind the counter.

'Yeah, except this is much more terrifying.'

I nodded. 'True. What do you want to drink?'

'A latte please.' As I stood he grabbed my hand. 'Fran, I need to ask you something.'

'What? What's wrong?'

'Nothing's wrong. I just...' He stopped, looked down at the tabletop, then back up at me. 'Will you leave us alone for a bit? Me and Jacob? Once he's here?'

My stomach dropped. I was desperate to see Jacob again, to spend some time with him. But how could I refuse? I owed him this.

'Okay.' My voice came out as a whisper.

'Are you sure you don't mind? It's not that I don't want you there. I just – I'd like a bit of time alone with him.' He shrugged. 'I don't know. It seems important.'

I nodded and stood, clasping my hands together. 'I'll just get the drinks.'

As I waited for the coffees I tried not to let the tears come. I was being ridiculous. It was a perfectly reasonable request. After all, I'd already spent time with Jacob on my own, and I was still going to get to see him. Why was I so upset?

I got back to the table and put the coffees down before I spilt them. But before I could sit, the bell above the door tinkled and both Will and I froze.

I looked up and locked eyes with Jacob. Seeing him standing there, so familiar already, made my heart soar. As the tension seeped from my body at the sight of him, I realised how scared I'd been that he wouldn't turn up.

But now, here he was.

Slowly, he approached our table and Will pushed himself up to standing. The café was small and it only took a few seconds, and as the two men stood in front of each other I was struck dumb at how similar they were. It was almost as though Will was looking into a mirror, at himself almost twenty years before.

I shivered.

Jacob held his hand out first, and Will took it in his and shook it warmly. 'Hi, I'm Jacob.'

'Will.' His voice cracked. Then Jacob turned to me.

'Hi, Fran.' He held out his hand to me, awkward. 'It's good to see you again.'

'You too,' I said, relishing the feel of his palm against mine.

We all sat and immediately I sprang up again. 'Coffee?' God, why was I so nervous?

'Oh, yes please. An Americano please.'

I walked back to the counter, my legs shaking, and looked back at the pair of them, two peas in a pod facing each other across the table. My heart ached for them both. What sort of way was this to begin their relationship: Will dying, Jacob knowing his father didn't have long left. It wasn't the most auspicious of starts. But at least it *was* a start.

By the time I arrived back with Jacob's drink, they were chatting. Will was asking about Jacob's job, and listening intently to the answers. I took two enormous gulps of my coffee and stood abruptly. Jacob looked up quizzically.

'Are you all right, Fran?'

'Yep. I...' I bent down and scooped my bag from the floor. 'I'm going to leave you two for a while, if that's okay. Give you time to get to know each other.'

'Er, okay.' Jacob looked at Will, who gave a little nod then looked at his son.

'That would be good, wouldn't it?'

Jacob nodded too. 'Yes, I suppose it would.' His words were so clear and well enunciated and I tried to imagine how different he'd have sounded with the clipped vowels of North London, if he'd have grown up with me.

'Righto, then.' Righto? Who was I, Enid Blyton? 'I'll see you in a couple of hours. I'll just be...' I flapped my hand. 'Around.' I turned to Will. 'I'll ring you, okay?'

'Thanks, Fran.'

My chest felt heavy as I walked away from the pair of them. The longing to stay, to drink in every detail I could about the son I'd only just found, was almost overwhelming, but I pushed it down, ignored it, until I got to the door and heard it close behind me. I walked briskly down the street, busier now, not thinking about where I was going. I listened to the pounding of my pulse in my ears, until I found myself standing outside the Natural History Museum. The magnificence of the building soothed me and I took a few deep breaths in the warm summer sunshine, feeling my heart rate slow and my breath return to normal. Everything would be fine. Will and Jacob would be fine. This was the right thing to do.

I spent an hour wandering round the rooms of the museum, studying the displays and admiring the sheer size of the blue whale suspended from the ceiling in the mammal room. I remembered the first time I saw it as a child of around nine, a day trip to London with school. Will stood next to me, my partner in everything, and we gaped up in awe at the majesty of it all. Afterwards we'd giggled at the human biology section and yawned at a talk about insects and eaten our lunch on the steps outside – jam sandwiches and cartons of juice and packets of cheese and onion crisps. I smiled at the memory.

I felt too jittery for another coffee, so I headed outside and bought an ice cream from the van and sat and ate it in the sun. The cool creaminess filled my mouth and I watched people go by – tourists, office workers, groups of teenagers – and wondered about their stories, their lives. I bet everyone had their own secrets to tell.

I was startled by my phone buzzing in my pocket and, licking the ice cream that had dripped onto my hand, I fumbled for it, answering it at the last minute. It was Will.

'Everything okay?'

'Yeah, fine. We just wondered where you were.'

'I came to the Natural History Museum. Are you done?'

'For now.'

'Oh.' I shouldn't have been surprised. I'd been worried it would be too much for him today, and now he sounded utterly wiped out.

'Shall we come and find you?'

'Is Jacob still with you?'

'Yes. He's got a couple of hours still until his train.'

I agreed to wait for them, and fifteen minutes later I saw them approach and stood to greet them. Both looked happy enough but I could tell it was a little awkward.

'All okay?'

They both nodded at the same time, and Jacob ran his hand across his cropped hair. 'Great.'

I looked from one to the other and realised. They were both the same. Neither found it easy to make small talk. They needed me.

We spent an hour wandering round the museum again, chatting. The constant movement, and the distraction, gave us something else to focus on, and made it easier for the two of them to talk. 'We came here as kids, do you remember, Will?' I said.

'I remember you being scared of the *T. rex*,' he said.

'I was not scared!'

He gave me a sideways glance. 'If you say so.'

'So you really were best friends?' Jacob said.

'We were. Even if she was really needy.' Will grinned. Jacob stayed quiet, staring into the display of bones in front of him, deep in thought. Will glanced at me, and I shrugged.

'So how come it all ended in such a bloody mess?' Jacob looked at Will. 'How come you left, and how come you' – he gestured at me this time – 'didn't tell him you'd had a baby? What happened?' His forehead creased and he looked lost all of a sudden, like a little boy who needed answers. Answers that, no matter how we framed them, would never be enough.

'Life happened,' Will said. 'I mean, my mum died, and me and my little brother Jim and my – my father – were all heartbroken. Your m— Fran – had gone off to university and then we moved to Australia, me and my brother and father.' He looked up at Jacob and then at me. 'We all do things we're not proud of. I wish I hadn't left the way I did, but at the time it felt as though I had no choice. But of course I did. And because of that, I never even knew about you. I knew nothing about you until...' His voice broke and he stopped.

Jacob nodded but said nothing.

'And I never stopped thinking about you,' I said, brushing my hand along his sleeve. 'Never.'

The silence between us was drowned out by the hum of voices around us, the sounds of laughter and footsteps echoing and bouncing off the high ceilings.

'If it helps, I never forgave myself,' Will said. 'And I didn't even know then exactly how much I'd lost.'

Jacob snapped his head up, his face resolute. 'Well, I'm glad I've met you both now, even if...' He stopped, but we all knew what he was about to say. Even if Will was dying. 'I'm glad. Thank you for finding me, Fran.'

I smiled, unable to speak.

I felt overwhelmed by the things I wanted to tell him, the things I needed to say. How could you possibly fill someone in on twenty-five years of your life when they haven't lived it with you? I wanted him to know about me, and my parents, and Kieran. I wanted him to really *know* Kieran. And I needed, with a feeling so strong it almost overwhelmed me, to know him.

* * *

As Will and I made our way home on the Tube later that day, I studied his reflection in the carriage window and went over the day in my head. It wasn't what I'd expected, but then how do you ever know what's going to happen in a situation like that? I was just glad Will and Jacob seemed to get on.

Will still hadn't said a word since we'd left Jacob at South Kensington Tube station. I was dying to know what he was thinking.

In his ghostly reflection, I saw him turn to face me. 'Thank you, Fran.'

I watched him, opposite me.

'What did you think of him?'

'He seemed...' He stopped, let out a breath. 'He was amazing. Just the fact that he exists is amazing.'

I smiled. 'I can't tell you how relieved I am to hear that.'

'Why, what did you think was going to happen?'

'I thought...' I stopped. 'I worried that by telling you about Jacob, you'd never forgive me, and I'd lose you too.'

I could see Will studying me in our reflection and I turned to meet his eye. 'Fran, I would never leave you. No matter what. At least, not by choice.'

20

Late August 2019

Sitting in the waiting room of the hospital, I found myself avoiding other people's gazes. I couldn't look into the eyes of a mother sitting with her daughter, wondering which one of them was ill. I couldn't catch the eye of the elderly couple when I was wondering why they'd got to live for so many years when Will's life was about to be so cruelly cut short.

Beside me, Will took my hand and gave it a squeeze and I glanced down at our fingers threaded together. Maybe, if I stared at our entwined fingers for long enough, the image would be seared into my memory and I'd be able to hold it there for the rest of my life, in a library of images I could borrow whenever I needed comfort.

Will's health had taken another, sudden, nosedive after meeting Jacob. His headaches got worse, and his vision started getting blurred, but perhaps most worryingly he was utterly exhausted all the time. At first we put it down to overdoing things, but it soon became clear it was more than that.

Fortunately, he had an appointment with his consultant already booked, who'd sent him immediately for some further scans to see what was happening in his brain. And now here we were, two days later, waiting for the results.

The consultant's door opened and the now-familiar face emerged. We stood and walked in, hand in hand, and sat down at the desk.

I found myself staring at the framed photo on the desk, at the half-dead plant on the windowsill, reading the inscriptions on the certificates behind the doctor's head proving his credentials – anywhere but at him. I tried to focus on his words, but it was hard.

Afterwards we stood and left and as we walked back towards the lift, still holding hands, I realised that I didn't have a clue what the consultant had just said. My mind had blocked it out in a bid to protect me from what was happening. I turned to face Will now. His face was drawn, his skin grey.

'So, what now?' I said, my voice a whisper.

Will stood, his shoulders hunched, his head drooped. 'I guess this is it. The beginning of the end.'

I felt tears prickle my eyes and I breathed in deeply through my nose, trying to get some oxygen to my lungs. 'But what did he say? Is there nothing they can try?'

Will gave me a strange look. 'Weren't you listening?'

I looked down, ashamed. 'I – I missed some of it. I was scared.' The words sounded pathetic even to my ears. It was Will going through this, not me. Who was I to play the scared card?

But Will didn't seem to notice. 'He said the tumour has grown faster than they expected and – well, the cancer has spread further. To my bones.'

I felt the ground tilt beneath me and I clamped my hand round Will's forearm to steady myself.

'What does that mean?'

I felt his fingers beneath my chin and he tipped my face up gently so I was looking him in the eye.

'It means I don't have long left. It means we've got to make the most of the time we do have, before I get too weak.'

'Did he say how long?' The words came out in short, breathy gasps.

'Weeks.' His voice cracked.

I've heard that when you think your life is about to come to a sudden end, images of memories flash before your eyes. As I stood there, by the lifts in the hospital, looking at Will, our life together spooled through my mind as though it were a film reel on fast-forward. The day we met, giggling little seven-year-olds who'd been thrown together by our mothers' friendship; stealing biscuits from the jar to eat in our secret den in the garden; taking money from my mum's purse to buy a bottle of Cinzano at fifteen and puking it up in a hedge three hours later; our first kiss at sixteen, the moment we both realised we meant more to each other than just childhood friends. The first time we slept together; kissing on the beach in Brighton; the promises we made to always love each other no matter what. The horror of realising Will had gone without a goodbye; the pain and the tears as I picked myself up and put myself back together again; and the meeting in the café that had thrown my life up into the air and scattered the pieces around for me to make sense of. We'd found each other again, and that should have been that. That should have been our story, our happy ending. But instead, this. This thing that had come between us and would tear us apart one final time, before we were anywhere near ready to be parted.

I pulled my hands from his and wrapped my arms round his neck, sobbing into his shoulders. I could feel his body shake next to mine and I knew he was crying too. I didn't care who could see us: the doctors and nurses streaming round us, patients being wheeled past, trolleys squeaking along the corridor. For now, it was just me and Will. Just us.

Finally, we pulled apart and Will wiped his face on his sleeve and took a long, shuddery breath in. 'That's better,' he said, attempting a weak smile.

He took hold of my hand again and when the lift doors opened we stepped inside, and I caught our reflection in the mirror. We were both blotchy and pale, our eyes rimmed red. We looked like ghosts and I wondered what I would have thought if the teenage me could have seen us now.

* * *

Summer rain always made me think of teenage me, sitting in my room listening to records as the rain hammered on the skylight, an accompaniment to the music my parents just didn't understand.

'It's the summer holidays,' Mum always said. 'You should be out and about, not cooped up in your room listening to this noise.'

'I'm fine, Mum, I'll go out tomorrow when it's stopped raining.'

'Well, make sure you do.'

Sometimes it was just me, indulging myself with my ever-growing vinyl collection, listening to all my favourites, The Wonder Stuff, James and the more obscure indie bands coming out of Manchester that I loved. Other times Will would be there, his socked feet up on the bed, hands behind his head, tapping out a rhythm on whatever he could find, asking me questions about every song I played.

'I don't get you and your obsession,' he'd say.

'Well, it's like you with your football, I guess.'

'But football's football. I don't get how you can get so excited about music. It's just sound.'

'I'm not sure you and me can be friends any more,' I'd say, laughing as he threw a cushion at me.

That's what I was thinking of as I lay in bed a few days after Will's devastating diagnosis, listening to the rain hammer on the windows of my flat and watching Will's chest move slowly up and down. He seemed to be sleeping more and more, and I tried not to think about how quickly he was going downhill. What I wouldn't give to be back in that teenage room now, a young Will winding me up.

He opened his eyes and turned his head, his face sleepy.

'You watching me again, Gordon?'

I smiled. 'Yep. Not much you can do about it.'

'Weirdo.' He closed his eyes again and I lifted the duvet and climbed out. 'You going?' he mumbled.

'Yep. Got to get to work. Someone's got to earn some money around here.'

'Good girl.' He turned over and peered at me through half-closed eyes again.

'Anyway, I've got a surprise for you later.'

'Oh?' He was more awake now, his eyes fully open. 'What is it?'

'Well, it won't be a surprise if I tell you, will it?'

'Yeah, but I hate surprises so now I'll spend the whole day worrying about it.'

I pulled my top on and checked my reflection in the mirror, slicking a bit of lip gloss and mascara on. I looked tired. 'Well, tough. You're just going to have to wait.' I leaned down and pecked him on the forehead. 'But it's a good surprise. It's meant to cheer you up.'

'I like being a miserable old bastard.'

'I know you do, but I'm going to give it a go anyway.'

When I got home later that day, Will was up and dressed, sitting on the sofa in the living room watching the news.

'Where's Kieran?' I said, peering round the living room door.

'In his room, I think.'

'Well, wait there. Don't come into the kitchen for a minute.'

'Okay.'

'Promise you won't?'

'I promise!'

I walked back to the front door and pulled it open and lifted the two carrier bags I'd left there in one hand, and held my other hand out. Elodie took hold of it. 'Now remember, totally quiet, okay,' I said. She nodded eagerly and held her finger up to her lips.

Together we crept along the hallway past the living room where Will was waiting, and into the kitchen. I closed the door and lifted Elodie onto one of the stools. 'Right, do you want to help me get all this ready for Daddy?'

'Yes!' She clapped her hands together and then stopped and giggled. 'Sorry.'

'That's okay. We just don't want to let Daddy know you're here yet. Right, let's get started.'

I pulled everything I'd bought out of the carrier bags and piled them on the side. I'd had stuff delivered to work over the last couple of days ever since I'd had the idea, and now food and paper plates covered the kitchen.

'There's loads!' Elodie said in a loud stage whisper. 'How's Daddy going to eat all of this?'

'I'm sure we can all help can't we?'

For the next twenty minutes I prepared everything I'd bought. Finally, satisfied, I stepped back to look. 'Ready?'

Elodie nodded and I handed her a piece of fabric. 'You hold this, and when we get to the living room, we'll open it up and put it on the floor, okay?'

'Like an indoor picnic?'

'Yep, exactly like that.'

'Okay.'

I opened the kitchen door and picked up the first tray, and let Elodie walk in front of me to the living room. She pushed the door open and as we stepped in I cleared my throat. Will looked round and, noticing Elodie, his whole face lit up. 'Els!' he said. 'When did you get here?'

'Ages ago. I've been doing secret things in the kitchen with Fran,' she said.

'Oh, have you now?' Will said, glancing up at me, his face a question mark.

'Yep. And I'm staying the night. Fran arranged it all with Mummy, didn't you, Fran?'

'I did indeed. I hope you don't mind. We wanted it to be a surprise.' The tray shook in my hands and I bent down to whisper to Elodie. 'Now, can you manage to spread that out on the floor by yourself?'

'Yep.' She opened the blanket up and dropped it to the floor and pushed the corners out, leaving the middle a crumpled mess.

'Let me help,' Will said, dropping to his hands and knees next to his daughter and helping her smooth it out.

I bent down with them and placed the tray down carefully. 'Now, I know you always wanted to go to New York, and it was on the bucket list.' Will nodded. 'Well, because you won't be able to get there now, I thought I'd bring New York to you. And I checked with the Bucket List Officials and they said it does count.' I smiled at Will and he grinned back.

'So, we've got...' I lifted the first plate from the tray. 'Hamburgers and hotdogs, clam chowder, bagels, and... hang on...' I stood and walked back to the kitchen and returned with a second tray. 'And also pretzels, cheesecake and Hershey's chocolate. Oh, and cream soda.' I opened a can of it and poured it out and stuck a mini American flag in the top, then sat back on my heels and watched as Will took in the array of food in front of him.

'Oh my goodness,' he said. 'You – you did all this for me?'

I shrugged, suddenly shy. 'Well, yes. I mean, I know you wanted to get our bucket list finished and I thought this might cheer you up. After – you know. Your news.'

He lifted his eyes away from the food and looked at me, his eyes shining. 'This is absolutely amazing, thank you, Fran.'

'Can I have a hotdog?' Elodie asked.

'Of course you can, darling.' I handed her a paper plate decorated with the American flag and stood. 'I'd better go and let Kieran know all this food is here. I think we'll need some help.'

Moments later as Kieran entered the room, his eyes opened wide. 'Woah!'

'Help yourself, it all needs eating.' I swept my hand across the blanket of food and watched as they shovelled food into their mouths like this was their final meal. I bent and picked up a bagel, pastrami dripping from its insides like a tongue, and took a bite. And I realised, as I stood there in my tiny living room, that despite everything, I was happy.

* * *

Later, with Elodie in her pyjamas and Kieran back in his room, Will and I chatted as the TV flickered in the background. The evening was warm now, rain having cleared the air, leaving it feeling fresher than it had in weeks. A gentle breeze blew through the open window, the blinds banging against the window frame every now and then.

'Today was brilliant, thank you, love,' Will said.

'You don't have to keep thanking me. I just wish we could have got to the real New York.'

'But this was the next best thing.' He rubbed his belly and I was glad to see him eating properly. It had been a while since he'd tucked into anything with such gusto.

Elodie was tucked into the crook of Will's arm, half asleep. Now she looked up at him, the blue light of the TV flickering on her face.

'Daddy, are you going to die soon?' She creased her forehead as she asked the question so innocently, as though it had only just occurred to her that something like that could happen to her daddy.

'Well. Yes.' He looked at me uncertainly. 'Yes, I am.'

Elodie studied him for a moment, trying to process what he'd told her. For a moment no one spoke. 'And when you do will you be up in heaven with Freddie?'

'Freddie?'

'My hamster, Daddy, you remember. He died and you said he was up in heaven and that he was watching over me to make sure I was being good. So does that mean he can look after you when you go to heaven too, and you can watch us together?'

Will looked as though, if you flicked him with a feather, he'd fall off the sofa onto the floor. He looked empty and shocked, yet at the same time, mirth formed crinkles at the corners of his eyes.

'Oh, Elodie, yes of course it means I can look after Freddie.' He hugged her again and she pulled away, then turned to face him again.

'Well, good. But I will miss you lots, so don't go yet, will you?' And then she snuggled back into his chest, her thumb stuck firmly in her mouth, and closed her eyes.

I wished with all my heart, as we watched her drifting off to sleep, that I could be as brave as a six-year-old.

21

Early September 2019

As a child, I had no idea of the worry and torment parents went through: their turmoil when their child got bullied or fell out with friends; the niggling doubts about first boyfriends or girlfriends.

It's not until you're a parent yourself that you realise the trouble you put your parents through, because you're now going through it yourself.

Until now I'd been lucky with Kieran. He was a good boy, mostly. Lazy sometimes, like most teenagers, but generally kind, funny and loving. And I had always relished being the most important person in his life.

Now, though, things were beginning to change and I wasn't sure I liked it. Kieran was spending more and more time with his father, away from me. Some of it out of necessity – when Will was having a bad day, it was much nicer for Kieran to be out of the house than to be caught up in the difficulty of illness.

But it was also, I had to accept, because he wanted to spend time with his father – and Sean, finally, seemed to want to spend more time with him. I'm ashamed to admit that some days, my jealousy made me behave like a belligerent child. Luckily, today was not one of those days.

'Thanks for having him,' I said as Sean brought Kieran home after a day out. This was the first time he'd come to the front door rather than just dropping him and waving from the car.

'No worries, we had fun,' Sean said, as Kieran slouched through the door and went straight to his room. I expected Sean to turn and leave but he lingered on the doorstep, his shoulder butted up against the doorframe.

'Everything all right?'

'What? Oh yeah. Good.' He looked down at the floor and bounced from foot to foot.

'Did you need to ask me something else?' I said impatiently.

'No. I mean, not exactly.'

'Sean, spit it out. Is there something wrong?' The mean part of me expected him to say he'd had enough of seeing Kieran and I was all ready for battle, to tell him how selfish he was, how I didn't need this, not right now.

But instead he said, 'I was just wondering. Maybe Kier could come and stay over sometimes. At my flat?'

I stared at him for a moment. This man, who had abandoned us when Kieran was just a few months old, and had hardly bothered with his son since, was now telling me he wanted me to let him sleep over at his flat? My immediate instinct was to tell him to sod off, but Sean was his father. Stopping Kieran from seeing him for my own selfish reasons would be completely unfair.

'Does Kieran want to?'

'I think so. He asked me, but I said I needed to speak to you first.'

'I see.' A silence fell between us. I knew I should probably invite Sean in, make him a cup of tea, sit down and talk it through properly, but I was exhausted, and the last thing I felt like doing was spending any time with him right now.

'Let me talk to Kieran, then. But if he's up for it and you're happy to have him, then I don't see why not.'

I was surprised by the look of gratitude in Sean's eyes. 'Thank you, Fran.' He looked up at me. 'I know I've been pretty shit up to now.'

'You could say that,' I said and regretted it immediately. 'Sorry, carry on.'

He cleared his throat. 'As I say, I know I haven't been the greatest dad in the world, but I've loved spending time with him these last few months. I've changed, Fran, I promise. Grown up, like, and even if you don't believe me, Kieran likes being with me, and I like being with him. We have fun.' He ran his hands through his hair. 'He's a great kid.'

'He is.' I let the fact that it was down to me and nothing to do with him hang unspoken in the air between us. When it became clear I wasn't going to be pushed any further on the subject, Sean spoke again.

'Right, I'll be off then. Let me know what he says, yeah, and maybe he can come next weekend?'

I nodded. 'I'll ring you. I promise. Bye, Sean.'

'Bye, Fran. BYE, KIERAN!' he called.

'Bye, Dad,' came the muffled reply.

And then he left, and I watched him as he walked down the street away from us, puffing on a fag, and wondered what I'd ever seen in him.

* * *

Thinking about Sean and Kieran always got me thinking about Will and his dad again. I'd been trying to remember how his dad had been with him when we were younger, trying to work out whether there were any hints of things that could have gone wrong later. Will's dad was often out at work, but when he was at home I remember him being properly present, engaging with his boys. He was someone who was fun and silly and always helped us build dens or climb trees. I remembered barbecues in the rain, soggy sausages squashed into sopping wet rolls as we huddled under an ineffectual umbrella, Alan refusing to give up on the idea despite the weather. I thought about him lifting me onto his shoulders when I was tired on a walk, the branches of the trees tickling my face as we passed; the swing he spent an entire day building for us in the woods behind our houses. I could picture the glee on his face when he saw our own faces, the happiness he'd given us as we swung through the trees. He was kind, softly spoken for the most part, and I couldn't imagine my father being friends with someone who had a dark side.

And yet.

There were flashes, from time to time. Flashes of memory that seemed to dissipate as quickly as they had formed. A look of rage on his face at some minor misdemeanour, a clenched fist when trying to suppress his anger. And there was something else there too, buried deep. Alan's reaction when Will got into a fight at school. The fight hadn't been Will's fault – in fact, it was less a fight than a beating, a boy called Gary who'd just wanted to have a go at someone and Will had been in the wrong place at the wrong time. I'd expected Alan to be cross and upset and his mum and dad both were, but later, when Will's mum had gone upstairs and I'd popped to the loo, I caught something. Hissed, angry words, a voice I barely recognised as Alan's. I'd peered through the gap between the wall and the door to see Alan holding his face right up to Will's, Will pressed back against the kitchen worktop. Alan looked like he might hit his son. Then it had all ended as suddenly as it started and I'd never really thought about it again.

So was there another side to Alan that Will had never told me about? If there was, it was clear Will still didn't want to talk about it.

I decided to ring Jim.

'You know he won't tell me, Fran,' he said, when I begged him to ask Will again what had happened.

'But you're his brother. And your brother is dying,' I said. I felt even more frustrated than ever.

'I know, and I'm sorry,' Jim said. 'It's just...' He hesitated and I listened to the air whistle through his nostrils as he decided what to say next. 'It's hard to explain. The thing I want more than anything else in the world is for Will to agree to see Dad, believe me. But I can't be the one to go against his wishes. Will's always been one hundred per cent loyal to me, and I might think he's being a stubborn arse, and that his reasons for not seeing Dad – the ones he's admitted to at least – are half-cocked, but they're his reasons.' He stopped. 'We've almost come to blows about this already, Fran, and I can't risk losing him over this when he's got so little time left anyway. I'm sorry.'

I understood Jim's reasoning, of course I did. It was the same as mine. We both loved Will and neither of us wanted to upset him.

And yet.

Circumstances change, and Will no longer had the benefit of time on his side.

I was more confused than ever about what to do for the best.

But I knew I needed to do something.

* * *

Two days later, Will and I were sitting in a North London pub, waiting for Jacob. Will looked weak and pale in the late summer sunshine that slanted through the window, and my heart clenched.

'You don't need to be so nervous, you know,' I said.

'I'm not nervous.' He ran his hands through his hair again.

'Good. You shouldn't be; Jacob's looking forward to seeing you again.'

Jacob and I had been texting each other to arrange to meet, and although he was reticent about hurting his parents' feelings – especially his mother's – he'd made it clear he was keen to see us both again sooner rather than later. *She'll be fine*, he assured me, on his latest text. *I'll talk to her.*

'I know,' Will said now. 'I just...' He stopped and I waited. 'I hate him seeing me like this. Only knowing me as this, this – weak, dying person. This isn't me.'

'Oh, Will.' I reached across the table and took his hands.

'I know I should be grateful we've met at all. But – well. This isn't the way I'd choose someone to think of me.'

I didn't have a chance to reassure him any more because suddenly a figure appeared beside us. Just like the other times we'd seen each other, my heart flipped over at the sight of my son, at the easy familiarity of his face. I stood and hugged him. He turned to Will.

'Hi.'

'Hello.' Will smiled weakly.

I hoped today they would get to know each other better so that Jacob could be left with a lasting memory of his father that meant something, but they needed to get over this awkwardness first.

'Can I get anyone a drink?' Jacob indicated our almost-full glasses.

'No, I'm fine thanks.' Will shook his head.

I watched as Jacob stood at the bar, his shoulders strong, the familiar profile of his face, and I smiled.

'What are you grinning at?' Will said, taking a sip of his pint, the froth sticking to his upper lip. He wiped it away.

'It feels as though I've known Jacob my whole life, and yet he's a virtual stranger.'

Will nodded and swallowed.

'I know you don't feel like that yet, but you will.'

His gaze moved to his son at the bar, and I watched a small frown flit across his forehead. 'I hope so.'

Jacob returned with a pint and sat down on the stool next to Will. 'So, big day.'

'Yeah.'

I resisted rolling my eyes at the fact they thought a football match was so important, and watched as Jacob took a sip of his pint. He looked so like his father, and yet there was more than that. It wasn't just in the familiar curve of his nose, or the flick of his hair. It was his gestures, the casual way he moved. I wished Will could see it.

'Reckon they'll do well?'

'Probably not. You know Arsenal; if they can mess it up, they will.'

Jacob grinned. I'd been happy to discover he supported the same team as Will, and had managed to get tickets for one of their first matches of the season. I hoped it would give them something to talk about. It seemed to be working so far.

I sat back and watched them, not really listening to their words as they discussed a sport about which I knew very little, despite Kieran's love of it. It didn't matter what they were talking about; the fact was they were talking, and they were smiling.

Pints finished, we made our way to the stadium past rundown houses with paint peeling off the window frames and tatty furniture dumped in front gardens that stood in stark contrast next to homes that owners were clearly proud of, vases of flowers bobbing in windows, front doors gleaming with fresh coats of paint; past second-hand furniture shops and launderettes, and neat blocks of flats, a mish-mash of flags flying from upper windows in the gentle breeze; past hawkers selling knock-off Arsenal shirts and scarves and posters, and kids kicking litter like footballs across the pavement. I took it all in as I hung back and let Will and Jacob stroll side by side, keen to let the pair of them spend as much time together as possible. I had all the time in the world to get to know our son. Will didn't.

The football match was more fun than I'd anticipated, and afterwards, as we made our way out of the stadium with a home team victory under our belts, the singing and jostling and the cheering seemed apt, somehow. A father and son memory they could both treasure for the rest of their lives, wrapped in a little bit of nostalgia.

'That was amazing,' Will said, stumbling a little as he slung his arm across my shoulders.

'You okay?'

He grinned. 'I'm great,' he said, stumbling again. 'Oops, must be the beer.'

Beside him, Jacob looked a little the worse for wear too, a matching grin on his face, his steps a little unsteady. I rolled my eyes.

'Why don't you two go and have a couple more drinks? I've got to get home for Kieran.'

'Yeah!' Will said, slapping Jacob on the back.

'Oh.' Jacob looked crestfallen. 'I've got to get a train back to Brighton.'

'Stay with us!' He looked at me. 'He can, can't he, Franny?'

My thoughts turned instantly to Kieran. He'd said he wanted to meet Jacob but was it fair to spring him on the poor kid like this? But then again, what choice did I have now when Will had already offered?

'You're more than welcome,' I said tentatively, placing my hand on Jacob's arm. 'But there's no pressure. And Kieran is there.' I gave Will a look but he didn't seem to notice.

Jacob didn't speak for a moment and I wondered whether he was considering what his mum might say. But then he gave a small nod. 'I'd really like to, if you're sure you don't mind?'

'Only if you don't mind a sofa bed in the lounge?'

'Fine by me.'

We said our goodbyes and as they joined the crowds of happy supporters wending their noisy way down the street towards the nearest pub, I stood and watched for a moment. I knew one day I'd look back on this moment and wish I'd remembered it better, appreciated it more. But for now, it was impossible to believe that this could be one of the last times that they would be together.

* * *

A couple of hours later I heard the scratch of a key in the lock and then a low giggle as Will and Jacob arrived home. Kieran looked up at me, eyes wide. I'd explained that Will had invited Jacob to stay and, while he was adamant he didn't mind, it was clear he was nervous about meeting his brother for the first time.

'Listen to the state of them.'

'I know.' I reached over and squeezed his fingers.

Seconds later they burst into the room, Jacob first, an exhausted-looking Will following. I leaped up and took his elbow and guided him to the sofa.

'Are you okay, love? You look...' I trailed off. I didn't want to say *terrible*, and I didn't want to embarrass him in front of Jacob. I knew how important it was to him that his son had some memories of him as Will, not as someone dying of cancer. But he did look awful, and I worried staying out had been a mistake.

'I'm fine,' he said, dropping to the sofa. He closed his eyes immediately and rubbed his neck. I glanced at Jacob, who still hovered by the door. He gestured me over and I followed him out into the hall.

'What is it? What's happened?' My voice was an urgent whisper.

He shook his head. 'Nothing to worry about. He just – he had a couple more pints and looked like he was going to pass out. And then he started speaking but the words made no sense. I – I didn't know if that was normal, or whether I should be worried.'

My stomach dropped to the floor. This was something we'd been warned about. The cancer was taking yet another hold of my Will.

'It's fine, don't worry. Thanks for getting him home safe and sound.'

'No problem.' He looked down at his feet, suddenly awkward. 'Is that Kieran?'

I clasped my hand to my mouth. 'Oh my goodness, I haven't even introduced you, have I?' I said.

'No. I...' He stopped. 'It's been a bit strange, knowing I have a brother.'

'I know. It is for Kieran too – it's always just been me and him. But he's excited about meeting you.'

'I am too. And a bit terrified.'

'Of a teenage boy?'

'They're the most terrifying of all.' He smiled. 'I guess it's all just starting to feel real now.'

I took his hand. His skin felt warm and fit perfectly in mine. 'Come on, let's go and meet your brother.'

We marched back into the room where Will was already fast asleep, his mouth slightly open. Kieran looked up from his phone and swung his legs to the floor.

'Kieran, this is Jacob. Jacob, this is Kieran.'

Jacob stuck his hand out and Kieran took it awkwardly.

'Hi.'

'Hello, Kieran. Your mum's told me loads about you.'

'You too.'

An awkward silence fell for a moment. I clapped my hands. 'Right, I'll get Will to bed.'

'Do you need a hand?' Jacob said.

'No, you stay here, chat to Kieran. It'll be easier without me watching over you.' I smiled. 'He won't bite.'

Together we hauled Will off the sofa and I walked him slowly to the bedroom, his head lolling against my shoulder. I could hear Jacob's voice, and the rumble of Kieran's voice in reply, and my heart filled with happiness.

Because despite the dark cloud of Will's illness hanging over us, I had, under one roof, something I never thought I'd have: my three boys.

I knew I would treasure the moment forever.

22

NOW

Late September 2019

'I need to talk to you,' Will said to me, one morning as he lay on the sofa. It was mid-September, two weeks since his and Jacob's football trip, and the air that trickled through the open window was still warm, autumn tugging at the edges of summer like a child on an adult's sleeve.

'Oh?' I looked up from the book I was reading and squinted at him.

He lifted his head and pushed his upper body up so he was resting against the cushion. He was pale, his skin drawn more tightly across his cheekbones, his collarbone visible, his shirt hanging off him. My Will. Always so strong and capable, now so diminished it was as though a light was flickering, about to extinguish.

'I'm moving into a hospice.'

'What?' I let the book drop into my lap and I studied him, aghast.

'Look at me, Fran. All I do is lie around all day, getting in the way. I'm no good to man nor beast. It's not fair on you or Kieran.'

'No!' The word left my mouth like a bullet. 'That's not true, we want you here.'

'I know you do. But I think it's for the best. For both of us. I mean, I don't want you to become my carer, wiping my bum for me, carrying me around, giving me medication. I...' He stopped.

'But I want to do all of those things for you.'

He shook his head. 'No, you don't. At least, you might think you do but you won't want to once you're doing them.' He dropped his head. 'Fran, I went through all of this with my mum, remember? I watched her body fade away to nothing, until she couldn't do anything for herself. My mum, who was the most capable woman I knew, couldn't even lift a drink or get out of bed by the end. It was awful; I don't want you to watch it happen to me.'

'But—'

'No, Fran. I've made up my mind.'

'But where?'

'Hampstead. It's not far. It's a nice place.'

'You've been to see it already?'

'Yes.' He sighed. 'I'm sorry. I went last week. I knew you'd say you didn't want me to go, but I have to do this. It's the right thing to do.'

'So when – have you sorted it all out, then?'

'Yes. I move in at the end of the week.'

Two days. Two more days and Will would be leaving me, physically at least. But it was more than that. The move would mark the next stage, when Will would be closer to the end. Closer to leaving us for good.

I didn't want him to go but I knew he was right. Over the last two weeks his body had grown weaker by the day, until some mornings he was barely able to lift himself from the bed. He did, of course, determined not to give in to it, but I could see the effort it took, and the pain it was causing him. I'd probably known, deep down, that this day was almost here. I just hadn't wanted to admit it.

'Come here.' Will held his frail arms up and I walked over and fell

into him, into the arms that once had held me so tightly and now felt
so light, so weak.

* * *

The day Will had moved into my flat just six months before had been
filled with laughter, happiness and hope. We'd missed so much time
together, but now here we were at last, making a fresh start, a new
beginning.

This time, moving his things from my flat into the hospice felt
horribly different. It felt like we were just waiting for the end.

Not that Will would admit to that.

Once his few boxes were unpacked in his new room, he peered out
of the window at the grey day where the clouds hung heavy over the
rooftops. 'So, who's up for a walk around the gardens? It looks nice out
there.'

I glanced round his room and wanted to cry. It was perfectly nice.
The whole hospice was perfectly nice. But it was what it represented.

A single bed butted up against the wall, because he'd never have a
need to sprawl across a double bed any more, or sleep next to anyone
else; plain walls, painted a soft grey and dotted with a few pinpricks
where a previous occupant had hung pictures. A wardrobe in the
corner, a chest of drawers, a velvet-covered chair and a small area for
making tea and coffee, then another door leading into a compact bathroom. And that was it. That would be the extent of Will's world until
his final breath.

I let out a strangled noise and Will looked at me quizzically.

'Are you okay, Fran?'

'What? Yes, sorry, I'm fine.'

'So will you come into the garden with me?'

'Of course I will. Don't you want to put everything away here first,
though? Make it a bit more cosy?'

He glanced round at the piles of clothes and bits and pieces and shrugged. 'Nah, it will give me something to do when you've gone home.'

I took a breath in and felt it catch in my chest. 'Okay, if you're sure.'

He held out his hand and I took it in mine, his skin dry and papery. We walked along the corridor and out of the main doors into the garden. The air was cool and damp and clung to my skin, making me shiver. I wished I'd put on something warmer than a jumper.

The grounds weren't very big but Will was right, they were pretty. Most of the flowers had died down by now, resting for the winter, getting ready to push their heads through the soil, show off their blooms again in the spring. A spring that Will would never see.

'What are you thinking about? You look melancholy.'

'I was just thinking how lovely the gardens are here.' A small fib to protect his feelings.

He studied me for a moment, as though trying to work out if I was telling him the truth. He chose to believe me.

'I think it'll be all right here. The nurses seem nice.'

'They do.' The conversation felt stilted, awkward, and I wondered whether we'd ever get back the ease we'd always had between us.

'Can we sit down?' Will led me to a bench and we lowered ourselves onto the damp wood. Beside me he put his head between his knees.

'Are you okay, love?' I rubbed his shoulder blades with the palm of my hand.

'My head's killing me.'

'Want me to call a nurse?'

'No, I just need a minute.'

I leaned into him, resting my cheek on his shoulder and clasping his hand as he inhaled deeply and squeezed his eyes tight against the pain. As we sat there, the cold air creeping through my jumper, the hum of cars passing on the other side of the hedge, I felt sadder than I'd ever felt in my life.

Will had been right, to come here. As these episodes increased, this was where he needed to be. He'd be in the best hands, safe hands, not somewhere he couldn't get help, or with someone who panicked at the slightest thing.

This was where he should be.

But I missed him already.

* * *

If I'd been worried about Will getting lonely, I needn't have. He was barely ever on his own. I visited him every day, and Kieran came sometimes, when he wasn't at school or with his dad. One day Amy came with Elodie, and I was pleased. Will would be glad to see her.

'How is he?' she asked as we walked towards his room where he'd spent the morning dozing.

'He's tired, but doing okay considering.' I looked at her. 'But don't be shocked by his appearance. He's lost a lot of weight.'

As we reached Will's door, Amy stopped and grabbed my forearm. 'I wanted to thank you.'

'Thank me? What for?' I couldn't for the life of me think what Amy might have to thank me for.

'For looking after Elodie. And Will. I don't think I could have done it. I...' She stopped, clasped her hands together. 'I always knew it was you, you know. I always knew, if you came back, he'd leave me for you.'

I stared at her, this woman who'd given her heart to Will once too, who'd had it broken and yet could still stand there and say thank you to me, and my heart swelled with respect for her. She was a good woman and I wondered whether, after this was all over, we might become friends.

I looked down at my feet, then up into her wide eyes. 'Thank you for bringing Elodie to see Will. It'll make his day.'

'I'd never keep her from him. She needs to see her daddy as much as she can before...' She stopped, not needing to finish the sentence.

'Ready?'

She nodded and turned to find Elodie, who was chatting to one of the nurses. 'Come on, darling.'

Elodie ran towards us, her bunches flying out behind her, and grabbed Amy's hand with one of hers, and mine with the other. I looked at Amy to see if she minded, and she shrugged and smiled. 'Let's go and see Daddy.'

I knocked on the door gently and pushed it open. Will was in his armchair, playing a game on his phone. He looked up as we entered and his face lit up as Elodie threw herself at him.

'Daddy!' She sat on his lap and put her arms around his neck and he held her, perfectly still.

'Be gentle with Daddy, Els,' Amy said, laughing.

'It's fine. She's fine.' Will smiled as Elodie rested her head against his shoulder. Her sunflower dress was hitched up to reveal her striped tights but she didn't care.

'Shall I...' Amy gestured towards the bed and my heart went out to her. She felt as awkward in this room as I had the first day. At least now it had a bit more character, a bit more of Will injected into it – his beloved Arsenal shirt signed by Ian Wright that I so hated was hung above the headboard, some framed photos were scattered across the top of the chest of drawers and a couple of Will's favourite prints were tacked up on the wall above his bed.

'Yes, sit wherever you can find space.'

Amy and I sat on the bed, side by side, and waited for someone to speak. If Will was surprised to see me and Amy together, he didn't mention it.

'So, how is it?' Amy's eyes wandered round the room.

'It's not as bad as I thought. Everyone's very kind.'

'And what are you doing? You know, to keep busy?'

'Ah you know, a few games of football, some basketball every evening and tonight I thought I might go for a jog.'

Amy's eye widened and she looked at me, confused, before realisation dawned.

'Hilarious, William.'

'Sorry. If you can't laugh you'll cry, isn't that what they say?'

She shrugged.

'There is stuff to do here, actually. I feel lucky, really, I'm one of the well ones so I'm left to my own devices most of the time, if I want to be. I spend a lot of time reading, playing games, watching telly. But it's only been three days, and I've been feeling pretty good, and Fran has been here every day so...' He trailed off.

'I'm glad.'

'Thank you, Amy.'

For the rest of the afternoon we played games with Elodie, talked about my job, and I told Amy all about Kieran. But I knew Will wanted to tell Amy about Jacob himself, so as the afternoon crept on, I stood.

'Shall I take Elodie for a walk outside and leave you two to chat for a while?'

'That would be great, thanks, Fran,' Will said, while Amy looked at me, her brow creased in a confused frown.

'Come on then, Elodie.'

Elodie jumped up from the floor where she'd been colouring in a picture and grabbed my hand. As I left, Will flashed me a grateful smile.

I just hoped Amy would be as understanding about Jacob as she had been about everything else.

* * *

'It's like a party in here,' I said, balancing a tray with six cups, a huge teapot, a pot of coffee and jug of milk and plonking it down on top of Will's chest of drawers. Will's small room had far too many people in it – he was in his chair, Mags and Rob were perched side by side on the bed, while Jim sat cross-legged on the floor. Music played in the background and the soft murmur of voices filled the room.

'Thanks, love,' Will said, reaching for my hand.

Everybody had come to see Will this weekend, and although the hospice didn't normally allow so many people at one time, they'd made an exception today because it was what they deemed a special occasion.

'What time's he arriving?' Mags said, checking her watch.

'About one.' I glanced at the bedside clock. Forty minutes until Jacob arrived. Mags and Jim had been desperate to meet him so I'd rung him a couple of days before and asked him if he was up for it.

'I'd love to,' he'd said, to my surprise.

'Are you sure your mum and dad won't mind?'

'They're fine,' he reassured me. 'I've promised Mum that you're not trying to take over from her and I think she finally believes me.'

'Thank goodness.' I had no desire to upset anyone.

We'd arranged to go out for lunch in a pub near the hospice. Fortunately Will was having a good day, having spent most of the previous one in bed, dosed up on painkillers. The shadow of it still hung on his face, although I suspected only I'd noticed.

'I'm so excited,' Mags said now.

'Just promise not to talk his ear off or try to read his aura or anything.'

'Course I won't. Oh, but that reminds me,' Mags said, pulling her canvas bag from the floor.

I rolled my eyes. 'Here we go,' I muttered under my breath, then watched in amusement as she pulled out a selection of strange items.

'So, I've got you a few things, Will, to make your room more' – she waved her hands around, her bangles jangling on her wrist – 'you know.' She picked up the first item. 'A scented candle, lavender and eucalyptus, which are both good for the immune system...' She rummaged through her bag again and pulled out the next items, which clattered against each other. 'A couple of crystals – clear quartz, which is an amazing healer, and ruby for energy. And one more thing. A faceted crystal to hang in your window to bring in energy from outside.' She stood. 'Can I?'

Will nodded his consent. 'Why not, anything's got to be worth a go, right?'

Mags beamed at me in triumph then turned to hook the crystal onto the top of the window by its ribbon. Rainbows of light danced around the room in the pale autumn sunshine. 'See, it's already working.' Mags smiled.

'Thanks, Mags. They're lovely. Only – what am I meant to do with those?' Will pointed at the crystals.

'Oh, whatever you like. I'll pop them next to your bed for now, but you can move them wherever you want.'

'Okay.' When he was sure Mags wasn't looking, Will flashed me a grin. We both felt the same way about Mags's obsession with alternative therapies, but neither of us were going burst her bubble. She was being kind.

For the next half an hour we drank tea and chatted, and for that half an hour life felt normal. As though there was no cancer to worry about, nothing hanging over our heads, clouding the future. I had half an eye on my mobile, waiting for Jacob's text to let me know he'd arrived and finally, the screen lit up.

'He's here. I'll just go and find him,' I said, leaping up from the floor where I'd been sitting next to Jim. I scurried along the corridor to the reception area and there he was. Our son. The sight of him made my heart leap every time. The sun shone through the double doors behind him as he stood, chatting to a nurse and, sensing my arrival, he turned and smiled, that smile of his father's that I'd always loved.

'Fran,' he said, planting a soft kiss on my cheek.

'Jacob.'

We held hands for a moment, until the nurse cleared her throat and said, 'I'll let you get on, then.'

'Sorry,' Jacob said. 'It was lovely to meet you.'

'You too,' she said, and hurried away.

'It looks like you've got an admirer,' I said, watching the nurse's retreating back.

'Oh, we were just chatting.' He grinned again, his face flushing pink. He seemed lighter, less serious than the last time I saw him, and I hooked my arm through his and said, 'Ready to face the music?'

'Don't make it sound so terrifying, I'm scared enough.'

'You'll be fine. They're all so excited to meet you.'

We made our way along the corridor and as we reached the door I gave Jacob's arm a squeeze and knocked to let them know we were there.

And then the door opened, and we stepped inside...

*   *   *

Later, after we'd all eaten our meals, I could see that Will was flagging. His face was grey and his head creased in pain.

'You all get back, I'll stay here and sort out the bill,' I said.

Jim glanced at Will and nodded. 'Come on, old man, let's get you back before you fall asleep.'

Normally Will would have come back at him with some jibe, but today there was no energy there, nothing extra to give. Instead he glanced up at his brother gratefully and took his proffered arm to pull himself up to standing. Then they left, Jacob on one side of Will, Jim on the other, leaving me with Mags and Rob.

'How are you feeling?' Mags said as we watched them make their way across the car park and climb into Jim's car.

'I'm all right.'

I felt her hand slip into mine and she rested her head on my shoulder. 'It's okay to not be all right, you know.'

'I know.' I carried on staring out of the window, not trusting myself to meet Mags's eyes. Mags knew me better than almost anyone else in the world. Better than my parents, even. There was nothing I could hide from her.

'Why don't you have a cry? Let it all out before you have to go back and put on a brave face for Will again?'

'I...' I stopped, then suddenly a huge sob erupted from my chest and I fell into Mags's arms, my whole body shaking. I didn't care at that moment about anyone else in the pub as the pressure and pain of the last few months flowed out of me, the tears soaking Mags's top. Slowly, finally, I felt the tears slow and my breath start to even out and I lifted my head. Mags stroked my face, pushing away the hair that had clumped onto my cheek and holding her palm against my face. 'Better?'

I nodded, not daring to speak.

'I don't know how you're coping with this, my darling,' she said, searching my eyes. 'But you're doing amazingly well. I'm not sure I could do it.'

I shook my head. We both knew Mags could cope with anything. But I was grateful for the sentiment.

'It's just so awful, seeing him go downhill so quickly.' The words came out broken as my chest hitched through the sentence.

'I know.'

'Were you shocked, when you saw him today?' It had been a few weeks since Mags had seen Will and I knew how different he must have looked.

'A little. But you mustn't focus on that. Don't think about how quickly he's getting worse, or what you've both lost already. Just think about the good times you've still got ahead of you.'

'I know. It's just so hard when...' I stopped, unable to finish the sentence. But it didn't really matter what I was about to say because the truth was it was all hard. All of it. The cancer, watching Will deteriorate before my eyes, listening to the pain in his voice when he spoke about Elodie, imagining life without him once he'd gone.

'Sometimes I almost wish I'd never met him again.'

'You don't mean that.'

'No not really. But I – I'd been without him for so many years. I was living, without him, happily. But now I have to cope with losing him all over again and I'm not sure I can do it.' My voice cracked.

Mags lifted my chin until I was looking at her again.

'Before you met Will, you were the saddest I'd ever seen you. You were getting through life; you weren't really enjoying it. You had Kieran, but he was the only thing in your life that gave you any joy. Now look at everything you've got. Will, for one, and when he's gone you'll have the happy memories of him. You've got Elodie, who clearly adores you, and you've got Jacob. None of that would have happened without William Poulton coming back into your life, so don't ever say you wish you'd never met him, do you hear me?'

I nodded. She was right, of course. Before Will, it had felt as though life would continue in exactly the same way for the next forty, fifty years until I died. Now, it might be painful, but everything was better. Everything.

And it wasn't over yet.

* * *

Mags and Rob popped back to the hospice to say goodbye to Will, Jim and Jacob, then left us to it.

'It was really lovely to meet you, Jacob,' Mags said, pumping his hand like a piston as her gaze lingered on his face a few seconds.

'You too,' he said.

Mags turned to me then. 'You just remember what I said, okay? Make the most of what you've got left. Promise?'

'I promise.'

Will had had a nap before we got back and I was relieved to see him looking a little more upbeat.

'Right, I'm going to have a beer, who wants one?' Jim said, pulling a box of BrewDogs from his bag.

'I will,' I said, leaning over and grabbing one.

'Please,' Jacob said.

'Will?'

'I probably shouldn't.'

'Ah, shouldn't schmouldn't. Why not?' Jim held one out and Will smiled and grabbed the can.

'Go on, then. I might as well live a little.'

We sat sipping our beers, the light fading outside the bedroom window and the candle Mags had brought sending a lovely, relaxing scent through the room.

'How's the bucket list going?' Jim said, taking a sip of beer.

'Not bad. We've still got about four things to go,' I said.

'Anything I can help with?'

'Not really.'

'What's this?' Jacob said.

'I can't believe they haven't bored you with the details of this yet,' Jim said.

'Oi, it's not boring!' Will said. He turned to Jacob. 'So, you know we told you about when me and Fran were together, when we were younger.' He stopped as realisation dawned. Of course Jacob knew about us being together. It's the reason he existed. Will cleared his throat. 'Well, anyway. When we were about seventeen we wrote a list of things we wanted to do before we were forty, which seemed ancient to us then. We found it recently and we realised we'd hardly done any of the things on there. So we decided to get them done before I – well, before I die.'

'Wow. So what sort of things are on it?'

'We've been skiing, and sky-diving,' I said.

'And we did an amazing zipwire a while back,' Jim said.

'We've eaten a dozen doughnuts each in a row and everything off the same menu – they were my choices, obviously.' Will grinned. 'Oh, and Fran humiliated herself by throwing herself around on a trampoline trying to do a backflip.'

'You said that counted!'

'It did. Doesn't stop it being hilarious, though.'

I stuck my tongue out.

'So what have you got left to do? Jacob said.

'I've lost track. But not much.'

I pulled my phone out and scrolled through to the list I'd copied on there. 'We've still got to see the Northern Lights, see a shooting star... get matching tattoos, oh...' I looked up. 'And get married.'

'I've been married.' Will raised his eyebrows.

'I know but I haven't.' I felt my face flush.

Will looked at me, and a silence fell across the room.

'Well, that doesn't sound too bad. I mean, it sounds like you've done pretty well already,' Jacob said at last, breaking the silence.

'Yeah, we've packed a lot in.'

'Not enough, though.'

'Will, don't become obsessed by it. It's not the be all and end all.' Jim took a swig from his beer and Will fixed him with a stare.

'It is to me. I don't want any regrets when my last days arrive.'

'Don't you think there are more important things to have regrets about?' Jim's voice might have been quiet but his words had power.

Will's face went white. 'Are you talking about Dad again?'

Jacob looked from me to Will and back to me again, his face confused. I gave a tiny shake of my head.

'Of course I am. What else would you have to regret?' Jim's face was dark.

'Why do you have to bring the mood down, Jim?'

'I'm not bringing it down, I'm just saying, that's all. I understand you want to get this bucket list done, but perhaps there are other things you should be focusing on at the same time. That's all.'

'I'm not seeing Dad!' The words shot out and ricocheted round the room.

'You've made that perfectly clear.' Jim's voice was clipped and I could feel the tension between them growing thicker, denser. Next to me Jacob sat back on the bed and stared resolutely at his can of beer.

'So why do you keep bringing it up, then?'

'Because someone has to. And everyone else is too damn scared of upsetting you.' He didn't need to look at me to tell me who he was talking about.

'I'm not scared,' I said, my voice quiet, 'It's just not my business.'

Jim gave a small shake of his head. 'I know. And I'm sorry. But someone has to say these things, so I'm taking it upon myself to do it.' He shrugged.

'But why?' spat Will. 'Why can't you just leave it alone?'

'Because you're dying, Will, and I won't sit around and let you do this to yourself – or to Dad – because of some stupid, mulish sense of pride.'

A silence fell, and I felt the atmosphere shift again. Will's face, which had been pale before, now had two blotches of red on each cheek, and a vein throbbed at his temple. I held my breath.

Finally, Will turned to Jacob. 'Sorry you have to hear this, Jacob, but it needs to be said.' He turned back to his brother. 'Do you know what Dad did, Jim?'

Jim met Will's gaze, his lips pressed firmly together. 'No, of course I don't. No one does because you refuse to talk about it. But I can't see how it can possibly be anything bad enough to warrant being cut off for twenty-five years.'

Will shook his head. 'No, I don't imagine that you can.'

'What does that even mean?'

'It means that you never saw the bad side of Dad. You were only fourteen when he made us move, when he ripped away everything we'd never known and loved. Yes, I know you missed your friends, but it was even worse for me. I was eighteen. I had Fran, I had – I had my whole life in front of me. Losing Mum had been hard enough. And then we left. Just like that.' He dropped his eyes to his lap. Neither I nor Jim spoke. Will looked up, his face defeated. 'I tried everything, Jim, after Mum died. I tried everything to get Dad to love me again, but nothing worked. It was as though, with Mum gone, his capacity to love had gone with her. And he took everything out on me. Not you. I sheltered you from the worst of it but he was awful. He drank too much, and when he drank too much he got angry, throwing things round the room and shouting. Mainly at me, but you must remember some of the times when we were both there?'

He waited for Jim to answer, and he gave a small nod. 'Some of them, yes.'

Will nodded in satisfaction. 'Well, then, hopefully you'll understand what happened next, and why I couldn't forgive him.'

'Go on.'

Will sucked in his breath and blew his cheeks out.

'Dad hit me, when he was drunk one night. I was willing to stay, before that, for you. But it was almost the final straw for me.' I held my breath, waiting for more. 'I was getting ready to leave. I knew he'd never hit you; he never laid a finger on you. I knew you were safe, even without me.'

'Is that it?' I could hear the contempt in Jim's voice. 'Dad hit you once and you don't speak to him for twenty-five years? I mean it's not great but...' He stopped, seeing Will's face.

'No. That wasn't it.' He took a deep breath. 'Dad said it was my fault that Mum died.'

Jim's face paled and his hand tightened round his can so hard it buckled.

'He didn't? He would never have said that.' Jim's voice was gravelly, as though he was fighting back tears, or anger. I held my breath.

Will nodded. 'But that's just it, Jim. He did. Dad blamed me for Mum's death.'

Jim stared at Will a moment. He clearly didn't have a response.

'What – why did he think that, Will?' My voice was raspy.

'Doctors said Mum took too many of her tablets, the day she died. A lot too many. They said she probably wouldn't have died that day, if she hadn't have taken them.'

'Mum took an overdose?' Jim sounded as distraught as me.

'That's what they said. But I didn't give those pills to her.'

'So who did?'

'No one, is my guess. Mum would have found a way.' He buried his face in his hands then looked up at us pleadingly. 'She was in so much pain, at the end.' He looked from me to Jim and then back again. 'I mean, you both saw her. She'd had enough. She wanted to go.'

'And Dad blamed you?'

'Yeah. He said it must have been me that gave her the tablets, because there was no way she'd have wanted to leave him.' Tears shone in his eyes and he looked away, over my shoulder. I wouldn't have been surprised if I'd turned round and seen the spectre of his mother standing there.

'So why didn't you just tell him that?'

'I did. He didn't believe me. But even if he had it was too late.' His voice cracked. I wanted to reach out and hug him, but I couldn't move. I was paralysed. 'I could never forgive him for that.'

'But surely you understood that he didn't mean it? I mean, the man was grieving. He'd just lost his wife.'

'And I'd lost my mum.'

'Me too, Will.'

The two brothers stared at each other for a moment. Eventually, Will spoke again, this time so quietly that Jim and I both had to lean forward to hear him. 'I couldn't forgive him, Jim. I couldn't.'

He shook his head and this time the tears came thick and fast. Jim wrapped his arms around his big brother, and Jacob and I just sat there helpless, lost, as they comforted each other. Finally, Will lifted his head, his face sodden. 'I would never have done that to Mum. You believe me, don't you?'

'Of course I do.'

He looked at me. 'Do you believe me, Fran?'

'I...' I stopped. I didn't know what to say. Throughout this whole conversation I'd been frozen in horror.

This was the reason Will hadn't spoken to his father? Because his father thought Will had given his mother the pills that ended her life early? I felt as though there was something blocking my throat and I swallowed, tried to get some air into my lungs.

'Fran, what's wrong?' Jim's face loomed in my peripheral vision but I couldn't look at him.

'I...' I started again, but the words got stuck again.

'Fran, you're scaring me now. What's going on?' Will's face was deathly pale and I knew I had to speak. I had to tell him the truth. I owed it to him.

Whatever it cost me.

'It was me.'

23

THEN

October 1993

The room was dim, the curtains drawn against the grey day, the only light coming from the small lamp on the bedside table. It was hot, the air dry, the radiator turned up to maximum. In the bed lay Will's mum, the shape of her body barely visible beneath the heap of covers. Her eyes were closed, her head turned away from me.

'Mrs Poulton?'

She turned her head and when she saw it was me she smiled and held her hand out weakly. 'Francesca. It's so lovely to see you.'

'It's lovely to see you too, Mrs Poulton.'

'Come on, love. You've known me almost your whole life, and I know you've never liked calling me Kathy, but won't you, just for now, for today? You make me feel like Alan's mother when you call me Mrs Poulton.'

My face felt flushed as I took her papery hand in mine. 'Okay, Kathy.' The name felt strange on my tongue, unfamiliar.

'Good girl.'

I sat down in the chair by her bed and listened to her laboured breathing for a few moments. I wondered how long it would be until that breathing stopped forever. Not long, I didn't think.

'Is William here?' She glanced over my shoulder.

'He's downstairs; he thought I'd like to come and see you on my own. I'm only here for a few days.' I didn't dare tell her about our row. Where was the harm in letting her believe we were still happy?

'Well, I'm glad to see you.' She looked at me again, her brow furrowed. Her eyes roamed up and down my body, and I felt my face grow hot.

'There's something different about you. What is it?'

'I...' I stopped. Could she tell? I shook the thought away. Of course not. But her roving eyes continued their journey from my face to my abdomen and down to my toes, then back up again.

'Fran, I'm going to ask you something, and I don't want you to get upset if I'm wildly wrong.' Her breath was laboured, the words coming out staccato.

'Okay.' My temple pulsed and my mouth felt dry.

'Are you pregnant?'

I sat for a moment, looking at her, at her searching eyes. Then I nodded, dropping my head. I felt a gentle squeeze on my fingers.

'How did you know?'

'I can just tell. You're – radiating light.'

I doubted that very much, the way I was feeling, but I didn't say so.

'So assuming it's my William's...' She paused and I nodded.

'Of course.'

'So what have you decided to do?'

'Do?'

She smiled weakly and I knew there was no point hiding the truth.

'I'm not keeping it.' The words caught in my throat and I swallowed. Kathy gave a small tilt of her head. I knew speaking took any spare breath she had so I filled the silence, justifying myself. 'I'm too young to have a baby. I just can't.'

She nodded. 'And what does William think?'

I hung my head. 'He wants me to keep it.'

A silence hovered between us, thick with anticipation.

'Will you think about it?' Her voice was so soft I had to lean forward to hear and even then I wasn't sure I'd heard right.

'About keeping it?'

She nodded again, words too much now. My head swam. This was exactly why I hadn't wanted anyone to know, why I hadn't asked opinions.

And yet I couldn't ignore Will's dying mother, could I?

Kathy took a deep breath in now, and grimaced, her hand fluttering to her chest. I waited for the wave of pain to pass and then she leaned slightly closer to me. 'I know you think this is the right decision but Will's about to lose me and it will be hard.' She drew in a rattly breath. 'I don't want him to lose everything.' She breathed out heavily. 'Just think about it, for me?'

I nodded. What else could I do? I felt an overwhelming urge to stand and leave, to get out of that room and gulp in lungfuls of fresh air greedily, but Kathy clung to my hand, her grip surprisingly firm. She wasn't finished yet.

'Will you...' She stopped, swallowed. Her eyes were huge in their sunken sockets, her previously thick hair nothing more than wisps around her face now. 'Will you help me?'

'Of course. What do you need? Water? Food? Medicine?' I looked round wildly, trying to see what was already in the room. But she shook her head.

'I can't go on much longer.' She breathed in deeply. 'It hurts too much.' Another breath, which sounded as though she had to fight to suck in the air. 'Will you give me my pills?'

'Where are they?'

She pointed towards the box on the dressing table across the room. I stood and lifted it and brought it over, lifting the lid. There was an enormous stash of medication, and I had no idea what any of it was. What if I gave her the wrong ones?

'Which ones?'

'See the pink ones?'

I picked up a packet of pink tablets and she nodded.

'All of them.'

'All of them? Are you sure?' I studied the packet, where it stated in thick black letters: *Only ONE to be taken every four hours. Do NOT exceed the stated dose.*

She nodded, her eyes pleading, and in that moment I realised what she wanted from me.

'I can't ask anyone else. Please?' A single tear slipped down her cheek and landed on the pillow and my stomach rolled over. How could she ask this of me? I thought of Will, and how devastated he would be when he found out his mother had gone.

But then again, she was almost gone anyway, and he knew that. We all knew it, which was why he'd asked me to come home to see her. She just didn't want to go through any more pain.

How could I refuse her?

I sat for a moment, holding the pills in my fist, my mind whirring, the ramifications of what I'd been asked to do paralysing me momentarily.

She was asking me to help her to end her life.

But she was dying anyway.

It would only be a matter of a few hours. Days, at most.

And she was desperate. Why else would she ask me such a thing?

One last look at her face made my mind up for me. I closed the lid of the box and reached my hand out, and dropped the pills into her open palm. Slowly, she closed her hand round the packet and smiled at me.

'Thank you, Fran. You're a good girl.'

I stood, desperate to get out of there, to be anywhere but here with this dying woman who'd meant so much to me throughout my childhood.

I leaned forward and kissed her forehead gently and then I turned and left the room. 'Goodbye, sleep tight,' I said, as I left the room.

'Bye, Fran. Thank you.'
She died the next day.

24

NOW

October 2019

All three men stared at me for what felt like hours, but could only have been a few seconds. I watched as, slowly, realisation dawned.

'You gave Mum the pills?'

'What? No! Fran?' Will looked desperately at me, and then back at Jim.

I nodded. 'She begged me to.'

'But... ' Will stopped. 'But how could you have done that?'

His face was etched with pain, the confusion sunk deep into the lines and contours of his face. The light from the candle cast half of his face in shadow.

'I'm so sorry.'

Nobody spoke for several minutes, the horror sinking in. Outside the room life went on as normal, nurses' muffled footsteps padding along the corridor, shouts and laughter from the common room, the hum of someone's TV a few doors down drifting in and settling among the motes of dust. And yet nothing and nobody within these four walls moved.

I knew how awful this was. I'd done something terrible, something I'd spent years trying to block from my mind, to convince myself that it didn't matter, that I'd done what I thought was for the best, that she had been dying anyway.

But now the consequences of my actions – the irreparable damage to Will's relationship with his father – had become clear, and that could never be undone. Even if I could get them to understand why I'd helped their mother, nothing could ever change what had happened as a result.

I couldn't look at either of them. I couldn't look at Jacob either, terrified of what I'd see in his eyes.

Will spoke first. 'I don't believe it.' His voice was hoarse. 'All this time. All this time you've known this and you've never told me.'

'Your mum made me promise. She was desperate, Will.'

He said nothing.

'If I'd have known the reason you didn't speak to your father, I'd have told you before. I swear. I just – you never told me.'

'She's got a point, Will.' Jacob's voice was quiet, but Will's head snapped up and he looked confused, as though he'd forgotten Jacob was even there. His eyes focused on his son now and his gaze softened.

'I'm sorry, son—' He stopped as he realised what he'd said. He'd called him son. Not Jacob. Son. Jacob said nothing and I reached out and held his hand. 'I'm sorry,' Will continued. 'You didn't need to hear all this, not now.' He glanced at Jim, who was watching me.

I squeezed Jacob's hand. 'I'm sorry too. This wasn't what I'd imagined for today. I should go.'

'No, don't.' Jacob looked round the room, his gaze resting on each of us as it passed. 'Things are never clear cut. When I found out about you and Fran' – he pointed at me and Will – 'I could have refused to get to know you. To have kept you out of my life and pretended nothing had changed. But knowing you were out there made me see the world differently, whether I wanted to or not. I couldn't have carried on the way I was without meeting you both. It was unthinkable.' He looked down at his feet, planted on the floor in front of him. 'What I'm trying to say is...' He stopped again, tucked one leg under the other. 'I guess what I'm trying to say is it didn't take long for me to realise that playing the blame game, and being angry changes nothing. Fran obviously did what she thought was right at the time. She thought she couldn't give me the life I deserved, so she made sure I got it. That was the way I chose to look at it, rather than focusing on the fact that she gave me away.' He took a deep breath and looked at Will, then at Jim.

'I get that this feels impossible to wrap your head around. What Fran did would probably sound terrible, out of context. But think about it. Do you really believe she would have helped your mum if she hadn't have thought it was the right thing to do at the time? Do you really believe she did it for any other reason than compassion? And as for what happened with your father afterwards – well. It seems to me that was between you, and nothing to do with whatever Fran did or didn't do. That was about your relationship with your father rather than anything else.' He stopped and shrugged. 'That's my opinion. For what it's worth.'

The three of us stared at him for a moment. I could hardly take it in. Jacob forgave me. Whatever else happened as a result of my confession, Jacob forgave me.

Would Will and Jim be able to do the same?

'Jacob's right, Will.' Jim's voice was quiet as he ran his finger round the rim of his beer can. He looked at me. 'I know you only did what Mum asked you to do. And let's face it, there's every chance she would have gone that day anyway. She was ill. She was dying.'

Will raised his eyes to meet mine. They were unreadable and terror pulsed in my throat as I waited for his verdict.

'I'm sorry, Fran. I didn't...' He stopped and ran his hand over his face. His eyes looked dark, exhaustion taking over. 'I know you were only trying to help. Mum was in terrible pain, those last few days, but she would never have dared ask us to help because she knew we'd refuse. You took away her pain, and that was all she wanted.'

I swallowed. Relief flooded through me that Will seemed to understand.

'But your father – everything that happened as a result...'

Will shook his head. 'My relationship with my father was damaged anyway, long before that. If it hadn't have been this, it would have been something else. Jacob's right about that. I was just looking for an excuse to blame him, to leave.'

I stood and walked across the room and kneeled down by Will's chair and laid my hand on his knee.

'I'm sorry. Truly.' Tears dripped down my face and landed on his trousers, soaking into the fabric.

'It's okay, Fran. Really.' He lifted my chin and planted a gentle kiss on my lips.

'Okay, enough of that,' Jim said, and I smiled at him.

Jim hauled himself to his feet and walked the few steps across the room until he was standing in front of me, then he hugged me tightly, holding on to me as though his life depended on it.

'Oi, I'm still here,' Will's voice piped up, and we both grinned at him.

'Sorry, mate,' Jim said, ruffling his big brother's hair.

As I took my place next to Jacob again I felt as though a weight I hadn't even known I'd been carrying had been lifted from my shoulders.

Will knew the truth, and he forgave me.

Jacob forgave me too.

25

Late October 2019

It was a big day. A huge day. One that I never truly thought I'd see.

Will was going to see his father.

A few days after the revelations about why they'd fallen out, I'd arrived with Kieran in tow to find Will looking brighter than he had in days. His eyes shone and a smile stretched across his face.

'You look like the cat that got the cream,' I said, pecking him on the cheek. 'Been chatting up the nurses again?'

'Yeah, they love me,' Will said. 'Hey, Kieran, how was school?'

'Yeah, fine.' He sat on the floor and pulled his phone out of his pocket, conversation over.

I rolled my eyes then turned back to Will. 'Anyway, what are you looking so happy about?'

'Jim just called.'

'Right?' Jim called every day to check on his brother, partly, as he admitted to me, to ease the guilt of being almost three hundred miles away. 'Presumably he had some news?'

Will smiled at me, his eyebrows raised in a question.

'Are you going to tell me or am I meant to guess?'

'We talked about Dad.'

'Oh?'

'Yeah. He – rather, I asked him if he could contact him for me.'

'Oh!' I hadn't expected that. After the other night I'd harboured a vague hope that Will might think about forgiving his father, but I hadn't expected him to come round quite so quickly.

As if reading my thoughts, he said, 'I know it's a sudden turn-around but let's face it, Franny, I haven't really got any time to waste, have I?'

'Well, no… So what did he say?'

'He said he'd already spoken to him.'

'And?'

'And he wants to come and see me.'

I stared at Will, unable to believe how calm he was being. After everything we'd been through, all the heartache, all the times he'd refused to even mention his father's name, now he was telling me he was going to see him, just like that?

'That's amazing, Will.'

'I hope so.'

I perched on the edge of his bed. 'So what happens now?'

'Jim's going to speak to Dad and ring me later.'

It was all happening so fast but Will was right. He didn't have any time to waste.

I just hoped he wasn't going to be left disappointed.

* * *

In the end, Alan came to visit just two days later. I was almost as nervous as Will about his arrival, although I could see the terror and apprehension in his eyes as the time approached.

'How long?' Will said for the twentieth time that morning.

I checked my watch. 'Half an hour.'

'Oh God.' Will's leg jiggled up and down. 'I haven't made a terrible mistake, have I?'

'No, Will. This is good. You're going to make amends with your father.'

'But what if he's still angry?'

'We've been over this, and you heard what Jim said. Your father's thrilled you want to see him. Why would he be angry?'

He shrugged. 'I've been awful.'

'None of this is your fault. None of it.'

'I know. Sorry. I'm just scared.'

We were silent again for a few moments, but after a while I couldn't stand the slow ticking of the clock painfully marking out the minutes until Jim and Alan's arrival any longer.

'I'm going for a walk round the garden, want to come?' Will could still walk, but not far, and had been given a wheelchair for me to push him round in. He said it made him feel like an invalid and rarely agreed to use it, but today he just needed to take his mind off the wait.

'Yeah, go on, then.'

We wandered slowly round the gardens, where the fallen leaves that covered the path despite the best endeavours of the gardener clogged the wheels of the wheelchair. Neither of us spoke. I tried to conjure an image of Will's father in my mind, but it was so long since I'd seen him the image floated away before it formed, lost on the breeze. I wondered whether I'd even recognise him after all these years. He was an old man now, in his seventies, and people change. I wondered what he'd make of Will. I knew Will was anxious about his father seeing him like this: weakened, defenceless.

'Can we go back inside?' Will said. 'I'm cold.'

He had blankets piled over his legs but he was right, it was chilly, the air still and damp, clinging to our skin and clothes, so I turned him around and walked back towards the house. I stopped dead just as Jim's car drove into the car park, and Will and I watched as he pulled into a parking space. Neither of them had seen us yet, and for a few moments nobody emerged from the car.

'Shall we go over and say hello?' I said.

Will shook his head. 'Let's wait.'

We stood and watched as Jim climbed out of the driver's side. Seconds later the passenger door opened and a slim man with wispy grey hair climbed out. He pulled his coat tighter round himself as a gust of wind caught him, and he looked around. Then, suddenly, his gaze stopped at the sight of me and Will. Even from this distance the recognition in his face was plain to see.

'Shall we go over there now?' I whispered.

Will looked round over his shoulder. 'This isn't how it was supposed to go.'

'It's okay, Will. It doesn't matter.'

He thought a moment, then nodded his head. 'You're right. Let's go and say hello.'

The walk across the garden and into the car park under the gaze of Jim and their father felt like the longest of my life, and as we approached I could see Will's knuckles turn white in his lap and his shoulders hunch. I stopped the wheelchair and Will pushed himself up to standing, unfolding himself until he was at least four inches taller than his father. For a moment they stared at each other, neither speaking, just searching each other's faces. Then, finally, Alan held his hand out for Will to shake. 'Hello, son.'

Will hesitated a moment, then held his hand out and took the older man's hand in his.

'Hello, Dad.'

I didn't know where to go, what to do. Should I leave them to it, let Alan push his son back inside, let them talk? I was about to make my excuses when Jim came over.

'Shall we go inside then? It's freezing out here.' He came round to the back of the wheelchair. 'Do you want me to push him?'

'Sure, thanks.' I stepped aside and once Will had taken his seat again the four of us walked back inside the hospice in silence.

Back in Will's room, I hovered awkwardly by the door.

'I'll just go and get some tea and cake,' I said.

Jim stood. 'I'll come with you.' Then he took my arm and we walked away, leaving Will and his father alone for the first time in twenty-five years.

'Do you think they'll be all right?'

'They'll be fine,' Jim said. He walked towards the front doors and steered me out into the cold again. 'I think we should just give them a while. Shall we go for a walk?'

'Sure.'

Jim hooked his arm through mine and we strolled along the street towards Hampstead Heath. The day had turned colder and people walking past looked as cold as I felt. I shivered.

'Here, have this.' Jim passed me his hat and I shoved it on my head gratefully.

'So how was Will this morning?'

'Terrified.'

'Dad was too.'

'What did he say when you told him Will wanted to see him?'

'He thought I was joking at first. I'd told him Will was ill a while ago, but I don't think he had any idea how ill.'

'You told him?' Will had made it clear he never wanted his father to know anything about him at all. Despite his good intentions, this felt like a small betrayal on Jim's part.

'Yeah. I know Will wouldn't have liked it, but it felt only fair to warn him that his eldest son was dying.'

'I suppose so. And it doesn't really matter now, does it?'

'No.'

We fell into silence for a moment. I desperately wanted to ask Jim whether he'd truly forgiven me for what I'd done to his mum. I knew he'd said he did, but I wanted to know whether he felt differently, having had time to think about it. Luckily, he brought it up first.

'I understand why you did it, you know.'

I turned to study his face – a face that was in some ways so familiar, so like his brother's but in other ways so utterly different. He turned to face me.

'Thank you, Jim. I loved your mum. I would never have done anything to hurt her.'

'I know.' He paused. 'She asked me too, you know.'

'Did she?'

'Yes. I suppose she thought a fourteen-year-old might be more willing to help out than Dad or Will. And even though I could see how much pain she was in, and she begged – properly begged – I said no. I just – I couldn't do it.' He stopped in his tracks. 'But you know what? I regretted it for years.'

I stopped walking and Jim stopped and turned round. 'I didn't know.'

'No, well, you wouldn't. I've never told anyone until now. But what I mean is I understand why you helped her. She was desperate. You just took away her pain.' He held out his hands and I took them in mine. 'We should have thanked you, really. You did what you thought was best.'

'It's the story of my life, isn't it? Making choices I've thought were for the best at the time, and then spending my life trying to block them out.'

'Do you mean Jacob?'

I nodded, words catching in my throat. 'I – I was terrified I'd lose Will if I told him about him. But I had to, didn't I?'

'You did the right thing. Will might not have time to get to know Jacob very well, but at least he got to meet him, to spend time with him. That means the world.'

We carried on walking, looping round the park and back towards the hospice. As we got nearer, I felt my heart rate quicken.

'How do you think it's gone?'

Jim shrugged. 'They've either killed each other or they're best friends. I wouldn't like to say.'

'God, I hope it's gone well. Will needs this. I think it will give him some peace.'

'Dad does too. It broke his heart the day Will walked out. I think he always thought he'd come back one day. It took him a long, long time to accept that he wasn't going to.'

As we stepped through the front door and made our way to Will's room, my heart thumped and my legs shook. What would we find when we got there?

I tapped gently on the door, pushed it open and stepped into the room, Jim close behind me. 'Is it safe to come in?' he said.

'Perfectly.'

Alan stood as we entered, and held out his hand for me to shake. 'Hello, Francesca. I'm sorry I didn't say hello before. It's lovely to see you again,' he said.

I shook his proffered hand warmly. 'You too.'

'So how's it gone?' Jim said, looking from his dad to Will and back again.

'Really well.' Will's voice was quiet. 'I – we've talked. And – well, let's just say we both know we made mistakes. But we're good. Aren't we, Dad?'

Dad. The first time he'd spoken to his dad in so many years, and yet it was as though that wasted time had slipped away, and all that was left was a desire to make things right again.

In normal circumstances perhaps there would have been years of recriminations, of discussion, or blame. But here and now, with Will dying, there was no time or need for any of that.

Will had his dad back. And Alan had his son.

* * *

Alan stayed for the rest of the day, and although I offered him a bed at my flat, he and Jim decided to find a B&B nearby to stay for a few nights.

'I'll come and see you tomorrow if that's okay?' Alan said, his voice still full of uncertainty at how much his son had truly welcomed him.

'That would be great, Dad. Thank you.'

Alan's face broke into a smile and as they said their goodbyes my mind wandered back to the past, a place where it had been a lot recently. I remembered times when the four of us were together, we'd play football in the park, Will out-skilling us all until we forced him to play on his own against his dad, me and Jim; of the time we built a den in the woods behind our houses, spending the whole day piling up branches and twigs into a sturdy structure we could climb inside. I remembered the times Alan had welcomed me into their house, helping me with my maths homework, making sure there was enough dinner for me, cleaning my shoes. Then I looked at this old man giving his son a hug goodbye after so many years apart and I felt torn by sadness.

We'd all wasted so much time. Time we hadn't appreciated until it had almost run out.

'Right, will we see you tomorrow?' Jim said as they prepared to leave.

'Yep, I'm here every day.'

'She was always a good'un,' Alan said, smiling as he reached out and hugged me briefly. 'Thank you for looking after my boy.'

After they had left, a few moments passed before either of us spoke.

'Well. How was it, seeing him again? As you expected?'

'Better. He – he wasn't like I remembered. He was softer, less combative.' Will picked the blanket on his knees. 'The trouble is, it just makes me feel more sad, that I was so hard on him for all this time.'

'Oh, Will, you mustn't think like that.' I dropped down to my knees and kneeled beside him. 'There's no point looking backwards, regreting anything. All you can do is look forward now, and enjoy the time you've got left.'

Will nodded. 'You're right. The trouble is, I'm worried it's running out even quicker than I'd hoped.'

26

November 2019

Each day I came to see Will, we settled into a kind of routine. I'd arrive and come straight to his room without any questions from the nurses, who knew me well by now. He'd be waiting for me and then we'd have a cup of tea and go for a walk in the garden. I tried not to notice that each day he seemed to grow a little weaker, to fade a little more.

So I was surprised when I arrived one morning in mid-November and there was a bustle of people outside his room. I hurried my steps as I approached, my heart thumping, expecting the worst.

'What's happened? Is Will okay?'

A young nurse I didn't recognise turned and spotted me and steered me away from Will's room towards the lounge area. 'Let's just take a seat in here a moment,' she said.

'What's going on? Is Will all right?' I could feel panic rising in my throat.

'Will's fine, don't worry.'

'Well, what's happened then? Why can't I go in?'

She looked awkward, her eyes flitting towards the door every few seconds, her gaze resting just above my shoulder. 'I – er, I'm not sure. I've just been asked to get you to stay here. Sorry.'

I felt sorry for her. The poor girl clearly didn't have a clue what was going on either.

'But Will's okay, is he?'

'Yes, yes, he's definitely fine. I – I just need to pop out for a moment. Can you wait here until I get back?'

'Okay.'

She scurried away, clearly relieved to have been given a pass to leave. I waited obediently where I was, watching some of the other residents coming and going. Some looked well, the way Will had looked when he'd first arrived, and it made me realise how much he'd deteriorated since then. Others were obviously much closer to the end, their tiny bodies frail and folded, and I had to look away, unwilling to imagine Will like that, just yet.

A few minutes passed and I grew impatient. Should I defy orders and go and see what was happening? But before I could make that decision, one of Will's nurses came into the lounge and sat down beside me.

'How's Will? What's going on?'

'Will's absolutely fine, don't worry about that,' she said. 'But he's asked if you'd do a favour for him before you see him today.'

'What do you mean?'

She handed me a piece of paper with an address scribbled on it. 'He says can you go here and collect something for him and then bring it back. Apparently they're expecting you.'

'I...' I didn't really know how to respond.

'I get the impression it's quite important.'

I sighed. I knew Will wasn't a fan of surprises, but I'd always quite liked them. This time, though, I was far too curious to enjoy it.

Perturbed, I tapped the address into my sat nav on my phone. It was about a mile away, a twenty-minute walk from here. I set off, the cold November rain driving at the back of my neck, and pulled my hood tighter. What on earth was I doing, going off on some wild goose chase when Will was back there, waiting to see me?

I hurried on, and was relieved when I arrived at Hampstead High Street and found the right address. It was a boutique. I peered back down at the crumpled piece of paper in my hand to double check it. Yes, this looked like the right place. I pushed open the door and went inside, water dripping from my coat and forming puddles on the pristine floor.

'Hello, how can I help you?' said a voice, and I looked up to see a woman I'd have guessed was in her late fifties, smiling at me.

'Oh, um, I'm not sure I'm in the right place.'

'Are you Francesca?'

'Oh. Yes. I am.' I looked around, bewildered, as though expecting to see hidden cameras recording me.

'How lovely to meet you. I'm Jennifer.' She walked forward and clasped my hand in hers then stepped away. 'Just give me a moment.' She disappeared through a door and I took the opportunity to look round the shop. There were a few racks of clothes – dresses, coats, bags, shoes – but all of them looked more expensive than anything I could afford. I turned at a sound to find Jennifer standing in front of me holding a package wrapped in brown paper. She held it out but before I could take it she glanced out of the window.

'Oh dear, I'm afraid this is going to get awfully damaged in this weather. Is your car nearby?'

'No, I walked here.'

'Hang on a tick, then.' She bent down behind the counter and produced an enormous dark blue bag into which she placed the parcel before handing it over again.

'Now, my instructions for you are that you're not to open it until you get back. Does that make sense to you?'

'I suppose so.' As much as any of this made sense.

'Great, well, I hope you enjoy it. And good luck.'

I turned, even more bewildered than before, and stepped back into the rain, which seemed heavier now I was walking into it, the raindrops pummelling my eyes and clouding my vision. Finally I arrived back at the hospice and as I stepped inside, a different nurse ran up to me.

'Is everything okay?'

'Yes, yes, grand.' She placed her hands on mine and smiled warmly. 'Now, William has asked me to ask you to put whatever is in this parcel on please.'

'Okaaay. Is there somewhere I can get changed or does he want me to strip off right here?'

'Ha ha, of course, follow me.'

She led me to a toilet. 'I'm sorry, this is the best I can do; all our rooms are full.'

'It's fine. Thank you.'

'Oh, hang on.' She scurried away and returned a few seconds later brandishing a hairbrush and a lipstick. 'They're nothing special but they're the best I could do at short notice.' I shot her a quizzical look but she said nothing more, just ushered me into the toilet cubicle. As I locked the door behind me, I sat on the closed toilet seat and reached down and pulled the paper-wrapped parcel out of the bag and tugged impatiently on the string tying it together. Then I peeled it open to reveal its contents.

There, nestled in tissue paper, was a slip of fabric, in a beautiful deep green. I stood to lift it out and the fabric tumbled to the floor like water, soft against my skin. It was stunning. But what was it for?

And then I noticed a note inside the tissue paper, a flash of pink. I picked it up and immediately recognised Will's scruffy scrawl.

My darling Fran,

Choosing something for you to wear is always a risky business. I wanted you to have something special so you'll always remember this day. I hope you'll wear it with pride.

If you do, then I have this question for you: Francesca Gordon, I love you more than I've ever loved anyone. I always have and always will.

Will you be my wife?

Say you will
Your Will xxx

I dropped the card to the floor and sat back down, my legs shaking. My breath was too fast and my head spun and I sucked in air greedily, trying to calm myself.

Will wanted to marry me.

And did this mean... could it mean... right here, right now? Is that what all this secrecy was about?

I wanted to run out of there and into Will's room and tell him of course I'd marry him, and that I loved him and that he didn't need to buy me expensive things to convince me to say yes. But he'd obviously gone to a lot of trouble to make this special, and had involved a lot of other people, so I'd do it his way.

As I undressed and slipped on the dress, I shook with nerves. Who else knew about this, who else would be there with us? Was Mags in on it? Elodie, Kieran, Jim? They must be. God only knew how Kieran had kept it secret. Would Jacob be there, and Alan?

I pulled the brush through my rain-dampened hair and slicked on some lipstick, grateful now for the nurse's kindness. I felt sick with anxiety, yet my heart thumped with anticipation as I let myself out of the cubicle.

'Oh, she's here!' Will's nurse ran over and clasped her hands together with glee. 'You look beautiful. Look, everyone, doesn't she look beautiful?'

'Gorgeous,' someone said and my face flushed.

'Oh, but have you seen the note? You've read the note, right?'

'Yes, I've read the note.'

'She's read the note, everyone!'

A cheer went up and I grinned. It seemed everyone was in on this, even some of the residents. 'Right, are you ready?' I nodded. Then from behind the throng of people gathering by Will's door stepped my father, wearing his favourite suit.

'Dad!' I ran towards him and hugged him tightly.

'Yes, well, right,' he said, patting himself down as I pulled away.

'You look smart, Dad, are you going somewhere?'

'Well, um…' He looked round, bewildered, for Mum, who stepped forward to save him.

'She's teasing you, Pete.' She rolled her eyes. 'Blimey, you'd think he'd understand your sense of humour after all these years wouldn't you?' She turned to me. 'Oh, love, you look absolutely gorgeous. Didn't he do well, choosing that all by himself?'

'He did, Mum.' I hugged her and she pressed her cheek against mine briefly. 'Right, shall we get going?'

Dad held out his elbow and I took it. 'Ready, love?'

'Ready, Dad.'

And then we walked into Will's room.

* * *

It was only a small space but it was packed: first I spotted Will, who was sitting on the edge of his bed, looking nervous in a dark suit that hung off his tiny frame; beside him stood Jacob, looking for all the world like his father had twenty years before, and Alan, who'd scrubbed up well in a shirt and tie. Kieran grinned at me, wearing a shirt I'd never seen before, Amy and Elodie were squeezed in next to the window and Mags, Rob and the kids were squashed by the bathroom door. There was also a woman I didn't recognise, who stepped forward and introduced herself as Sandra. 'I'm the registrar, it's lovely to meet you,' she said, and shook my hand warmly.

My father walked me the few steps to the bed, and Will stood up, holding on to a frame.

'I can't believe you've done this,' I said, blinking back tears.

'I can't believe you said yes,' he replied, his eyes shining. He pressed his forehead against mine for a moment.

'Okay, I think we'd better get on with this while I'm still standing,' he said to the room.

'Are you sure you don't want to sit down? I'll sit too?'

'No. I'm going to stand proudly while I marry the love of my life,' Will said, and I pressed my hand against his that was gripping his frame.

The ceremony was lovely, the words barely registering in my mind as I looked round the room at all the people I loved. I could hardly believe this was happening, and before I knew it, Will was slipping a ring onto my finger. It was antique gold with tiny emeralds embedded in it. It was beautiful. Then he handed me a plain gold band to give to him.

We were married.

'Well, that's another one ticked off the bucket list,' I said, smiling.

Will leaned over and kissed me gently on the lips. 'That's not the only one I've got planned today.'

'You're kidding? I think getting married might be enough for one day!'

'Hang on.' He beckoned to the nurse, who stood outside, and she nodded. Moments later a man walked in carrying a large bag. His arms and neck were covered in tattoos.

'I know we've got rings, but I want something even more permanent to take with me,' Will said.

'Our matching tattoos,' I said, realisation dawning.

'Matching tattoos,' Will confirmed. 'I know it's not exactly traditional but not a lot about today is traditional so I thought what the hell. What do you say?'

'I say let's do it.'

* * *

After we'd had our tattoos –our initials, entwined, small and tasteful on the inside of our wrists – and hugged everyone, I could see that Will was flagging.

I grabbed a glass and a spoon and banged them together until everyone looked at me.

'Today has been brilliant,' I said. 'I can't believe you all kept this from me – especially you, Kier,' I said, and Kieran grinned. 'But it's more than I could ever have dreamed of.' I turned to Will and raised my empty glass. 'This man has made me happier than I ever thought possible, and the fact that I can call myself his wife is—' My voice broke. 'It's incredible.' I cleared my throat and looked up. 'But I think it's time to get the groom to bed and say goodnight. To Will!'

'To Will.'

As the room fell into silence, Will cleared his throat and pushed himself to standing again with the help of his metal frame. His hands gripped the metal tightly, his knuckles white. 'Fran, you are and always have been the love of my life. Thank for you making my dream come true.'

Then, exhausted, he dropped back into his chair, a faint smile on his face.

I couldn't look at him because I knew I'd burst into tears. Memories of the Will I'd always known – the football player, lean and strong, and even the Will I'd met just nine months before – kept flashing through my mind and I struggled not to compare them to this tired, frail man who sat in the chair before me.

But he was still the boy I'd loved since I was seven years old.

* * *

Half an hour later, when everyone had gone, leaving just me and Kieran to say goodnight, Will seemed to perk up a little.

'What a day,' he said, reaching out to grab my hand lightly.

'I can't believe you organised all of that,' I said.

'I had a lot of help. But it was important. I wanted to let you know just how much you mean to me.'

'Well, thank you. It was amazing.' I studied the ring that sparkled on my finger and felt a shiver of delight.

'Plus, of course, we've ticked two more off the list.'

I rolled my eyes. 'You and that bloody bucket list.'

'I know it doesn't matter so much to you, Fran, but for me it's a symbol. If I can just complete it, I'll feel I've achieved something. I know it sounds stupid.'

'It doesn't sound stupid, love. I'm sorry. And I'm glad we've almost completed it too. Although...'

'What?'

'Haven't we still got two pretty impossible ones left?' I thought about the list and the two remaining things we hadn't completed: see the Northern Lights and spot a shooting star.

'Yes, I guess we have.' Will pulled me closer and pressed his lips on the back of my hand. 'But at least we've done the most important one. I can live with that.'

'Actually, I've got a surprise for you,' Kieran said.

'What, love?'

'Hang on.' He bent down and reached under Will's bed and pulled out a black case that I recognised at once.

'Your telescope!'

'Yep. I read something the other day that said there was going to be a meteor shower tonight so I dug it out. I thought – well, I thought we might see one.' He shrugged. 'Worth a go anyway? If Will's not too tired?'

My heart swelled with pride that my boy could be so thoughtful.

'Let's do it,' Will said.

Kieran assembled the telescope and set it up at the window, angled upwards. He peered through and moved it around to get a better view.

'Here you go.'

I took Will's arm and helped him up to standing, and then across the room. I supported him as he bent his head over to look through the lens. He felt light as air beneath my hands and I knew if he fell I could easily support his weight.

'Can you see anything?'

'Not yet.'

'It can take a while.'

Kieran and I sat patiently while the minutes ticked by. I didn't dare let go of Will's arm.

Suddenly, he jerked and lifted his head with excitement. 'I saw one!'

'Where?'

Will pointed somewhere to the right and Kieran and I squinted into the darkness just as a flash of white zipped through the sky, clear as anything.

'There, I saw it,' Kieran said excitedly.

Will smiled. 'That was amazing, but I think I need to sit down now.'

I led him back to his bed and he lay down, his head propped on the pillows.

'Thank you, Kieran.'

'S'okay. I'm glad it worked.'

'It was very thoughtful; I'm very proud of you,' I said, ruffling his hair.

'Get off!' he said, ducking away from me.

I turned back to Will, who was already dropping off to sleep, his eyes opening and closing. I leaned over and gave him a gentle kiss on his head. 'Night night, husband.'

'Night, wife,' he mumbled through the thickness of sleep.

Then Kieran and I crept out of the room, leaving him to rest.

27

Christmas Eve 2019

When I was a child I always looked forward to Christmas Eve. It was my favourite day – the anticipation reaching fever pitch, the excitement of Christmas Day still to come.

This year, though, was a different kind of waiting game.

This year we were waiting for Will to die.

Every morning I'd wake up in the bed where I'd slept alone for so many years, and the empty space beside me would feel overwhelmingly huge. For a few seconds I'd lie there, wondering where Will was, whether he was making breakfast or having a shower, before reality came crashing back in and crushed the air from my chest.

Would today be the day? Or would we have one more day together? As Christmas approached it felt like opening some sort of horrific advent calendar. A countdown to the end.

Every day since our wedding I'd rung the hospice each morning to see how Will was, and spent as much time there as I could. Some days i went alone in the precious hours after work, while other times Kieran and I would sit peacefully with Will, just spending time together. Elodie and Amy visited regularly and, to my utmost joy, so did Jacob, when he could, and Alan.

In fact, Alan had been to visit Will almost every day, and the pair had spent hours talking: about their shared past, their separate pasts, and everything in between.

'I can't believe I wasted so much time being so stubborn,' Will said to me one evening as we sat in the darkness of the garden, wrapped in coats and blankets. 'All this time, I could have had my father.'

'We said no regrets, remember,' I said, laying my hands gently on his shoulders and nuzzling my nose into his thin hair.

'I know, I know. And I'm trying. But it's really hard. We've hardly got any time left.'

'But at least you've got him now.'

He nodded as we headed back inside.

On Christmas Eve, I woke up with the same feeling of dread as I did every morning. Would this be the day that I rang to hear bad news?

Climbing out of bed, I resisted the urge to call straight away. Mornings were a busy time at the hospice, getting everyone up and dressed and fed. I'd give them a bit of time.

I padded through to the kitchen. It was early and Kieran was still asleep and the flat felt quiet, as though it was holding its breath. There were no signs of Christmas in here apart from a half-eaten box of Celebrations on the side. I stuck my hand in and unwrapped a Bounty and chewed it half-heartedly. I made coffee and walked through to the living room and switched on the Christmas tree lights. They sparkled in the darkness of the morning and I decided not to switch on any more lights. Instead I sat on the sofa and sipped my coffee and let my mind drift to Christmases past, and happier times. Last Christmas my life had been so different. Will and I had just met again, and we were happy, looking forward to spending the rest of our lives together after so long apart. There had been no Jacob, and no Alan either, both of those secrets still hidden, waiting to be revealed. How much life had changed in a year.

My thoughts raced then right back to 1993, and the Christmas I'd spent away from home, Will gone, me pregnant. No idea what my future held or whether I'd ever see Will again. This year, I was faced with the prospect that Will could leave me again, and this time forever, but at least now I knew he loved me. I was certain about that, and I always would be. My mind rewound a few more years, to the Christmas my family and Will's had spent together when we were ten, Kathy cooking the turkey and my Mum cooking the starter and pudding. Will and I had been thrilled to be together on Christmas Day for the first time, and even Jim hadn't been too unhappy about having to share his big brother with me. He was used to it by then. I remembered the lights on the tree, the paper chains strung across the ceiling, the Queen's Speech as we stuffed Quality Streets in our mouths, and the hours we spent in Will's room, playing with my new record player, listening to the latest Prince album.

Suddenly my thoughts were shattered by the sound of my phone ringing and I leaped up, almost knocking my coffee over. I dug in my dressing gown pocket for my mobile and glanced at the screen. It was the hospice.

My heart dropped to my feet.

Was this it? Was this the call I'd been waiting for?

Why else would they ring at seven o'clock in the morning?

With shaking hands I answered the call and held the phone to my ear. 'Hello?'

'Hello, Fran, it's Katie.' Will's nurse.

'Hello, Katie. Is it Will? Is everything all right?'

The tiny hesitation told me everything I needed to know.

'I think you should come in as soon as you can.'

I tried to speak – there were so many questions I needed to ask. How long did he have? What had happened? Should I let everyone else know? But none of the words would form and instead my throat closed up.

'Fran, are you there?'

I swallowed. 'I'm on my way.'

I don't know what happened over the next few minutes. I must have got dressed, and I woke Kieran, and I called a taxi, but I don't really remember any of it. All I can remember is thinking that time was ticking, relentlessly passing, and we might be too late.

I must have called Alan, Jim and Amy, and Jacob too, but I don't remember what I said or how they replied. But by the time we pulled up in the car park of the hospice, I was beside myself with fear.

Kieran and I ran from the taxi into the hospice and as we entered the main doors, Katie came to greet me, her face serious.

'Is he...' I stopped, unable to say the words.

'He's waiting for you.' She walked ahead of me and beckoned for me to follow. I leaned on Kieran for support. My boy, my precious boy.

As we reached Will's door, I was struck by how different this moment felt to just a month before, when the place was filled with excitement, and we were about to get married. My thumb felt for the ring on my finger and my heart rate slowed slightly. Everything was all right. Everything would be all right.

I stepped into the room and there was Will. His head was propped up on pillows and the room was hot, the heat from the radiators making it difficult to breathe. An image of his mum, Kathy, flashed into my mind then and I shook it off as I walked towards his bed with shaking legs. I perched on the edge, careful not to make him jump, and watched his chest rise slowly up and back down, the covers barely moving. His face had a yellow tinge, and his hair, which had thinned so much, was like a halo round his head. I reached out and stroked the side of his face and he opened his eyes a little.

'Fran.' His lips were dry and cracked and the sound was so quiet only I could hear it.

I lifted his hand up and pressed my lips to it. 'I made it, Will.'

A wisp of a smile flitted across his face and I listened to the whistle of his breath, in, out, in, out. 'Happy Christmas, darling,' I whispered.

His eyes flickered and his lips moved but I couldn't hear the words. I leaned forward and held my ear to him. 'Finish... the... bucket... list.'

I lifted my head and smiled, nodded. 'Of course I will.'

'I love you.'

'I love you too, Will.'

And then his breath slowed, and his head dropped and, with barely a whisper, Will left.

And my world dropped away.

I sat, motionless for a moment. I felt Kieran move behind me and place a hand on my shoulder and I lifted my hand and covered his. Tears were falling down my face, but I couldn't move, not yet.

'Mum?'

I turned and Kieran's arms were round me and I held him tightly, as though I would never let go. 'I love you, Mum.'

'I love you too, darling.'

I don't know how long we sat there, but the next voice I heard was the nurse's.

'Fran?' I looked up.

'He's gone.' My voice was nothing more than a croak.

She nodded and stepped towards me and hugged me. 'There are some other people here to say goodbye. I'll go and tell them, shall I?'

'Yes please.' I couldn't bear to break the news to anyone else. Saying the words out loud would make it all too real. Moments later Jacob, Jim and Alan crept into the room. The three men stood there, respectfully, each one broken in their own way.

'Can we...' Alan indicated the bed where Will lay. I looked over. He looked so peaceful it was hard to believe he was gone.

'Go, go and say your goodbyes,' I said. I stepped out of the room on shaking legs. Amy was waiting near the entrance, Elodie on her lap.

'I didn't know what to...' Amy trailed off and I nodded.

'Is Daddy dead?'

'Yes, I'm afraid he is.' I kneeled down beside her and cupped her hands in mine. 'But he told me to tell you he loves you very much.'

She nodded and looked down at her shoes. 'Has he gone to heaven to be with Freddie?'

Despite everything, I smiled, and Amy smiled too. 'Yes, darling, that's exactly where he's gone, to look after your hamster. So at least they'll have each other.'

She sat for a moment more, then hopped off Amy's lap. 'Good. Freddie will be happy to have Daddy there.'

And that was the end of that conversation, for now at least. I wished I could deal with it as well.

* * *

I imagined I'd spend the time after Will died grieving and crying. But the reality was much more mundane. After Will left us, the rest of the day felt like a whirlwind of admin, of answering questions, of filling in forms. It seemed too prosaic to feel like the end of a life.

But I was sure that the grief was all to come and, to be honest, I was glad of the distractions.

It wasn't until later that evening as I sat at home, Kieran in his usual armchair and the space next to me on the sofa empty, that I thought about how much things had changed since Will had come back into my life.

Before, I'd been merely existing. I'd had Kieran, of course, and Mags was wonderful, always. But other than that I'd had a job I tolerated, a barely existent social life and there'd been no man on the horizon for years.

Meeting Will again had changed my life beyond recognition. Now I had Jacob, as well as Jim, Alan, Elodie and even Amy, who was slowly becoming a friend. My life was full of people I cared about, who knew Will as I knew him, and who loved him in their own way. Kieran had even got his dad back, as much as I'd tried to resist it for so long, and he was happy.

So even though my heart ached with sadness, and I knew there were many, many months of grieving and mending left to get through, at least I wasn't on my own.

Now, I had an army of people to be there for me, to love me. And I was lucky.

I hoped Will knew what he'd done for me, before he died.

I owed him everything.

EPILOGUE
NOW

March 2020

I tipped my head up and stared at the sky, at the great wall of light, like lasers dancing. It was magical, the greens and reds and yellows lighting up the night sky, guiding the way.

'Wow,' Kieran breathed beside me.

I squeezed his hand.

Despite the cold, I felt a warm glow of pleasure as I looked around me. Here, in the freezing grey of an Icelandic winter, were all the people who'd meant so much to Will. Jacob, Alan, Jim, Karen and the girls, Amy and Elodie. We'd come to fulfil his final, dying wish, together. To see the Northern Lights.

'Will would have loved this,' Jim said, his face lit up.

I nodded, the tears threatening to come again. It had only been three months since Will had died but unbeknown to me he'd put some money aside during his last weeks especially for this trip so I had seized the chance. He must have known he'd never make it, that he would never quite finish the list.

But he'd wanted us to do it for him. How could we refuse?

So here we were, all together, watching the sky. I couldn't help wondering whether somewhere up there he was watching over us, happy that we'd done as he'd asked. Mags would have said he was.

I wasn't so sure. But for now, faced with this natural extravaganza, I was happy to believe anything was possible.

'Ready?' Jim said beside me.

'Ready.'

I picked up the jar next to me and stepped forward.

'It's time to say goodbye to Will,' I said, shouting into the wind. 'He always wanted to come here and see this' – I indicated the sky above our heads – 'but he never quite made it. So we've brought him here to say farewell.'

I held the jar up and unscrewed the lid and beckoned Alan, Jim and Jacob to come forward. Between us, with all four holding on to the jar, we threw Will's ashes up, watching as the tiny specks whipped and whirled and floated into the air, and up, up, into the sky.

'Goodbye, Will. May you always be free.'

Goodbye, my love. Goodbye.

ACKNOWLEDGMENTS

Writing a book is quite a solitary experience, and even as you type the words 'The End', you still have no idea whether anyone will ever want to read what you've written. Which is why I'm starting these thank yous with my best friend Serena. She's mentioned in all my acknowledgements, but always at the end, and I'd hate her to think she was an after-thought. So thank you Serena for always reading everything I write, for always supporting me and believing in me. It means the world.

I also have to thank Sarah Ritherdon, my editor, for loving Fran and Will's story so much and helping me bring it into the world. I'm sorry for making you cry, but I'm also not really sorry. It was completely intentional. Thank you also to the whole team at Boldwood, who have made me feel so welcome.

When I'm writing about things as important as illness, or adoption, I like to make sure I've got the details right. I did quite a bit of research into brain tumours and although I know every single case is different, I hope Will's story rings true. Thank you to Margie Harris, who talked me through everyday life at a hospice, and also to Venessa Collins who helped me with the details of the adoption storyline. Your help is hugely appreciated, and anything that's not factually correct is my fault – deliberate or otherwise.

As always, thank you to the fabulous book bloggers who support me, especially Anne Cater (Random Things Through My Letterbox), Linda Hill (Linda's Book Bag), Rachel Gilbey (Rachel's Random Resources) and the book community in general. Thanks to Katy Regan and Rowan Coleman for always listening to me moaning when I'm struggling, and the fabulous Savvy Author group on Facebook. And while we're on the subject of Facebook, some of the groups I've recently joined have been so wonderfully supportive, especially the lovely Anita Faulkner from Chick Lit and Prosecco, and the ladies who run the Friendly Book Community and The Fiction Café. It's lovely to have a space to meet readers, fellow authors and chat about my books.

I can't leave this without saying my thank you to my boys: Jack, Harry and Tom. You inspire me every day – and yes, Jack, a few of Kieran's mannerisms *may* have been based on you! Love you all.

MORE FROM CLARE SWATMAN

We hope you enjoyed reading *Before We Grow Old*. If you did, please leave a review.

If you'd like to gift a copy, this book is also available as an ebook, digital audio download and audiobook CD.

Sign up to Clare Swatman's mailing list for news, competitions and updates on future books.

https://bit.ly/ClareSwatmannews

ABOUT THE AUTHOR

Clare Swatman is the author of three women's fiction novels, published by Macmillan, which have been translated into over 20 languages. She has been a journalist for over twenty years, writing for Bella and Woman & Home amongst many other magazines. She lives in Hertfordshire.

Visit Clare's website: https://clareswatmanauthor.com

Follow Clare on social media:

facebook.com/clareswatmanauthor
twitter.com/clareswatman
instagram.com/clareswatmanauthor

ABOUT BOLDWOOD BOOKS

Boldwood Books is a fiction publishing company seeking out the best stories from around the world.

Find out more at www.boldwoodbooks.com

Sign up to the Book and Tonic newsletter for news, offers and competitions from Boldwood Books!

http://www.bit.ly/bookandtonic

We'd love to hear from you, follow us on social media:

facebook.com/BookandTonic

twitter.com/BoldwoodBooks

instagram.com/BookandTonic

Printed in Great Britain
by Amazon